Explosive Reprisals

Crime Scene Kosovo
Book 3

Tasmin Turner

Wish Books

EXPLOSIVE REPRISALS

CRIME SCENE KOSOVO BOOK 3

by Tasmin Turner

Also in paperback
ISBN 978-1-9911924-7-9

For more information see www.wish-books.com

Cover Design by 100books.com

People and Places

People
- Alexei Georgiev, Bulgarian financial adviser
- Angela Keys, office assistant, OIDC
- Andrea Gulaj, Kosovo police officer in Driton Kupi's group
- Axel Delcroix, international prosecutor
- Bo Westergaard, Head of Mission, OIDC
- Brad Harris, Deputy Head of Mission, OIDC
-Briz Prela, Kosovo police officer in Driton Kupi's group
- Caitlin (Kit) Chase, lawyer from New Zealand working in the Office of the Chief International Prosecutor in Pristina, Kosovo
- Christina Wackernagel, international prosecutor
- Don Edgson, canine unit leader and general dog handler, US military on secondment to EUFOR
- Driton Kupi, Kosovo police captain
- Dua Rexhepi, Albanian intern with the international prosecution office, OIDC
- Eva Refazo, Chief International Prosecutor, OIDC

- Fatmir Hoxhaj, Kosovo police officer in Driton Kupi's group
- Father Peter, Russian Orthodox priest and chess exponent
- Dr. Jyoti Prabhu, International Coroner, Pristina
- Lira Siliqi, popular singer in Kosovo
- Mal Mala, crime boss, Pristina, Kosovo
- Matthew (Matt) Hackman, Major, Special Investigations Branch, British Military Police, EUFOR
- Milon Kastrati, Kosovo police officer in Driton Kupi's group
- Natalia Marin, Romanian friend and member of the khash group, dream therapist, and tarot card reader
- Owen Reese, Sergeant, Special Investigations Branch of the British Military Police with EUFOR
- Rosalyn Chase, Kit's mother in New Zealand
- Sergei Sokolov, Russian intelligence officer, also known as Oleg Anton Soroka
- Silver, alias of Russian hacker
- Valon Rama, Kosovo police officer
- Vernon Chase, Kit's estranged father
- Visar Dreshaj, Pristina politician

Animals
- Bambino, Eva's rescue dog
- Max, Belgium Tervuren, military police canine unit

Places
- All Gem Hotel, high-end hotel in Pristina
- Black and White Café, café in midtown Pristina
- Dukagin Resort, hotel in Dečani, Kosovo
- Mother Teresa Boulevard, main pedestrian mall in central Pristina

- One-up Café, popular café in Pristina
- Orchid Oasis Resort, luxurious health resort in Hua Hin, Thailand
- Prince Hotel, casino hotel on the outskirts of Pristina
- Pristina, capital city of Kosovo
- Task Force Headquarters, upmarket apartment rented by Matt Hackman in Pristina for informal task force meetings
- Dečani Monastery, Orthodox Serbian Monastery in Kosovo

Organizations

- European military and police force (EUFOR), engaged in law enforcement in Kosovo during the post-conflict period
- Kosovo Liberation Army (KLA), an ethnic Albanian separatist militia that sought the separation of Kosovo from the Federal Republic of Yugoslavia and Serbia
- The Organization for International Development and Coordination in Kosovo (OIDC), an international organization assisting with the administration of Kosovo during the post-conflict period. Its European headquarters is in Berlin, and its international headquarters is in New York.
- Khash, a Russian philosophical system based on applying lessons from the game of chess to life

Background

During the 1998–1999 Kosovo conflict, ethnic Albanians opposed the Serbian Government of the former Yugoslavia in Belgrade. Kosovo broke away and sought to set up an independent state, which Serbia did not recognize. Allied forces drove Serbian forces back following a humanitarian crisis. International organizations stepped in to support the government in Kosovo. This story is set in a fictionalized post-conflict Kosovo.

Chapter One

P*ristina, Kosovo. Spring 2002*
In a military Jeep, Assistant Chief Prosecutor Caitlin "Kit" Chase and EUFOR Sergeant Owen Reese drove through the rain-drenched streets, carefully avoiding potholes. The cold spring downpour beat against their windshield, causing the wipers to move back and forth in a steady rhythm. While Owen, dressed in his camouflage uniform, kept a vigilant lookout for any dangerous vehicles ahead, Kit exuded an air of legal professionalism within the plain interior of the vehicle. She sported a beige trench coat over her navy suit and held onto her briefcase tightly.

Following a tense meeting at the prosecution office in Mitrovica—a hotspot for ethnic tension in the northern region of Kosovo—they were now on their way back to Pristina. The area was always on edge, with constant clashes between the majority Albanian residents and the Serbs who viewed Kosovo as a rebellious province. Although NATO had intervened to quell the violent conflict between Kosovo and Serbia, a lasting peace remained out of reach. Numerous international missions had been deployed in an effort to restore stability to the region, though locals tended to see them either as saviors or invaders.

"So, Visar Dreshaj invited you to a casino with him tonight," Owen said, his voice edged with concern. Under Owen's army fatigues, his muscular build spoke of his rugby days back in Wales, and his short-cropped hair and intense blue eyes projected a no-nonsense attitude tempered by years on the field and in the kitchen before his police service.

"He invited me months ago when he helped us with a criminal case," Kit clarified. Kit's fair skin, sprinkled with freckles, and her weary, turquoise eyes contrasted sharply with her crisp professional attire, hinting at her struggles to adapt to Kosovo's relentless pace since her arrival from New Zealand. "Just because he's a minister in the Kosovo government doesn't automatically mean he's up to no good." Sensing Owen's discomfort, she reassured him, "Don't worry, I'll handle it with care."

Owen's grip on the steering wheel tightened. "Kit, you risk compromising your impartiality between Kosovo and Serbia for short-term benefits. Don't risk your reputation by being seen out socially with a politician at a casino!" Owen leaned in closer to Kit. "I know we're not supposed to talk about our monitoring operations out in the open, but I've heard rumors about high-stakes games happening at this casino. Some people think it's just a front for something more dangerous... like organized crime."

Kit's heart rate spiked, the words hitting too close to a past she fought to bury. Memories of whispered deals and clandestine money transfers flashed through her mind. "Accusing Dreshaj of being involved in organized crime is a serious claim. He's a politician, not a criminal," she said, her voice steadier than her pounding heart.

"But maybe that's the perfect disguise," Owen countered, his eyes narrowing. "I worry about you, Kit. You're playing a dangerous game here and not just at the casino tonight."

Kit hesitated, her thoughts tangled with the upcoming event and its critical stakes. Her boss, Chief International Prosecutor Eva Refazo, viewed Visar Dreshaj as a pivotal ally, and missing a chance to network at this level wasn't an option. However, feeling the weight of Owen's inquiry too close to her own hidden truths, she needed a swift diversion.

Turning towards Owen, she let the professional mask slip just enough to reveal a more vulnerable side. She reached out, her fingers brushing his arm with a feigned casualness that belied her calculated intent. Her eyes locked onto his, shimmering with a mix of challenge and charm. "There are better things on my mind right now," she murmured, her voice a seductive lilt that she rarely allowed herself.

Owen's reaction was immediate, his usual guarded smile broadening into a more genuine expression of intrigue. "I like the sound of that," he replied, the usual tension between duty and desire melting into palpable excitement. As they leaned in, the professional world with its threats and alliances receded, replaced by the personal realm of possibilities and the unspoken questions of what might come next.

Approaching Pristina, the drizzle transformed into a full-blown storm. The city's dim lights blurred through the Jeep's rain-streaked windows. Owen's quick reflexes saved them from a near collision with another vehicle at a roundabout while Kit caught sight of a familiar sculpture. Painted in vibrant colors, the bold letters spelling "Newborn" marked a landmark close to her apartment. By the time they found parking and dashed through the downpour to her building, they were soaked, out of breath, and laughing.

The atmosphere was electric as the elevator ascended. Kit couldn't resist touching the wet fabric clinging to Owen's chest, her fingertips tracing the hard lines of his muscles underneath. His sharp intake of breath reverberated through the compact space, amplifying the tension between them. As the elevator announced their arrival, Kit's hands, now trembling, fumbled in her bag for the keys. Her heartbeat hammered in her ears, mirroring the anticipation that hummed between them. The usually familiar action felt like defusing a bomb—one wrong move and everything could explode.

The door swung open, and they stepped into her apartment, leaving behind the downpour that had soaked them to the bone. The air inside was warm and inviting, a stark contrast to the chilly rain outside. Owen's arm snaked around her waist and drew her in closer to his sturdy body. Their gazes locked, and sparks flew, a storm of desire that threatened to consume them. With each breath, their passion rose like the wind outside, building into an unstoppable force.

Owen effortlessly lifted Kit, her legs wrapping around his waist without hesitation. Their kiss was as intense as the storm outside. They shed their drenched clothes, leaving a trail on the hardwood floor that led to the bedroom. As they surrendered to their shared desire, Owen protected Kit's body with his own, creating a shield behind which nothing else mattered except for what they experienced in the moment.

As Owen's hands explored, Kit's eyes briefly revealed a

shadow of her concealed past—fleeting and vanished like lightning streaking across a tumultuous sky. "There is so much you don't know," she whispered, her voice tinged with a hint of sadness that colored her longing. Although Owen heard her, the intensity of their closeness muddled her words in his mind, leaving him puzzled yet more intrigued.

In the thick of their embrace, a cool greenstone pendant pressed between them, its presence insistent. A gift from Kit's mother, the pendant wasn't just an adornment but a symbol of her complex dual existence. It connected her to New Zealand, a life she thought she had left behind but which still clung to her, represented by the stone's tranquil coolness against the heated chaos of their current moment.

The scent of Owen's aftershave mixed with the ozone from the lightning, creating a heady aroma that reminded Kit of their first physical connection. It had been a dangerous assignment that brought them together, an irrevocable bond forming between them. And now, as they yielded to their desires, an unspoken power play danced between them, Owen, with his need to protect her, and Kit, fiercely independent yet secretly craving the safety he offered. In this moment, they were two sides of the same coin, finding comfort and understanding in each other as they delved into the intricacies hidden beneath the facade.

As the intensity of their love-making died down, they collapsed onto the bed, their limbs intertwined in the aftermath of their passion. Owen cradled Kit, his breath warm against her neck. Their chests rose and fell in unison, the scent of rain and sweat combining to create an intimate and primal fragrance. Kit nuzzled into Owen's chest, finding comfort in the steady beat of his heart.

As the rain outside softened, Kit exhaled contentedly, her body languid and satiated. Despite the peaceful moment they shared, her mind was elsewhere. She couldn't stop thinking about Sergei, her captivating nemesis. His amber eyes seemed to pull her away from Owen's comforting arms. Even in these intimate moments, she couldn't escape his persistent image. Sergei, the manipulative Russian intelligence officer, was the enemy she had faced off against. He was responsible for the murders of Serbian farmers in Staro Dorbi, part of a mission to disrupt Kosovo's fragile peace. Caught between Owen's unwavering love and Sergei's dangerous charisma, Kit struggled with a difficult decision. She knew she needed to stay true to herself despite societal expectations and norms that were pulling her in conflicting directions.

Kit lay restlessly in bed, her inner turmoil raging between her free-spirited desires and her sense of responsibility to stand up for what is right. She longed for a love that would consume her, drive her to reckless adventures. But amidst the chaos of her desires, she also felt the weight of responsibility on her shoulders. Her quest for balance was never-ending, a delicate dance between heart and duty that left her restless and yearning for more.

After Owen left for work, Kit checked the time on her watch. His presence seemed to linger in the apartment as she prepared for her evening at the casino—Pristina's latest hotspot, and possibly a cover for illegal activities. But that wasn't her problem tonight; she reminded herself that she was off-duty. This was a rare opportunity to relax and enjoy herself without any professional expectations weighing her down.

As Kit gathered her belongings and prepared for the evening, her phone chimed, cutting through the silence. The screen lit up with a message from Silver—the enigmatic Russian hacker who had become an indispensable ally.

Silver, in her twenties, was an unconventional figure: slim with piercings and tattoos, her blonde hair styled in a modern asymmetrical cut with an undercut. More than just a brilliant hacker, she moonlighted as a waitress and served as Sergei's asset. Now, she had become Kit's confidante and accomplice.

Silver had been Kit's secret weapon, masterfully redirecting illicit funds into legitimate channels and significantly boosting Kit's finances. Although Kit had decided to return the principal amount to Kosovo's coffers, she couldn't resist keeping the accrued interest, stashing it away in a secret account for emergencies. Yet Silver, so often veiled in cyberspace, captivated her thoughts. Could Kit ever fully uncover the true identity of her elusive benefactor, or would she find herself entangled in her schemes, risking unforeseen consequences?

Kit's ethical compass wrestled with the tempting offer of $15 million in local currency that Silver had discreetly set aside for her. As a prosecutor, Kit understood the dangers of such a decision. The money held potential both to support noble causes and to fulfill her personal dream of opening a café bookshop in Auckland. The possibilities were endless and tempting.

Silver's message reappeared, succinct and cryptic, showcasing her mastery over discreet communications. Moments later, Silver's voice filled the room, carrying an icy note from Moscow. "We need to discuss your investments. Can we meet in Istanbul Airport? I have a lay-over coming up."

Kit felt the weight of her casual suggestion like a coin tossed into the air, uncertain where it would land. "What happens after Istanbul?" she asked, her voice slightly trembling as she tried masking her apprehension.

"That's up to you," Silver replied, her tone as measured and cool as the shadowed corners of a poker room. "You can join me or do something else that weekend."

Kit paused, Silver's proposal echoing in her thoughts. She shifted the conversation toward her immediate plans. "I'll be at the casino tonight." The notion of Istanbul—and the implications it might hold—lingered in the back of her mind, something to mull over later.

Silver's voice carried a hint of caution, "Be careful not to flaunt your wealth at the casino. It can attract unwanted attention. Remember, you're supposed to be a public servant, not a queen of diamonds parading around."

Acknowledging Silver's advice, Kit chose a sophisticated black ensemble for the evening. After ending the call, she stood before her wardrobe, contemplating her choices. She settled on a simple yet elegant black dress paired with low-heeled stilettos and selected a modest evening clutch. These items were not just fashion choices but her costume for the night ahead, carefully chosen to blend discretion with style.

Kit smoothed back her auburn hair and touched the greenstone pendant hanging around her neck, a reminder of simpler times, now another prop in this drama. Just as she finished adjusting the necklace, her phone buzzed—displaying Visar Dreshaj's name at the perfect moment. In that moment, Kit couldn't help but remember Mrs. Dreshaj, always in the background while her husband took center stage.

She picked up her silk shawl and evening bag and ventured out into the night, filled with anticipation. A sleek limousine awaited her at the curb, its shiny chrome accents reflecting the streetlights. The driver maintained an air of professionalism as he opened the door for her to step into a world of privilege and luxury engulfed by scents of leather, cologne, and tobacco.

"Good evening, Kit," Visar greeted her, a hint of an old-world charm in the kiss he carefully placed on her hand. Visar Dreshaj was a former academic and member of the Kosovo liberation Army, sometimes known by his nom de guerre, "the Inspector." He had a wiry build and an alert face, with slightly tousled dark brown hair. When not composing poetry or playing the violin, he practiced target shooting. Previously, he had provided Kit with confidential information to help her criminal investigations. While some of Kit's senior managers might disapprove of her outing tonight, she was not one to play by the rules. Besides, her immediate supervisor, Eva Refazo, encouraged the contact.

"Are you excited for your first Kosovo casino experience?" Visar asked.

"I can't wait." She grinned, her defences down for a moment.

As the car eased forward, escorted by a convoy of security, Visar shared plans for the evening. "My cousin will be there, as will a former Kosovo beauty queen—Lira Siliqi."

Kit nodded, her thoughts adrift—not on pageantry, but on Owen's absence and Silver's habit of disguising herself as a waitress. It was a life of contrasts Kit knew all too well.

"What's on your mind?" Visar's voice cut through her reverie.

"A friend who'd enjoy this evening," she said, leaving the depths of her thoughts unvoiced. Bringing Silver further into this intricate web of Kosovar politics was an entanglement best avoided.

Their conversation flowed with ease, carefully steering clear of their intertwined histories and complex current ties. Visar's genuine interest in her professional insights went beyond mere pleasantries. He knew the power of knowledge, and Kit's experience was invaluable. Yet, even as she engaged, her mind occasionally drifted to her Russian contacts—each one instrumental in shaping her into the adept legal strategist she was today. No longer a green newcomer, Kit was a survivor, sculpted by secrets and wisdom hard won.

As they left the bright lights behind and drove through the rain, Kit felt her pulse quicken in anticipation. Tonight, she felt confident that she could navigate a path through glamour and ambition.

At last, they reached the grandiose Prince Hotel, its entryway guarded by pseudo-classical pillars. Above the red-carpeted entrance, a neon sign flickered—"Prince Hotel"—while another boasted, "For the game of your life!" A member of the close protection team opened the car door for Kit and sheltered her with an umbrella, while another did the same for Visar. Together, Visar and Kit made their way into the casino. Artificial palm trees stood sentry at the doors, leading inward where slot machines with names like Joker Spin and Wild, Wild West tempted patrons. Beyond, a room brimming with gambling tables invited high stakes, and off to one side, a restaurant beckoned to the famished. Those in search of a night's rest could find solace at the hotel reception.

Despite its garish exterior, a thrill ran through Kit's palms, the magnetism of the games challenging Silver's cautions against a display of her wealth. The echo of her recent windfall lingered in the recesses of her mind, stoking the embers of temptation.

A man with a broad smile made his way toward them, his wiry frame and amiable grin mirroring Visar's. Although his hair was cropped short and threaded with silver, the familial ties were unmistakable. They greeted each other with a solid handshake and affectionate backslaps, their rapport immediately evident.

"Let me introduce you to my cousin, Luli," Visar said, gesturing to the newcomer.

Luli's smile was warm as he reached out to Kit. The conversation flowed in Albanian while Visar translated for Kit, explaining that Luli would furnish them with complimentary gambling chips for the night.

"It seems my first casino visit will be a lucky one." Kit grinned. "Thanks to your cousin, I'll be trying my luck."

"Let's indulge in a drink first and enjoy the entertainment," Visar suggested, leading the way into the bar area.

On the raised dais, the most glamorous woman Kit had ever seen was singing. Platinum blonde tresses framed her flawlessly made-up dark brown eyes. Lips painted a glossy red added to her charm. Clad in a short, black miniskirt, fishnet stockings accentuated by stilettos, and a form-fitting, red camisole, she exuded an intoxicating allure. A classic beauty mark adorned the left side of her lower lip, while an emblematic tattoo of the double-headed eagle, symbolizing the Albanian heritage of Kosovo, graced her upper arm. Lira's face possessed an intriguing duality—a look of innocence paired with an undeniable knowing. Kit knew instinctively that many men would find her utterly irresistible.

"Lira Siliqi is one of our finest performers," Visar said, his voice tinged with pride. "She's popular in the UK and even won a beauty pageant a few years ago."

"I can see why," Kit observed.

Three men sat at a table close to the podium. Kit's gaze settled on one particularly striking man, his eyes locked on Lira's mesmerizing performance. He exhaled smoke in slow, thoughtful streams and cradled his whiskey, the low bar light casting deep shadows across his sharply defined features, lending him an air of mysterious allure. Lira's voice seemed to weave around him like an enchantment, drawing him deeper into its melodic embrace. Kit watched, captivated by the unfolding scene.

"Notice the admirers?" Visar remarked as Kit's gaze lingered on the men. "They're off-duty police officers. Rumor has it that one of them is quite taken with her."

"The one sitting at the front?" Kit observed the striking man, apparently in his early thirties, neatly attired in a fitted suit that hinted at regular visits to the gym. The other two men, though similarly well-dressed, looked older and bore the marks of fatigue around their eyes.

"Valon Rama? He's known as a trustworthy man, particularly in challenging situations," Visar commented. Valon, with his athletic build, thick dark hair, and penetrating brown eyes, naturally drew people in. His presence, when coupled with Lira's, created an unmistakable aura of charisma. "That man sitting beside him is his police captain, Driton Kupi," Visar added.

Kit's attention shifted to the figure next to Valon Rama. Driton Kupi, in his early forties, held a commanding presence even while seated. His robust frame and the authoritative ease of a police captain were evident, yet his steel-gray eyes flickered with an untamed spark. His closely cropped, dark hair lent him a polished look, contrasting with the slight hunch of his broad shoulders as he leaned forward to engage with his colleagues. Though Driton exuded a subtle yet potent power, it was clear he was not just a man of the law but a worldly figure, his demeanor hinting at depths not immediately apparent. Valon Rama might radiate overt charisma, but

Driton Kupi commanded a more understated, compelling force.

"So, that's Kupi," she said thoughtfully. Lira's performance captivated the smoky room, her voice shifting seamlessly from soft and alluring to bold and commanding as she delivered the ballad. Throughout her set, her gaze often lingered on Valon Rama. Kit found herself curious about the finer details of Lira's presentation—her choice of hair extensions, the fragrance enhancing her allure—each element adding depth to her enchanting stage persona.

"So," Visar interrupted, pulling her attention away from the stage. "How much do you want to bet tonight?"

"Remember the complimentary gambling chips your cousin gave us?"

"Yes. Would you prefer to use those first?"

"How many did we get?"

"Around 200."

"That was incredibly generous of him."

"He's a great host."

"I'll start with those chips tonight and see where the evening takes us," she said, gauging her approach.

The band stopped playing and the musicians set down their instruments. Valon Rama had joined Lira on stage, sharing a moment while she lit her cigarette.

"Care to try your luck at the roulette table?" Visar suggested.

"Sure. What are the usual stakes here?"

"It varies," he replied. "With high rollers around, the stakes can escalate quickly. Just like anywhere else, really."

"Do you see any big spenders here tonight?"

"I was about to say no, but look who just walked in. That's Mal Mala."

As if on cue, the atmosphere in the room subtly shifted.

Four men entered through the grand front entrance, their confident strides echoing on the polished floor. The leader, a man in his early forties with sharp features, commanded immediate attention. His dark brown hair, styled into a distinctive widow's peak, accentuated his piercing gaze and thick, intimidating eyebrows. Clad in an impeccably tailored suit, he exuded an undeniable air of authority and menace.

Behind him, two men whose broad statures and alert demeanor resembled bodyguards moved with a deliberate sense of purpose, their eyes scanning the room. The aura they projected was unmistakably dangerous, their appearance akin to that of seasoned gangsters.

The group made their way to the bar. The leader swiveled in his seat, his calculating eyes sweeping over the patrons—a predator sizing up his environment. Kit's eyes inadvertently met his, and a wave of discomfort swept through her. His probing look gave her the unsettling impression that he was evaluating her, possibly mistaking her for Visar's new interest. Turning away to regain her composure, she couldn't resist the urge to glance back, curious about his next move.

His scrutiny didn't linger on her for long. Instead, it shifted to assess three men positioned strategically nearby: Visar's security detail. Kit noted a similar assembly of guards encircling Mal Mala, their demeanor just as vigilant. Meanwhile, his remaining companions appeared preoccupied, one engaged in a hushed phone conversation and the other briskly typing on a smartphone, likely handling other urgent affairs. Across the room, Lira and Valon continued their lively discussion by the band area, seemingly oblivious to the charged atmosphere the newcomers had introduced.

Kit shifted uncomfortably in her seat. "That guy over there makes me uneasy," she confided to Visar.

"Rightly so," Visar responded seriously. "But you're safe with me."

"I know about your Kosovo Liberation Army background, but I guess even that doesn't deter everyone," Kit said, trying to lighten the mood.

Visar raised his eyebrows in mock surprise. "I was actually referring to my role as a minister. Though, it hasn't stopped assassination attempts in the past."

Kit frowned. "You enjoy trying to shock me, don't you?"

She noticed their three guards shift from relaxed to alert, the room's tension mounting.

"Do you feel it too?" she asked.

Visar smiled, gesturing openly. "Lira used to date Mala, but now she's with that bodybuilding police officer. It's stirred up quite the storm among the local bosses."

"His police colleagues are here too," Kit noted.

"What could go wrong?" Visar joked lightly, though his tone suggested concern. "Mala's group outnumbers Valon's."

As Valon's associates tensed up, watching the crowd at the bar, Kit sighed. "I was hoping for a relaxed night at the roulette or slots. Think they might be armed?"

"Definitely. Everyone here likely is."

Around them, others began to take notice. One couple quickly left; a small group of men followed suit.

"I'm feeling really uneasy. Should we leave?" Kit asked.

"Under normal circumstances, I'd say yes. But leaving now might complicate things for my cousin. It could escalate tensions if I'm not here," Visar explained.

Kit's mind started racing and she fidgeted with her bag. She thought of Owen and his advice against going out with

Visar to the casino tonight. He might have been right. She wondered if she should text Owen to come and pick her up —but that would upset Visar. Kit pulled out her mobile phone and checked messages. She ignored those about work and quickly sent a message to Owen, *Things are getting tense here—not sure what's going down.*

Within a few moments a message came back from Owen. *Are you okay?*

Yes—it's probably fine but

Visar snatched her phone from her grasp and quickly scanned through the messages. He turned off the phone and put it in his pocket.

"Excuse me," Kit said. "That's my phone."

"I know. You don't need it now. You're with me, remember? There's no need to text your boyfriend to come pick you up."

"Please give me back my phone." Kit's voice shook with anger as her cheeks flushed red.

"Not yet," Visar replied coolly.

Kit decided she would go to reception and find a telephone. Before she could move, Visar reached out and placed a hand on her arm. "It may not be safe for you to leave right now. I wouldn't want you caught in any danger."

Kit froze in shock as she looked at him. "Do you really think there might be shooting?"

"It's happened before."

"Why did you bring me here if you knew this was a possibility?"

"I never said I knew it would happen tonight. As I said, it's happened before."

"And you're so calm about it?"

"I've been through worse," he replied calmly.

Kit remembered that during the conflict, Visar's nickname was "the Inspector," referencing his role in the Kosovo Liberation Army. He had seen plenty of action.

She extended her hand towards him. "Please, just give me back my phone."

Visar reached into his pocket to fetch the phone. "There are several reasons why it may not be wise to call your boyfriend right now."

"If you insist, but I think you should take me home."

As they conversed, Kit noticed Mala rising from his seat, flanked by his companions, making his way towards Lira and Valon. Raised voices emanated from the other side of the room.

"Here they go," Visar muttered with a tight smile, his usually composed expression faltering for a moment. "You'd better come with me now," he said. Without hesitation, he grabbed Kit by the elbow and ushered her towards the bar. She tried to ask questions, but he remained silent as they quickly made their way across the room. "Stay here and take cover," Visar said before he headed back towards the opposing groups. The bartender was already systematically moving the top-shelf liquor lower, bracing for trouble.

Kit fidgeted, unease prickling her skin. "I can't shake the feeling that something's about to happen here," she confessed to the bartender. It was Gavin, whom she recognized from team visits to the Hopscotch bar in Pristina. Gavin, with his towering frame and hearty Scottish brogue, leaned closer, his eyes twinkling with a mix of concern and intrigue.

"Mala is a notorious kingpin from Peja," he said. "Ever since Lira began her gig here, he's been chasing her. They were involved once, but now she's dating Valon Rama." Gavin's intel was consistent with what Visar had shared with Kit earlier.

Before Kit could inquire further, chaos erupted. Mala grabbed Lira and tried to drag her towards him. Valon intervened by forcefully pushing Mala away, but Mala responded with a quick punch. The tension between the two groups became palpable as they faced off. In the midst of it all, Kit caught a glimpse of Visar and his cousin rushing towards the escalating fight, accompanied by their security teams.

The melee escalated at an alarming pace, a chaotic blend of flying chairs, broken glass, and wild punches. Kit, Gavin, and the other patrons and staff scrambled for cover as the fight erupted. Visar's security team quickly formed a barrier around him while Valon's allies joined in around him. Mala's agility was impressive despite his size, effortlessly dodging and striking back with precision. The altercation devolved into an all-out brawl with no holds barred, as fists and kicks flew unrestrained.

Kit's sense of alarm increased as she watched the chaos unfold from the safety of the bar. This volatile situation could easily escalate into something dangerous. Suddenly, Gavin grabbed Kit's arm and pulled her to the side. A loud crash issued as someone threw a chair into he bar. She met his gaze with astonishment and gratitude—she hadn't expected him to act so swiftly, potentially saving her from harm.

"Thank you, Gavin, that was close," she breathed out, still shaken by the narrow escape. "I don't care what Visar said; I'm calling the police. This situation's out of control." Reaching for her mobile, she realized it was missing—likely overlooked in the midst of the commotion when Visar neglected to return it.

"Can you call the authorities?" she implored Gavin.

"Uh, negative," he said. "It's my rule of thumb not to

involve the cops. I'll never get another gig if I'm known for calling in police when fists fly."

"Then, where's your landline?"

Gavin gestured towards the far end of the bar where an antiquated phone hung on the wall. Crouching, Kit navigated the chaos toward the phone. Gripping the receiver, she dialed Owen's number.

"Reese," his voice echoed on the other side.

"Owen, it's chaos here," Kit said, struggling to keep her voice even. "A brawl's broken out. They're armed—it's a powder keg. We need backup immediately."

"Location?"

"Hotel P—" Her sentence was severed by a series of sharp reports, unmistakably gunfire, followed by the sound of shattering glass. Darkness engulfed the room, pierced only by the dim haze from the city's neon lifeblood. Disoriented and temporarily blinded, Kit struggled to see as the staccato gunfire was replaced by the hum of the now-dead telephone line.

Gavin's muffled curses filtered through the chaotic room, his voice a low growl. Kit couldn't see anything, relying on her memory and the sounds around her as she guided herself back to the safety of the bar. "Are you still convinced we don't need the police?" she whispered.

"This is uncharted territory," Gavin replied.

Gunshots rang out again, accompanied by shouts and a loud scream—Lira's unmistakable cry of fear. In the midst of the chaos, lights flickered on to reveal Luli's silhouette against the turmoil, desperately trying to fix the fuses. The fuse box itself was evidence of the violence, damaged by a stray bullet. Kit could make out Albanian voices shouting. Minutes later, the distant wail of sirens began to slice through the clamor.

Crouching, Visar sprinted toward the dubious safety of the bar. "Cops are en route," he gasped, pressing Kit's mobile back into her hands before his grip shifted, insistent on her arm. "Luli's got a back exit—my guys are bringing the car around now."

"Is anyone injured?" Kit asked.

"I think at least one person is hurt," Visar replied.

"Gavin, can we give you a lift back into town?" Kit asked the bartender.

"Thanks, love, but it would look like I was fleeing the scene of the crime. Better stay put; the police will want my statement."

A narrow doorway flanked the left of the bar, leading to a corridor. On one side were the restrooms, and on the other, an exit door that Visar flung open for Kit. Stepping outside, the night air felt like salvation after the chaos, and she inhaled deeply, her breath shuddering with relief. With a growl of the engine, Visar's car tore around the corner, skidding to a stop beside them. He gestured for her to get in, and she slid into the backseat, the leather cool against her skin, Visar close on her heels.

The pulsing lights of police cars blinked in the distance as they circled to the rear of the building and darted out through the service exit. The car followed a shadowy road beside the railway, then streaked toward the highway leading back to Pristina.

Settling into the seat, Kit let out a centering breath. "I was actually looking forward to some gambling tonight. It's a pity about the fire fight."

"We'll find a better night for it," Visar offered in a comforting tone. "Perhaps I could tempt you with a nightcap at a bar I know, a more low-key one."

"Thanks, but I think I'd better head home. My nerves are shattered," Kit replied, fatigue edging her voice.

Visar murmured instructions to the driver, then reclined into the car's shadows. "Your cousin—do you think he's okay that we left?" Kit inquired, recollecting his earlier unease as the situation grew heated.

"Once the Police got involved, our continued presence at the scene could've complicated things," Visar said.

Kit gave a small nod, her mind circling around the edges of the night's events and their implications.

"I'd hoped tonight would leave you with such a sense of gratitude you might reward me with a goodnight kiss. How do my chances stand?" he teased lightly.

Her irritation flickered back. "I'm not over you confiscating my phone and ignoring my requests to have it back."

"But I returned it, didn't I?" he countered.

"Eventually, but the damage is done—the evening's tarnished. So, no kiss," she said, crossing her arms.

"And what would have happened without that scene back there?" he prodded, a note of playfulness in his voice.

Kit offered no reply, merely shrugged and turned her gaze to the window where the drizzle persisted. She concealed her smile from him, letting the night's shadow be her accomplice.

Chapter Two

Valon Rama exited the Pristina Police Station and made his way to the car park. He ran through his plans for the day, smiling as he thought of meeting Lira Siliqi. Lira lived nearby with her mother and two sisters. He found his pace quickening at the thought of spending time with her later. They would go to a café. He would listen sympathetically to her talk about weekend plans and her latest gigs. His face lit up as he imagined her tossing her hair back and batting those long dark lashes at him over macchiato.

Her beauty, a magnet for stares, had caught Mal Mala's eye. What she had seen in Mala, Valon couldn't fathom, but their past connection had faded, leaving only Mala's bitterness in its wake. Since shifting her affection to Valon, Lira's fear of Mala's retaliation had grown. Their love had become a focus for Mala's animosity, culminating in the firefight at the casino.

Valon could sense the unease in Mala's movements; despite the presence of Driton and the police, his attack was alarming. As Valon's boss and head of the Police unit,

Driton Kupi often teetered on a thin line between providing safety for others and accepting bribes. Although Valon had not participated in any extortion tactics like his coworkers, he found little comfort in that fact as he braced himself for what was to come.

Despite being aggrieved by Mala's animosity, Valon's love for Lira kept him grounded. He braced himself for another confrontation that seemed inevitable, though he couldn't predict when or where it would occur. If facing Mala was necessary to ensure Lira's safety, he would do so without hesitation. These thoughts wrestled with his concentration as he geared up for an intense training session at the gym.

He was almost at the parking lot, which was located behind the shops on the main road. Students headed to their favorite after-school hangouts, like the nearby snack bar or gelato stand. Spring had arrived in full force, with intermittent showers puddling on the sidewalks. His keys jingled in his pocket as he approached his car. A vibration from his mobile phone caught his attention.

It was a text from Lira. He couldn't help but smile at her greeting, *Hey babe, what's up?*

Not much. Coffee later? he responded.

Sure, came her answer.

See you in a few?

I love you forever, darling.

Me too.

We'll be in love for all time.

See you later. His smile turned into a grin as he ended the conversation. Lira's dramatic declarations of love sometimes made him roll his eyes, but he couldn't resist her enchanting beauty and the way she loved him. If only he could express his feelings for her as passionately as she did for him.

As Valon approached a foreboding black vehicle, he noticed two figures emerging from its shadow. The pair seemed tense and jumpy.

"Valon Rama?" one of the men asked, his pale face glistening with sweat. Valon's thoughts were jolted back to reality.

"Yes, wha—" His words were cut off as the men opened fire at close range.

Multiple bullets found their mark in his upper body, one rebounding off a graffiti-covered wall behind him. The spray-painted words "Every spring has its story," now served as the backdrop for a tragedy. Another shot tore through his shoulder, causing blood to spatter against the wall.

"God, no!" Valon cried out as he collapsed onto the wet pavement. Panic erupted and people scattered in every direction. Within moments, the sound of approaching sirens filled the air, growing louder by the second.

"We need to get out of here," one of the attackers growled, quickly stowing his weapon out of sight. They rushed back to the car and jumped in. The driver expertly reversed, disappearing through a different exit, tires screeching as they sped away.

Valon lay sprawled out on the ground, his face contorted with pain, his life draining onto the wet pavement. As the sound of his attackers' departure faded, the passers-by who had initially taken cover began to cautiously gather around the fallen figure.

Chapter Three

In the Organization on International Development and Coordination (OIDC) headquarters, prosecutors gathered around a table, their faces etched with concentration.

The walls of the meeting room were made of see-through glass, a nod to modernity in the otherwise aging, repurposed building.

Sitting at the head of the table with her sharp legal mind and impressive reputation, Eva Refazo commanded attention. Her appearance was formidable, although slightly disheveled. The dark clouds outside seemed to match her grey business suit, and a white ruffled shirt peeped out from under her jacket. With her reading glasses perched on her nose, she scanned over her team while holding a pencil above her legal pad. Under the table, Bambino, her faithful scruffy terrier cross with a grizzled muzzle, lay quietly next to her black stilettos. On the table, an unopened pack of cigarettes and a plastic cup filled with black instant coffee served as evidence of the demanding nature of her job.

Kit sat beside her, her auburn hair pulled back in a sleek

ponytail. She was absorbed in the screen of her mobile phone, while her dark business suit seemed to absorb the harsh lighting above. The only hint of softness was the emerald sheen of her silk blouse. Across from them, their efficient assistant Angel typed away on her laptop, her blonde locks falling in front of her face. She was dressed casually in a cashmere sweater and chic slacks, a stark contrast to the formal atmosphere of the room.

Across the table, the newest member of their team, Dua, a young Albanian woman with lustrous, short black hair and doe-like brown eyes, sat silently, notebook in hand. Axel Delcroix, a dark-haired French man in his mid-thirties, murmured into his mobile phone, oblivious to the buzzing of activity around him. A woman, Christina Wackernagel, lean and sharp-featured in her forties, was absorbed in a stack of reports, her highlighter dancing over the pages.

"*Buongiorno*, good morning," Eva greeted her team warmly, her light Italian accent adding a melodic quality to her words. "I'm excited to introduce our newest intern, Dua Rexhepi, from Albania. She has a law degree from the US and is ready to get started."

Dua smiled shyly and replied, "Thank you, Eva. I am thrilled to be here."

"To start, Dua will be working closely with Kit. As we progress, we'll find other ways to utilize your skills."

Kit briefly looked up from her phone to acknowledge Dua's arrival, a welcome event in the busy office. "Welcome, Dua," she said as she shifted her focus back to the demanding case at hand. "Your timing couldn't be better. We have a huge caseload."

Dua nodded eagerly, her eyes lighting up with anticipation. "I'm all set to help out with anything," she declared.

Eva glanced at the stack of documents cluttering the

table. "Right now, we're deep into tracing the paper trails of several judges. It's meticulous, critical work, given the irregularities we've observed in case assignments."

Intrigued by the challenge, Dua leaned in. "I can't wait to start. What's our first move?"

"Our primary suspect, Judge Tirol, has returned to Austria to face charges," Eva explained, her voice tinged with the gravity of their task. "Though he's back home, we're convinced he wasn't working alone. His ability to manipulate case assignments suggests a wider network."

Dua nodded, recalling a news segment she had seen. "I remember reading a piece about that scandal."

"Yes," Eva said. "And it's not just Tirol. Our former mission chief Mueller and his deputy are also caught up in extradition issues and a money laundering case related to public utility deals in Kosovo."

Kit, who had been listening intently, chimed in, "Exactly. Those kickbacks are just the tip of the iceberg."

Eva sighed, her frustration palpable. "Power tends to corrupt. Following the scandal, our entire senior leadership was overhauled. The new acting head came in from OIDC's New York office, and the deputy was pulled from Berlin."

Angel, leaning against the doorframe, smiled wryly. "Quite the drama unfolding, isn't it?" Her Yorkshire accent softened the edge of her words, adding a light, humorous note to the meeting.

Despite only being in his mid-thirties, Axel looked tired in his slightly too snug white shirt and well-worn navy suit. "At least we managed to hold onto our jobs," he said.

Eva offered a thin-lipped smile. "There was a moment

when I wasn't sure I'd have a job to come back to. They put me on administrative leave for a couple of months when I dared to publicize the bribery allegations."

"I'm glad you're back," Kit said. "Things were hectic here without you." During Eva's absence, Kit had been given the role of acting head and chief prosecutor. Now Kit understood first-hand the many responsibilities that Eva had to manage—from personnel issues to prosecuting cases and handling political challenges with higher management.

"Speaking of which," Eva said, toying with her cigarette packet. "We may have a busy week ahead of us—there was a shooting incident at a casino on the outskirts of town. A few arrests were made, but ultimately, no charges were filed." Eva glanced at Kit with a questioning look. "Eyewitnesses reported seeing the Minister of Energy and a female associate at the scene. They left swiftly before the police arrived."

Kit cleared her throat and shifted uneasily. "Could we possibly discuss this later?"

"Sure," Eva replied, giving Kit a pointed look. She paused, collecting her thoughts, before continuing, "One of the persons of interest was a police officer, Valon Rama. He was involved in a confrontation with Mal Mala, a man tied to organized crime and extortion rackets around Peje and with business ventures in Pristina, like the One Up Café. It seems both were linked romantically to a former beauty queen, Lira Siliqi. Members of Rama's police unit also got involved in the melee," Eva explained. "Sadly, the same Valon Rama was the target of an assassination just yesterday. Two unidentified assailants shot him in a car park off the main avenue. He was dead on arrival at the hospital."

Kit frowned, her expression somber. "That's really unfortunate."

"Yes, bad things do happen to good people. Quite frequently," Eva said. "Kit, can you follow up with your EUFOR police contacts and find out what's been going on? If they've formed a task force to locate the killers, I want you on it."

Kit looked down, scribbling notes on her pad. Her involvement with Owen Reese was common knowledge in the office. The Kosovo prosecutors were in the thick of the criminal investigations, dovetailing with the police, ensuring proper handling of evidence, and upholding the integrity of criminal procedures.

Kit was certain Eva harbored suspicions about her recent visit to the casino. In their organization, the OIDC, fraternizing with local power players like Dreshaj was generally taboo, yet his insights had proved crucial in advancing their last few investigations. Kit felt her pulse quicken with the thrill of rule-bending—this audacity had been instrumental in cracking their previous cases. She resolved to clear the air with Eva later, away from the curious ears of their colleagues.

Axel's gaze cut across the room to Kit, his eyes sharpening with pointed accusation. "Using your personal connections again to get a leg up with the local police, Kit?" he remarked, loud enough for only her to hear. His tone mixed skepticism with a hint of envy.

Kit met his gaze with a nonchalant shrug. "Perhaps." Axel's veiled jabs never failed to irk her, stemming, she presumed, from Eva's tendency to entrust her with high-profile cases, leaving him to muddle through mundane legal proceedings. As Axel's stare intensified, a mix of irritation and defiance spurred Kit to act. Under the table, she stealthily texted Owen. *Hey, I was just assigned to Valon Rama's murder task force, if it exists?*

Owen's response was swift, *No official task force yet. Join our briefing, tomorrow.*

Will do, she responded, lifting her eyes back to the meeting.

Dua observed the office's interpersonal dynamics with a smile.

"Do you need me to research the land records?" The slender blonde woman broke her silence. Christina Wackernagel, from Germany, excelled at tasks that required careful attention to detail. Dependable as the sunrise, her uncanny knack for spotting the smallest inconsistencies made her an asset in dealing with land-related cases. Kit was always relieved when Christina was roped in to sift through the mass of cadastral records, as this kind of work was not her forté.

Eva nodded, "That would be excellent, Christina."

Christina wrinkled her nose in frustration. "The reliability of records here is questionable. During a visit to the land registry, I watched them alter documents right in front of me. It seems some are acquiring lands through possession, disregarding legal processes—unthinkable in Germany."

Eva, leaning back in her chair with a wry smile, nodded understandingly. "Around here, I'm rarely surprised by anything. Dua, while you're digging into your research, keep an eye out for any irregular land inheritance cases. Coordinate with Christina on this; we need to ensure there's no foul play."

"I'll keep that in mind," Dua replied, making a note to prioritize this issue.

Clearing his throat, Axel interjected, "I've heard rumors of a march tomorrow to protest Valon Rama's murder. Might be a good opportunity to scope out any suspicious characters. I could attend, if you like." His gaze shifted to Kit, gauging her response.

Eva jumped on the idea, "Sounds like a plan, Axel. Why don't you and Kit work as a team on this."

Kit frowned as she shot a disgruntled glance at Axel. He was well aware that she'd been assigned the Rama case, and yet here he was, muscling in on her turf. But as much as she hated to admit it, he had a point. The protest could provide valuable insights, and she had been so caught up in other matters that the march had slipped under her radar.

"Are we, as OIDC personnel, permitted to attend local demonstrations and protests?" Dua inquired.

"We're allowed to observe but not participate," Eva said.

"That distinction can be a blurry one," Christina said.

Kit silently planned to give Axel the slip at the earliest opportunity so she could launch her investigation unhindered. Her first order of business would be to reach out to Owen and garner any inside information he might have. If Axel got lost in the process, all the better.

"Alright then," Kit conceded. "See you there, Axel." *Or maybe not*, she mused.

"I saw in some local news," Dua interjected. "The march is set to start at noon from the spot where Rama was killed. There's a large turnout expected."

Kit assessed Dua with newfound interest. Having a team member fluent in Albanian could prove helpful for insights from local sources. She decided to approach Dua later, when Axel wasn't within earshot, and invite her to join Kit at the protest.

"Kit, we have another matter for your attention. We've received a request to reinstate the international arrest warrant for Sergei Sokolov, the suspected organizer of the Staro Dorbi killings."

"Mmhm," Kit acknowledged non-commitally, her mind whirring. "The Russians kicked up such a fuss last time about his diplomatic immunity that we had to withdraw the application while you were on leave. They're sure to do that again, so it seems a waste of resources chasing the Interpol red notice."

"I'm aware," Eva replied. "But our new boss from Denmark doesn't want to let the Russians off the hook for serious crimes. Can you revisit this issue, and we'll discuss it further?"

"Alright," Kit agreed, making a mental note. Her mind was already buying time for this task, which would reverse a favor she'd done for Sergei, her confidant and key ally from her last case. Convincing the mission head against pursuing the warrant was critical to avoid agitating the Russians. That her personal life sometimes conflicted with her professional one made her jittery, risking exposure. Her bond with Sergei had metamorphosed her from a naïve New Zealand lawyer into a canny legal operative.

"We have court appearances scheduled for defendants who are implicated in a range of serious crimes. Axel, could you handle that? It's crucial someone from here attends to oppose any bail request. They're clear flight risks."

"I'll check the hearing schedule," Axel offered. "We've got the Rama support march tomorrow, remember."

"We have to ensure that gang remains locked up," Kit emphasized. "You can't afford to miss that hearing, Axel. If they manage to get bail, they could vanish into thin air again."

"*N'inquiète pas*," Axel replied in his native language. "Don't worry, I've got it under control."

As they wrapped up the meeting, Kit lingered and

signalled Dua. "Could you join me in my office? I'd like to discuss a task with you," she said.

Chapter Four

The Black and White Café was already buzzing with the aroma of freshly brewed coffee when Kit arrived the next morning. She was dressed in a chic black leather jacket, and she spotted Dua waiting for her at a table near the window.

After exchanging greetings, they placed their drink orders. Kit stuck with her usual Americano, while Dua chose a small espresso. As they drank their coffee, Kit outlined her plan.

"I need you to take some photos during the march," she said in a low voice. "Try to be inconspicuous."

"Of what exactly?" Dua asked, her eyes narrowing with curiosity.

"Everything and everyone," Kit replied.

"Ah, I see," Dua nodded. "And do you often gather your own evidence?"

Kit smiled, impressed by Dua's observation skills. "Only when necessary."

"But wouldn't the police take care of that? And what about privacy concerns?" Dua persisted.

"We work closely with the police; this is just an additional tool for our investigation. The photos won't be used in court," Kit clarified, pausing to savor her coffee. She had started smoking as a way to cope with stress, but now she was trying to cut down to just a few cigarettes a day. However, the aroma of her coffee made her crave a smoke. "Listen, I'm trying to quit smoking, so let's finish up before I give in and light up. It's almost noon; we should get to the crime scene early."

Dua nodded and hastily downed her espresso. They left some money on the table for the waiter and headed towards the place where the march was set to begin. When they arrived, the scene was already buzzing with activity. Memorials and pictures were propped up against the wall near where Valon had been shot. A large portrait of the victim hauntingly gazed into the distance.

"Looks more like a shrine than a crime scene," Kit said.

"He was so handsome and a respected police officer ... such a loss." Dua sighed. "I hope they catch the ones responsible."

"We will," Kit assured her. "We definitely will."

"What about Axel? Should we be expecting him here?"

"I'm sure he's around somewhere," Kit replied, scanning the crowd. "He'll find us."

Kit and Dua situated themselves a reasonable distance from Valon's makeshift shrine, keeping an eye on the gathering protesters. Slowly but surely, the crowd grew until there were nearly 2,000 people. Organizers had even arranged for T-shirts bearing Valon's name and banners decrying his murder.

"Let's get closer to the front," Kit suggested, beginning to weave through the throng. She spotted Visar Dreshaj among the crowd, along with several other prominent politicians and a host of other public figures and celebrities. Given the recent gossip about her and Visar's visit to the casino, she decided to keep a low profile, staying to the side where she could still observe the demonstration.

"If you spot anything interesting in Albanian on the banners, let me know," she said to Dua.

The pair of them meandered with the crowd, purposefully staying away from the frontline. Periodic chants of "Rama! Rama!" rang out.

"Valon Rama was a hero to the people," Dua said. Kit took a quick glance at the crowd, searching for any familiar faces, but no one seemed suspicious. "It seems like this gathering is a reflection of public opinion. The police are under pressure to find the perpetrators."

"News reports say that some people suspect that Mal Mala is responsible, but he's already fled the city." Pointing towards the front line, Dua continued, "And there's Valon's girlfriend leading the protest."

Kit spotted Lira, who looked drained. Her previously vibrant face was devoid of makeup and obscured by dark sunglasses. Her hair was tied back tightly to reveal her unadorned features. The image of Lira onstage at the casino —commanding the room with her glamour and talent— flashed through Kit's mind. Now, Lira looked fragile, almost childlike, and Kit felt a pang of sympathy for her. It was a stark reminder of the importance of cherishing the moments spent with loved ones. The future, she knew, was unpredictable.

Almost instinctively, Kit reached for her phone, checking for any new messages.

"I thought I might see you here," came a familiar voice from behind her.

She looked to the side, her heart jumping at the sight of Owen in his EUFOR uniform, with another officer in tow.

"I was just thinking about you," she admitted, lightly touching his arm.

Owen flashed a smile at her, but then the seriousness in his expression returned. "This is a sad day. Rama was one of their finest."

"Lira's clearly heartbroken," Kit said.

"They say she's now under the protection of the head of Rama's unit," Owen added.

"Kupi?"

"Yes, Driton Kupi. He's always just a few steps behind her."

Kit glanced toward Lira and recognized the man she had seen with Valon Rama at the casino. She nodded, absorbing the information. "What does being under his protection imply?"

"It suggests he acts as her guardian in public contexts—and beyond that, I'm not entirely sure," Owen admitted, clearly puzzled by the nuances of local traditions.

"Things are changing now," Dua interjected, catching their attention.

Owen looked over at the young Albanian woman, noticing her modern outfit of cropped jeans and a jacket with a faux fur collar.

"I apologize for not introducing you two earlier," Kit said. "Dua is our new intern from Albania. Dua, meet Sergeant Owen Reese. We often collaborate on cases, right Owen?"

Owen and Dua exchanged a handshake. "Pleased to meet you," he said.

"Dua has been instrumental in helping me with some research," Kit continued. "She's been translating billboards and keeping us informed about local Albanian news relevant to this case."

"Glad to have your help, Dua," Owen said. "Kit, I received your message about being assigned to this case. There's a meeting later today at the office; can you make it?"

"I'll be there," Kit assured him. "Also, we need to keep a lookout for Mala and his crew. Dua mentioned he might have already left Pristina."

"If he has, it won't be for long. He runs his operation from here, and he's likely just laying low for now," Owen speculated. He paused and discreetly scanned the crowd, his gaze settling on a small group. "There they are, behind you. Don't look now, but those four are part of his gang. They might not be directly involved in the killing, but they're definitely his men."

Kit glanced around discreetly, taking note of the men Owen had pointed out. They were smoking and talking amongst themselves, positioned away from the protest but still aware of their surroundings. The usually busy shops had quieted as people joined the demonstration. Kit nodded in understanding as she caught sight of the men.

"End corruption! Justice for all!" voices rang out from the crowd.

"I'll catch up with you later, Kit. We need to patrol near the government buildings. Come by our office in about an hour," Owen suggested.

A voice with a distinct French accent cut through the rising clamor of the rally. "I have been looking for you, Kit," Axel panted, his appearance slightly disheveled as if he had been sprinting through the crowd. His eyes held a hint of urgency mixed with a challenge.

. . .

"Thanks, Owen. I'll catch up later," Kit responded, her voice calm but her eyes alert as she gave a subtle nod toward Dua, signaling an exit strategy. Owen nodded, understanding the cue perfectly, and drifted away to join a group heading towards the stage.

"Hello, Axel. Just wrapping things up here, right, Dua?" Kit kept her tone light, but her stance was guarded.

Dua nodded, glancing between the two lawyers.

"Seen anything interesting?" Kit asked, turning to Axel, her question laced with a double meaning.

"Not yet," Axel admitted, his gaze scanning the crowd before settling back on Kit. "But Rama drew a big crowd, didn't he? We might be able to see something useful for the case. I'll hang around and see what else I can find out." His voice lowered slightly, suggesting he knew more than he let on.

Kit's eyes narrowed for a moment, picking up on the hint. "Good luck with that," she said curtly, before turning to Dua. "Let's head out."

As they walked towards the main street, Dua pulled out her phone and checked a new message. "Do you mind if I meet a friend for coffee? I'll be quick."

"Go ahead," Kit replied, understanding the flexible nature of their break times. "Everything settled in your new place?"

"Almost. Just the basics for now," Dua said as they walked. "I'm still setting it up."

"Take your time," Kit said.

"Thanks. Besim's helping me. That's who I'm meeting for coffee."

"At the One Up Café?"

"Yeah, he's on a break too. We met in English class," Dua explained just as they reached the café. She spotted

Besim across the street and waved. "Gotta go, Kit. See you back at the office."

"Sure, I'm off to the police meeting shortly," Kit replied as Dua crossed the street to join Besim, who was waiting with a friendly smile.

As Kit approached the EUFOR Police Headquarters, a sense of unease gnawed at her. Watching Dua disappear into the crowd at the café to meet Besim, Kit was struck by a nagging feeling of familiarity. Her gaze fixed on the café's sign—One Up. A chill of recognition raced through her; that name had come up during a recent office meeting. One Up wasn't just any café—it was owned by Mal Mala, the prime suspect in the murder of Valon Rama.

Could this seemingly ordinary café be hiding something more sinister, masked by the comforting aroma of coffee? Her heart skipped a beat. Was she overthinking this, seeing connections where there were none? Yet, the more she pondered, the more an insidious dread took hold. Was she on the brink of uncovering a hidden element of the case, masquerading behind casual coffee meetups?

Chapter Five

As dusk gave way to night, the tree-canopied avenue, a stone's throw from the main street, felt like a secret corner of Pristina. The noise of traffic was drowned by the rhythmic pulsation of music from local clubs and bars.

The Mamba Club held a corner spot in the city's vibrant nightlife hub, hidden behind a screen of trees and unkempt gardens. The club had a Caribbean theme with its indoor-outdoor seating, wooden floors, and tropical decor. Coloured lights wound around trees and the billboard out front, creating a luminous oasis against the darkness of the nearby street, lit only by a single, dim streetlight. But within the club, the ambiance was warm and electric. Tonight, the Mamba Club was booked by a group celebrating an engagement within the Siliqi family. A group of young women danced in a line while men and couples lounged at tables or atop barstools, drinking and smoking.

Seated alone at the bar, Lira was a solitary figure clad in black. Her blonde hair was pulled back with a black bow, and she wore a black miniskirt, tights, and thigh-high boots.

A faux black lambskin jacket kept the chill at bay. A cigarette in one hand and a cocktail in the other, she was periodically approached by her sisters and cousins, coaxing her to join them on the dance floor. She always refused.

Her thoughts were interrupted as Driton Kupi slid into the seat next to her. He draped an arm around her shoulders and planted a kiss on her cheek. Her eyes, lined with smudged eyeliner, looked up at him.

"Driton, how did you find me?" she asked.

"Your mother mentioned you were here. Do you mind if I join you?" Before she could answer, he had already flagged down the bartender and was lighting a cigarette.

With tears in her eyes and a runny nose, Lira used a tissue to dab at her face. "It was heart-warming to see such a turnout at the march for Valon."

"Yes, it was moving to see so many people rally behind Valon and our cause," Driton agreed.

Lira took a slow sip of her cocktail, her gaze drifting over the bar without focusing, her eyes slightly watery.

Driton's voice trembled as he spoke, "I miss Valon everyday. He wasn't just a friend to me; he was like a brother." A tear rolled down his cheek, but he quickly wiped it away. "Valon once confided in me, saying that if anything were to happen to him, he would…" His words trailed off as the memory of their conversation overwhelmed him with emotion.

Lira leaned towards him, her hand resting on his arm. "What did Valon say, Driton?"

"He actually… I can barely even say it… he said that if anything ever happened to him, he would give me his blessing to take care of you."

Lira gasped and pulled back. "Valon would really say something like that?"

"I swear it on my life, Lira. He did."

"But you're engaged," she pointed out.

"That's not going as planned."

"Have you told your fiancée?"

"No, but that doesn't matter now. People will understand." He turned towards her, emanating warmth. Despite her inner turmoil, she found solace in his presence.

Lira's voice shook as she spoke. "I feel completely broken," she admitted, her emotions too complex to make sense of. "I've cancelled all of my performances for the next month. I can't even bring myself to sing. My grief for Valon is consuming me."

"I completely understand, Lira. I am also struggling with intense emotions. But I only ask for the opportunity to stand by your side and keep you safe."

Her large, brown eyes, rimmed with smudged kohl, searched his face. "I have something to tell you about, Valon. Let's step outside where our conversation won't be easily overheard."

Driton nodded in agreement and dismounted his barstool. He offered her his arm for support as she stood, swaying slightly on her high heels. She gathered her bag and jacket, and together, they crossed the worn but sturdy floorboards. As they exited the room, filled with loved ones and acquaintances celebrating, they were met with sympathetic glances from those who noticed their departure. A few whispered conversations took place before the party continued with its lively energy.

Outside, the air was refreshingly cool, a gentle drizzle misting down on them. They stood under one of the sparse streetlights, their figures illuminated by the twinkling lights strung along the low fence encircling the club's front porch. Driton lit her cigarette before sparking one for himself. For a moment, they stood in silence, Lira's gaze wandering beyond the budding spring leaves to the pockets of darkness. He resisted the urge to reach out to touch her, to brush his fingers through her golden hair and bask in her alluring presence. The next move was hers to make.

"I need to talk to you about Mal," she started. "We had a short relationship. Just some casual meet-ups for coffee and drives, nothing serious. But when I ended it, he didn't take it well. I realized he wasn't the right person for me. Thankfully, I met Valon shortly after... and no one measures up to him, you know?"

Driton nodded, indicating for her to continue.

"Mal turned nasty. He kept calling home, demanding to speak with me. Eventually, my mother and sister blocked his number to spare me. One day... and I swear this is true... he purposefully drove at me with his car. I was just walking home. It was a terrifying experience. And then there was the incident at the casino... I'm certain Mal played a role in Valon's death. I'm truly scared, Driton."

"You have nothing to fear, my dear. I won't let him or anyone else harm you. He's been spreading lies and threats about me too. He knew Valon and I were in the same police unit, keeping people safe from him and his gang."

Lira moved closer, resting her cheek against Driton's chest. He gently wrapped his arms around her, kissing her forehead as he gazed out into the darkness.

"I didn't want to cry. I want to be strong."

"You're stronger than you know. And I didn't plan on doing this either," he said, lifting her tear-streaked face to meet his gaze. He kissed her tenderly, his lips briefly exploring hers before pulling away. "You're the most stunning woman I've ever met. Most importantly, you have a good heart."

"I'm not sure I can navigate this alone," she admitted.

He gently tilted her head to rest against his chest. "You don't have to face this alone. I'll stand by you, no matter what. And Mal will get the punishment he deserves. He will pay for his actions. In full."

Chapter Six

The next evening, Driton waited at the family farm, a bottle of rakia and five shot glasses set out on the table. He pulled the curtain aside and peered out the window. His breath fogged up the window pane, which he wiped clear with his sleeve. Glancing at his watch – an expensive-looking Rolex knockoff from the market – it was 9:45 p.m.. They were late. Anger and unease swirled in his gut. He poured himself another shot of the fiery drink and downed it.

The farm was owned by his family, who had already gone to bed, their snores emanating from another part of the house. The moment the liquor hit his stomach, he regretted it – a burning sensation spread inside.

At last, the sweep of headlights cut through the darkness along the long drive, closely followed by another pair. The vehicles crunched over the gravel before coming to a stop in front of the farmhouse. Driton set down his glass and went to the door.

The family's dog was dozing on a blanket on the porch,

chained to a ring next to a water bowl. The dog barely stirred as Driton opened the door and positioned himself at the top of the steps to await the arrivals. The two unmarked police cars pulled up alongside his own, and several men disembarked. They approached the house single file, each offering a greeting as they stepped inside.

There was a hearty exchange of backslaps and handshakes, although their gazes held a noticeable chill. This was Driton's elite police team.

"Evening, brother," Driton greeted each man. "Had your meal yet?"

"Sure thing, Chief," one of the men replied. "We had *iftar* before coming."

It was the holy month of Ramadan, a time of daylight fasting in the Islamic world. While much of Kosovo maintained a secular lifestyle in post-Socialist Yugoslavia, there was a growing adherence to Islamic observances that had been re-introduced from the earlier Turkish Ottoman Empire's 500-year rule. The breaking of the fast at sunset, called *Iftar*, was often a time for extended families to gather and dine together at local restaurants, fostering community spirit.

The men entered the rustic, comfortably furnished room and sat down around the table. Driton poured them all a shot of liquor.

"Thanks for coming," he said.

"Is tonight the night?" asked Briz Prela.

Driton nodded curtly before asking, "Did you do what I asked?".

"Yes, boss," Briz said. He was a fair-haired man with small freckled hands, the accountant of the group.

"What kind of device did you find?"

"It's an anti-tank mine that my cousin took from the Serbs on their way out of Kosovo after the war. He's got a weapons cache in a cave. Some of the munitions came from the war, and he imported others from Albania.

"It's none too soon, boss," said another man at the table. Andrea Culaj, Driton's deputy, was a shorter, well-built man with a five o'clock shadow and thick dark hair.

"Why do you say that?" Driton asked. He rummaged in his pocket for cigarettes. Briz pulled out his own packet and offered one to him. Driton took it and lit up. Two of the other men followed.

"I heard from a couple of good friends in town that Mal Mala has been talking openly that he intends to take you out, just like he did Valon."

"Screw that," said Driton and spat into the corner of the room. "What else?"

"Just that he's going to get you—probably a drive-by shooting, or he'll send a team to take you out on your way to work," Andrea said, looking down at his hands as if he didn't want to see rage cross the other man's features.

Driton's whole body tensed, but he remained expressionless, toying with his glass and his cigarette.

"But why is he so hostile?" asked another man, a new recruit called Milon. "What changed? I mean, I know you don't get along and your—you know, business interests—are different. But things are getting out of control now."

"I told you what's going on, Milon. He's clearly behind the killing of Valon—he's bragging about it around town," Andrea said.

"He threatened Lira, as well. I'm going to hurt him badly for that alone—and what he did to Valon, that's unforgivable. Everyone knows it, and everyone expects me to do something about it," Driton said in a leaden, monotone voice that held menace in every syllable.

The men glanced up at Driton. There was a silence, and then Andrea spoke. "He threatened Lira?"

Driton nodded. He had not made a secret of the fact that he intended to start seeing her. Whatever happened in Pristina, someone saw it and would tell. Of course, he realized that the men knew that he had a long-standing girlfriend, Adrienne, as well as a fiancé, Darlene. He treated them all well, according to his code of ethics. The women knew about each other, while they pretended not to. He was fond of each one. But his passion was for Lira. He would do anything to protect her and to pay back Mala for hurting her so badly by taking away their team member, Valon. Everyone loved Valon, including Driton.

"Don't get me going on that now," Driton said. "I'm going to explode if I talk about it. Tonight is for acting, not talking. Tonight is for explosive reprisals." He took a deep breath and poured himself another shot of spirits. After downing the glass, he continued, "What about the payments from the supermarkets? Did they pay the protection money this month?"

Briz reported, "We got about half of the regular payments, boss. But some of the owners were afraid of Mala. They said they already paid him a hefty price, and they couldn't afford to pay both of us this month."

Driton thumped his fist down on the table. He made the bottle jump, and one of the empty glasses that was still on the table toppled over. One fell to the ground and smashed. "This man pushes me to the limit. Over the limit. We need to teach him a lesson that he won't forget."

The men looked at him and nodded. "We're ready," Andrea said.

"This man shows no respect—he needs to learn the hard way," Briz said.

"I know where we can pick up the device and the weapons, like Briz said," Fatmir said. "I can bring them back and set them up." Fatmir was the mechanic of the group.

"Where?" Driton asked.

"It's in a disused mine about 20 minutes' drive from here."

Driton was quiet for a moment and then looked at Milon. "You haven't said much tonight, Milon. Are you up for this?"

"Sure, I'm up for it," Milon said, but there was a quiet reserve in his voice that gave Driton pause.

"You sure? If you've got something to say, say it now."

"Of course, I'm behind you 100%, Chief," he said. "But I was just wondering... Is it possible to meet with Mal? Discuss these problems and reach an agreement? Maybe split our territory so we don't have to work against each other?"

"Come on, bro – we went past that point months ago," Fatmir said. "You heard what Andrea said. Mala's planning a hit on our chief. That's not empty talk. We need to show him what's what before he attacks again."

"He's affecting our bottom line," Briz said. "We're providing a good service to people, businesses. They're grateful enough to pay well for it."

"He arranged for Valon's murder, and he'll do the same to Driton—or any of us, if he can," Andrea said.

"And he threatened Lira," Driton said.

"No, no, you're right," Milon said, looking down at his glass as he turned it in his fingers.

"I'll drive," Briz said, looking around the table. "Who wants to come with me? Fatmir?"

"Sure," he said and got up from the table.

"Alright," Driton said. "We'll meet you at the Prince Hotel in about half an hour, switch the cars, and drive into Pristina." He thumped his rakia shot glass down on the table and stood up. "Let's get this done."

Chapter Seven

The clock struck midnight, yet the One Up Café was still buzzing with activity. In one corner, a group of young men lounged on low chairs and a couch, passing around shisha pipes filled with fragrant tobacco that had been cooled through bubbling water. Other groups, mostly men with a few women sprinkled in, sat at more western-style tables drinking coffee and small glasses of hot back tea.

Dua's friend Besim weaved effortlessly between the tables, balancing trays of olives, sheep cheese, pickles, and other snacks while the aroma of freshly baked pizza and garlic lingered behind him. With a flick of his wrist, he smoothly transferred another tray onto a different table before delivering all the snacks to their intended recipients.It was Ramadan, and increasingly after the conflict, Kosovars were observing the practice of fasting during the day of the holy month of the Islamic calendar. This meant that they enjoyed time with friends and family even more after the sun had set, often staying up late with extended meals and drinking tea and coffee.

Besim felt his mobile phone vibrate in his pocket. Hoping it might be a message from Dua, he cleared some tables, and, after returning the dishes to the kitchen, went outside to check his phone. It would just be for a couple of minutes, he told the other waiter. This was also a chance to light up. Although some customers smoked the shisha pipes, the café staff were not supposed to smoke on the job.

He pushed through the back door at the rear of the café's kitchen. The night outside was cool and fresh, although a taint lingered from the local lignite-burning power station.

"First things first," he said to himself and dug a cigarette packet out of his pocket. Besim lit a cigarette with a lighter and got out his mobile phone. It was a message from Dua apologizing for not meeting him earlier in the evening, as she had been tied up in the office. She suggested meeting tomorrow evening instead, during his dinner break.

Keeping the cigarette in the corner of his mouth, he started typing a message accepting Dua's suggestion, until his attention was caught by screeching tires of two vehicles as they swung around the corner into the car park. The lights of the vehicles were switched off. Under the dim light of a lamp, Besim could see that the number plates had been removed from the type of vehicles used by the Kosovo Police. The drivers and passengers were dressed in the dark tactical gear of a special ops police team, their faces covered by balaclavas. He stepped back into the shadow of the corner of the building and dropped his cigarette with its glowing tip onto the ground, pressing firmly but quietly onto the concrete with his foot. He slipped the mobile phone back into his pocket and watched.

The cars halted at the rear of the parking lot. Three men got out of a car and removed a heavy box out of the trunk. The other men sat in the darkened interior of their vehicle, watching and waiting. Besim saw another man from the parking lot approach the waiting vehicle, and ask what was happening. The driver waved him away and said gruffly, "Police business." Seeing the balaclava-clad men and hearing the terseness of the reply, the man shrugged and walked away, leaving the area of the café car park altogether.

The three men with the box went through a rear entrance into a utility area under the staircase that led to the next level of the café restaurant. Besim figured that it must be some kind of police operation, but he couldn't imagine what they would be doing wearing tactical gear and carrying a box. He could hear them whispering urgently amongst themselves. One man stumbled on the doorstep, and there was a scuffling sound.

"Shit!" the man exclaimed, his voice muffled.

The other man said, "Be careful, Briz! Do you want to blow us all to hell?"

"Sorry, man, I didn't see that step."

"Just shut up and hurry, you two. Driton's going to kill us himself if we mess this up."

"Just wait, I have to get this door," said the shorter man.

There was a scuffling sound and then the sharp crack and splintering noise of a crowbar being applied to a door.

"Can you make more noise," said one of the men. "I don't think the whole neighborhood heard."

"You're a pain, Fatmir. Why don't you do it yourself."

"Just shut up," said the other man.

"Stop complaining."

Besim shook his head and smiled. These cops seemed panicked and not at all professional. They must be on some high-stakes operation, and he didn't want them to know he was there watching and listening.

The back door opened, and a shaft of light shot out into the darkness where Besim was sheltering. The other waiter appeared, wiping his hands on the black apron. "Hey, Besim, stop texting your girlfriend. I need your help inside. Another group just arrived for a meal."

"Yeah, sure," Besim said. He knew it was best to keep out of police business and didn't comment to the other waiter about what he'd seen.

"So, how's that hot girl you've been dating?" the other waiter continued. "Is she coming in to see us tonight?"

"Ah, maybe," Besim said. He was distracted now, trying to refocus on his work "She's working pretty full-on in the office these days."

"Which office?"

"The OIDC, the Organization for International Development and Cooperation."

"We don't need them here anymore since we won the war against Serbia," the other waiter said. "But it's still cool that Dua's getting international experience. And earning a good salary."

"It's an entry-level job," Besim said.

A man at the head of a family table signalled to a waiter to take their order, so Besim excused himself and went over. He was preoccupied with what he'd seen the men doing outside and still feeling uncomfortable with what they were up to. He took mental note of the order for the table and went back to deliver it to the kitchen.

A couple on the other side of the café ordered espressos, so Besim went over to the large Italian coffee machine behind the bar. It was the pride and joy of the owner, Mal Mala. He remembered the day when Mala had bought the impressive machine back in the trunk of his SUV in an old box, covered with blankets. Besim had brought the box inside and set up the machine. He polished it and admired the gleaming chrome surfaces. Having a great coffee machine gave the café a competitive edge against others nearby. A friend of the family had worked in a restaurant in Germany and helped show him and another couple of servers how to use the machine. He deftly ground the coffee dose and slotted the dispenser into the coffee machine, and he switched on the water.

The sound of tires screeching drew Besim's attention. He saw the shadowed outlines of two cars driving past the window. *If they were trying to avoid notice, it would make more sense to drive slowly*, he thought. That was unless they really had to get away quickly.

Later, when Besim tried to describe what happened next, he said it was as if time slowed down, and all the oxygen had been sucked out of the room for a moment that hung in a void like an eternity. Then the air came roaring back ahead of a blast with a brutal, stunning force that threw him to the ground, smashing tables and chairs. The cheerful, buzzing café was gone, replaced by a pile of smoking rubble. The shock wave pummelled Besim's body inside and out. In one heartbeat, he was crafting a rich cup of espresso behind the bar; in the next, a cataclysmic eruption of brilliant light and scorching heat catapulted him through the air. He hovered in a surreal, dream-like freefall until the base of his skull brutally collided with the shelf behind the bar, and he crumpled to the ground. Now, all was eerily silent.

Besim sensed a weight bearing down on him, pressing the wind out of his lungs. He fought to dislodge it, but his body refused to obey. Sight and hearing had abandoned him; all he knew was the crushing mass pinning him down.

Chapter Eight

K it's bedroom was a serene space of simple design accentuated by crisp cotton sheets and a plush duvet, the perfect setting for restful sleep. The open window brought in a touch of the outside world, with shadows dancing across the room and a gentle breeze hinting at approaching rain.

Despite the tranquil setup, sleep remained elusive. Kit lay awake, tempted to check her phone for messages. Adding further disruption to her sleep was Owen, who had been more frequently joining Kit overnight. Her train of thought was interrupted by a distant noise, possibly thunder or an explosion. A few moments later, her phone started ringing, followed by Owen's. The sound of sirens sliced through the night as Kit, now draped in her silk gown, reached for her phone.

"Bloody hell," Owen grumbled, still groggy with sleep. His gaze fell to the vibrating device on the nightstand. "It's Matt," he said.

Without another word, he answered the call. "Major, this is Reese speaking," he greeted, tone professional despite the disarray. He nodded. "Understood, sir. I can be at the location in ten minutes."

Meanwhile, Kit noticed the caller ID on her own phone. It was Eva on the other end. She retreated to the living room for privacy.

"Eva, what's going on?" Kit inquired sharply, the color draining from her face as she was drawn to the window. "You can't be serious. That's... that's appalling. I heard the sirens, and even the explosion, but I couldn't be sure of the cause."

"You need to go to the One Up Café—it's not far from you," Eva said. "Find Dr. Prabhu from the city morgue. We're expecting casualties; your job will be to confirm any fatalities."

"OK," Kit said. "Is the area secure yet?"

"Still unclear. Major Matt Hackman is on point for that and a response team is on their way."

"Do we have leads on the motive?"

"Not yet," Eva replied. "That's what we need to find out."

"Terrorism, hate crimes, gang violence... it could be anything."

"Indeed."

"Will you be there, Eva?"

"Possibly later. The head of staff is arranging a crisis control room at headquarters. I need to offer guidance to our higher-ups. There are concerns about this causing another round of hostility, especially if the Serbs are involved and it incites demonstrations and retaliatory strikes."

"It seems improbable that the Serbs would target a café, especially at this time of day, doesn't it?" Kit pondered while biting her lip.

"I tend to agree, but you never know who might have been targeted there."

"What do you mean?" Kit was starting to look for her clothes. She chose the black slacks, roll neck top and black jacket with loafers that she often wore to crime scenes. In the distance she could hear more sirens. The café was no more than a kilometer or two away.

"It could have been an assassination attempt against a local politician, say. But I'm going with an organized crime related hit. The One Up Café is owned by Mal Mala, who is a reputed crime boss."

"Yeah, but a lot of real estate around town is owned by people associated with crime. That doesn't mean there's a connection to him," Kit said. She tied back her hair in a ponytail and moved some stray tendrils to one side with a hair clip, with the phone still pressed between her ear and shoulder.

"Well, let's go into this with open minds and see where the facts lead," Eva said. "The police will gather evidence to identify the culprits. It's important that proper procedures are followed for chain of custody, so we can ensure accurate testing in the labs and use the evidence in court."

"Will do." Kit was now putting together her satchel ready to leave.

"Oh, and send me regular updates. I'll be in the situation room and pass them on to mission leadership."

Owen appeared in the doorway in his uniform, the picture of readiness.

"I've got this," Kit assured Eva. "You'll have the latest as soon as I know." With a final glance at Owen, she ended the call. "How in the world did you manage to get dressed so fast?" she inquired, raising an eyebrow.

"Look who's talking," Owen retorted with a playful smirk. "I've never seen a woman get dressed as fast as you."

"Is that so? You've been keeping a tally, have you?" Kit bantered.

Owen only shrugged. "You know what I mean."

"I do," she replied, her gaze drifting to her reflection in a nearby mirror. Dressed for the occasion, devoid of makeup tonight, she exuded efficiency. Her freckled skin was naturally radiant, requiring no enhancements, especially when she was on duty.

Chapter Nine

Kit and Owen reached the crime scene to find the area already secured by police tape. Major Matt Hackman was positioned by his Jeep, flanked by Don Edgson and his Belgian Tervuren, Max. Emergency services swarmed the location: fire crews, Kosovo police, and ambulances buzzed with activity. Among the responders, Kit noticed Dr. Prabhu, the coroner.

Don Edgson, a lanky Texan who looked like he'd misplaced his cowboy hat and boots, stood attentively beside Matt. His piercing blue eyes scanned the chaos, missing no detail. Max, sat by his side. Resembling a slimmer German Shepherd with a rich mahogany and black coat, Max faced the turmoil, alert and focused.

Kit was surprised to see Matt leaning against the military police vehicle. He nodded to Owen as he arrived, and Owen stood to attention. As far as Kit could remember, Matt was always first on the scene, giving orders and taking action. Yet tonight he was almost lounging on the Jeep and talking philosophically to Don.

"My wife told me the other night about a Sherlock

Holmes detective novel. Apparently, his assistant, Dr. Watson, had expected Sherlock Holmes to plunge headfirst into a crime scene, but rather Holmes took his time, staring at the sky, the ground and the opposite houses. Having finished his scrutiny he proceeded along the path, keeping his eyes on the ground." Matt looked up. Kit could see signs of sleeplessness on his face. He had dark rings around his eyes and his usually clean-shaven face had signs of stubble.

"Sir?" Owen said.

Matt looked at him. "I thought I might try the Sherlock Holmes approach this time, Reese. What do you think?"

"I'm not sure what you mean, sir," Owen said.

Kit surveyed the scene, only paying partial attention to what Matt was saying. The emergency vehicles had parked around the centre of the bomb blast, the One Up Café. It was gutted and open to the night. Many buildings around it also appeared to be damaged. They would need to get moving quickly, before the evidence was compromised and the crime scene contaminated. Kit felt her phone vibrate and checked. It was a message from Dua. *Kit, I'm at the café looking for Besim. Are you here?*

She punched back the reply. "Yes, I'm across the road with the military police. Come over now." Kit knew it was good that Dua was already on the spot. But her stomach churned as she realized that Dua's friend Besim may have been working at the café when the explosion happened. She looked up and could see Dua hurrying across the road, with the flashing lights, and glowing debris behind her. Owen looked at Kit questioningly.

"While the two of you play detective, I need to begin gathering information for my report," Kit stated. "Eva is currently in the situation room with our mission's senior management, eagerly awaiting an update."

"Sir, I think we should see if there are any secondary devices at the scene," Don said. Max whined.

"You're right, Captain," Matt said. He took a deep sigh and seemed to shake his head briefly, as if to clear it. "We need to establish a command post. The building over there by the park looks like as good a place as any. Check the area for any secondary devices. Take whatever help you need for that. Also secure the roof of the building, we going to have to go up there to survey the scene in its entirety."

"I'm on it," Don said. "I think we need two other canine units, with dogs certified for explosives. We have to cover this scene quickly before something else happens."

Matt nodded curtly and continued to give instructions.

"Sargent," Matt said to Owen. "Coordinate with emergency services, request bomb technicians, other law enforcement officers and EMS personnel. Remember that safety comes first. The bomb squad should coordinate with the canine units to find any secondary devices. Also try to recover any evidence near the primary blast."

"Looks like emergency services are already here, sir," Owen said. "I'll coordinate."

"As a priority, we need to identify scene hazards, such as structural collapse, blood-borne pathogens and hazardous chemicals as well," Matt continued. He seemed to be back in control.

"Right away, sir," Owen said. He moved away to the vehicle, picked up the radio telephone and started making calls.

"Dua, can you make a list for me of all the buildings that have been damaged by the blast?" Kit said. Dua didn't immediately respond. She was squinting into the night, across the road, breathing shallowly through her open mouth.

"Besim, he was there in the café," she said. "I tried to reach him earlier but he didn't reply—he always replies. I'm afraid that he might have been caught in the blast."

When Kit looked at her, her normally pale face was even more pallid. She touched Dua reassuringly on the arm. "Don't worry, if he's here they'll find him. The best thing we can do right now is our job."

Dua was calling Besim's number repeatedly but there was no reply. *This is a lot to put on to a newcomer,* Kit thought. It seemed not long ago that she herself was the newest person on the job and overwhelmed by the violence that she had encountered. She looked up at Matt, who was now acting more like his old self. He was on the mobile radio phone, issuing orders. He had seemed like another person a few minutes ago, standing there quoting Arthur Conan Doyle. Although maybe he had a point—perhaps it was better not to rush ahead. They should do a proper evaluation of the scene at first. Mistakes had been made before by rushing in too fast.

"Someone needs to check for evidence before it's compromised by firefighters or the med techs moving victims." Kit said. *Or before another device goes off,* she thought.

"Kit, it looks like there's a lot of damage to other buildings. The café a couple of doors down, the fitness club, the night club—they're all trashed," Dua said.

"Okay, you make a quick survey of what the damage seems to be. Keep your distance though, we don't have the all clear yet, and there could be secondary devices or active shooters around," Kit said.

"Speaking of which," Owen said. He handed them both Kevlar vests to put over their civilian clothes.

"Owen, you're coordinating with the med techs at the

moment. Would you mind asking them to keep an eye out for Dua's friend, Besim. What's his second name, Dua?" Kit said.

"Besim Krasniqi," Dua replied.

"Besim Krasniqi, early twenties, about 5' 9", dark hair, average build," Kit said, looking enquiringly only at Dua in case she wanted to add something.

"Yes, he works at that café. I haven't been able to reach him," she explained to Owen.

Owen cast a worried look at Kit and then nodded. "Sure, I'll ask them to keep an eye open for anyone matching that description. If I hear back, I'll let you know right away."

"Thanks," Kit said. Neither of them said anything more, but with a detonation of this size, it was clear that there were going to be casualties. Kit aimed to keep Duo busy at a distance. She didn't want her to go anywhere near the café in case Besim was there.

"Okay," Kit said briskly. "Dua, you do a quick check of how many businesses and buildings have been affected and let me know. Then I want you to go to the command centre that Matt and Owen are setting up over there." She indicated with a movement of her head towards the building where Matt said they would set up the centre. "I need to find Dr. Prabhu as soon as possible. But first I need to brief Eva on what's happening so that she can pass the update to the situation room back at the mission."

Dua nodded and slipped the vest over her leather jacket. Although layered, the vest hung loosely around her petite frame. Kit adjusted the straps for her before donning her own vest. It offered protection against active shooters and flying debris from potential detonations. However, without helmets or additional protective clothing, their safety was still not assured. Kit tried to clear her head, focusing on the task at hand rather than worst-case scenarios – they were in risk mitigation mode now.

Dua stood looking over the road towards the tangle of fallen girders and walls. Even though the all clear had not been given, the emergency services were still at work. EUFOR personnel worked to secure the area and to look after the safety of the first responders, but they couldn't stop the medics from trying to rescue people. Kit noticed Dua's tense posture and saw that she was on the brink of dashing back across the road.

"Dua, I need that information right away. You need to make a list of all the businesses affected by this. Also, see how many onlookers there are, and their distribution around the scene. Maybe even take some photos if you can. It's possible that the perpetrators are still nearby. Eva is waiting to hear from me about this."

Dua looked up at Kit, her eyes were smudged with tears. "If he was there—I don't know what I'll do. Besim is such a nice guy, you know, he would never hurt anyone. I think I should go over there and see if I can find him."

"Dua, you are not going over there," Kit said firmly. "I need that information—the senior leaders at the mission are waiting for this. There's nothing you can do—emergency personnel are there now. They will let Owen know as soon as they have any news about Besim. Can you do that what I asked?" Kit asked, pulling out her mobile phone and preparing to call Eva.

Dua was trying to reach for a tissue under her Kevlar vest. "All right—I guess I can do that."

"Good. I'll be giving Eva updates, so let me know what you find out. Don't forget about the photos."

Kit called Eva and briefed her on the current status of

the crime scene. "It's a freaking mess, Eva," she said. "It's possible that Dua's friend was injured—he's a waiter at the One Up Café. "

"*Madre mio*," Eva said, reverting to her native Italian in moments of stress. "I hope not. Keep her away from the crime scene itself."

"I'm trying to—but she keeps wanting to go over there. Even if Besim is not injured, there are casualties. This was a busy time at the café. Clearly the intention was to kill or maim as many people as possible. The nearby buildings have been trashed as well. I've got Dua doing an overview of the damage to the block, and checking who is in the group of onlookers."

"Good. We're doing what we can on coordination here. The military patrols have been stepped up in case this is an opening attack for hostilities between Serbia and Kosovo. But so far, there doesn't seem to be any unusual activity, apart from this explosion."

"Matt and Owen are already here, setting up a makeshift command center. Don, along with other canine teams is sweeping for additional explosives. They haven't ruled out snipers, either."

Kit, charged with adrenaline, was hardly recognizable as her younger self who had fainted at the sight of the Staro Dorbi massacre. Yet, she hesitated to get closer to the blast site.

"What do they think may have caused the explosion?" Eva inquired.

Kit's focus wavered. "One sec, let me ask Owen." She signaled to Owen. "Eva's asking about the cause of the explosion."

"We're not certain, but it seems to be an IED—an

improvised explosive device. Whatever it was, it had the force of a modified anti-tank mine or something similar."

Relaying this, Kit added, "They're still trying to lock down the scene. The injured are being taken to the hospital."

"Tell Matt to secure that scene fast. They might be trampling on evidence as we speak," Eva insisted.

"I see Dr. Prabhu over there; I'll check with her first about the casualties. Hopefully, by then, I'll muster the courage to survey the damage. Frankly, I'm dreading it."

"I understand, but we need to focus on our role of helping to manage the crime scene and facilitate the collection of evidence and working with the Coroner. Those are our priorities. Of course, the first responders' job is to save lives," Eva said.

"Understood," Kit said.

"There's a lot of talk going on here at headquarters. We need to keep everyone in the loop in case there are decisions need to be made at this level. I'll pass on the news. Please call me back when you know more."

"Will do." Kit hung up and spoke to Owen. "I'm going to have to go over there to the detonation scene. How long till we get the all clear?"

"I don't know—maybe half an hour. There is a lot of ground to cover first."

"I don't think I can wait that long. The med techs are already working to try to save lives. That's great but probably they are compromising the evidence. Plus, Dr. Prabhu and I have to fill out the paperwork for the casualties."

Owen's gaze settled on Kit, fraught with concern. He offered no false comforts or platitudes, only a grave nod. "Maybe you could join the doctor at the ambulances first. Help with the preliminary checks on the casualties before they're sent to the morgue. With any luck, we'll have the green light to secure the crime scene by then."

"Why didn't I think of that?" Kit responded, her grin a slice of bravado in the grim setting. They both understood it was a façade, yet necessary to keep the edge of panic at bay. Covering the distance between them, she leaned in and whispered, "Right now, I'd much prefer to be in bed with you." Even through layers of Kevlar and tactical gear, proximity to Owen ignited a warming flush across her skin.

"Me too," he said roughly, his voice laced with a yearning that matched her own. But the moment shattered by Max's barking from about fifty meters off. Their attention snapped to the canine, hearts hitching with the threat of another device. Don's voice crackled over the radio, reporting Max's alert to Owen

"Okay, I'll let you deal with that," Kit said. "I'd better head over to Dr. Prabhu by the ambulances. I've asked Dua to assess the extent of the damage in the block and then come back to your op center. She shouldn't stumble upon her friend from the café—especially if he was involved in the incident."

The memory of her own first encounter with a scene of carnage flashed through her mind. She wished someone had shielded her, or at least prepared her for the brutal reality she'd faced. Matt had tried to dissuade her, yet she'd stubbornly pushed to go. It had cost her dearly. With a nod to Owen, she pivoted towards the coroner, only to pause and look back over her shoulder.

"Have you ever seen Matt act like that before?" she asked.

"Act like what?"

"When we arrived, he was leaning against the Jeep, lost in a story about his wife reading Sherlock Holmes. It's not like him to be so detached. He's usually the one in command. Now he seems back to normal, but it was odd, wasn't it?"

Owen's expression acknowledged the shared concern. "I know what you mean."

"Just keep an eye on him, okay?"

A slim, blonde woman in mock camouflage gear materialized behind Kit, breaking into their conversation. "Who are we keeping an eye on?"

Kit turned to find Zena Lace Letalova, the last person she wanted to see right now. Lately, Kit had come to recognize a jealous streak within herself she hadn't known existed. She couldn't shake the suspicion of an unspoken history between Zena and Owen, despite his assurances of mere camaraderie. Those early morning training sessions they shared seemed suspect.

Forcing a smile, Kit greeted her. "Zena, I'm surprised to see you. I thought desk assignments were keeping you busy."

"Profiler's work is never done," Zena replied briskly. "You look like you're heading out?"

"I am, to the ambulances, unfortunately." Kit fought the childish impulse to keep Zena away from Owen. If there were something between them, neither could she stop it, nor would she give them the satisfaction of seeing her insecurities.

Zena looked at Owen. "Is the crime scene accessible yet?"

"Not yet," he answered.

"Well, then, do you mind if I wait with you? I'd prefer to avoid an... explosive entrance." She let out an uneasy laugh, brushing Owen's arm.

Kit's smile strained, but she didn't let it slip. "Staying put is wise, Zena. I'm off to the site now."

She pivoted sharply and strode off, Zena's voice trailing after her. "But I must get there soon. The psychological profile requires a first-hand look."

Kit made her way to where Dr. Prabhu stood by the crime scene perimeter near the last ambulance, her presence marked by a calm authority. Dr. Prabhu, with her lustrous black hair secured away from her face in a tight braid, was clad in surgical gear and a clear plastic coverall that spoke of grim tasks ahead. Despite the chaos, her face lit up with recognition as Kit approached.

"Ms. Chase, a sight for sore eyes," Dr. Prabhu greeted her, the warmth in her voice a stark contrast to the cold scene around them. "I wish our meeting wasn't under such circumstances."

"The feeling's mutual, Dr. Prabhu." Kit noted the blood that had already stained the doctor's gloves, foreclosing the possibility of a handshake. "It's a horrendous scene."

"Among the grimmest I've encountered," Dr. Prabhu agreed solemnly.

A heavy silence descended upon them as they took in the devastating scene before them, illuminated by the flashing red and blue lights of emergency vehicles and the harsh glow of streetlamps. The wreckage periodically succumbed to gravity, sending up clouds of dust that obscured the destruction in a ghostly veil. Kit caught a glimpse of something in her peripheral vision – the glistening pools of blood now collecting in the gutters, warped and distorted by the overhead lights. She turned away, her stomach churning with the knowledge of what was beyond her line of sight – the gruesome imagery of dismemberment and death.

The horrifying reality of the situation threatened to break through her composure. It was Dr. Prabhu who had guided Kit through her first autopsy, preparing her for the visuals she would encounter. But nothing could have truly prepared her for this mass casualty event.

Her thoughts drifted to Sergei, her mentor turned enemy, whose lessons on mental fortitude suddenly seemed critical. If there was ever a moment to employ that discipline, to focus on her objectives and stay strong, it was now.

Kit nodded towards an ambulance nearby. "I was just speaking with EUFOR. We agreed that I should start confirming deaths for some of the bodies already extracted from the debris. We're still waiting for clearance from the bomb squad before I can enter the crime scene and search for evidence."

"Sounds like a good plan," Dr. Prabhu said. "I was waiting for a prosecutor to come from your office. Let's make a start."

"There's one more thing. We are keeping an eye out for the friend of one of our new interns. He worked here." She corrected herself, "He works at this café. His name's Besim Krasniqi. He's about 5' 8", dark brown hair, probably in his early 20s."

Dr. Prabhu shook her head. "I've seen victims who could fit that description. We haven't identified them yet though."

Kit lingered in silence. The hope for easy identifications dwindled in the face of such tragedy.

"Let's take a look, then. There might be IDs on them. I didn't know Besim well, but I saw him from afar, so I might recognize him."

"You might not be able to discern faces, but IDs are a possibility," the coroner concurred.

A stretcher arrived, hauled by two med techs; one, with sweat matting his dark hair to his forehead, signalled to Dr. Prabhu. "Doctor, we've retrieved more of victims."

Doctor Prabhu cautiously unzipped the body bag to inspect its grim contents, her expression settling into a troubled frown. She then gestured to Kit, an unspoken invitation to come forward.

The chaotic flicker of police lights and the crimson flash of ambulances twisted together, sending a wave of dizziness over Kit. Acrid smoke lingered in the air, clinging to her, mingling with the metallic tang of blood that now smeared the rubble at her feet.

Observing Kit's pallor, Dr. Prabhu extended a tissue. "This might help," she offered.

Kit accepted it, bemused, until the doctor clarified, "It's infused with peppermint and eucalyptus –helps against the odors."

Kit inhaled the scent from the tissue, a cautious sniff that transformed into deeper draws of the mentholated air. The eucalyptus and peppermint mingled, transporting her to her aunt's sunlit garden, where as a child, she had plucked peppermint leaves under a towering eucalyptus tree. For a brief second, she was swathed in the comfort of those memories, insulated from the present horror. Then she opened her eyes, the garden receding, but her senses steadied.

"Thank you," she said, attempting to hand back the tissue.

"Keep it," Dr. Prabhu insisted, her smile gentle. "It helps, doesn't it?" There was solace in knowing that even the coroner employed small acts of self-care amidst the turmoil.

With renewed focus, Kit returned to the grim task.

Together, they confirmed three sets of remains for transport to the morgue. Although the exact identities were obliterated by the explosion, the coroner would later rely on DNA analysis to determine who they were. From what little Kit could piece together, the victims appeared to be young men.

Despite the lack of an all-clear, the medical team rushed in to tend to the survivors of the blast. After 45 minutes, Owen's voice came through on the radio, bringing a mix of relief and caution. He reported that no additional IEDs had been found by Don and his dogs, giving them the green light to move in. However, they still needed to remain alert for potential snipers or other threats.

According to Kit's watch, it was 3:45 a.m. She could feel exhaustion setting in, like the disorienting effects of jet lag. She hadn't been able to sleep more than an hour and her clothes were now sticking to her body with sweat. It seemed unlikely that she would have a chance to rest much during the rest of the night.

Chapter Ten

Kit trudged wearily up the stairs of her apartment, her fatigue weighing heavily on her shoulders. It felt like an eternity ago she had been cocooned, warm and safe, beside Owen. While the investigation so far had confirmed multiple casualties, Besim's the fate remained uncertain. Kit climbed the final step and, summoning her dwindling strength, inserted the key into the lock. Slipping inside, she locked the door behind her, shutting out the unwelcome dawn that cast its cold light into the room.

Exhausted but unable to sleep, Kit's eyes fell on the drawer. She hesitated before pulling it open, revealing Dr. Maria Montenegro's old sleeping pill bottle nestled among other forgotten items. The therapist had once been a beacon of support, guiding Kit through past traumas and the chaos of her father's sudden reappearance. But now, the memory of Maria's betrayal—her involvement in a high-level conspiracy and blackmail scheme—tainted any sense of comfort. With a resolute breath, Kit shut the drawer. She would just rest, if not sleep, for a couple of hours.

Brushing her auburn hair before bed, Kit's thoughts drifted to her late sister Patricia, their childhood games, and the laughter that now echoed sadly in her mind. It was a brief respite from her relentless chase. Amidst these memories, Natalia Marin's face surfaced. The dream therapist's guidance in Ljubljana had been a safe haven, untouched by Sergei's deceptions.

Kit paused, her hand hovering over her phone. When they had exchanged numbers, it seemed simple, yet their connection was complex. Natalia's business card, once forgotten, felt reassuring in her hand. Opting for a message, Kit typed swiftly, hoping Natalia could once again shed light on her dark path.

In her message, Kit recalled their meetings in Ljubljana, and asked Natalia if she would be available sometime to talk. She was surprised to hear back within a few minutes. It was Natalia asking if she could call now. Kit's heart quickened as the phone rang, her mind already formulating her move. With the possibility of a crucial trip to Thailand to rendezvous with Silver on the horizon, she made a mental note to explore the possibility of a session with Natalia upon her return. She would pay, of course.

Natalia mentioned she had been writing in her dream journal when Kit's message arrived. Hearing Natalia's voice, Kit's shoulders relaxed, and a smile softened her face.

"Sorry to disturb you so early," Kit said, her voice tinged with the exhaustion of a long night. "I just got back from an all-nighter. I won't go into the details. But our meeting in Ljubljana has been on my mind. I'd love to connect again, whether in person or online. Another tarot reading would be amazing, and I'm eager to learn more about dream work."

"I'd love to," Natalia said. "In fact, as fate would have it, I'm coming to Pristina soon. I've got a job interview lined up with a wellness center that's working with a lot of PTSD patients. They'd like to start offering dream therapy."

"You're coming to Pristina? Fantastic!" Kit exclaimed. This was better than she had hoped.

"In fact, I was thinking about contacting you. It seems that synchronicity is at work. Did you ever uncover the identity of that deceptive Queen of Cups from your tarot reading?"

"I did, big time. I'll tell you all about it when we meet. And listen, if you need a place to stay during your visit, I have a spare bedroom. You're more than welcome—in exchange for a dream therapy session, of course."

Gratitude filled Natalia's voice as she accepted the offer. "I'd love that, Kit. I'm looking forward to it even more now. Speaking of which, have you heard from Sergei lately? I was wondering how he is."

Kit's stomach did a flip at the mention of Sergei, her thoughts veering towards that enigmatic figure. "No, it's been rather quiet on the Sergei front. I'm sure he'll resurface eventually. Things have been hectic at work, so I haven't had the chance to contact him."

After Natalia mentioned her upcoming visit to Pristina, Kit shared her own plan to return from Thailand around the same time. They discussed possible dates, and despite her exhaustion, Kit felt a spark of excitement. Being with Natalia always brought comfort and understanding, a much-needed respite after everything that had happened recently. She looked forward to the trip more than ever. Plus, she was eager to learn more about khash philosophy after her intriguing encounter with Father Peter, the enigmatic Russian Orthodox priest and Sergei's mentor.

"Natalia, before I let you go, have you heard any more about Father Peter since we met in Ljubljana? I was fascinated by him and the story about those Rasputin Manuscripts."

Natalia chuckled. "Your intuition is working overtime, Kit. I heard he's at the Serbian Orthodox monastery in Dečani, Kosovo, overseeing the restoration of religious icons. That's his specialty."

"Wow, so he's actually in Kosovo!" Kit sat down, absorbing the news. "That's incredible."

As the call ended, Kit felt a quiet reflection settle over her. The conversation had sparked a current of anticipation, electrifying the night air with the promise of the journey ahead. She contemplated the converging paths in Pristina, where answers awaited, and old mysteries might finally find resolution.

Chapter Eleven

K it, already running on empty, set aside the allure of sleep. She received an urgent message that the task force was convening. Quickly, she showered and donned a fresh outfit. Her office attire was carefully chosen—a sleek, dark green jacket paired with tailored wool slacks, complemented by a crisp white blouse and elegant black heels. A touch of makeup, strategically applied, aimed to conceal the dark circles beneath her eyes.

She headed to the operational hub of the task force, located within the EUFOR police headquarters in Pristina. Kit slipped into the room, blending into the back rows. About eight officers, stationed at desks or lingering at the edges, focused on Major Matt Hackman. Positioned in front of a cluster of images and schematics pinned to the white-board, the fatigue etched in his eyes mirrored Kit's own exhaustion.

"Let's get started on mapping out the area," Matt announced, his voice strong despite his obvious fatigue. "We're facing a triple murder, at least. Three lives taken, four people fighting for their lives in the ICU, and five others struggling with serious injuries. The One Up Café is our main focus." He traced a path across hastily drawn maps and diagrams, outlining the key points of their investigation.

"According to our forensics team, it looks like the explosion was caused by an IED made from an anti-tank mine," Matt explained, gesturing towards the individuals marked as A, B, and C. "We're currently trying to gather information from potential witnesses who might have seen something before the incident. A confidential source reported seeing two vehicles similar to those used by local law enforcement arriving just before the explosion. The suspects inside were wearing balaclavas. Another witness, watching from across the road, confirmed this account."

Kit raised her hand, which Matt acknowledged with a nod and introduction. "Thank you, Ms. Chase from the Chief Prosecutor's office."

"We're about to apply to court to keep the witness identities under wraps," she said, sharing the information provided by Eva earlier.

"Perfect," Matt said. "We should drill deeper into their stories and pull in any others near the crime scene."

Before Matt could go on, Owen said, "We've got another lead, sir. There's talk of a stash of weapons—anti-tank mines included—in a cave on the outskirts of town."

"That could be the source of our IED," Matt speculated. "Dispatch a search team. Bomb squad, sniffer dogs, the works. I want every nook and cranny inspected."

At Matt's instruction, the room started buzzing, ready to unearth this secret cache. Kit's eyes, accustomed to being amongst a sea of male faces in law enforcement meetings, noted another woman among the ranks—a blonde with her hair gathered into a club at the base of her neck.

"We should check into anyone with grudges against the café's owner, Mal Mala," Zena Lace Letalova said. "That could be a motive for the bombing."

The suggestion resonated with Matt, "Get into profiler mode, Ms. Letalova. But Mala wasn't the only victim. We need a list of possible targets present in the café."

"That would be a long list," Kit said.

Zena nodded. "Maybe. But if we can tie any of those suspects to police vehicles, we've got our lead."

Kit shrugged, glancing at her notes to hide her irritation. She was still annoyed about how Zena had been hovering around Owen the night before. Her pen tapped rhythmically on the page, a subtle response to Zena's insight.

"Anything else?" Matt asked.

"We've been interviewing people who saw the explosion in the area," an officer said. "So far nothing really helps."

"Keep going," Matt directed. "Talk to the victims in the hospital and see what the neighboring businesses have to say. Look for any grudges or disputes that might hint at a motive. Form a team to go through the statements thoroughly. I want every detail sorted out. Report back to me by the end of the day."

"We've hit a bit of a snag," Owen interjected. "Our potential eyewitnesses are reticent to come forward."

"Fearing reprisals, no doubt," Zena said.

"Exactly," Owen confirmed. "The specter of organized crime and rogue elements within the Kosovo Police loom large. It's got them spooked, too frightened to say what they know."

"Right, people," Matt said. "We need to find a way to reassure these witnesses. Offer them protection and anonymity. If necessary, get creative. There's plenty to be getting on with. We should have more information from forensics soon."

As the cacophony of footsteps and voices filled the room, Kit felt the weight of the investigation on her shoulders as lead prosecutor. Her mind raced, desperate to find a path through the possible dead ends for the sake of the victims, both present and future. Political pressure to make arrests was inevitable, and public concern was at its peak. Time was slipping through her fingers, and she needed a breakthrough—fast.

As the team dispersed to chase their leads, Kit stared at the map on the whiteboard, a gnawing sense of unease in her stomach. She suspected the treacherous web of crime, corruption, and explosives stretched far beyond their current grasp. What they didn't know, she feared, could be the key to stopping a ticking time bomb.

Chapter Twelve

That weekend, Matt invited his coworkers over for a grill party at his house. After working around the clock for over a week, they needed a break to relieve tension and build some team camaraderie. The pressure of gathering evidence and assessing leads in the bombing case had been relentless. While eyewitness statements pointed to Driton Kupi's group, they still needed solid evidence to directly link them to the crime.

Kit pulled on her embroidered, distressed jeans, a black tank top, and a linen shirt. She chose her favorite boho-style purple boots to complete the outfit. After brushing her hair back and tying it up, she added some lipstick and eyeshadow. A spritz of her addictive amber fragrance finished her look. She grabbed her bag, a bottle of Merlot wine in a brown paper bag from the diplomatic sales shop, and headed out the door.

Catching one of the plentiful taxis from the rank close to her apartment, she headed over to Matt and his wife, Sylvie's, house. Together with their son, David, they lived in a three-bedroom house in Sunny Hill. There was a garden out the back where Matt had set up a grill. Kit recognized some of the vehicles parked on the street as belonging to colleagues, with OIDC, EUFOR and diplomatic plates. Owen was already there, as well as Eva, and she was surprised to see Dr. Prabhu's car. The weather forecast had been cloudy, and she noticed they were gathering.

Kit let herself in the gate and walked up the stairs to the main entrance. The door was ajar, and she rang the bell. Sylvie greeted her and gave her a swift kiss on one cheek.

"Kit, great you could make it," she said.

"Hi, Sylvie. I bought something for the party," Kit said and pressed the bottle into Sylvie's hand.

"Thanks very much," she said. "You didn't have to, but it will come in handy."

Sylvie wore her blonde hair up in a messy bun, looking as if she had either just got out of bed or was ready to go out to an expensive nightclub. She was wearing faded blue jeans and white sneakers, like last time Kit had seen her a few weeks ago, and over the top she wore a loose gathered floral tunic. Kit noticed a small but noticeable bump on Sylvie's belly, which had not been observable before. She didn't want to mention anything, but Sylvie noticed her lingering gaze. "Yes, you're right, Kit," she said. "We've got another one on the way."

"How wonderful, congratulations!" Kit said and embraced Sylvie warmly. "I don't know why Matt didn't say anything."

"Matt doesn't always say what's on his mind," Sylvie said, her blue eyes sparkling. "You must know that having worked with him for a while."

Kit shrugged. "Business is business, I suppose. None of us talk about our private lives that much."

A blonde toddler with a halo of fine hair and a face

smeared with chocolate ran up to his mother and wiped his chocolatey hands on her jeans, looking up at her with an adoring smile.

"David, do you have to do that? Mummy is supposed to be hosting a party," Sylvie said, rolling her eyes at Kit and laughing. "Excuse me, I better go change my jeans. Just head through into the garden. Matt will be starting the grill soon. Some of your friends are already here."

"Thanks, Sylvie, I'll do that." Kit passed by the kitchen counter and watched as Sylvie disappeared through a door with David in pursuit. She then made her way towards the garden, ready to join the others.

It was the first time that Kit had been inside Matt's house. She had seen him briefly in his garage a few months ago to discuss another case. The living space was open plan, with a compact kitchen opening directly into a dining room, from which the lounge flowed. The patio doors were open, and she could walk through directly into the garden. It was fully fenced, with several mature fruit trees and a small vegetable garden.

On the paved area, Matt was working at a mobile barbecue grill. Owen was close by, preparing food for Matt to roast. Zena Lace Letalova stood not far away, nursing a glass of wine and watching Owen work. Kit suppressed a surge of irritation and took a deep breath. She tried to switch into her neutral strategic mode, as Sergei had taught her. First, look over the scene of battle, before you react. Over to the left, she could see her colleagues from the chief prosecutor's office. Dua was talking to Eva, animatedly. Eva dropped a tasty morsel to her dog Bambino while Axel and Christina were talking over a plate of hors d'oeuvres. On the other side of the garden, there were a few small groups of people, talking. Kit recognized Don Edgson and other members of the official task force. She went over to Eva and Dua.

"Hi, how's it going, you two?" Kit said. "Looks like I just arrived at the right time."

"*Ciao bella*," Eva said. "Yes, it looks like Matt is doing a great job with the barbecue. I hope lunch is ready soon, I'm starving."

"Me too," Dua said.

"Any news about Besim?" Kit asked.

Dua frowned. "I was just filling in Eva about that—he's in intensive care. But thank goodness, he's doing better. He had serious concussion and had to have surgery on his arm."

"Oh, I am sorry, Dua. But at least he seems to be doing better than some of the other victims." *Meaning that he is still alive*, Kit thought.

"We have to see how much use he can get back in his right arm," Eva said. She pursed her lips. This was a serious injury for someone who earned his living as a waiter. Besim might not be able to work anymore, and paying jobs were hard to come by in Kosovo. Plus, the café would be out of commission for months.

"Well, thank you my friends," Dua said. She tossed a glance over towards where Matt was working at the grill. "Looks like food is up. Eva, can I get something for you?"

Kit felt a firm pressure on her right shoulder and turned around, to see Owen holding a plate of grilled meat and vegetables for her. She took the dish and kissed him on the cheek.

"The way to a woman's heart is through her stomach," she said.

"I thought that might be the case." Owen laughed.

Eva eyed Kit's plate. "Yes, perhaps a small piece of steak and some of that corn looks good," she said to Dua.

"Our private task force hasn't met for a while," Kit said quietly.

Eva nodded. "*Sí*, I was thinking about that."

"We haven't had to yet, as the official task force is currently working well," Owen explained. "But there could be news from our headquarters in Berlin that may not bode well for us."

Kit looked at him curiously, taking a delicate bite of her charred and buttered corn cob.

"What kind of news?" Eva asked.

"It seems like something has happened that Matt wasn't pleased about. He wouldn't tell me what exactly, but he did mutter something about budget cuts," Owen replied.

"That's concerning," Kit remarked, wiping her mouth with a napkin. "What do you think might be going on?"

"There have been talks about restructuring and reducing funds. We should receive more information soon," Owen answered.

"I found it odd that Matt decided to throw a party in the midst of such a significant investigation. Do you think he may give an update?"

"I doubt he would do it here—but something has unsettled him. He seems quite preoccupied at the moment."

"I'll try to get it out of Matt," Eva said. "I didn't hear anything from our political advisers in-house, but that's not really unusual. Either they don't know, or they're keeping all the juicy news to themselves."

A deep voice interrupted their conversation, and Kit looked up to see Matt standing behind them. He was wearing khaki pants and a red polo shirt. She turned her attention to the grill, where Dua had taken over and was serving plates of food to the other party guests. "What's going on?" Matt asked, joining the group.

"Well," Owen stammered, his cheeks turning slightly red. "I was just mentioning that there could be some news from Berlin."

Matt scowled. "I can't stand the way those people do business. They have no idea what it's like trying to solve crimes in the field."

"Is there some kind of political game being played in Berlin?" Kit asked.

"It seems like it," Matt replied, taking a draught from his beer bottle. "It's not confirmed yet, but there's talk of cutting funding for our anti-crime unit and downsizing staff. They want us to focus more on monitoring and mentoring local authorities."

"That's a bit premature, isn't it?" Kit interjected. "Maybe in another five years or so..."

"There's nothing concrete yet," Matt continued. "But one of my sources in Berlin says this is in the works."

"What does this mean for our jobs?" Owen asked.

"Possible job cuts," Matt answered grimly. "It may not be our team specifically, but it will definitely change the way we operate if these reforms go through."

They all stood around quietly for a moment, lost in thought.

Finally, Angel joined them as well. "Who's interested in participating in our charity raffle?"

Intrigued, Kit asked, "Which cause are we supporting and how much are the tickets?"

She couldn't help but hear Sergei's words repeating in her mind: it's not about the cost, but about how much you're willing to pay.

"We're raising funds for a recycling project," Angel explained. "Tickets are 10 Euros each."

"I'm in," Kit declared, pulling out a bill from her purse.

"Why are you spending on a raffle when there's talk of layoffs?" Axel asked from behind her. He had been hovering around their group, listening in.

Kit shrugged nonchalantly. "Let's turn things around," she suggested. "Instead of giving less when someone threatens to cut funding, let's surprise them by giving even more."

Axel looked confused. "I don't understand your reasoning," he said sceptically. "Is Berlin monitoring our participation in this raffle? Is this some obscure lesson from law school in New Zealand?"

Kit laughed at his cynicism. "Nope," she replied, "just my own way of thinking."

"I'm with Kit," Eva chimed in firmly, turning to Angel and requesting fifty Euros worth of tickets. "We need to stay true to our intentions."

Axel scoffed at their enthusiasm. "Gambling is a waste of money," he said loftily. "If we invested that money instead, we'd see better returns."

"Everyone has their own opinions," Kit responded.

Owen watched with amusement as the group bantered back and forth. "I can spare 10 Euros for a good cause," he said at last. Kit grinned at him with approval.

"And what about you, sir?" Owen turned to Matt.

Matt looked pained as he admitted, "I'm no high roller. One Euro is my maximum bet."

Angel handed out the raffle tickets with a reassuring smile. "No pressure, Major," she said comfortingly. "You can always change your mind later."

"At least he's being honest about it," Kit commented.

"I'm just as straightforward," Axel interjected defensively. "Does that earn me your approval?"

Kit laughed and turned away dismissively.

"I think he might have a crush on you," Angel whispered conspiratorially, nodding towards Axel.

Kit cringed at the thought.

Meanwhile, Axel had redirected his attention to Matt, asking about their ongoing bombing investigation. Kit bristled at his boldness—she was the one assigned to the case, after all.

"As I mentioned earlier to Eva," Matt patiently explained, "we'll be searching a cave where explosives may be stored. We're still trying to link our suspects directly to the crime scene."

Axel appeared intrigued by this update and offered to assist in analyzing any evidence they found after the operation. However, Kit doubted whether he would actually have the courage to go into a potentially explosive-filled cave.

"I'll be there during the operation," she said confidently. She noticed Don watching them from across the yard; his bomb-sniffing dog, Max, would likely join them on-site.

Eva suggested that Axel could help document any evidence they found afterwards.

Zena approached Owen and lightly touched his arm. "Hey Owen," she said, "I'm leaving soon for training on advanced hostage negotiation tactics. We can hit the gym when I get back."

Kit couldn't resist asking, "Where will the training take place?"

"In Istanbul. An FBI specialist will conduct it there," Zena replied.

"And where specifically?"

"It'll be held with the Turkish counter-terrorism unit."

The first raindrop hit the metal grill with a loud hiss, cutting through the background chatter like a warning.

With each subsequent drop adding to the chorus, Kit felt the weight of responsibility for the upcoming operation settle upon her once again. The light but constant rain seemed to dampen the carefree mood of the evening, foreshadowing possible turbulent weather ahead. She watched as the droplets scattered across the yard, reminding her of the explosive situation they would soon be facing not only in the cave search operation, but also within their team dynamics. Taking a deep breath, Kit made a conscious decision to tread carefully in both areas.

Chapter Thirteen

The atmosphere at EUFOR Police Headquarters was electric the following morning. Inside the somber building, a team of highly trained officers, accompanied by canine units and explosives experts, eagerly awaited their daily briefing. The day's agenda was critical: investigate a possible cache of weapons hidden in a cave on the outskirts of Pristina.

Kit silently slipped into the back row, clad in a pair of khaki cargo pants, a navy windbreaker, and sturdy hiking boots. Instead of her usual legal briefcase, she carried a worn leather satchel filled with tools for gathering evidence. Following closely behind her was Dua Rexhepi, wearing an oversized tan jacket to keep out the morning chill.

Major Matt Hackman stood at the front of the room, morning light casting shadows on his grizzled face and emphasizing his stern jawline. The briefing room was quiet and tense as Major Hackman revealed new information that added a grim layer to the case. The presence of PETN in Kupi's police vehicle suggested guilt, but it was his recent chaotic personal life that hinted at a deeper motive. The altercation with Mal Mala, café owner and crime boss, and the untimely death of Kupi's team member, Valon Rama, suggested a possible revenge-driven motive fueled by grief. Rumors circulated that Mala may have orchestrated Rama's death out of jealousy and sparked a cycle of retaliation. As forensics lined up with Kupi's potential for revenge, the lines between personal vendetta and criminal behavior began to blur, setting the stage for an investigation into the murky depths of emotions like jealousy and vengeance.

Major Hackman turned to Owen. "Sergeant, did you speak with Kosovo's chief inspector for minerals, mines, and explosives?"

"Yes, sir. PETN is only used as a detonator in Kosovo and is placed in cords to ignite the main explosive charge. Possessing larger amounts is illegal and prohibited for police use," Owen replied.

"Correct. The Kosovo police should not have access to PETN," Matt confirmed. "There have been no reported thefts of the substance, and it cannot be obtained in large quantities from detonator cords."

Kit paused, pen poised over her notebook. "Can someone explain the difference between PETN and TNT?"

Owen stepped in. "PETN is more sensitive and reacts faster than TNT. Its detonation speed is quicker, leading to more destructive outcomes. And due to its intense combustion, there may be no residue left at the scene of an explosion."

"Considering the activities of the Kosovo Liberation Army during the conflict, they could have potentially used both PETN and TNT, possibly hoarding some illegally within the country," Kit suggested.

"So, the illegal use of PETN could be linked to stockpiles from the conflict era, or there may be involvement from insiders within the ministry," Owen added.

Kit paused, then looked up, a new question in her eyes. "And where do antitank mines fit into this? Could they have been used in conjunction with the PETN for the explosion we're investigating?"

Owen nodded, understanding the direction of her thoughts. "Indeed. Antitank mines, especially those leftover from conflict eras, can be modified to include a PETN trigger mechanism. It's a deadly combination, harnessing the mine's destructive capacity with PETN's fast detonation speed. This could explain the extensive damage and the lack of residue at the scene."

Matt added, "That's a solid theory. The antitank mine could act as the main explosive charge, with PETN serving as the detonator. Given their availability from the conflict era, it's plausible that our culprits combined these elements for maximum impact."

"I'm leaning towards the theory of conflict-era stockpiling," Matt concluded, taking note of key points on the investigation board. The statement hung in silence for a moment before Matt shifted his gaze back to the team.

"Alright, let's get moving. Our next stop is a location just outside of town where intel suggests explosives may be stored illegally," he instructed. The room sprang into action, the sounds of chairs being pushed back, bags being zipped up, and last-minute conversations filling the air.

Kit stood. "Let's go, Dua. It's time to leave." The rest of the task force began to file out of the room. Outside, a line of Jeeps awaited them in the cool morning air. Owen was in the driver's seat of the first vehicle, double-checking its controls before they set off. Matt hopped into the passenger seat, while Kit and Dua climbed into the back. As soon as the last door slammed shut, the convoy rumbled to life and started on their way to the cave—the main objective of today's mission.

As they made their way down the highway out of Pristina, the city gave way to the sprawling countryside. Their vehicle rumbled over the pot-holed roads, jarring them as Owen wrestled with the steering to navigate the rough terrain.

In the back, Kit passed Dua a clipboard with a checklist. "Evidence, Dua," Kit said. "We have to maintain the chain of custody by documenting every item of evidence found-who found it, where and when. Lose that, we lose court-admissible evidence."

"I see," Dua replied, hesitating. "Maybe I should shadow you for the first few times, so I can see what we need to do."

Kit nodded, looking out at the lush fields. Spring always had a way of injecting optimism into even the bleakest corners. Today would have been such a day, had the circumstances been different.

"I'm looking forward to working with the police dogs," Dua spoke up again, breaking the silence. "Do you think I could take some photos of them?"

"Absolutely, they're amazing animals," Kit said.

"Why are they coming with us today?" Dua asked.

"To detect explosives, and as a safety precaution in case there are guard dogs at the cave," Owen said while keeping his eyes on the road. "Maybe you can ask to take some pictures before they get to work."

Matt grunted in response to the discussion, lost in his own thoughts.

Dua nodded. "I won't get in their way while they're working. I just have a soft spot for dogs. It's sad to see all the stray ones on the streets."

"Trained police dogs are a world apart from strays," Owen remarked.

"During my visit to Sarajevo, I saw packs of wild dogs roaming the city," Dua recalled. "It was terrifying when they started chasing after me."

"That's why we occasionally have to cull them here," Owen explained.

Dua furrowed her brow, imagining soldiers hunting down the stray dogs. She fell silent, focusing on the checklists and preparing for the challenging day ahead.

"I've heard that certain groups use dog fighting rings as a form of gambling," Kit mentioned. "But there are efforts to change things for the better with new animal welfare legislation."

"And caged bears are also a worry. Luckily, an NGO called Green Tracks is actively working on improving their situation."

Owen signaled for a right turn and the rest of the convoy followed suit. Kit looked at Matt and asked for his views on the situation.

"I came across an Interpol report on Mal Mala yesterday," Matt answered. "He's connected to various illegal activities, including animal trafficking and cruelty. But it goes deeper than that; there are suspicions that he is involved in smuggling valuable cultural artifacts into the black market. The report mentioned Serbian Monasteries in Kosovo as potential targets. However, no one is willing to testify against him due to his ties with organized crime."

Matt's words hung heavily in the air, painting a disturbing picture of their conversation. One particular statement caught Kit's attention—Natalia had mentioned that Father Peter was currently staying at Visoki Dečani Monastery, working on restoring priceless religious icons. She couldn't help but wonder if he could be in danger from this criminal group.

"Even though Mala was a victim of the bombing—his café was destroyed—we can't overlook his involvement in illegal activities," Kit said.

"He's not an innocent victim," Matt confirmed.

"The world isn't divided into just villains and heroes. Most people fall somewhere in between. But for now, let's stay focused on our mission," Kit said, glancing down at the dossier in her lap.

The car fell silent except for the hum of the engine and the occasional splash of water as they drove through a puddle. Kit found her thoughts drifting to the bombing, the victims, and the strange twists this case was taking them. The explosive reprisals of Kosovo's underworld were as deep and tangled as the roots of the old trees that lined their path. And much like those roots, Kit knew they'd have to dig deep to unearth the truth.

"We're getting close," Owen said checking the GPS coordinates. "I think that's the site ahead." He indicated an opening in a rough cliff face just ahead. Kit could see that although there was no real road, vehicles had driven there recently, leaving a path in the grass.

"Let's stop before we get much closer," Matt said. "We need to look for evidence starting now, including tire tracks and things that the offenders could have dropped."

Owen pulled over to the side, and the following vehicles

did likewise. Kit and Dua slid out of the Jeep and stood to one side.

"Let the military police go first, Dua," Kit said to her softly. "We'll follow and help to document any evidence that they might find."

The officers gathered around Matt for instructions. He told one group to review the tire tracks and photograph them. Another forensic artist was already sketching the scene ahead, while another team was assembling lights and other equipment to go into the cave. Don waited to one side with Max. The dog's ears were pricked, his stance alert, and his eyes were on the cave entrance. He sniffed the air, his muscles taut with readiness, as he gave a single bark. Don moved cautiously, his eyes scanning the ground for any unusual signs.

The team, tense with anticipation, edged closer to the cave's shadowy mouth. Kit noticed Dua's knuckles whiten as she clutched her camera, eyes wide with a mix of fear and determination.

"He's picking up the scent of explosives already," Don whispered, casting a quick glance at his alert dog.

Suddenly, a chorus of barks erupted from the mouth of the cave. "Don, we might have company. See if there are any guard dogs," Matt instructed, his eyes scanning the rocky terrain.

"On it, sir," Don responded, motioning for the two dog handlers in army gear to step forward. One was lean, while the other was more muscular. They prepared their tranquilizer guns and tasers, accepting a bag of meat from Don as bait. "It could just be hunger that's driving them."

The handlers moved cautiously across the rough terrain towards the source of the barking.

"This is scary, isn't it?" Dua whispered.

Kit placed a comforting hand on her shoulder. "It's all part of the job," she reassured Dua. "We can trust our team; they know what they're doing."

The group was on edge for several minutes until the handlers reappeared, leading two formidable dogs: German Shepherd and Rottweiler crosses. Despite their initial hostility, the dogs had mellowed out after being given some food and didn't object to being secured in crates.

"These poor creatures must have suffered so much," Dua said in a soft voice, imagining the cruelty they must have endure.

"It's a sad reality that owners of properties like this often abandon their dogs to guard the area without making proper arrangements for them. And since rabies is prevalent in this part of the world, we must proceed with caution. However, we've taken responsibility for the dogs now, although there was one younger dog who managed to escape," Don explained.Kit made a mental note to add animal cruelty to the list of charges they could bring against the perpetrators.

"Have you checked for any explosives at the entrance?" Matt asked Don.

"We've cleared the cave entrance and a little way inside. There may be booby-traps further in. Max has indicated the presence of explosives."

"Alright, Sergeant, let's proceed with caution then. We'll need you and bomb disposal to go first; we'll follow behind doing a sweep for evidence. Kit and Dua, I want you both to wait at the entrance until I give you the all clear," Matt said.

Unable to contain her reaction, Kit squared her shoulders and fixed her gaze on Owen. "I hope that decision isn't because we're women," she retorted firmly. "If your team is going into the cave, we should be right there with you."

Owen met her stare with an indifferent shrug. "He's calling the shots. And honestly, I don't want either of you exposed to unstable explosives."

Irritation flashed across Kit's face before she could reel it back. She tried to take a more objective view, imagining the situation as a game of chess—weighing each move, the pros and cons. While her pride yearned for the thrill of being one of the first to enter the cave, but another part of her saw an opportunity in waiting outside, in scouring for evidence that others may overlook.

"Fine," Kit said, after a pause. "Just remember that any evidence needs to be photographed and catalogued properly."

"Roger that," Matt said in, his voice booming as he turned to the men. "Remember, preserve the evidence. The lawyers will be on our tails to document whatever we find."

The men fanned out, making their way towards the mouth of the cave. The bomb disposal team took the lead, with the canine unit close behind. Matt and Owen trailed, keeping a safe distance while maintaining a protective flank. As the men disappeared into the shadow of the cave, Kit and Dua changed their focus to the area outside.

"While we wait," Kit suggested, her eyes already scanning their surroundings, "why don't we scour the vicinity for anything they might miss?"

"Such as?" Dua shot back, her eyes narrowing with curiosity.

"A tossed cigarette butt, or imprints from a getaway vehicle," Kit said. "Even an old soda can could contain traces of DNA. Let's split up—you take the right, I'll cover the left. As soon as we get the all clear, we follow the others into the cave."

"Okay, I'll let you know if I find anything," Dua said.

They parted ways, and Kit followed a rough path that cut through low bushes. The trail seemed to have been recently used, but the ground was too compact to identify any footprints. Despite this, she had an intuition that there could be something worth finding among the bushes.

Kit's pace slowed as her phone buzzed, vibrating abruptly in her pocket. Without breaking stride, she fished it out, expecting Owen's signal. Instead, "Vernon Chase" flashed on the display, jolting her heart against her ribs. She slowed to focus on the call.

"Hello?" Her voice came out as a whisper.

"Kit, it's Vernon. Your father." The voice, deep and edged with a shrewd tone that she remembered all too well, held an unfamiliar timbre of age. "Am I catching you at a bad time?"

"Could say that," Kit answered, voice flat. "How'd you find me?"

A scratchy chuckle vibrated through the speaker. "Your mother. She refuses to be our go-between. And I'm not far away. In Thailand," he announced, as if it were a casual remark. "We need to talk. In person."

"About what?" Suspicion sharpened her tone.

"It's serious—not for the phone."

Her silence stretched out, a tightrope between curiosity and caution.

"I'll consider it," she conceded at last. "But I'm working right now."

"I wouldn't expect otherwise," he said, softer now. "Think on it, okay? It's high time we untangle our past."

"Maybe," she allowed. "I'll be travelling myself soon. We might work something out."

"I'll send the coordinates. See you soon, Kit."

The line went dead. His final words hung in the air like a ghost of affection. Pocketing the phone, Kit pushed forward, her focus back on the mission. But Vernon's plea stayed in her thoughts, an enigma that threatened the walls she had painstakingly built.

Kit froze as she caught a glimpse of movement near the edge of the cliff. Acting on instinct, she immediately crouched low, blending in with her surroundings. A man emerged from between the trees, carrying a suspicious black box and a rifle slung over his shoulder.

Kit's eyes followed him until he passed, then she scanned the bushes for a hidden path to follow him. She quickly typed out a message to Owen: *Suspect approaching. Armed. Left side of cave. 50m out.*

She silently pleaded for Owen to check his phone, but there was no reply.

Bending low, Kit retreated, taking a detour that brought her closer to the man. Through the foliage, she could make out his clothing—camouflage pants, black T-shirt, khaki vest. His hands moved swiftly, connecting the black box to a wire hidden in the brush. It was a detonator. The realization crashed into her—someone was onto their convoy, an explosion imminent. The man's profile sliced through her memory, a match to a suspect from the briefings.

With phone in hand, she took a risk and quickly sent out messages to her contacts, Owen and Dua, urging them to evacuate as there was an imminent threat of detonation. Time was running out and every movement felt like a dangerous gamble. She had to make a decision—confront the suspect or seek cover. In a panic, she sent another message to Angel and Eva, requesting back up. Thinking fast, she stood up and approached the man. He had a stubble and battle-weary lines on his face, but his eyes gleamed with determination.

"Hi," Kit said loudly and cheerfully. "I think I'm lost. Can you help me?"

The sound of her voice seemed to jolt the man as if from a trance. He whipped around, squinting into the sunlight, an ugly curse slipping from his lips. But undeterred by her efforts to distract him, he jammed his thumb down on the device in his hand. The low, ominous rumble echoing from the cliff made Kit's blood run cold. The bastard had detonated an explosive in the cave, right where her team had ventured.

Chapter Fourteen

"No..." The word dissolved into the roar of the blast. Kit staggered as pebbles and dust showered down, the cliff face dropping debris. She fumbled with her phone, the screen a blur of desperate swipes. Silence reigned—no messages, no calls. A visceral fear clenched her gut, images of Owen and her team—possibly buried, wounded, gone—flashing in her mind's eye.

Frozen, her gaze caught on the man's—her shock mirrored in his wide eyes. But he was next to irrelevant now. Adrenaline shattered her paralysis, her legs surging towards the explosion, while he fled in the opposite direction. Kit's only focus: the victims of his lunacy.

Her phone buzzed against her palm. A message from Angel: *backup incoming.* Kit's thumbs flew, *Explosion. Need immediate help.*

She stumbled, nearly twisting an ankle, her breaths sharp. Her sole mission: to reach those caught in the aftermath.

Emerging from a cloud of dust, Kit's first sight was Dua,

standing a few meters from the cave's mouth, clutching a trembling puppy. Dua's eyes flashed with alarm at Kit's approach. "There's been an explosion. It must've been a trap."

"It was deliberate," Kit countered, her voice edged with urgency. She didn't pause to question the puppy in Dua's arms; the urgency was too great. "I saw the bomber with the detonator."

Relief flooded her when Owen emerged, half-carrying Matt through the settling dust. Matt's head was bloodied, his arm torn, his eyes glazed with shock.

"How bad is it?" Kit's eyes darted over them, assessing.

"I'll live," Owen grunted, his voice strained as he adjusted Matt's weight. "Matt's got a head wound, might be concussed. We need to check for others—and for secondary devices."

Kit's attention split as Matt mumbled incoherently, trying to focus. "Who did this?" he managed to ask.

"A suspect I recognized from our briefings. Late 30s, male. I tried to distract him—too late."

Owen winced, both from Matt's weight and the question. "Distract him? With what backup?"

"It was all I could do," Kit replied, her gaze flickering to the ridges above, where danger might still lurk. "Backup's incoming."

Dua, cradling the puppy, perked up at the sound of distant sirens. "They're almost here."

Kit stepped back, her gaze sweeping the terrain. It was too easy to tunnel vision on the immediate crisis and miss the bigger picture. Sniper vantage points, potential IEDs— she knew they were not safe yet. Above them, the bushes rustled ominously, a reminder that they might still be in someone's crosshairs.

"Let's move out. Meet the ambulances on the road. Staying here is too risky—snipers, IED, you name it," Kit said.

Owen, face drawn, nodded sharply and they picked up their pace. Dua's voice trembled slightly, "And Don, Max, the rest?"

"Professionals are on their way for them," Kit assured her, propelling Dua forward with a gentle but firm hand. Despite their narrow escape from the blast, their safety was not guaranteed.

Catching sight of the puppy again, she raised an eyebrow. "What's that?"

"A stray," Dua said, hugging the animal closer. "She needs care."

"Okay, but keep her close," Kit said, her mind still on more pressing dangers.

They reached the EUFOR vehicles just as the rescue convoy skidded to a halt. Owen, supporting Matt, moved towards the paramedics who rushed over. Another ambulance crew beckoned Owen inside for a check-up.

Angel and Axel arrived in an OIDC Jeep, scanning the scene urgently. Kit briefed them and the newly arrived officers, "We have a fugitive, possibly armed. The cavern is compromised," she explained to Officer Atay, the attending Kosovo police officer. "This wasn't an accident."

The magnitude of the situation was palpable. With Matt incapacitated, Kit felt the weight of responsibility. The explosion's aftermath demanded a multifaceted response – search and rescue, forensic analysis, bomb squad, and a manhunt. It was a job for the whole team, and more.

With urgency in her voice, Kit relayed the situation to

the police—several officers were still trapped within the cavern.

"Officer Atay," she cautioned, "this was no accident. We have an armed perpetrator at large, and the cave may not be structurally sound."

She considered the scale of the destruction. How much evidence had been lost in the explosion? How much dangerous materiel remained? A multi-pronged response was required: a rescue team, a forensic sweep, bomb disposal, and a manhunt. This level of coordination typically fell to Matt, who, now injured, was out of play.

"We need a senior officer for the police response," she pressed Atay, who nodded. He extracted his radio phone and stepped aside to call headquarters, his conversation lost in the surrounding chaos.

Dua's eyes widened with a haunted look. "This is just like the café all over again," she murmured, her composure wobbling. Kit watched her fight back tears, then regain control. "I've got your back," Dua said, securing the puppy in their Jeep.

"Stay here, support the police when they arrive," Kit instructed. "Check with Owen for a headcount. We're missing officers."

Kit's gaze returned to the cave's dark mouth, a leaden dread settling within her. Where were Don, Max, and the others?

Angel and Axel joined them, concern etched on Angel's face, while Axel's demeanor was all business. He was coping unexpectedly well with the situation. "Update me," he said, pen poised over his notebook.

Angel clutched her bag tightly, her worry palpable. "Are you two okay?" she asked, voice trembling.

"We survived," Kit answered, her voice betraying her

worry. "But there may be casualties. We need more forces—police, possibly military." She paused, considering their next moves. "Major Hackman would normally oversee this. The blast hit him; he's with the medics now, alongside Owen. Let's hope their injuries are minor."

Kit caught Owen's eye; despite his wounds, he flashed her a reassuring smile as a medic attended to his head wounds. His thumbs up sign galvanized her own resolve. She nodded to him, a silent pact to discuss everything later, and refocused on the task at hand.

As the highest-ranking official on site, Kit's next steps were crucial. She turned to Angel. "Update Eva—mission leadership needs to know immediately. Alert Dr. Prabhu too; let's hope we won't need her expertise, but we need to be prepared for casualties. And keep an eye out for secondary devices."

The enormity of potential loss bore down on her, the nausea almost crippling. Kit steadied herself with deep breaths, fighting off the dizziness. She scrolled through her messages aimlessly, using the mundane action as a grounding moment.

Priorities crystallized in her mind: secure the site, aid the wounded, preserve evidence. Her own eyewitness account might be pivotal in court.

Don emerged then from the cave, a ghostly figure covered in dust, hobbling and clutching Max. Kit's caution evaporated; she sprinted to them. "Don, thank God. What's the situation inside?" His dazed eyes worried her, but his voice held steady.

"It was rigged to blow. Saved by Kevlar," Don managed, his pain evident. Max whined softly, wounded despite his protective gear.

Guiding them towards the medics, Kit pressed for more information. "And the team? Bomb squad? The police?"

Don's expression darkened. "It's bad. Some are trapped behind rubble. The bomb squad's gear is solid, but the others..." His words trailed off into a bleak silence.

A muttered curse escaped Kit's lips. The reality was stark—they had blundered into a deathtrap.

The day seemed never-ending, filled with a constant stream of work and responsibilities. Kit took charge of the rescue operation, a role she hadn't anticipated. Despite her personal feelings towards Axel and Zena, she put them aside to focus on the tasks at hand. The entire team worked together, including staff from the international prosecutor's office and the police. They combed through the site for any evidence, finding tire tracks and some seemingly insignificant items like a discarded soda can and cigarette butts that may have been left behind by the culprits.

But hopes of finding solid leads from the cave were dampened by a series of internal explosions. Among the scattered debris were fragments of explosive devices, a disturbing mix of grenades and antitank mines. Some had detonated while others remained intact, seemingly waiting to be triggered.

Kit's heart pounded as she surveyed the chaotic scene, feeling the weight of the day's events pressing down on her. The harsh reality of their situation hit hard, but there was no time for despair. With a final glance at the wreckage, she steeled herself for what lay ahead. Next, she would face the consequences in the fluorescent-lit executive office during the inevitable debrief, where senior management would make critical decisions and judgments. The praise and blame that would follow were part of the job, but today, they felt especially heavy.

With effort, Kit straightened up and headed towards the makeshift command center, ready to confront whatever awaited her. The day might have been ending, but the battle for accountability and justice was far from over.

Chapter Fifteen

As dawn broke the next day, Kit plunged into the demands of her duties. Angel briefed her on a scheduled meeting with the Head of Mission, Bo Westergaard, and his deputy, Brad Harris. She had interacted with them in the past, notably when she defused a tense situation involving an international warrant during Eva's leave. After her instrumental role in exposing corruption within the former leadership, Kit preferred a strategy of discretion. She zealously guarded her personal privacy from her superiors' prying eyes.

Stepping into Eva's office, Kit found the chief international prosecutor absorbed in reviewing a thick dossier of case files spread across her desk. "Good morning, Eva," Kit greeted her, noting the intensity of Eva's focus.

Eva looked up, her expression a blend of concern and resolve. "*Buon giorno*, Kit. Pristina's still reeling from the latest blasts. It seems you became OIDC's unintended representative in the chaos."

Kit eased into a chair, the leather worn from years of crisis management. "I kept the lines open for mission leadership. Dua was there too, and later Axel and Angel," Kit said, trying to shrug off the attention.

Eva acknowledged this with a nod. "Westergaard is personally grateful. You're being called a hero for your actions. He's eager for a first-hand account."

"The 'hero' title belongs to the team. Dua and I were just lucky to avoid the worst."

Eva's voice carried to the adjacent office, "Angel, see if Dua can join us, please."

Angel appeared in the doorway, concern creasing her brow. "Dua's not in yet. She mentioned visiting Besim at the hospital this morning."

Kit's features softened. "Yesterday hit us all hard, especially with the casualties and injuries. Dua was good at the site, but she might find solace checking in on Besim and caring for that puppy she found."

Eva gave a sympathetic nod. "I understand. But today, the spotlight is on you." Her expression then turned more serious. "The unfortunate part is that Major Hackman is under fire for allegedly failing to secure the site properly before the team entered the cave."

Kit sighed, shaking her head. "It's tough to see how he could have done things differently. Someone had to go in to inspect for explosives. We just didn't expect that one of the criminals would return to the site with a detonator. That set off the other explosives. I fail to see how Matt could have anticipated that."

"I know it can be difficult to make decisions in the field. They say that he should have secured the perimeter before even going into the cave." Eva said.

"For goodness' sake, how could he have done that without calling a full operation. They just don't have the personnel these days."

Eva shrugged. "You know I have the greatest respect for Matt. I'm sure he did the best he could—the best anyone could."

Kit looked down and picked at her nails. She had torn several the day before.

"Did you hear anything from Owen?" Eva asked

"Yes, he texted me this morning. He's been discharged from hospital with a few bruises. Matt's still there being treated for concussion."

"Could you get an update on the injured officers? I think Westergaard is going to ask about them."

Kit pulled out her mobile phone and sent Owen a message asking if there was any news about the patients.

"There's a press briefing later in the morning, as well," Eva said. Kit silently rolled her eyes—she wanted to avoid attention from the press.

"You don't need me to go to that, do you?" she asked with a hint of reluctance.

Eva considered her, the early sunlight creating long shadows on her desk. "Your witness account could lend credibility to Westergaard's statement. Just stand beside him, let your serious expression convey the gravity of the situation."

"But being a key witness and the lead prosecutor—it's awkward, don't you think?" She frowned, the sound of the detonation replaying unwillingly in her mind.

Eva tapped a rhythm on her desk surface, thinking. "A media frenzy around you wouldn't be helpful. It might be time to pass the torch to avoid the appearance of a conflict."

A wry smile flickered on Kit's lips, betraying her internal unease. "Uncharted territory, huh? Who's in the running to replace me?"

"Axel is the logical choice, despite your reservations. He

arrived at the scene minutes after you, and with Dua's support, they'd manage."

Frustration simmered within her. "But the case— I've managed the evidence from the start."

"That's precisely why Axel should step in before your testimony complicates matters."

Kit's phone buzzed with grim updates before she could mount another argument. *Three lives lost. Don's stable. The officers are recovering. And Max—the surgery went well at the vet's. He's fighting.*

And Matt? She typed hastily, her concern evident as she shared the information with Eva.

Matt's out of danger but grappling with the aftermath of the blast. The concussion's severe.

Eva sighed, a somber shadow crossed her features. "These are testing times," she murmured.

"They may test us more than we expect," Kit replied, a grim edge to her voice.

Within the hour, Kit and Eva were ushered into the spacious office of the head of mission, Bo Westergaard. His executive aide, the epitome of efficiency, showed them through the door, where the deputy head, Brad Harris, was already seated. Westergaard was of average height, with silver hair off-set by a rugged complexion, lined from many campaigns. In his mid-50s, he still exuded a youthful vitality.

Westergaard's resonant voice vibrated through the room as he stepped forward to greet them. "Ladies, please, make yourselves comfortable. Can I offer you a cup of coffee?"

Kit and Eva answered in the affirmative and passed their requests to his assistant. It was a hospitality far beyond what Kit had become accustomed to under their previous superior. Jacob Mueller had upheld a stern business-like façade, but what he got up to outside the office was something quite different.

Brad Harris, a recognized figure from the New York OIDC liaison office, greeted them with a warmth that felt genuine. His legal expertise resonated with their own, fostering a sense of professional camaraderie rarely seen from others in senior management.

Cream leather couches and a grand desk set a professional tone in the office, while vibrant art from local talents broke the monochrome with life. Kit nestled into a couch, a cup of Westergaard's assistant's freshly brewed coffee warming her hands. The rich scent stirred her awake, yet tension lingered in the air—a stark reminder of yesterday's chaos.

Westergaard's expression was grave. "Kit, detail the explosion at the cave for us. You were there—how are our people doing?"

The room's atmosphere tightened as Kit delivered the grim news, "Three officers didn't make it. The other four are critical but stable. Her vivid account of the events, culminating in her eyewitness story of the perpetrator's final act, darkened the atmosphere further.

Eva continued in a steady voice. "The bomber is one Andrea Culaj, Driton Kupi's right hand in his underground network. Our intelligence places him deep in the hierarchy."

Brad Harris leaned in, eyes sharp and focused. "Reasons for Culaj being there?"

"It's uncertain," Eva responded. "He might've been securing or retrieving something from the explosives store, or he knew we were coming and tried to cover any connection to the café bombing."

Brad's next question was weighty with implication. "Are we looking at Kupi's men as rogue elements in Kosovo's police?"

"Possibly," Eva conceded. "There are reports of masked men in police-type vehicles at the café bombing site before the blast. They may have been laying the bomb."

"And their motive?" Bo Westergaard asked.

Eva's answer was succinct. "Gang-related disputes."

That notion—of corruption within criminal justice units—sent a chill through Kit. In some ways, it mirrored the shadowy nature of their own off-books task force. She masked her unease with a sip of coffee, seeking a brief solace in its aromatic warmth.

"We shouldn't overlook the personal angle between Mala and Kupi," Kit redirected the dialogue, easing away from sensitive lines of thought. "A murder within Kupi's circle points to Mala. There's friction over control of protection rackets in certain areas, and both have connections to a prominent singer. It's personal as much as professional."

Westergaard grunted, recognition crossing his features.

"Now," he scanned their faces, "are we poised to bring this to court?"

Kit and Eva exchanged a meaningful look, the weight of Westergaard's question hanging between them. Eva spoke, her voice steady, "Evidence is being pieced together. We're tracking the suspects' communications. With Kit's ID of Culaj, we have enough to arrest him—potentially flipping him against his accomplices. Forensics is leaving no stone unturned at the blast sites. We expect to link the perpetrators to the crime soon."

The room fell quiet, digesting the update.

"We must move quickly," Westergaard urged, his tone firm. "The public eye is critical. We can't afford missteps. Apprehend Culaj and shake down the others for intel. What's the link between the police vehicles and the café bombing?"

Kit responded with a hint of defiance, "Sir, they've been cautious, but it's possible they tampered with the vehicle logs on the night in question. It's standard procedure for the police station to keep records of vehicle usage, and we're pushing those in charge for answers. But there's a strict unspoken rule, similar to the Italian *omertà*. Breaking it is our current struggle."

"The situation does sound challenging, Kit," Brad said. "Yet, as Bo emphasized, we must expedite the prosecution of this case."

Westergaard changed the subject. "However, Kit," he began, "Your commendable efforts have not gone unnoticed. I received reports about your quick thinking at the site of the explosion. Your efficient coordination with the police and emergency services likely saved lives and preserved crucial evidence."

Surprised, Kit glanced down at her notepad, feeling a slight blush creep up her cheeks at the unexpected praise. "Thank you, sir. I believe anyone in my position would have done the same. I was fortunate to not be inside the cave when it blew up."

"These are trying times for our international police force," Westergaard acknowledged, his gaze drifting towards the window. He stood up and walked over to take in the view of Pristina sprawled out before them. "There's talk of budget cuts, as you're probably aware. And now, with the cave disaster, those voices are getting louder. Some are saying that Major Hackman should have taken more precautions to secure the scene and prevent our officers from walking into danger."

"Especially since we knew there may have been explosive materials inside," added Brad Harris.

"Predicting the contents of that cave without venturing inside was near impossible," Eva said. "Our bomb disposal and canine units were on site specifically to detect and neutralize any explosive threats."

"We were caught off-guard by the presence of a man with a detonator," Kit added.

Westergaard turned back to Kit, a question burning in his eyes. "But you didn't go inside the cave. Why not?"

"The specialists were there for that purpose. Major Hackman had instructed Dua and me to enter only once the all clear was sounded. In the interim, we decided to scan the vicinity for any potential evidence related to the case."

"And that's when you spotted Culaj armed with the detonator?" Brad queried, redirecting the conversation back to the primary suspect.

Kit nodded. "Yes, sir."

"We're facing a difficult situation, to say the least. The café explosion was only the beginning; we walked right into another trap and lost three more lives. Our actions have only made things worse," Westergaard said. His gaze was still fixed outside the window, while he clasped his hands behind his back. Kit understood that he used "we" as a reference to Major Hackman's involvement. Avoiding eye contact, Westergaard knew the message he was about to deliver wouldn't be well-received.

As he continued, it became clear that he was hinting at a potential solution, "This tragedy occurred at a time when our budgets are under intense scrutiny. Hackman is approaching retirement and placing him on administrative leave during his hospitalization may help limit the damage to both our reputations. While he may have served well in the past, this incident requires a thorough investigation, including any role he may have played."

Kit could sense where this was heading and asked cautiously, "If Major Hackman is replaced, who would take over?"

Westergaard explained, "The British will likely send someone new, but it could take months. In the meantime, his deputy could fill the position. With budget cuts looming, most of the police work may be handed off to local authorities while international forces step back.""So, this situation could be viewed as an opportunity to side-line Major Hackman," Eva inferred, a note of cynicism in her voice.

"Could be," Brad admitted. "But it's far from an ideal or convenient one. We all wish the circumstances were different."

"No argument there," Kit concurred, her thoughts heavy with their predicament.

"It's a regrettable state of affairs," Eva said. "Major Hackman maintains a solid working relationship with our office, and that role that will now fall on Sergeant Reese, at least temporarily. However, there's another issue I'd like to bring up. As Kit is the primary eyewitness at the cave, it would be wise for someone else from our office to spearhead the prosecution. If and when the case goes to trial—presuming they don't all plead guilty, which would be a first—she'll have to give testimony."

Westergaard turned back to face them, his gaze landing on Kit. "That sounds logical—are you okay with this, Kit?"

Kit shrugged. "I'd prefer to lead the prosecution, but it's impossible for me to cross-examine myself."

"And who do you suggest take the lead now?" Brad inquired.

"Axel Delcroix," Eva proposed. "He's energetic and motivated."

At this, Kit barely suppressed an eye roll, hastily lowering her gaze to her legal pad. She bit back the retort that she was more energetic and motivated than Axel. Westergaard nodded, and apparently ready to move on to his next appointment, turned his attention back to the daily schedule that lay on his desk.

Westergaard paused, weighing his words with the gravity of the moment, "Let's proceed with this transition swiftly and carefully. Major Hackman's years of dedication are not forgotten, but it's imperative that we act promptly and adapt our strategies to ensure justice in light of recent events. Axel will lead the prosecution in the interim, and let's focus on collaborating closely with local authorities to maintain the momentum of this investigation."

Eva rose from her seat, murmuring "Yes, sir," signaling that their meeting was over. As they began their descent down the stairs, Kit turned to Eva, a wry smile tugging at her lips. "I suppose this makes me the star witness."

"It seems so, doesn't it?" Eva responded. "Do you want us to assign a protection detail to you, in case this puts a target on your back?"

Kit wrinkled her nose in distaste. "You know how I feel about having a tail. No thanks." Then, a thought struck her —this could be an opportune time to visit Silver and maybe meet up with her father in Thailand. "Eva, I've been meaning to bring this up. I've got a significant amount of unused annual leave. With all that's happened recently, I could really use a break. And now that I'm no longer leading the case..."

"How long do you need?" Eva asked, a note of resignation in her voice.

"No more than a week. Maybe two," Kit replied, her voice trailing off. She tried to figure out how long she might need for her personal business.

"Alright, but no extensions beyond that," Eva warned. "Make sure you brief Axel and Dua on the case before you go. You need to be back in Pristina as soon as possible to prepare for giving testimony. Make sure you're reachable at all times."

Kit nodded her assent, a sense of relief flooding her. "Thanks, boss," she said, already picturing herself relaxing in Thailand away from the stresses of Pristina. She was also quietly relieved that the issue of reissuing the red notice with Interpol for Sergei Sokolov's arrest hadn't come up. Clearly, there were more immediate concerns monopolizing the management's attention.

Chapter Sixteen

Istanbul, Turkey

Kit pressed her forehead against the plane's cool window and peered down at the buildings, winding streets, and sparkling blue water of Istanbul, which sprawled beneath her like an unfurling magic carpet. She couldn't believe she was finally here, however briefly. The city, previously known as Byzantium, then Constantinople, the heart of the Holy Roman Empire, was a place where history, culture, and continents converged. As the plane descended towards Atatürk Airport, she could almost feel the energy of this metropolis pulsing through her veins. She could sense that this trip would be full of adventure and discovery.

The steward collected her empty tray, previously laden with an array of the mouth-watering Turkish delicacies served in business class. A lingering taste of baklava, the sweet, sticky, nut-filled pastry, still teased her palate. Her newfound wealth was a secret she clung to, allowing her to afford these small luxuries, like the business class seat she now occupied.

A four-hour layover awaited her before the long haul to Thailand, where she had agreed to meet her estranged father, Vernon Chase, for the first time in over two decades. The reunion had played on her mind. Once Eva green-lit her time off work, Kit didn't delay. She'd set the meeting with Silver and even succeeded in connecting with Vernon to confirm arrangements with him. When she booked her business-class ticket to Thailand, Turkish Air had provided her with first-class service.

As the flight swooped low over the Isthmus, Kit drank in the view of ferries skimming across frothy waves and the bridge that swarmed with traffic. She yearned to explore this enigmatic city, but she needed to focus on the task at hand.

After plane touched down on the tarmac, Kit descended the cold metal stairs onto a VIP shuttle—CIF in Turkey. A perk reserved for business class passengers, this service promised a swift transfer to the terminal. Not that it mattered much—she didn't plan to set foot outside the transit area today.

Atatürk Airport, situated on the European side of Istanbul and just 15 miles from the city center, was alive with people. As she exited the shuttle, Kit was over-whelmed by the vast crowd. She made her way towards the international transfer area, joining the long line for security clearance before reaching the departure gates. Her boarding pass in hand, she passed through the checkpoint and found herself surrounded by a whirlwind of faces and clothing from all corners of the world. The mix of languages and accents created a chaotic symphony around her, making her stand out with her auburn hair and freckled skin among the sea of travelers.

Security clearance complete, Kit rode up the escalator to the sprawling main concourse of the international departure area. The duty-free shops were spread out like a maze, offering everything from high-end, global brands to unique Turkish products. She glanced at her watch, knowing that her body clock hadn't yet adjusted an hour ahead during her short 90-minute flight from Pristina.

Kit had agreed to meet Silver at the Turkish Air Business Lounge in half an hour, giving her just enough time to make a quick detour through the enticing fragrance section. A purchase in hand, she set off to find the grand entrance to the Turkish Air lounge. Kit tucked away her carry-on and jacket into a locker before stepping into the lounge, eyes scanning the area for any sign of Silver.

The lounge was expansive, stretching out over three sprawling floors. Across the room, tables and chairs arranged by the window offered views outside, punctuated with stations serving coffee. A sweeping staircase invited exploration to the lower floor, while vast metallic lattice arches created a spectacle above, inviting natural light into the lounge.

"Where would Silver sit, if she was here?" Kit wondered. The lounge was crowded with businesspeople, families, couples, and individual travelers. She didn't see any familiar faces. *Silver might not even be here,* Kit thought, *or she might be disguised.* She decided her best course of action was to wait for Silver to make contact.

Completing a round on the first floor, Kit noted the coffee and cake service, as well as a light lunch option being served at the counter, comprising soup, salad, and bread. After passing by the restrooms, she descended to the quieter, less populated lower level. She claimed a corner sofa by the window—a spot that offered her a clear view of the room and some privacy from other guests.

After pouring herself a cup of coffee and grabbing some nuts, she took a moment to relax and enjoy her first sip. She knew there would be numerous emails waiting for her from work, but this break was reserved for her, and she intended to make the most of it. Whatever happened, her priority was to spend time mulling over the main issues in her life.

As she waited in the sanctuary of the business lounge, Kit couldn't shake the sense of guilt of her illicit fortune. It was a result of her involvement in blocking a money laundering scheme, and she knew that it could all come crashing down at any moment. She had carefully spread her riches across various accounts to remain undetected. But now, exposing this hidden wealth could destroy everything she had worked for and leave her open to prosecution.

Kit's strong moral compass compelled her to ensure that the original sum of money ended up back in its rightful place in Kosovo. Her commitment to seeking justice was constantly at odds with her involvement in the criminal underworld, even if she was only on its fringes. Navigating this dangerous world tested her ethical boundaries. And her connection to Sergei, a man associated with a brutal massacre, caused her great internal conflict. He had introduced her to a thrilling, lawless lifestyle that was far from her previous pursuit of justice. In order to survive, she had to compartmentalize her life, but this created issues in her personal relationships, in particular her relationship with Owen and those closest to her.

Sitting there, Kit's racing thoughts were about to be interrupted by Silver's arrival. Silver, a key figure in the realm of illegal money and criminal activities, held both the key and the lock to the secrets she sought. Meeting Silver was a crucial step deeper into the maze that could either trap her further or help unravel the dangerous patterns surrounding her. Kit faced choices that would have lasting consequences on her life and the undercover world she had entered.

Kit was lost in thought when she heard a woman's voice calling out, "*Privet krasavitsa*, hello beautiful." She looked up to see Silver approaching. Her ash blonde hair was styled in an edgy undercut and she wore minimal silver jewelry with distressed jeans and a black T-shirt. Over it all, she had on a short, black leather jacket. Small braids with beads were woven into her hair, adding a touch of uniqueness.

As Kit stood up, the two women leaned in for a hug.

"I wasn't certain you would come," Kit said.

"Why wouldn't I? I'd cross oceans just to see you," Silver replied, her Russian accent flavoring her words.

Kit gestured towards the coffee station nearby. "Would you like some tea or coffee? I have a couple of hours before my flight. How about you?"

Silver's gaze fixed on the nearby stand. "Ah, Turkish delight—my favorite." She reached for the silver tongs, serving herself a large piece of the sweet confection before pouring a cup of hot, sweet Turkish tea.

Resettling opposite Kit, she asked, "How have you been?"

"Hectic at work, you know how it is," Kit replied. It felt like a bland response, but she couldn't think of a better one. She didn't want to relive the fraught crime scenes she'd left behind.

"Likewise," Silver acknowledged, taking a sip from her tea. "Though, I've been busy in other peoples' offices, mainly." She laughed. Kit guessed she was referring to her profession as a hacker. "Plus, my waitressing gigs keep me entertained."

"It's a good cover."

"It's more than that. I enjoy it. What about you? What do you enjoy?"

Her question got Kit thinking. "You know, I've been mulling over that." She retrieved a caramelized sugar lump, stirring it into her coffee, an occasional habit she'd picked up in Pristina. "I'm not sure. I've always felt a passion for justice, since law school. But it felt more like an abstract concept then. Now, it's visceral. An intense desire to set things right for victims."

Silver nodded. "You're following your dreams. I approve."

"Kosovo has been a crash course in self-discovery," Kit said.

Silver's turquoise eyes shone under the daylight filtering in from the expansive windows. They sat in comfortable silence for a few moments.

"I love travelling," Kit continued, a wry smile playing on her lips. "Join the organization, see the world, meet people... and prosecute them." She chuckled at her riff on an old recruitment slogan.

"That's right, the opportunity for travel is all yours now. You're no longer tied to a regular job, just like me." Silver chuckled.

Kit, still grappling with the reality of her newfound freedom, replied, "I'm still wrapping my head around that. Just before you arrived, I was thinking about how I'm supposed to declare my income at work. Can you imagine what the auditors would say if they saw all my accounts?"

Silver smirked. "I suggest they never find out. Remember, you're working because you choose to, not because you have to. You're free to leave if you wish."

Kit nodded thoughtfully, then added, "True, I could leave anytime. But technically, I may have committed a crime."

At this, Silver arched an eyebrow and retorted playfully, "There's no proof of criminal damage. They'd have quite the challenge tracing where the money went, accounting for the accrued interest, and figuring out its final destination. It's nearly impossible to prove anything. And there's no victim to complain. In fact, they should thank you for returning millions to Kosovo."

Kit let out a laugh. "It's rather ironic, isn't it?"

"If you say so," Silver responded. She then leaned forward, hinting at a new topic. "I thought we might discuss some ideas to help manage your investment portfolio."

Kit's eyes widened. "A portfolio? Now that sounds important."

Silver shrugged. "It should be a portfolio—you can't put all your eggs in one basket. Art, for instance, can be an excellent investment. You can store it in a Freeport area to avoid tax for the foreseeable future. Diversifying into different cryptocurrencies is another strategy. It's also sensible to put funds into property. Or what about the idea of setting up a trust fund for your family?"

Kit leaned back, considering the propositions. "You've already turned an enormous profit in such a short time. Could you earn even more if we reinvested a few more million?"

Silver responded with a casual shrug, her hands spread wide. "What a wonderful idea. But I got lucky that time. I might not be able to repeat it. What I did was a calculated risk and it paid off, but safe investments should also be part of your strategy. We will need time to teach you how to buy and sell on different exchanges."

"Absolutely!" Kit grinned widely, leaning back in her seat. "I guess I need to come up with a believable story about the source of the money."

"That's where the art investments could be useful. And if you decide to leave your current job, I could arrange some contracts through my family connections in Russia. They can be quite lucrative."

"Mmm," Kit hummed thoughtfully. She made a mental note to find out more about Silver's family connections. "What if I set up a charitable foundation to support a cause?"

"Could work," Silver agreed. "You should make a list of things you want your foundation to do, and we can look into setting something up. Maybe funded through offshore shell companies."

"I wonder about a foundation to fund law enforcement projects."

"That way you could be more independent with your work."

Kit was acutely aware that her newfound wealth required careful management; its virtual existence was as volatile as the winds of fate. She knew all too well how swiftly money could vanish, especially with the kind of high-stake contracts that were part of this shadowy world.

"A budget and some regular cash flow are essential," Silver remarked, the cadence of her voice betraying a hint of something more than mere professional concern. She reached out, her fingers resting gently on Kit's hand in a gesture that was tender yet charged with unspoken intent. "We can tackle this together. There's much I can show you."

At Silver's touch, Kit's heart skipped, an involuntary response she chastised herself for even as she pulled away, her discomfort concealed behind a neutral façade.

"Silver," she began, her words laced with hesitation, "I'm not sure what impression you've got... about us. I need to be clear—I'm with someone now."

Silver withdrew her hand smoothly, her expression unfazed. "I understand," she said, and there was a cool acceptance in her tone that belied the warmth of moments before. "No pressure intended. Let's just say I find both the project and your involvement... intriguing."

Kit laughed nervously. "So, I'm a project now?" she quipped, trying to steer them back to safer waters.

"Why not?" Silver shot back, her grin impish. "Let's see how much money we can make for a naive young lawyer and what she'll do with it."

"Then you'll know all my secrets and you could blackmail me."

Silver looked at Kit, a quizzical expression on her face. "In Russia, we have a term for this—*kompromat*, compromising information. But no, this is not like that. We're friends, there no strings attached. I operate under the radar too. It's not in my interests to expose my friends."

Kit glanced up at the sky through the arching skylights, watching the rain showers pass by outside. She thought about Sergei, who had introduced her to Silver and a philosophy where everything in life was up for grabs.

"This is all too complicated," she murmured, standing up from her seat. "I need another drink. I love the lemonade they serve here." Kit made her way to the drinks station and poured herself a glass of fresh lemonade, its citrus tanginess offset by the cool mint leaves and ice cubes.

Returning to her seat, she found Silver engrossed in her

mobile phone. "Let's change the subject," Kit suggested, setting her glass on the table. "I'd like your views on something else. I haven't heard from my father in about 20 years. He left us—my mum, sister, and me—when he and my mother's marriage fell apart, and he moved to Australia. Recently, he got back in touch with my mum and wants to meet me. That's why I'm heading to Thailand, apart from meeting you. It's halfway between Australia and Kosovo."

"What does he do now?" Silver inquired, still scrolling through her phone messages.

"He used to work in defense contracting. Probably still does."

"What kind?"

"He was always secretive about his work. I know he had dealings with military officials in both New Zealand and Australia."

Silver frowned, her eyes narrowing slightly. "When did he first contact you?"

"I spoke to him directly for the first time about a week ago, but he had already been in contact with my mother for a few weeks," Kit replied, her eyes downcast.

Silver paused, holding her phone in one hand. "What's his name?"

"Vernon Chase."

After Silver typed his name into a search engine, she handed her phone to Kit who scrolled down the list of profiles. "There are a few Vernon Chases on social media—is he any of them?"

"I'm not sure. Remember, I haven't seen him in 20 years and some of these online profiles don't even have photos. Given his line of work, he's probably cautious about his online presence."

"Do you have a picture of him?"

Kit pulled out an old family photo from her wallet and handed it to Silver. It showed Kit's parents with her and her sister in a formal setting, presumably taken in the early 1980s.

"I like your mother's hairstyle," Silver remarked, studying the photo.

"Yeah, big hair was in fashion back in the day. She still styles it that way."

Silver handed the photo back to Kit, shaking her head slowly. "Why does he want to see you now, after all this time?"

"He says he's been reflecting on his past and wants to reconnect with his family."

Silver gave her a sidelong glance. "If he really is your father, I can understand your desire to meet him."

Kit frowned. "What do you mean, if he's my father? Who else would he be? He even video called my mum. She recognized him."

"And he suggested meeting at a resort just outside of Bangkok?" Silver inquired.

"Yes, at the Orchid Oasis. He said it's the best wellness resort around."

"I've heard of it. My cousin stayed there before. It's a high-end place."

"And did your cousin like it?" Kit asked curiously.

"Yes, she did. She's a model and Orchid Oasis offers some excellent detox treatments. But I wonder about his intentions," Silver added seriously.

"I know. But I feel I have to see him," Kit said. "He's been part of my life, whether I like it or not."

Silver was quiet for a moment, her fingers flying across her mobile's keyboard. After a short pause, she looked at Kit. "I should go with you."

Kit looked at her in surprise. "What, to the Orchid Oasis? But what about your plans? Aren't you going to see a client?"

"I can delay that for a few days. I could use a little relaxation myself," Silver said. "Besides, you might need back-up with this stranger who claims to be your father."

Kit was about to ask if Silver could afford the resort's hefty price tag but then decided against it. Money was clearly no object with Silver, who could seemingly magic it up whenever she needed to.

"Sure," Kit agreed, Silver's unspoken concerns hanging between them like the silent prelude to a storm.

Chapter Seventeen

The Orchid Oasis Resort, Hua Hin, Thailand

Several hours later after their flight from Istanbul to Bangkok, the two women travelled to the Orchid Oasis. The tropical scenery unrolled like a film reel as they wound their way down the resort's palm-lined driveway, a vibrant tableau that might have served as a sultry backdrop to a movie. Kit surveyed the sprawling exclusive wellness resort from behind tinted windows of the sleek limousine that had collected them from the airport.

Silver sank into the plush leather limousine seat, her denim-clad legs stretching out before her. The loose-fitting T-shirt made her seem just another weary traveler, yet her eyes — sharp and scanning — missed nothing of the passing landscape. Kit, seated beside her, mirrored Silver's relaxed pose, her hands resting in her lap. But there was a readiness in her posture, an alertness that belied her calm exterior. The limousine glided down the drive, its tinted windows a barrier to the outside world. Yet, even as the vehicle insulated them from the outside world, the plush interior couldn't cushion the silent acknowledgment between them that this was no ordinary journey to a resort.

The Orchid Oasis, against the Andaman Sea, was a mirage of elegance. The resort's organic gardens boasted dazzling colors and graceful residential wings scattered across the grounds. As the limousine pulled up, Kit caught a glimpse of the sea, a vast stretch of blue that was both a tranquil backdrop and a reminder of the dangerous currents that swirled beneath their mission. Leafy curtains hid gyms and pools reflected the sky, beckoning invitingly.

Kit and Silver exited the limo, greeted by the comforting warmth of Orchid Oasis. The weather felt heavy with humidity, a marked contrast to the crispness of Kosovo at that time of year. But it was the aroma that struck Kit, a heady blend of blooming tropical flowers, smoky incense, and the sharp tang of anti-mosquito coils—the olfactory signature of Thailand. Here, the line between leisure and work was blurred, and they were prepared to play their roles in the unfolding story that awaited them.

A line of staff wearing radiant smiles and traditional Thai attire waited to receive them. The receptionist seamlessly updated Kit's reservation to include an extra bedroom in their private garden pavilion. No mention of costs was necessary; the silent swipe of Kit's card spoke of affluence and the simplicity of such transactions between women of their means.

Kit leaned in, her voice a low murmur meant for Silver's ears alone. "We'll settle accounts later."

Silver's shrug was dismissive, yet there was warmth in her eyes. "We're beyond keeping score at this point, don't you think?"

A fleeting memory of bank accounts swelling under

Silver's deft touch crossed Kit's mind. "True," she acknowledged with a conspiratorial smile.

"As for indulgences," Silver's voice dipped into a playful tone, "I insist on treating us to the next round of pampering. Consider it an investment in our well-being."

Later, after they had unpacked, Kit and Silver immersed themselves in the relaxed vibe of the resort's open-air terrace bar. The area was enveloped by a billowing canopy, presenting a stunning panorama across the lush grounds, stretching out to the beach and the ocean horizon. At the bar, tucked into a cool alcove, the bartender's graceful choreography was a sight to behold as he deftly navigated the arrangement of bottles and glasses. Adjacent to this, in the outdoor kitchen, the chef and sous chef were artfully preparing various snacks and light meals. Kit savored her refreshing pineapple banana smoothie, while Silver relished the crisp taste of her detox green juice.

"Think they're hiring?" Silver mused, nodding her head towards the bar.

"Maybe," Kit replied, her gaze fixed on the horizon. A few fishing boats bobbed lazily in the water, their efforts to catch the day's bounty a contrast to the serenity of the resort. Her brow furrowed. "Sorry, I'm not very talkative. I can't help but wonder about my father. I just don't know what to say to him."

"Maybe it's more about what he has to say to you."

Kit sighed. "I can't shake the feeling that he wants something."

"Well, I guess we'll find out soon."

Kit extended her hand, seeking Silver's across the table. "I'm glad you're here. I mean, if something happened to me, no one would know right away. The team back in Pristina would have no way to reach me quickly."

With her free hand, Silver set her empty glass onto the table, her laughter offering a touch of comfort. "Relax, I'm here for you. When is he supposed to get here?"

"Tomorrow, he said," Kit replied. "He'll come find me."

A pause fell over their conversation as a resort employee arrived, his arms laden with orchids. "Ms. Chase, that gentleman over there sent these," he indicated with a discreet gesture.

Kit's eyes landed on a figure dressed in a faded music festival T-shirt and khaki cargo pants, perched on the edge of the dining area.

"Could that be him?" she whispered, her heart skipping a beat.

Silver glanced over. "Looks like our guy."

Kit's expression tightened, a knot of anxiety in her belly. "I'm not sure I can face this now. Leave it to him to mess up the day of our meeting."

"We don't have much choice," Silver remarked, lifting her glass in a half-hearted salute toward the enigmatic figure approaching them. "Back in Russia, we'd drown such worries with enough vodka to make us forget our own names."

"That does sound appealing," Kit admitted, the corner of her mouth quirking up in amusement.

"Lucky for us, I got a bottle back at duty-free," Silver confessed, her smile edged with mischief.

"Ever the strategist," Kit acknowledged, her smile warming as she felt a flicker of gratitude. "A little liquid bravery might be just what I need right now." But before Kit could reach for an alcoholic drink, the man stood and strolled towards them, his casual manner masking the years between them. Kit groaned softly as she turned away, wishing for another day, another moment. He loomed closer, casting a shadow that felt like the past reaching out to her.

"You must be Kit," he said, extending a hand. His hair, a faded version of Kit's own auburn, complemented his warm voice, which felt like an invitation.

Kit narrowed her eyes, not at him but against the piercing sunlight, her posture unyielding. "And you are?"

He chuckled. "Isn't it about time for a hug, daughter?"

When Kit didn't make a move to get up, Vernon Chase slid a third chair to the table. "I apologize if I've made a mistake," he began, his voice carrying the undertone of an Australian accent. "You are Kit Chase, aren't you?"

Kit's grip on her glass tightened, her knuckles paling. "Yes, I am, and you have made a mistake, Vernon. More than one."

Retreating slightly, Vernon ran his fingers over the delicate petals of the orchids he had sent to the table. "I knew this wouldn't be a walk in the park," he conceded. "But I'm glad you made time to meet me. Whatever questions you have, I'm ready to answer, Kitten." She flinched at the old pet name.

"Don't call me that," she snapped, the words coming out sharper than she intended. "Let's start with why you left me and my mother. Were you even aware that my sister died? You were absent when Mum needed you the most. And now, out of the blue, you want to see me? Sorry if I find it hard to believe that you've suddenly discovered your paternal instincts after all these years."

Vernon absorbed her torrent of words, his eyes flicking towards Silver in silent inquiry.

"If you prefer, I can give you two some privacy," Silver offered, pushing her chair back with the intent to depart.

"No," Kit said firmly. "You've earned a place in my life." Her gaze swung back to Vernon, icy and accusing. "Unlike you, Father; where were you when I needed you?"

Vernon returned her look, his smile strained. "I owe you an apology. I wasn't there for you and your mother when you needed me the most. I heard about Patricia's passing and I'm truly sorry for the pain you and your mother endured. I also lost a daughter, and also grieved. At that time, I was unable to explain the circumstances, and even now, it's difficult for me to talk about it."

Kit snorted contemptuously. But before she could confront him further about his absences, his eyes darted towards Silver again. She shrugged and spread her hands in a sign that all of this was not her concern.

"You're Russian, aren't you? It sounds like it from your accent," Vernon asked.

"I can be whatever you want," she countered evasively, her voice taking on a heavy London accent.

"Vernon, you haven't earned the right to be called father, or dad," Kit interjected. "You need to start explaining, and fast. My friend is staying. I want a witness to whatever tall tales you're about to tell. Maybe I should even record this conversation."

"There's no need," Vernon assured her. "When I left New Zealand, I was involved in a highly classified project for the Five Eyes programme. The situation was becoming precarious, and I had to leave abruptly, assuming another identity for a while."

"Why was it so dangerous?" Kit pressed.

"Originally, the Five Eyes programme was just the UK and the US, but post-World War Two, it expanded to include Australia, New Zealand, and Canada. We share signals intelligence. I was heading a cyber defence project for the programme in New Zealand and Australia."

Kit's eyes flicked to Silver, who was idly tracing her fingers around her smoothie glass. She looked disinterested, perhaps even bored, but Kit knew better. This was when Silver was at her most alert.

"There were implications across all the alliance countries. I can't say more, except that we had to counter the surveillance capacities of our adversaries."

"I don't recall that being in the news," Kit said.

Vernon gave a wry smile, and Silver snorted in agreement. "Of course not," he confirmed. "It was top-secret, eyes only. Hence the name. Do you recall anything about the Rainbow Warrior bombing?"

Kit nodded. "Of course." That was an incident where French military intelligence was caught bombing a protest vessel berthed in Auckland, New Zealand, before it went to protest against French nuclear tests in the Pacific Ocean.

"French intelligence was interested not only in opposing Greenpeace's environmental actions but also in understanding the Five Eyes operations. The incident with the Rainbow Warrior showed just how quickly things can spiral out of control in the Pacific," Vernon continued.

"*Operation Satanique*, the Satanic Operation, they called it," Silver murmured, her tone carrying a hint of disdain.

Kit frowned. This exchange was feeding her doubts about Silver and now, Vernon. Silver had mentioned working as a contractor for the Russian GRU military intelligence, and now it seemed there might be a possible link between Vernon's work in defense and Silver's interest in her, Kit.

"This is all sounding a bit fantastical, Dad—or whoever you are," Kit said, scepticism tinging her words.

Vernon nodded understandingly. "This is a lot to take in, I know," he conceded. He turned and surveyed the kitchen. "I'm famished, and it's dinnertime. Let's continue our conversation at the restaurant in the main building."

Kit nodded, and they walked back to the resort together. They ascended to the open-air patio overlooking the gardens and the sea beyond. She needed to think clearly, yet her mind was reeling. Her mother had always portrayed Vernon Chase as a villain, and though she had a few hazy memories of him from her childhood, they had long been locked away. Or so she had thought.

"I feel like I should be dressed more appropriately for dinner," Kit said.

"You're fine," Vernon assured, casting her a quick glance. Kit was in a batik-printed muslin dress and strappy sandals, while Silver had donned cut-off jeans over her bikini with a loose tunic on top.

Silver suggested a secluded table at the corner of the restaurant terrace. The waitress, clad in traditional Thai silk dress, presented them with the menu and informed them of the day's specials. Despite the previous unsettling conversation, Kit realized she was starving and jet-lagged from the journey. She ordered grilled fish with spicy vegetables. Vernon chose steak, while Silver went for tempeh curry.

"Wine here is pricey and not that great," Silver advised. "I recommend trying one of their mocktails. We'll drink the Vodka later."

"I fancy a beer," Vernon countered.

"The Singapore beer is decent," Silver suggested.

Kit agreed with Silver's recommendation and ordered a mocktail mojito with crushed ice and refreshing mint.

As they settled down and browsed the menu, some of the tension in Kit's gut relaxed. But she knew she had to stay focused. She needed to learn as much about Vernon Chase as possible.

"I understand this is all hard to swallow," Vernon admitted after they had placed their orders. "I'm willing to undergo a paternity test to prove my identity to you."

Kit nodded slowly. "That might be a good idea," she finally conceded.

"I'll arrange it," Vernon said.

The waitress returned, bearing the appetizers. Kit took a moment to appreciate the array of exotic-to-her fruits and vegetables along with the marinated seafood.

"The food in Kosovo isn't bad," Kit admitted, "but this tropical fare is great."

"I understand," Vernon sympathized. "Stress from work, excessive drinking, and lack of sleep can necessitate a detox. That's why I like to come to this spa. Get away from everything," he added.

Kit felt a whirl of emotions as Vernon continued to talk about reconnecting with his first family. His life, his experiences, everything felt so alien and yet deeply personal.

"I started smoking in Kosovo," she confessed suddenly. "It's not really my style – or at least, it wasn't."

"Wait till we start the detox therapies tomorrow," Silver commented casually. "Eat well while you can. I'm starting a low-calorie diet tomorrow too."

Kit turned to look at Vernon. Her father. The man who, despite the years of silence and distance, felt strangely familiar.

"So, why contact me now after all these years?" she asked.

"Want the long story or the short one?" Vernon asked, taking a hearty bite from his steak.

"The short story before I finish my main course. And by dessert, I'd like to hear the long story," Kit said, her fingers playing with the bag containing her cigarettes.

"The short story is, I need your help," Vernon said. He paused, cutting another piece of steak. "The long one? I want my family back."

"Did you remarry?" Kit asked, her heart pounding in her chest at the prospect of these revelations. She had wondered about this over the years but there had been no way to find out more.

Vernon put down his knife and fork, his gaze lost in the dwindling sunset. "Yes, I did. No more kids, but she had two from a prior marriage. That relationship didn't last either. There were other romantic interests along the way."

"And how did you mess up the second time?" Kit asked.

"The same as the first," he admitted, "Long hours, too much travel. Indiscretions on both sides. It isn't easy to mesh two lives together."

Kit nibbled at her food, her mind whirling. She hated to admit that she could relate to Vernon's story. She and Xander hadn't been able to make it work with the distance, once she left New Zealand.

"I see," she said, stirring her fork in her food. "And what's this help that you need?"

Vernon didn't answer immediately, glancing at Silver who was fully engrossed in her vegan dish.

"She's not going anywhere," Kit said, "If you want to talk to me, you talk to her as well."

"So, you want a witness to our conversation?" Vernon asked, arching an eyebrow.

"Considering you turned up out of nowhere after twenty years, what do you expect?" Kit retorted.

Vernon sighed, "Fair enough. I hope your friend can respect confidentiality."

"Confidentiality is my middle name," Silver said, her Russian accent more pronounced. Kit wondered if she was trying to make Vernon more nervous on purpose. Kit held back a smile, letting the conversation lapse into silence. Silver traded in confidential information.

Vernon changed the subject then, and for a while, he regaled them with stories of his exploits in Australia and the Pacific area. He shared stories of visits to Bangkok, Manila, and Wellington.

Wellington, New Zealand's capital city. The thought stung. He was so close, just an hour away in Auckland. He'd been recruited by the defense department in Australia and was obliged to keep many of his operations a secret. He'd spent time with the Aboriginals, even 'gone walkabout', as they call it, wandering freely and living off the land in the vast Australian outback. It was during one of these periods that he decided to contact his first family again, he said.

Kit listened, her mind grappling with everything he shared. "It was during an initiation ceremony with the Aboriginal elders," Vernon was saying, "Lying there in the Australian outback by the river, covered in red ochre, listening to sacred tribal chants, I felt a strong connection between us. I had to see you and your mother again."

How long had taken him to dream up this highly unlikely explanation, Kit wondered. She looked at Silver to see what her expression was. Silver's face was unreadable. Kit could guess that she was probably still ruminating on the information about the Five Eyes spy network that Vernon had worked for.

"This was before the news came to me—my latest assignment in connection with Kosovo," Vernon said. When the waitress came to take their next order, he skipped dessert. "Dragon's Well tea, if you have it," he said.

The waitress nodded without comment and looked at Kit. The detox program didn't start until the next day, so Kit decided to order crème caramel, which was on the menu for the Western guests. Silver ordered a plate of tropical fruit.

"And what is that Kosovo assignment?" Kit asked. *Perhaps now we're getting to it*, she thought, *never mind the tales of walkabouts in the Australian outback and the call to return to his first family.*

"We received a request for extradition for a Kosovo Serb currently living in Australia. He and his family had joined the refugee program during an early wave of migration during the Balkans conflict."

Kit's gaze locked with his, an unspoken question swirling in her eyes. News of an extradition request for a prosecution of this magnitude should have pinged on their radar. It was supposed to run through their office, after all. She was almost certain that her boss, Eva, wouldn't have missed this. "Name?" she asked.

"Petr Simić," he replied. "Used to lead a Serbian battalion up north. Accused of war crimes in Kosovo."

"Where's the request from?" she probed, her mind already sifting through the potential implications.

From the table's edge, Silver lifted her head, a crease of concern etched between her brows.

"Here's where the fun begins," he began, leaning back in his seat. "It's straight from the Kosovo Ministry of Foreign Affairs."

Kit blinked. "But the international community hasn't

even fully acknowledged Kosovo as a member state. They're not authorized to have their own foreign affairs ministry."

"I know, it's a cluster mess over there. But our government recognizes Kosovo as an independent state. We correspond with their ministry," he explained.

"I work in the office of the chief prosecutor, yet this is news to me."

"They're laying the groundwork for a war crimes tribunal in Pristina. Separate from any other court or international body."

"And Simić? His crime sheet?"

"Ties with Serbian Tigers. Massacres in three villages, minimum. Led a clean-up operation, wiped bodies off the map and dumped them in mass graves over in Serbia. Allegedly."

Kit frowned. "This independent tribunal business, it was always more talk than action. Never seemed a solid plan."

"One of their issues was the prohibition on trials *in absentia*. If they bring Simić to Pristina, they can prosecute," he said.

"But this implies a whole new legal framework, separate from the existing system which isn't all that broken."

"That's why it's on the quiet. We don't want the Serbs getting a whiff of this yet." His gaze shifted to Silver, now engrossed in her phone. "The US is pushing this, with Australia's support. The idea is to help Kosovo move forward, support their economy, by bringing alleged Serbian war criminals to justice."

"I... I'm struggling with this," Kit admitted. "This is an odd way to drop such a significant proposal. How can I be sure that you are actually my father?"

"I've agreed to a paternity test. But anyone with eyes

can see the family resemblance." He gave a casual shrug, a touch of a smile on his face. Memories fluttered through Kit's mind as she gazed at Vernon, echoes of the past etched on his face. His resemblance to the man in those old family photographs was apparent, from the wiry build to the auburn hair that resembled her own. Her mother's lineage held nothing but English roses, leaving her father as the only source of her fiery locks.

"So, what do you want from me?" Kit asked, breaking the silence.

"Nothing immediate. But when it's time to bring our man in, we'll need your office and EUFOR on our side. The new Minister of Foreign Affairs is already looped in."

A frown creased her brow. "Who?"

"Visar Dreshaj. You didn't know?"

"But he's the Environment Minister and Deputy Justice Minister."

"There's a cabinet shuffle in the works. Our Prime Minister got the scoop from the Kosovo Prime Minister. Not public knowledge yet, but all part of the grand design."

Kit sank back into her chair, the revelation landing heavily. Dreshaj was the closest thing she had to a friend in the Kosovo government, and he hadn't breathed a word of this. It'd been a few weeks since they last spoke, but still. An independent war crimes tribunal in Kosovo was headline material, steeped in controversy. It made sense why Vernon was wary of Silver. Russia wouldn't take kindly to the initiative, likely arguing against a fair trial for a Serb accused of war crimes in Kosovo.

"One more thing," Vernon added. "My security clearance is up for review. They know I reached out to you. Aussies can be sticklers about these things. There's a chance they might poke around in your business."

At this, Silver abandoned all pretence of disinterest. "They can't investigate her. She's not even an Australian citizen."

Vernon shrugged. "I know, it's absurd. But I'm mentioning it just in case. They might not even reach out. But I know they tend to contact family during vetting. With Kit in Kosovo and potentially tied to a high-profile, covert operation, they might get curious."

Kit groaned. "Your timing's a bloody nightmare." As if she needed Australian intelligence officers digging into her past now. She was starting to regret bringing Silver along after all. Not that she doubted Silver's ability to cover her tracks, but questions would be asked. "Do they know you're here, Dad?" Kit asked.

"If they do, it's not from me," Vernon replied. "I wanted to give you the heads up, just us two." He paused, then broke into a smile. "So, this is what it takes to get you to call me 'Dad' again. You used to call me 'Dad', and I'd call you 'Kitten.' Remember?"

Kit rolled her eyes, an exasperated sigh escaping her lips. The term of endearment had slipped out unintentionally, but he was right. It'd been years since anyone called her "Kitten." Everyone always seemed to twist her name into whatever they preferred, like Sergei insisting on calling her Katarina. The nickname 'Kitten' transported her back to childhood days in New Zealand. The three-quarter acre plot with a backyard. The sandpit, the flowerbeds, the vegetable garden. The laughter as she and her sister ran through sprinklers on sweltering summer days while Vernon manned the barbecue and their mother looked on, her smile as warm as the sun. Those were the carefree days she missed.

As the waitress set down a tray of exquisitely arranged

desserts, she politely asked Silver to put her mobile away. The resort had a no-device policy in public spaces, ostensibly to mitigate stress among guests. Kit suspected it had more to do with protecting the privacy of their high-profile patrons.

"Is there a smoking area?" Silver inquired, and the waitress pointed them to a patio on the floor below.

Kit had plenty in her life she didn't want investigators digging into. Her connections with Sergei Sokolov and Silver, along with the dirty money involved, could make for some uncomfortable questioning. She could feel her stomach churn with the threat of exposure, and she pushed the inviting dessert away.

"I need a smoke more than this dessert," she said.

"Take your time," Vernon responded, sipping on his green tea. "Your desserts will be here when you get back."

With a small sigh, Kit grabbed her bag and followed Silver through the side exit. As soon as they were through, she confessed, "The last thing I need right now is an audit by the Australian security services. This whole situation is a bigger mess than I thought. My father appearing out of nowhere, this news about the new Kosovo war crimes tribunal—the timing couldn't be worse."

"Don't worry about it," Silver said, leading them to the open-air patio, adorned with rattan chairs and ashtrays. "We came here to gather information, and we have. Let's sleep on it, enjoy our spa treatments tomorrow."

Kit managed a small sigh, pulling out her Vogue cigarettes. "This habit is costing me too much."

"Smokes are not that pricey in Kosovo, though."

"True. Living there has saved me quite a lot." Sudden laughter erupted between them.

"You can save your salary, but you don't really need to now," Silver said.

"Right. Let's find some time to review my investments. I might need to move more into confidential accounts now."

"That was the plan," Silver said.

"I think I need that vodka shot now," Kit decided.

"That's why I bought it," Silver said with a smile.

They sat in silence for a moment longer, before Silver finally said, "I'm going to have to tell Sergei about this."

"I haven't heard from him for a while," Kit said, a note of worry in her voice. "Are you sure you have to?"

"Yes. He's been deep undercover for a few months. But we have a protocol for urgent situations."

"Crap and double crap," Kit grumbled, stress making her language coarse. A need to speak with a therapist tugged at her, or even better a tarot reading from Natalia. But a knot of tension within her eased. At least she now knew why Sergei hadn't been in touch. How much of this would she tell Owen? Her father's surprise appearance was a given, and probably about the extradition. But how much more?

Chapter Eighteen

The early morning light infiltrated the pavilion through the sleek slatted blinds, nudging Kit from her sleep. She felt groggy from jet lag, and the vodka shots she had shared with Silver hadn't helped. The night before, Silver had retreated to her room for some phone calls in Russian after their drinking session, while Kit had excused herself from Vernon saying that she needed to think about everything he had said.

"See you tomorrow. I'm going for a tai chi class on the beach first thing," Silver had said before closing the door between their rooms.

Kit had surrendered to sleep quickly, wanting to escape the whirlwind of thoughts that were still spinning in her head. Her absent father's sudden attentiveness, the threat of an Australian security check, the irregular war crimes tribunal brewing in Kosovo, the extradition request for Petr Simić, and Sergei's undercover operations all fought for attention in her mind. Then she remembered Owen. She quickly messaged him about her arrival and exhaustion.

After popping a melatonin pill in an effort to get over the jet lag, she drifted off to sleep.

Silver's ongoing phone conversations in Russian had punctuated the night, drawing Kit out of sleep occasionally. Groaning, she tried to bury her head deeper into the pillow. Sergei Sokolov was a name that topped her mental list of concerns, eliciting a kind of addictive craving. His absence brought peace, yet his presence made her feel more alive. His place in her life was an enigma she struggled with.

Upon checking her messages, she found one from Natalia confirming her travel plans to Kosovo, and another from Owen, who was keen to know how her meeting with her father went. She replied, *He looks like me, so I guess he is my father. He offered to take a paternity test to prove it. I'm going to take him up on the offer but at this point, there is little doubt that he is who he says he is. Also, there's a Kosovo connection. Will fill you in when I see you. Hope all is well in Pristina.*

Rubbing her face, she made her way to the bathroom and then to the kitchenette. While there was no coffee, the room note suggested lime juice in hot water was a healthy substitute. Sipping on the warm, citrusy drink, she sat on the porch overlooking the vibrant tropical garden. Golf carts occasionally passed by, ferrying workers around the extensive resort. In the distance, she spotted Silver moving with graceful determination at her tai chi class by the lower pool. Kit wondered if the woman ever rested.

Upon considering sending a message to her mother, Rosalyn, about meeting Vernon, she hesitated. The impact such a revelation could have on her mother after all these years was something she needed to consider carefully.

Silver returned from her exercise session, clad in loose Thai pyjamas and sea grass flip flops. She handed Kit her phone so she could read a text on it. "There's a message for you from Sergei," she said. "He wants to meet you in Bulgaria."

The fact that Sergei had called weighed heavily on her mind. Bulgaria, which had seemed so remote, now pressed in on her with urgency. Standing, she ran her fingers along the cool teak railing of the porch, seeking a sense of stability. The distant sound of golf carts shuttling back and forth was drowned by the pulsing in her ears. She had to clear her mind.

Deciding that the news warranted an indulgent pause, Kit left the warm remnants of her lime drink untouched. Draped in thoughts heavier than her silk dressing gown, she padded to the pavilion at the back. The lush tropical landscape momentarily calmed her anxieties. "Prepare the pool, please," she phoned the on-call valet, needing the quiet solitude and the therapeutic touch of warm water.

On the back terrace, the outside world receded, replaced by an intimate sanctuary she had requested. The valet had prepared the scene to perfection, with the soothing scent of eucalyptus and citronella oil burners. He presented a tray with a refreshing fruit cocktail and a plate of freshly cut mango and papaya. A plush cotton towel and bathrobe awaited her on a rattan chair. "Anything else, madam?" he inquired.

"No, thank you," replied Kit. As he retreated, she slipped out of her dressing gown and the familiar aroma wrapped around her, softening the sharp edges of her thoughts. The warmed pool beckoned, a place to ponder Sergei's message and the looming Bulgarian encounter.

She stepped into the pool, its temperature designed for relaxation. Sampling her tropical cocktail, she eased herself into the water, her hair twisted atop her head.

The words of the onsite guest services coordinator echoed in her mind. The radiant Thai woman in her forties, Muki, had shared her insights, "When life's exhaustion disconnects us from our essence, it's crucial to care for our body, mind, and emotions. Only when these align can our relationships flourish. If we're drained, we have little left to offer others." She had pinpointed Kit's exhaustion with uncanny accuracy. Undoubtedly, many resort guests shared similar feelings. Her father must have, too—why else had he been here before?

The distant rhythm of the waves provided a soothing soundtrack as the tepid water embraced her. She took a deep breath, reflecting on her past neglect to visit an Asian spa while in New Zealand. With her work in Pristina accelerating and her relationships demanding more, she recognized the need for this respite more than ever.

A voice interrupted her thoughts. "Those lamps might repel the mosquitos, but they attract the moths." It was Silver. "See, one of them just did a kamikaze dive into the fire."

"I know the feeling," Kit said. She looked up to see Silver standing naked with a shot glass of vodka in her hand.

"Mind if I join you?" Silver said. Without waiting for a reply, she tossed back the shot and walked to the steps on the other side of the large pool. Kit noticed her lean muscular thighs. Her breath caught as she noticed Silver's piercings weren't limited to her ears and nose. A silver bar pierced her navel, and there was a ring in the outer folds of her shaved vulva. Lines of tattoos trailed up the inside of her left arm and snaked around the back of her neck where a new ladder of intricate lines and Thai letters formed a lattice.

"Do you like my new tattoo? I had it done a few weeks

ago. Some places have a monk visiting to do the *Sak Yant* for a donation to the monastery."

"What does it say?" Kit asked.

"It's a Buddhist prayer for good luck. Let's see if my luck with you changes today."

"What do you mean?" asked Kit. But she knew.

"You remember that kiss we had. The night of our first operation together—you ran through that killer—what was his name now?"

Kit remembered the night vividly. It was when they finally got evidence of the corrupt money laundering scheme, the night they arrested the crooked international leaders, the night Raco the assassin had tried to kill her but instead she ran him through with a blade—the night that Silver had kissed her.

She shrugged. Kit didn't want to invoke Raco's presence by saying his name there in the Orchid Oasis. "Do you want to try again?" Silver asked.

Kit shivered, in the warm tropical arm and tepid water around her. "I've... I've got a boyfriend."

Silver shimmied closer in the fragrant water.

"It doesn't matter. This is different." Silver's arms were reaching around Kit's neck. She grabbed a handful of damp auburn hair and tilted Kit's head back, easing into a slow, luxuriant kiss. As Silver's lips met hers, time seemed to slow and the world beyond them blurring into an indistinct haze. The warmth of the tropical air and the heated water surrounding them faded into the background. Silver's hands, cool and confident, pulled her closer.

Kit's heart pounded in her chest. She had always admired Silver for her courage and tenacity. But this, this was uncharted territory. There was an odd comfort in the fact that the rules here in Thailand were different. It was just her and Silver, in this tranquil resort, far removed from their real lives.

She tensed momentarily before melting into the kiss. Silver's lips were soft, the scent of her skin carrying a hint of the fragrant flowers that surrounded them. Kit felt a strange but soothing warmth spread through her, a sensation she hadn't felt before. Silver was right—this was different.

Silver pulled back slightly, her icy-blue eyes gleaming in the candlelight. "Are you okay?" she asked, her voice barely above a whisper.

Kit nodded, her eyes still shut. She felt disoriented, her mind trying to reconcile the unexpected intimacy. She opened her eyes, meeting Silver's steady gaze. Silver's platinum hair, twisted into a top knot and adorned with jade chopsticks and white orchids, added an ethereal aura. The sight took Kit's breath away.

With a soft smile, Silver traced her fingertips gently down Kit's arm, sending shivers down her spine. For a moment, they simply stayed there, their faces close, their breaths mingling, the ambient noises of the resort a distant hum in their secluded oasis. Whatever was to come, right now, in this moment, they had found a unique comfort in each other's arms, an unspoken understanding that bridged the gap between their two worlds.

Chapter Nineteen

K it let the rest of the day wash over her in the Orchid Oasis. It was a welcome reprieve from the emotional whirlwind of events that had unfolded earlier that morning and the night before. Silver had been thoughtful, guiding her through spa treatments to help reduce the stress and fatigue she was battling from her job in Pristina, the reappearance of her father, as well as coming to terms with the new dimension to their relationship.

Later in the afternoon, Silver proposed they meet at the resort's secluded waterfall. Hidden away in the heart of the lush tropical gardens, it was one of the few places in the resort where they could enjoy privacy amidst the vibrant sounds of nature. Silver joined her at the foot of the waterfall, where a natural pool had formed. Overlooking this beautiful sight, a Thai-style gazebo offered a comfortable setting for their discussion, equipped with plush outdoor seating, a low teak table, and a carafe of hibiscus tea.

"Managing your assets—your considerable assets—is key," Silver suggested, her playful twirling of a hibiscus petal between her fingers belying the seriousness of their conversation. "Diversification is crucial. If the Australian government probes your finances, they must find nothing amiss, nothing suspicious concentrated in one place."

Kit let out a sigh, the weight of her financial future pressing down. "I understand the need for security and smart investment. But how?"

Silver's expression shifted to one of empathy as she began to outline a strategy in her measured voice. "You're sitting on substantial liquid funds. But it might be wise to look at tangible investments as well."

"Such as?"

"How about rare books? There's a solid market for them," Silver proposed.

Kit's interest piqued. "Like a café that deals in rare books, you mean?"

"Exactly," Silver said. "It's an elegant solution. A café that specializes in rare books could be a legitimate front. You'd have a reputable business, a cozy place where coffee and wisdom are equally valued. Patrons could enjoy a latte before perusing first editions. The high value of rare books means a small inventory can justify sizable funds." Silver sipped her drink as she segued into another topic. "And then there's freeports. Picture them as vaults—discreet, fortified, and under the radar—ideal for stashing artworks and other valuables. They operate outside of the usual tax jurisdictions, perfect for your needs."

Kit grappled with the thought. "But isn't art meant for display?"

Silver's soft laugh echoed, "Not always. For some investors, art is just a financial bet. They buy, not for display, but for its anticipated future value."

Taking in the concept, Kit asked about the safety and

privacy of freeports. Silver assured her, describing the high-security measures and anonymity they offered.

Intrigued, Kit considered. "This seems like a path I could explore. I want my funds to make the world a better place."

"I can see you becoming quite the art connoisseur, Kit," Silver said with an encouraging smile. "But beyond that, think about your idea of setting up a foundation. Something that embodies your zeal for justice."

Kit's eyes sparkled at the notion. "That's appealing. It could be something like, Justice Pursuit International, JPI for short. This could channel my funds into something meaningful."

"JPI has a ring to it," Silver conceded.

Kit's mind raced with the possibilities. "JPI wouldn't just be another non-profit. It would operate on a project basis, taking on cases or causes that lack attention or funding. We could hire experts—investigators, lawyers, even lobbyists—to work on assignments with tangible goals: freeing the wrongfully convicted, lobbying for legislative changes, or funding legal battles for the underrepresented."

Silver leaned in, her interest evident. "An agile operation, picking up where traditional justice leaves gaps."

"Exactly," Kit affirmed. "And with JPI, our work would be discreet. Our projects would be carefully selected, and while we'd maintain transparency about our goals, the source of the funding would remain confidential. We'd employ a tight-knit team, all trusted associates. They'd be brought in on a need-to-know basis, paid well for their discretion and expertise."

Silver nodded, a gesture of approval. "A tight ship, then. But you'll need a solid plan to keep things from getting muddled."

With resolve, Kit pulled out a notebook and pen from her bag, setting them down beside the pool with deliberate care. "We'll draft it the old-fashioned way. No digital footprints, just ink and intention. Every strategy, every mission, starts here—on paper."

Silver chuckled. "Just don't misplace that paper. And don't let it get wet."

Kit began outlining her financial landscape, drawing circles on the page that represented her known assets. "These first two are my legitimate income and investments—nothing to hide here." She added more circles, linking them with arcs. "And these," she continued, "represent my other assets. These are trickier to manage."

Silver interjected with a suggestion that resonated with the then current banking practices. "For the funds you wish to keep private, we could use offshore bank accounts and shell companies. They offer layers of anonymity and can be quite difficult to trace." Silver then offered a tailored strategy for funding Kit's justice-oriented ambitions. "To fund your foundation, consider using these discreet financial pathways. They can be set up through international banks that specialize in private wealth management."

Kit tapped the pen against the paper. "What's the best way to move forward?"

Silver leaned back, her gaze thoughtful. "I have connections that could be useful. My family works with an accounting firm known for their expertise in international finance. I'll introduce you to someone who can guide you in more detail."

Kit's smile was a mix of relief and gratitude. "That would be fantastic, Silver. Expertise is exactly what I need." Then, with a slight tilt of her head, she asked, "But what's in all this for you?"

Silver's grin was genuine and warm. "Consider it an investment in our relationship. You're expanding my network to New Zealand, and possibly Australia. And Vernon has already proved to be a treasure trove of information, if reluctantly. For me, this is about the long game—building connections rather than accruing wealth."

With a mischievous grin that marked the end of their serious conversation, Kit flicked fragrant water at Silver, eliciting a burst of laughter from them both. The light-heartedness was interrupted by a man's voice, "Sorry to crash the party, kids, but it's time for me to hit the road."

Kit clasped her notebook, now a trove of clandestine strategies, and slid it into her tote with a care that betrayed its significance. She then faced Vernon, who had found his way to their secluded slice of the resort's gardens. His carry-on bag, a testament to the transience of his visit, trailed behind him. This place had become the backdrop for a reunion two decades in the making, one that had unearthed layers of emotion she wasn't prepared to confront.

"This has been... enlightening, Vernon," she began carefully. "Not all the revelations were welcome, but they've certainly painted a clearer picture. I'm glad we met." Her mind buzzed with the implications of the Simić extradition —a heads-up that was perhaps the most tangible outcome of their encounter.

Vernon paused, the lines on his face softening. "It was good to see you, Kitten. You won't lose me again. That's a promise. My disappearing act is over," he said, but the ease of his words didn't quite reach his eyes.

Kit took a step forward, closing the distance. "That promise better hold, Vernon. There's more to uncover, more I need to understand."

Silver's voice was a gentle nudge, reinforcing the sentiment. "Keep in touch, Mr. Chase—she's your daughter, after all." Kit appreciated Silver's nudge, but also recalled her words about the value of Vernon's intelligence.

A half-smile flickered across Vernon's face—a silent acknowledgment. "Count on it," he said.

He then pivoted, pulling his luggage behind him, his silhouette shrinking as he approached the office to check out. Kit watched him go, a complex feeling weaving through her. Beside her, Silver stood in solidarity.

And with Vernon's parting promise still echoing in the air, Kit began organizing her departure from the Orchid Oasis haven. Her next destination was Bulgaria, where Sergei awaited, and her thoughts were a whirlpool of recent revelations that reshaped her understanding of her past and tinged her future with a sharp sense of uncertainty.

Silver scribbled down a contact—Georgiev and Associates Financial Services—on a slip of paper, along with a Sofia phone number, and slid it across to Kit.

"Silver is a handle, right? What's your actual name? I'll need it for the financial adviser," Kit asked, her gaze not leaving Silver's face.

There was a brief pause, a shared look of trust, as Silver began to speak. Kit leaned in, the moment stretching between them, a secret about to be revealed.

Chapter Twenty

Sofia, Bulgaria

Fresh from her flight from Thailand, Kit found herself outside the Quartz Palace Hotel's grand entrance in the heart of Sofia. The place buzzed with activity, framed by diplomatic buildings, trendy shops, and lively bars. Chestnut and linden trees lined the streets, providing a sense of tranquility amidst the city's pulse. Pulling her luggage, Kit made her way inside, where the reception area boasted a sleek wood finish. A young, sharply dressed receptionist welcomed her and promptly handed over the key to her room. It was an impressive suite that balanced comfort with a touch of Eastern European flair, showing signs of history without feeling outdated.

Kit made herself a robust cup of instant coffee using the suite's amenities. Mug in hand, she sank into the plush armchair and pulled out her phone. The message from Sergei was still there, as clear as when Silver had first prompted the contact back at the Orchid Oasis. The message was succinct, with just GPS coordinates in the

Bulgarian countryside and a simple order for the following day: *Driver at your hotel at 9 AM. Come alone.*

She turned over the details she'd gathered about a Bulgarian firm charged with overseeing the Abramovs' financial affairs in Europe. In a few days, she was to sit down with Alexei Georgiev of Georgiev and Associates Financial Services. Silver had vouched for Alexei's skill in managing her increasingly intricate financial portfolio, with his Abramov connection suggesting reliability—a notion that resonated with Kit's layered past.

Before leaving Thailand, she had pieced together more of Silver's story. Tatiana Abramova, her full name, was the offspring of the renowned Abramovs, emblems of Russian prosperity. Her father, Nikolai Abramov, had built a vast empire in the wake of the Soviet Union's collapse, branching into metals, oil, and telecommunications.

Nikolai was as celebrated for his philanthropy—establishing schools, hospitals, and cultural institutions—as he was infamous for his vast wealth, with reactions ranging from praise to suspicion. His wife, Olga, with a history in the KGB, had transformed her espionage skills into a shield for their empire. Their sole heir, Tatiana, known as "Silver," earned her reputation not just as an affluent heiress but also as an astute hacker and tactician. Her nickname was both a nod to her family's roots in the metals trade and her distinct role within the Abramov lineage.

As Kit pondered this web of influence, she couldn't help but speculate on how her upcoming meetings with Sergei and Alexei Georgiev would redirect her journey. While uncertainty cast a long shadow, it was entwined with the thrill of unknown opportunities.

With a quick tap, she sent a nonchalant *What's up?* to Sergei's latest contact number. She waited, half-expecting the immediate arrival of a reply, but there was only the hush of unmet anticipation. Exhaling, she put the phone down. There was nothing predictable about this situation.

Hunger pangs interrupted her thoughts, a reminder of her neglect to eat amid all the strategic plotting. Local eateries beckoned, yet the importance of staying under the radar was clear. She opted for the safety of anonymity, steering clear of unnecessary exposure before meeting Sergei.

Her decision made, Kit lifted the hotel's phone. "Hello, room service?"

The next morning, Kit savored the last morsels of her continental breakfast in the sprawling hotel dining hall. Retreating to her room, she readied herself for the day ahead and organized her overnight satchel.

Every time she prepared for a meeting with Sergei, it felt like venturing off the edge of the known world. Each encounter was full of mystery and uncertainty. She carefully chose her outfit for the day, putting in more effort than usual. Memories of their last rendezvous in Ljubljana resurfaced, where he had surprised her with a collection of designer clothes at their hotel. She slipped into her fitted jeans and soft cashmere top, completing the look with her stylish leather jacket. The excitement ran through her veins like bubbly champagne.

Sergei had planned for a local driver to assist Kit during her stay in Bulgaria. As she stepped outside the hotel onto the cobbled sidewalk, the driver was waiting to take her into the unknown. Kit settled into the plush leather seat of the limousine while Ivan Petrov, Sergei's trusted driver, took his place behind the wheel. Despite his role as a chauffeur,

Ivan's strong physique and impeccable appearance hinted at a potential for much more. His sharp gaze conveyed intelligence and potential danger, making him an intriguing ally or potential foe on Kit's journey through Bulgaria.

The ride was both enjoyable and informative as he pointed out various landmarks, including the beautiful Orthodox Christian churches that dotted the landscape. Kit listened intently, her thoughts drifting to a certain Russian person who had played a significant role in her life.

The lush Bulgarian countryside unfolding before her eyes was a welcome respite from her work-laden life in Pristina and a contrast to tropical Thailand. She sighed as she pulled out her mobile, eyes scanning for new messages. Owen's text simply read, *I miss you.* She responded in kind, making a mental note—she needed to have an honest conversation with Owen. Soon.

Kit's journey from Sofia to the Damascena Rose Centre sliced through the Bulgarian countryside, a stretch of time she used to gear up for the meeting ahead. Ivan drove with an effortless precision that betrayed his experience. They spoke little, the weight of the impending rendezvous hanging over Kit.

Upon arrival, the centre presented itself: a curious blend of tradition and allure amid the rural backdrop, gleaming under the scrutiny of the sun.

Ivan's voice cut through the silence. "We're headed straight to the restaurant, if that's okay with you, ma'am."

He parked swiftly in the lively lot, and they moved together, weaving through the clusters of cars. The entrance was a grand overture, bronze statues welcoming them to a domain of culture and leisure—a museum, a café, and a gathering place wrapped in one. The air was ripe with the scent of nascent roses, a fragrance that beckoned Kit forward. A nod and a couple of words to the clerk, and they were through, the expanse of the grounds swallowing them whole.

The restaurant stood in the embrace of an artificial lake, a secluded spot veiled by greenery and the quiet company of swans. Crossing the wooden bridge, Ivan led Kit to a pond side restaurant, secluded and cooled by a breeze—a perfect spot for discreet conversations and hidden agendas.

A sense of vertigo washed over Kit as she noticed a familiar figure lounging at a table, his gaze fixed on her. Her driver discretely melted into the background. Time stretched, her senses heightened, and a wave of warmth surged through her, flushing her cheeks. Before she knew it, her feet were carrying her at a swift pace towards Sergei.

He stood up from his seat at the table, looking much better than their last encounter when he seemed frail and worn out. Now, he appeared at ease with a light grey shirt that hugged his well-defined chest and charcoal slacks that highlighted his slim waist. His hair, once sprinkled with grey, now had golden accents. Kit couldn't help but stare at him hungrily.

She happily threw herself into his arms as he accepted her embrace, although his face hinted that he would have preferred a more reserved greeting in such a public place.

"Katerina, you look absolutely stunning," he remarked. His compliment made her laugh, and their eyes locked. Life without Sergei felt incomplete.

"Your message caught me off guard. What brings you to Bulgaria? Why did you choose to meet here?"

Instead of answering with words, he slid a small package across the table towards her.

"Ah, typical Sergei. You always keep me on my toes."

He smirked and replied, "So I am predictable after all."

"Alright, I'll take the bait." She succumbed, fingers unfurling the delicate gold wrapping tied together with a red silk ribbon. She held her breath, thinking but not daring to hope that it could be an engagement ring. In those moments while she unwrapped it, her imagination conjured up visions of a life in a dacha near Moscow with Sergei, his gifts, meeting his parents, rendezvous with Silver, perhaps even visits from her mother. Yet, she reminded herself to resist, to draw out their courtship before accepting any such proposal.

Her fantasy came crashing down when the package revealed not a ring or jewelry, but a beautifully carved wooden bottle bearing a crimson rose motif. Inside was a small glass vial containing a clear liquid. An unreadable Cyrillic certificate nestled beside it.

"It's pure Bulgarian rose oil," Sergei clarified, seeing her confusion. "Its value surpasses gold; in case you wonder about the size of my gift."

Drawing a deep breath, she could catch the faintest hint of a honeyed rose aroma from the sealed vial, a delicate whiff that conjured a leisurely stroll in a dew-kissed garden.

"Wow," she breathed out. "It's incredible. I can't wait to try it properly."

"This is part of my mission here," he explained. "I'm officially on the hunt for the finest rose oil for a new perfume blend for a Moscow perfumer."

"So you say," she said, remembering that Silver had said he was undercover. "The real story?"

"I really am hunting for the finest rose oil for research purposes. Not much different."

"Research?"

"There's a research institute in Moscow. They're exploring some of the more eccentric theories of Nikola Tesla and others."

She remembered. "They had an exhibition on Tesla in Ljubljana when we were there, but we never got to see it." Memories of their time together tightened her throat.

"Indeed, he was a man ahead of his time, a Serbian American. Our research follows his insights, like harnessing free energy. He believed the beauty and scent of roses had medicinal properties, and sunlight could be used as food."

"Sunlight as food?" she asked, incredulous.

Sergei nodded, just as their first course arrived, accompanied by a local wine. He had ordered already. They ate in silence for some moments, save for the clinking of cutlery and occasional comments on the food.

"Plants draw energy from sunlight, and we consume it indirectly," he mused.

"I haven't forgotten what I learned in high school biology," she retorted. The pedantic side of Sergei could get on her nerves.

"This is far more nuanced. And classified," he said, ignoring her barb. Sergei served Kit before himself, pausing to regard her with a penetrating gaze. "Do you ever reflect on our time in Ljubljana? I don't mean the Tesla exhibit."

"You mean the forbidden books exhibit?"

His laughter echoed as he raised his glass in a toast. "If that's what you want to call it."

She took a sip of her wine, feeling its warmth ease her inhibitions. "It's hard to talk about," she admitted with a slight tremble in her voice. "I can't decide if what you gave me was a gift or a nightmare. Or perhaps it was both." Her face darkened as she spoke, the memories flooding back. "Sometimes I can't shake the feeling that we're reliving that night, that dangerous encounter. And yet here we are, in a peaceful rose garden, sipping wine. It's enough to make me question my sanity."

She remembered the night in Ljubljana when, in Sergei's arms, under carefully calculated pressure and the influence of a cocktail of drugs, she had experienced an out of body event. In that state, she had uncovered the key to cracking the money laundering case she had been working on—the pi numerical sequence that Silver used as a password for illicit financial accounts. Sergei had compared her experience to a pawn being promoted to queen in a game of chess.

"Have you ever encountered another equally defining and intimate event?" His voice was intense, probing.

Kit stayed silent, opting instead to breathe in the calming fragrance of rose oil, allowing it a moment to relieve the tension.

"Why do we keep coming back to this?" she pondered out loud, her voice laced with a newfound vulnerability. "You slipped something into my Mojito, didn't you? Leaving that vial for me to find was intentional—a clue for the morning after."

"I wanted to put your mind at ease about what had happened," he said, his tone matter of fact and unapologetic. Then, changing the subject, he asked a question she didn't expect. "Do you wish to find peace and heal from what happened that night and everything that followed?"

Tears brimmed in her eyes as she nodded slightly, her cheeks warming with emotion. "Yes," she whispered. "That night, it... it jolted something inside me. It opened unexpected doors, financially and beyond. But it also left a wound. It's complicated my relationship with Owen, my trust—it's all tangled now." Her words dissolved into the charged silence, the depth of her turmoil beyond what words could convey.

"I can imagine," he sympathized. "Remember the Tesla quote I mentioned earlier? I was thinking... perhaps you'd be open to another experience together, as intimate as before, but with the intention of healing."

"With the roses?"

"Exactly. Our institute is investigating the biological healing potential of certain plants, but personal experience is the true test."

"I'm suddenly not hungry anymore," she confessed, pushing her food away. Two swans had approached the edge of the restaurant, their gaze fixed on the bread. "You're not having my meal," she informed the birds playfully.

"The swans remind me of the Greek myth of Leda and the Swan. Zeus turned himself into a swan and..."

"And had an interesting encounter, as you'd put it," she finished his sentence. One of the swans craned its neck, reaching for the bread. "There's something about you, Sergei, something addictive. I know you're bad for me, but I can't seem to resist," she confessed. "But you never reveal your feelings for me. It's like you're manipulating me, while never exposing yourself. You thrive in the shadows, pulling strings."

"You could be right. I sometimes struggle with expressing my feelings. I prefer to convey them through actions rather than words."

"Sounds like many men," she said.

"Consider this", he suggested smoothly, "I may be guiding you to discover aspects of yourself that you've kept concealed."

"And what might those be?" she inquired, her tone laced with a mix of skepticism and intrigue.

"The parts that resonate with the teachings of the khash philosophy and its benefits," he replied cryptically.

Kit paused, mulling over his words. In the silence, her eyes traced the contours of his face—a face that wouldn't be out of place gracing the covers of fashion magazines. His hair, now fuller and longer than last time she had seen him, framed his compelling amber eyes. Her attention was momentarily captured by his lips, their sensuality pulling her thoughts away from the conversation. He leaned forward, capturing her hand in his and carefully turned it over, his touch tender, sparking a cascade of emotions within her.

"Are you trying to read my palm?" Kit half-teased, one eyebrow arching in playful challenge.

"Not exactly," Sergei responded, his voice low. "I'm tuning into your energy."

"It's true, you do help me touch a part of myself that seems elusive to everyone else. Even my former psychotherapist, Dr. Montenegro, couldn't reach that depth. The only other person who gets close is Silver."

"Are you addicted to Silver as well?" he inquired, a note of curiosity in his voice.

"Perhaps," she replied, feeding the swan a piece of her flatbread.

"Did the two of you become lovers?" His question was direct, his gaze unwavering, his hand still holding hers.

"Didn't she tell you?"

"I'd prefer hearing it from you. I promise, I won't react negatively."

"We did share something in Thailand..." Memories flooded her senses, the tropical nights, the aroma of coconut oil, the laughter of the Thai women, the sensation of tension unwinding during their massages.

"Silver is outstanding in her field, a true maestro in hacking and finance," he acknowledged with a respectful nod, tactfully steering clear of probing into Kit's personal connection with her.

Kit couldn't help but smile at the mention of her friend. "She really is exceptional."

The conversation shifted seamlessly. "You're considering putting your windfall to good use?" he inquired.

"Exactly. Once back in Sofia, I'm meeting with an Abramov family accountant," Kit explained. "I'm toying with the idea of a café, maybe a bookstore, or a blend of both."

"That shouldn't need too much investment," he observed, sipping his wine thoughtfully.

"She did hint at the arts, rare books especially," Kit added.

He nodded, setting down his empty glass. "And Owen? Does he know of these plans?"

Kit withdrew her hand, a slight tension in her voice. "Owen's in the dark. How do I even begin to explain my financial life? It's a gray area, legally speaking."

"No justifications needed here. I admire your initiative, Kit. You took the opportunity and made it yours. And as for the delicate matter of your finances, Alexei Georgiev will be a key. His reputation precedes him in managing things for the oligarchs."

A momentary silence fell between them before he broke it, "Whenever you're ready, we can talk it through."

She eyed him critically. "That's just it, isn't it? Whenever I need to talk, you're submerged in work, unreachable."

He offered an apologetic smile. "I'm sorry, *malishka*. Fieldwork doesn't always allow for communication. You understand."

"Let's just focus on the present, enjoy our coffee and the surroundings here," she proposed, eager to move past the discomfort. She recognized her tone had been more pointed than she intended, especially when, often, their time apart was filled with her own commitments or with Owen.

Following their meal, they took a tour of the Damascena Rose Center, marveling at the reconstruction of traditional rose oil distilleries. Large copper vats lined the building for the distillation of organic rose oil. On the ceiling were frescoes depicting rural life in earlier centuries.

As they approached the expansive conference center, Sergei's hand found the small of Kit's back, gently guiding her closer. "What's the status of the international warrant against me?" he inquired, breaking the quiet between them.

Kit tensed at the question. Conversations with Sergei invariably came with strings attached, an exchange of favors. The crunch of gravel underfoot punctuated their stride toward the center, passing a shop that boasted a wide selection of local essential oils, rose and lavender prominent among them.

"It's a complicated situation," Kit explained. "The new head of the mission, Bo Westergaard, wants to reinstate the warrant, but they have more pressing issues to deal with at the moment. I'll do my best to delay them. However, with Eva back in charge at the office, they might push for reactivation."

"I appreciate the heads-up," he replied. "Keep me informed, especially if reinstatement becomes likely. My government will contest it, but I'd rather avoid any surprises during my travels."

Kit reflected on the battle to clear Sergei's name from Interpol's red notices. It had been a precarious endeavor, balancing the geopolitical muscle of Russia and its Serbian allies. The corridors of power in Kosovo were rife with figures whose histories were marred by the conflict, many vulnerable to accusations themselves. But with persistence and savvy negotiation, the former head of the OIDC had relented, withdrawing the warrant under the nebulous term "technical reasons"—a diplomatic smoke screen for the reality of political leverage.

In the perfumed Bulgarian Rose Centre boutique, Kit indulged in a fleeting escape. The air was thick with the fragrant promise of the assorted cosmetics on display.

"My mother would love this," Kit mused, her gaze dancing over the neatly arranged products. "She runs a small gift shop with some herbal products in Auckland."

Sergei regarded her thoughtfully. "Perhaps she should consider adding Bulgarian rose items to her inventory?"

The suggestion caught Kit off guard, yet the idea resonated with her. "That's actually a great idea," she conceded. As they browsed the shelves, Sergei's adept commentary on the rose products intrigued Kit. She watched as he deftly navigated the array of rose oil products, his fingertips gliding over the labels with an assured touch that suggested a depth of knowledge. He paused to lift a small vial, holding it up to the light, the liquid inside capturing the glow like a gemstone. "The distillation process for this particular oil," he began, his voice a soft baritone that seemed at odds with a rugged scar that just peeked above his collar, "requires a precise temperature control to maintain its integrity."

She couldn't help but raise an eyebrow. This was Sergei, a man whose dossier as a GRU operative was filled with cold tactical assessments and covert operations—a man more at home in the gritty underbelly of international intrigue than the fragrant aisles of a boutique. Yet here he was, speaking with an artisan's passion about floral essences, revealing layers and a finesse that no file could capture. It was these contradictions, she realized, that wrapped him in an ever-deepening enigma, each facet he revealed adding to the complexity of the man she thought she knew.

He picked up a jar of rose cream. "This is one of our bestsellers. I have a feeling it will be popular in Auckland as well." Her surprise was clear, but she decided to trust his expertise and ended up purchasing multiple jars. When they finished their shopping, Sergei refused to let Kit pay, his manner confident and insistent despite her protests.

The scent of Bulgarian roses clung to the bags in her hand as she left the boutique. Sergei's proposal still hung between them, lingering in the space.

"The rose is more than just a symbol of beauty, Kit," he had said. "If you come with me to Plovdiv tonight, I can show you its deeper powers. It may even surpass the revelations we discovered in Ljubljana." His tone was gentle, yet his offer was clear: a life-changing experience awaited her. A thrill rippled through Kit, her heart racing with anticipation. This was the opportunity she had secretly craved, a chance at something profound and potentially life-altering. Aware that her next choice might not be the most prudent, she found herself reveling in the loss of restraint. The wildest part? She felt no urge to pull back. "That does sound intriguing," she conceded, her fingers lightly brushing his arm.

"Excellent. I'll arrange for the suite. But first, I'll instruct Ivan to pick you up tomorrow morning post-brunch for your trip back to Sofia. You'll come with me in my car now." He turned to her, his eyes asking, "Is that alright with you?"

"I suppose so," Kit answered, her voice on the edge of uncertainty. She was treading a dangerous line, the pretense of resistance barely disguising her intent. "I suppose you're on an undercover mission at the moment."

"That's right. Duty calls tomorrow." He spoke briefly with Ivan in fluent Bulgarian before he placed a call—presumably to the hotel. He then guided her to his nondescript yet classy black S90 Volvo sedan.

"Ever been to Plovdiv before?" Sergei asked.

"No, it's my first time in Bulgaria."

"Plovdiv has a charming old city centre," he enthused. "I think you'll like it. The drive is less than an hour, so sit back and enjoy."

Kit placed her bag at her feet, buckling up in the vehicle, her eyes meeting his. "There are things I'd like to discuss with you. Off the record." She smiled, knowing that their whole relationship was off record.

"We have time," he said. "I'll drive while you tell me about it."

Kit inhaled deeply before diving into the murky waters of her latest case. "It looks like we're dealing with two rival factions. One side's dirty cops, the other's under Mal Mala's flag. The evidence is scarce, which means no solid case yet. The bombing took innocent lives, and a second explosion at a disguised armory has Major Hackman wrongly accused. As a direct witness, my job as prosecutor just got harder. Mala himself, he's despicable, involved in everything from animal trafficking to stealing cultural artifacts."

"Ah, this is about the Mala Café incident and Kupi's gang, yes?" Sergei's accent tinted his words with a note of curiosity.

"That's the one," Kit confirmed with a nod.

"And this Valon Rama, the respected Kosovo officer was caught in the crossfire, I think?" Sergei's eyes narrowed, fitting the pieces together.

"You've got it right," Kit said, impressed by his grasp of the situation.

"I take it your suspects are under watch," he surmised, his tone matter-of-fact.

"Yes, we have surveillance on them. But it's possible they know we're listening," Kit replied, her brow furrowing slightly.

Sergei's eyebrow quirked up. "You are searching for solid proof, perhaps someone from the inside who is willing to come forward? Though, such individuals are not easy to find."

"We've got a few witnesses who saw police vehicles at the scene before everything went up. Now, we need forensic evidence that links Kupi and his men to the actual explosives used," Kit explained, her frustration barely concealed.

Sergei's question came thoughtfully, "Do you consider a link to terrorism possible, or is it strictly a local vendetta?"

"It seems like a dispute between local factions. And in the midst of it all is Lira Siliqi, local chanteuse and ex-beauty queen, caught up in the turmoil. Several of the involved men have been linked to her romantically."

"That does complicate things," Sergei acknowledged. "Would it be helpful if I used my contacts to find out more?"

"That would be fantastic," Kit replied, allowing herself a moment of vulnerability in her glance. Sergei would be her confidential informant. That could justify a lot.

"And you think these bombs have an international connection?"

"It's a possibility we can't ignore."

"What do they construct the device from?"

"Seems they've repurposed an antitank mine."

Sergei's reaction was subdued, yet his distaste was clear. "That is barbaric, especially for use on civilians."

"And to top it all off, there are talks of cutting our task force's budget right when we need it the most."

"Why would they decide to cut now?" Sergei asked.

"I wish I had the answer. Do you have any insights?"

He shook his head slowly. "Political games, perhaps? It is often the case."

"And don't forget, I'm a direct witness to the second explosion," Kit pointed out, her tone edged with bitterness.

"You are fortunate not to have been in the cave. But being a witness is challenging, no?"

"I saw the bomber. Only reason I wasn't in that cave when the bomb detonated was because I was outside with my intern. They've pulled me from leading the prosecution since I'm a key witness," she shared, her gaze distant.

Kit opened up about her concerns: Hackman's precarious position, the strain he was under, and her struggle with how to use her newfound resources.

"Now is the time to think about what you truly value, Kit. What do you want to stand for?" Sergei's suggestion was gentle, encouraging introspection.

"At the moment, my values seem to be all about bringing criminals to justice. That is, unless I'm romantically involved with them," she joked, though her laughter was strained.

"Are there others?" Sergei's expression was lightly teasing.

"No, just you. And there is Owen, as you know..." She hesitated, a flush on her cheeks, before regaining her composure. "And then Silver in Thailand, but that was different."

Sergei offered a small smile. "Life is complex, isn't it?"

"Above all, I value justice and the environment. And I aim to live a life that's rich with purpose."

"There is your answer," Sergei suggested softly. "Use your means to support these causes. It will give you a sense of purpose."

After a few quiet, thoughtful moments, Kit voiced her idea, "What if I started a trust fund to support our task force in Pristina; and another for environmental protection? I could call it Justice Pursuit International, JPI."

"You've overcome significant challenges before, and this will be no different." Sergei reached over, giving her hand a reassuring squeeze. "I'm proud of you, Kit. You're not that young lawyer who fainted at a crime scene anymore."

"I didn't faint at the sight of blood—it was the brutal murder of a young girl." She shook her head, pushing away the memory, and the fact that he had been implicated in it. He glanced at her, a silent understanding passing between them.

"I know, Katarina," he said softly.

Kit decided to change the subject. "Did you know that Natalia is moving to Pristina? She's got a job at the new wellness center as a dream therapist. I was hoping she could help me since my previous therapist, Dr. Montenegro, turned out to be linked to the criminals we were pursuing."

"That's intriguing," Sergei said with interest. "Working with Natalia seems like a wise choice."

"And she told me Father Peter is currently at the Dečani Monastery in Kosovo, restoring religious icons.

Natalia and I plan to visit him. But the thought of Mala's gang might be targeting these sacred relics is worrying. They'd fetch a fortune on the black market."

Without warning, Sergei swerved. He pulled the car over onto the side of the road, turning off the engine. He turned towards Kit, his brow furrowed with concern. "Why didn't you tell me this before?"

She shrugged, taken aback by his sudden reaction. "I'm telling you now. We've had much to discuss, given your lengthy radio silence," she retorted, a hint of reproach creeping into her voice over Sergei's lack of communication.

"Dečani should be secure; it's guarded by EUFOR forces. But Mala... he's ruthless. I know his reputation. And you're targeting his rivals?" His question carried recrimination, as if she should be doing more to counter Mala rather than hunting down the rivals who had bombed his café.

"We can't ignore the bombings, Sergei, whoever owns the café. Innocent lives were lost, officers were injured."

Sergei ran a hand over his jaw thoughtfully. From Kit's vantage point, she could almost visualize the complex mesh of cogs and gears spinning in his mind, each strategic element working to fall into place.

"I need time to think for a moment," Sergei said, his voice heavy with concern. "Father Peter has been my mentor for years. Having him in the heart of Kosovo makes me uneasy." He got out of the vehicle and paced restlessly on the gravel outside on the layby. Kit watched, feeling a sense of unease settle in her stomach at the sight of Sergei's agitation.

Ignoring the knot in her stomach, Kit followed as he walked. To their left, a forest of Bulgarian pines towered, filling the air with the scent of fresh pine resin. "What's wrong?" she asked cautiously.

He glanced at her, his brow furrowing even more deeply. "It's not your visit I'm worried about, but Father Peter... he may have some incredibly rare manuscripts."

"The Rasputin Manuscripts..." Kit repeated softly. She remembered the stories Sergei had told her, tales of original documents discovered by Rasputin's own son, containing cryptic secrets of the khash philosophy.

"Mala mustn't get hold of them. It's not just about the money and the cultural heritage, but the power that these manuscripts can convey to the careful reader," Sergei said, his gaze fixed on her, intensity burning in his eyes. "I like to believe I'm well apprised of most things, but I can't keep tabs on Father Peter's every move. My undercover work, my silence... it all limits me. That you've brought this to my attention, I'm... grateful."

The rest of their journey was shrouded in a heavy silence, each lost in their own thoughts. They finally reached an imposing hotel in Plovdiv, where the exterior's traditional allure seamlessly transitioned to a sophisticated and stylish modern interior. As they entered, the receptionist acknowledged Sergei with a discreet nod. Walking in his wake to their room, Kit wrestled with an undercurrent of embarrassment, conscious of the eyes that might question her company. Yet, as they moved through the lobby, a quiet reassurance took hold—here in Bulgaria, she was a ghost, her identity shielded from prying eyes.

They stepped into the elevator and Sergei pressed the button for the top floor. He turned to her and smiled, clearly putting their unsettling conversation about Father Peter and Mala behind them, at least for now.

"I hope you brought the rose oil I gave you," he reminded her.

"Of course," she replied, digging through her bag.

Before she could find the oil, Sergei moved closer and pinned her against the mahogany-lined walls of the elevator. He tilted her chin up and kissed her tenderly, exploring every curve and crevice of her mouth, filling the space around them with an electrifying silence.

Chapter Twenty-One

Plovid, Bulgaria

They crossed the threshold into the palatial hotel suite. The first wave of sensation to wash over Kit was an intoxicating bouquet of roses, mellowed by a sensual undernote of sandalwood. It was like a warm, soft embrace—an invitation to relax, to let go. The ambient lighting lent the room a sense of intimacy, the shadows playing on the elegant corners and surfaces, creating a cozy palette of twilight hues.

Sergei helped Kit slip off her jacket, his fingers grazing her arms with a light touch as he placed it upon the coat stand. She drifted towards the center of the room, her gaze sweeping across the decor that melded mid-century modern flair with traditional Bulgarian elements.

With the skill of someone who had performed the gesture countless times, Sergei opened a bottle of chilled rosé. Its ruby hue caught the light as he poured the wine into two glasses. The gentle whisper of half-drawn drapes seemed to murmur secrets to her, and the plush luxury of the Berber carpet caressed her feet. Beyond the lounge was a spacious bedroom, beckoning with silent promises.

Soft candlelight flickered in every corner, casting a warm and soothing glow throughout the room. Bouquets of roses in shades of red, pink, and white created a fragrant display. The stereo played an ethereal melody, its gentle rhythm reminiscent of a distant memory. Underneath the main tune, there was a faint drone that added to the hypnotic atmosphere of the room, inducing a sense of relaxation.

Sergei approached her then, his eyes gleaming in the mellow candlelight. With a tender touch, he tucked a loose strand of her hair behind her ear.

"Do you like it, Katarina?" he asked, keeping his gaze locked on hers. "I made this for you, for us to enjoy today."

"It's amazing," she admitted, her voice barely audible. "The aroma is unlike anything I've ever smelled before, and the music... it speaks to me on a level I can't quite explain."

With each word that left her lips, she took in another deep breath, fully immersing herself in the intoxicating fragrance, soothing music, and warmth of Sergei's presence. She was completely under the spell of this beautiful day, surrounded by an exquisite atmosphere and the man himself.

Sergei's smile sparkled like a warm flame as he gently brushed his fingers against her cheek, stirring a whirlpool of emotions within her. "The music is tuned to 639 Hz, also known as the heart-healing frequency," he explained in a soothing tone. "And the scent that envelops us is a combination of three Bulgarian roses—the passionate red rose, the vibrant pink Damascena rose, and the serene white Rosa Albus. Together, they create a heavenly symphony with a grounding note of Mysore sandalwood from the protected forests of India."

Kit savored a long sip of her rosé, the vibrant flavors dancing on her tongue. With each mouthful, she felt the tension in her body unraveling. As she placed the glass back on the table, she couldn't resist wrapping her arms around Sergei in a tight embrace. Her cheek pressed against his crisp shirt, and she breathed in his signature scent of vetiver cologne mingled with the aroma of roses surrounding them. Eyes closed, she whispered of her longing, "I've missed you so much. I hate being apart from you, even though I know it's necessary."

She felt him hug her tighter and took a deep breath as he kissed the top of her head, his words echoing in her ears, "I've missed you too."

"Why does it have to be this way?" She sighed against his chest.

"It doesn't have to. You don't need to work anymore, if you don't want to," he murmured, his voice gentle yet insistent.

Kit pulled back slightly to look into his eyes, searching for his true meaning. "Are you saying that if I stopped working, we could be together more?"

A soft smile curved Sergei's lips. "Yes. We could be together, without as many interruptions."

She sighed again, with a note of resignation. "I know... I just need more time to figure things out."

Sergei nodded, understanding her internal conflict. "I'll be waiting. Would you like something to eat or drink? On my last trip to Turkey, I bought the finest rose Turkish delight," he offered, his tone light and inviting as he gently extracted himself from her embrace, turning to the treat.

Lured by his suggestion, she reached out to the delicate

silver tray. The rich, rose-colored Turkish delight, lightly powdered, tasted like a sweet symphony of rosewater in her mouth, elevating her senses to a new level of sublime. The memory of Silver making the same choice in the Istanbul airport business class lounge flashed into her mind. She was savoring the treat when Sergei said, "We could go straight to the bedroom now. That would be my preference."

Her response was simple: "Let's..." As she spoke, her resentment and arguments began to dissolve like a sugar cube in hot tea. She silenced her phone and looked up at Sergei. Her eyes were caught in the amber depths of Sergei's gaze. They both knew that this time together should not be interrupted by work or outside distractions.

"I have prepared the room for our pleasure today. The healing I promised will be enhanced by the rose."

"I'm ready for it," she said.

"If you have the rose oil, I can mix it with some pure carrier oil by the bed."

She reached into her bag and drew out the wood-encased vial. He accepted it with a gentle, "May I?" Following her approving nod, he walked to a small crystal flask and added three drops of precious rose oil. After sealing it with a glass stopper, he tilted the flask, letting the rose essence blend with the carrier oil. He set the flask aside and carefully returned the wooden vial to her handbag. The room filled with the soothing melody and the ambrosial scent of roses, creating an inviting atmosphere. "Take your clothes off and lie down on the bed," Sergei murmured, his voice deep and inviting.

A delicious light-headedness washed over her, a consequence of the wine's subtle influence, mingling with the intoxicating essence of roses and the hypnotic hum of the music.

"What are you going to do?" she asked, her shirt unbuttoned, slipping away to reveal her white lace underwear. Her curiosity was laced with anticipation.

"I'm going to give you a massage with the rose oil I've just combined with this excellent carrier blend," he explained.

Kit's soft moan voiced her approval, "That sounds fantastic—just what I need." Discarding her jeans, she lay face-down on the bed. A part of her started thinking of the future, doubting that this would ever happen again. Sergei was an enigma, poised to disappear into the unknown wilds of Eastern Europe, to resurface at a place and time known only to him. But those were future uncertainties. The present moment was hers to live and treasure, whatever the future held.

"Would a khash expert approve?" she asked, her question carrying a twinge of jest, although she was genuinely curious. She had no doubt that Sergei had planned every his every move today.

A rustling sound, reminiscent of discarded clothes, was her only answer for a moment. Time itself seemed to have slowed, letting every moment stretch into an eternity. Kit reminded herself to breathe.

"A khash master would have already visualized the scene in detail, fully committing to the successful execution of their intent. Once the plan has materialized, what remains is to embrace it and experience it fully," Sergei's voice filtered to her as if through liquid, its soothing resonance making her skin tingle.

"That sounds like a great philosophy. I must learn more about it," she chuckled lightly.

"You're about to," he replied, a smile audible in his voice. "An important part of our philosophy is how to heal past wounds. If you allow me, I'd like to help you do just that. Now, relax. Notice your breath and the sensations in your body."

A brief pause filled the room as he reached for the bedside table, turning up the volume of the music. "The Solfeggio energy healing music will provide a sound bath."

"I have no idea what that is," Kit confessed. "But it sure sounds good."

Taking a sideways glance at Sergei, she found him standing in his designer shorts, rubbing the oil meditatively between his hands. His dedication to physical health was evident in his toned physique.

"You're not going to run off again after this, are you?" she asked, a trace of vulnerability seeping into her voice.

Leaning closer, Sergei's whisper brushed against her skin, "Focus on being present here and now, not on what might happen in the future or what happened in the past. But to answer your question, no, I don't have to rush off anywhere after this. For now, no more talking, just feeling."

He placed his hands on her back, palms down, and started to knead her tense shoulders gently. His hands were slick but not overly oily, maintaining enough friction to work deeper into her muscles. As Sergei's strong, confident hands traced her body's curves, the soothing rhythm of the music and the calming scent of the rose oil carried her further into a realm of pleasure.

"Only to the edge of pain, but no further," he breathed in her ear. A retort formed on her lips, but the intoxicating essence of rose oils and the magic of his touch silenced her. She surrendered to the sensations, sighing as she relaxed. "Keep breathing," he urged in a whisper. "Just feel what you're feeling. I'm here with you, no matter what, and so is the rose."

She focused on her body, following his instruction. His hands traveled down her spine, exploring the curves and planes of her body, reaching the base and then splaying out onto her buttocks. A wave of tension washed over her. Memories flooded in, vivid recollections of her last intimate encounter with Owen. Why did she have so many doubts about their relationship?

His hands glided further, pressing into her upper thighs, the tension making the muscles taut. Acupressure points yielded under his skilled touch, releasing the pent-up energy. Amidst the pleasure that made her skin tingle, memories of her father, Vernon Chase, invaded her thoughts. Her mind wandered, free-associating, traveling back to the time of her childhood. She felt the sting of abandonment as she recalled him leaving their family without a word. Self-doubt gripped her, filling her with the nagging sensation of not being enough, like she was the cause of her parents' separation. If only she had been a boy, would things have been different?

With each rising wave of memory, her body tensed, her breaths grew ragged, hitching in her throat. A stifled sob escaped her lips as Sergei's hands massaged her calves, his rhythm alternating between light and deep strokes, skirting the border of pain and then retreating. The tension slowly eased as he worked his way around her ankles, sparking a warm surge that traveled up her legs, pooling into her hips.

"Focus on the breath," she reminded herself, her own whisper barely audible. As he worked his way up her spine, kneading the tension from her neck muscles, she found herself sinking deeper into relaxation, opening herself up to a level of pleasure previously unknown. His thumbs traced the occipital ridge at the back of her head, eliciting a gasp of delight from her.

"It feels so good," she breathed, her voice a soft sigh echoing her contentment.

"Turn over," he commanded gently. With her eyes still shut, she obliged, her body rolling over effortlessly. He had unhooked her bra while massaging her back, and now, she slid it off, letting it drop to the floor. A gentle tug at her panties and they too joined her bra. Peeking through half-lidded eyes in the dim light, she saw that Sergei, too, had shed his remaining clothing.

"Yes please," she murmured in assent. He anointed his hands afresh with the fragrant oil and began tracing gentle but firm circles around her breasts, centering on her sensitive nipples. Deep breaths carried away the tension that had held her body captive. The rich aroma of the precious rose oil enveloped her, offering a sense of safety she couldn't recall ever experiencing.

"Are you ready to go further?" His question arrived softly, spoken into the intimate silence they shared. "A bit more,' she found herself whispering back. After a few moments, she took his hand, guiding it to the soft mound nestled between her thighs.

"A Yoni massage," he noted with a soft smile, recognising her invitation.

"I don't mind what you call it," she responded, her own smile echoing his.

"The rose between the thighs," he mused, his hands delicately tracing the contours of her intimate anatomy. "Just like a flower, the petals cannot be forced open."

"You can say that again," she quipped, a quiet laugh punctuating her words. His soft chuckle added to the symphony of sensations she was experiencing, each caress, each touch unfolding a new note of pleasure. "I never want this to stop," she confessed.

"There's always more to explore, further to go..." he promised, his words filled with the excitement of endless possibilities.

He lifted himself up, planting kisses across her body until he reached her mouth. She welcomed him eagerly, letting go of any worries about the past or future. All her reservations about relationships, social perceptions, and potential outcomes faded away. In that moment, nothing else mattered except for the soft hum of the heart frequency music and the intoxicating scent of roses guiding her on a journey of pleasure. Their tongues intertwined in an intimate dance of desire.

"Are you ready?" he asked, pausing briefly.

"Yes," she exhaled, filled with anticipation. When they finally joined together, it felt like rays of sunlight illuminating her hidden depths. A fleeting thought crossed her mind—*Could I get pregnant?* But she pushed it away just as quickly. The thought disappeared into the fragrant air, replaced by a simple mantra: *Everything is as it should be.*

Kit's body moved in sync with Sergei's as he quickened his pace. The healing soundwaves and the sweet smell of roses enveloped her, creating a feeling of safety that allowed her to fully surrender to the moment. It was a reminder that she often felt most secure when she let go of her guard. For now, it was enough. As pleasure washed over her, she was transported to visions of sunlight dancing on water and a peaceful beach lined with palm trees. She existed simultaneously in the physical world and ethereal realm, experiencing both intense physical pleasure and cosmic sensations. Her teeth sank into his neck, tasting salt and iron, grounding her back to reality. The bite pushed him over the edge and he climaxed, convulsing involuntarily. When she opened her eyes, he was laughing and wiping at his neck with a pillowcase. "I'm glad that you're laughing," she said with a touch of regret in her voice. "I didn't mean to bite so hard."

He responded with a tender kiss and rolled off of her. "I might have to wear polo necks for a few days," he joked.

"I'm sorry," she apologized again. "People will think that you have been attacked by a vampire."

"Or something." He chuckled, filling the room with his laughter.

He got up from the bed, and grabbed a small bottle labelled 'lavender oil.' He put a few drops on a linen hand-kerchief and pressed it against the bite mark. "Just watch, the lavender oil will heal the wound quickly and there won't be much bruising." She noticed his neck already looked less inflamed.

"That was one of the wildest experiences I've ever had," she blurted out, immediately regretting her words. She didn't want to give him the satisfaction of knowing he could affect her so deeply.

"I'm glad you enjoyed it," he replied. "Care to join me in the shower?"

He didn't wait for her answer as he adjusted the music and diffuser before heading towards the bathroom. The interior was luxurious, with marble-tiled walls and a spacious rain shower, complete with separate nozzles and jets. It felt like a private oasis, with soft light filtering through green-tinged glass bricks. A spa bath occupied one corner of the room.

Kit joined Sergei in the shower and immediately sensed a change in the atmosphere. The smell of roses dissipated, replaced by a subtle vanilla scent. She pulled her hair into a bun and stepped under the warm water. As she stood next to him, she couldn't help but admire his toned, muscular body as the water cascaded down his skin.

He turned on the rainfall shower-head and began lathering her body with a designer shower gel using a marine sponge. She enjoyed the sensation of his hands on her hips as he kissed her softly. Turning her around, he gently washed her back while she relaxed and felt the foam trickle down her body. He pressed against her from behind, kissing her neck as she pushed back against him, savoring the feeling of his slick and firm physique against hers. Then, he activated the side jets, lifting one of her legs onto a tiled ledge as he nestled closer between her thighs. In that moment, Kit felt completely comfortable with her body, free from any insecurities or rush to finish their intimate encounter. He matched her movements, driving deeper into her as she pushed back against him. The combined feeling of the warm water cascading down her body and Sergei's steady rhythm sent her spiraling into a pleasure unlike any she'd ever experienced before. Their breaths synchronized, ragged and uneven, the steam and the warmth encapsulating them in their own little world.

Surrounded by the ever-changing hues of the shower jets, the familiar touch of Sergei's hands, and the intoxicating scent of vanilla, the bathroom felt more like a luxurious retreat than an ordinary hotel room. The tightness of their embrace, coupled with the new position, intensified the electricity between them.

Sergei's hand glided over a breast while his other hand

moved lower down her abdomen, teasing her sensitive skin. Her sharp intake of breath and the added stimulation sent shivers down her spine, bringing her closer to the edge. A low moan escaped her lips, reverberating through the steam-filled room. She held onto the shower wall for support, relishing the coolness against her heated skin.

Her legs trembled as pleasure surged through her body. Sergei's relentless movements elicited a whimper from her with each thrust. His warm breath tickled her neck and his grip tightened around her, signaling that he was also close to losing control.

A wave of ecstasy washed over her as she climaxed, her scream muted by the sound of the shower. Sergei followed suit soon after, his own release matching her intensity. They clung to each other as they rode out the waves of pleasure, their heavy breathing filling the otherwise silent bathroom. The shower jets had stopped changing colors and now emitted a soft blue light, casting a dreamy glow over them.

Once their breathing had returned to normal, Sergei turned her to face him. His gaze met hers with a tender expression. He leaned in and softly captured her lips, holding her in a deep, lingering kiss. "That was amazing," he whispered against her mouth. She could only nod in agreement.

After they had finished washing each other and the water had gone cold, they stepped out of the shower. Sergei wrapped a warm towel around her before securing one around his own waist. He then guided her back into the bedroom, where the scent of roses still lingered in the air. The evening was far from over, and they were just getting started.

. . .

As the sun began to set, they found themselves sitting on the hotel terrace, watching the pulse of the city unfold beneath them. The sky was painted in hues of orange and red, while the streets were alive with locals scurrying through the offerings of the evening. Sergei had somehow managed to produce a couple of steaming mugs of coffee from their suite's machine and handed one to Kit. With her damp hair plaited against her skin, she seemed to be at peace for a moment. Meanwhile, Sergei kept a watchful eye, his gaze sweeping over the landscape like a hawk.

"So, what's new in the Chief Prosecutor's office?" he asked, breaking the ice.

Kit frowned into her mug. "We're in a standoff over the bombings—pressure's mounting to act, but we're still grasping for solid evidence," she admitted, tracing the ceramic rim with her fingers.

"Ah, but you have the luxury to strategize now," Sergei mused, his accent adding a velvet touch to his words. "In chess, the wise player sizes up the adversaries—seen and unseen—before striking. Who do you think is lurking in the shadows of your battlefield?"

Kit's eyes darkened. "It's a web of criminals and undiscovered traitors. The obvious threats are clear—past defendants with grudges, potential bombers. But it's the silent ones I can't identify that haunt me—those who pretend to be allies."

Sergei nodded. "And beyond the courtroom, couldn't friends, those you trust, turn on you if certain secrets were revealed? Like a GRU informant or hidden assets?"

Her eyes met his, a flash of alarm passing through them, quickly masked. "You play a dangerous game, Sergei. And yes, there are parts of my life that must remaincompartmentalized, sealed away. It's... complicated."

"The art of war often is," he murmured, a hint of solidarity in his voice. "But I suspect it's the thrill of the chase that has you hooked."

Laughter, brief and unguarded, escaped her lips. "A huntress thrives on pursuit," Kit conceded, a fleeting smile crossing her face. "Caitlin 'of the Chase'—it's a fitting nickname."

She leaned into the twilight, her resolve hardening. "And that's precisely why withdrawal isn't an option—not yet."

"And what about Officer Reese?" His eyebrow arched curiously as he regarded her over his steaming café lungo.

She exhaled deeply, pausing to collect her thoughts. "It's complicated. I realize that you and I don't exactly fit the conventional mold for a future together. I mean, I hope that we will always share a bond..." Her gaze met his briefly before dropping back to her coffee. "I sense Owen is someone with whom I could build something more permanent, you know..."

Sergei nodded, allowing her to gather her words.

"Technically, I suppose I have strayed in my commitment to him. I'd be devastated if he did the same to me—in fact, I was jealous of him and this woman, a psychological profiler with the service. It feels like you and Silver exist in a parallel universe, detached from my everyday life back in Pristina."

"Undercover agents often feel like that," Sergei said.

"I can imagine," she mused. "At some point, I suppose, I need to start planting roots—I have dreams of having a family..." Her mind drifted back to their earlier intimate encounter. They had not used protection and it seemed that Sergei expected her to either be on some kind of birth control or know when she was not in her fertile time of month. She flushed, uncharacteristically and added, "But not yet."

As dusk turned into night, passion once again consumed Kit and Sergei. Their connection was deep, their understanding of each other more profound than ever before. Sergei cradled Kit, his touch gentle, yet conveying an intensity that left her breathless. Hours passed in shared intimacy, blurring the line between night and day. She felt that he had delivered on his promise to provide her with a rose-infused healing.

When morning arrived, sunlight streamed through the open balcony door, illuminating the room with its soft, warm light. Sergei was the first to stir, awakening Kit with a tender kiss on her forehead. "Good morning, Caitlin of the Chase," he murmured playfully, an echo from their conversation the previous day.

Kit stretched and smiled, her gaze meeting his. The morning felt serene, unhurried, a sharp contrast to the restless pace of their previous night. They indulged in a leisurely breakfast, savouring the Bulgarian *banitsa*, a traditional cheese pastry from the region, and sipping hot coffee, while discussing everything from local culture to global politics. Their companionship felt comfortable, natural, as if they had known each other for years.

Later that morning, they took a few hours to explore more of Plovdiv's winding streets. Sergei was her guide, showing her around the Old Town. They paused at the Roman Amphitheater, one of the city's crowning jewels. The hushed atmosphere enveloping the ancient monument seemed to slow down time itself.

"Your trip to Dečani Monastery with Natalia," Sergei broached the subject, replaying their previous conversation. "When is it happening?"

Kit shrugged. "Soon," she replied. "I'm back in Pristina tomorrow and Natalia arrives the day after. We might go over the weekend."

"And what about Father Peter? Have you talked to him?" Sergei asked.

Kit shook her head, realizing that she still had a lot of planning to do.

"I'll handle it," Sergei said. "I need to be there for security reasons, especially with the manuscripts involved."

Kit's emotions were in turmoil as she processed this information. She had just come to terms with the fact that she wouldn't see Sergei for a while, and now he was dropping another bombshell—he was coming to Kosovo this weekend. With the Interpol Red Notice against him potentially up for renewal, their interactions would have to be hidden from prying eyes, except for Natalia and Father Peter who were part of their tight-knit team.

Finally, Sergei broached a subject that still hung between them. "There's one more thing we haven't discussed," he said in a low tone, searching Kit's eyes for a sign of readiness. "It's about the reappearance of your father. And the news he bought."

She exhaled, a slight nod acknowledging his statement. He had left this difficult topic until last. "Silver mentioned that she was going to tell you about it," she replied. "The Simić extradition, the tribunal... it's a lot to take in."

As they walked, the remnants of their shared night seemed to fade into the background, replaced by the stark reality of daylight and the shadows it cast. Plovdiv's Roman Theatre loomed beside them, its ancient pillars a stark reminder of how the world had changed through history.

"The extradition issue, it's a diplomatic tightrope," Sergei said.

"And with Dreshaj stepping into Foreign Affairs, it changes everything," Kit said, tensing.

Sergei and Kit had reached a secluded narrow alley, the clamor of Plovdiv's morning market a distant hum behind them.

"A war crimes tribunal in Pristina..." he began, the words tasting of the geopolitical turmoil they implied. "It's a bold move, and not without consequences."

Kit watched him closely, her arms crossed against the chill of the morning and the unease that settled in her chest. She knew all too well what was coming.

"Russia's stance is clear," he continued, his gaze steady. "We support Serbia, so a Kosovo war crimes tribunal—whose sovereignty we do not recognize—will not be taken well. It undermines the International Criminal Court's authority, and of course this should have been discussed first at the UN Security Council."

Kit felt a tightness in her throat. The implications were far-reaching, and her role in the international prosecutor's office made her directly involved. "They bypassed us too," she said, the betrayal evident in her tone. "Ignored our jurisdiction. Eva will need to know about this, even if my father shared the information in confidence."

Sergei nodded. "I must report this to my command. They will see it as an affront to Serbia, and a provocation that cannot be ignored. Things could get messy."

"I'm not happy about it either. For me, this is about

justice. The US and Australia are using Simić as a political pawn."

Sergei's expression remained unreadable. "Justice in the international arena is rarely free from politics."

Kit sighed, knowing her own report to Eva would require a delicate balance of facts. "It's personal because of my father's involvement, as well as my own work."

Sergei reached out, his hand briefly touching her arm, a fleeting gesture of support. "We both have our roles to play. For now, we do what we must."

The conversation inevitably turned to the subject of Vernon's security clearance and what it could mean for Kit. The possibility of her past—her financial entanglements and their shared secrets—being exposed was a specter that loomed large over them both.

The time for parting came all too soon. It was as if someone had thrown a bucket of icy reality over her. Sergei pulled Kit into his arms, his embrace a stronghold in the whirlwind of emotions swirling within her. The sting of goodbye was now tempered by the promise of another meeting at Dečani. She watched him recede into the distance, his silhouette slowly melting into the city's backdrop. A question tugged at her. What would she tell Owen about what had happened? The two spheres of her life were hurtling towards a seemingly unavoidable clash.

The arrival of Sergei's driver broke her from her reverie. They embarked on the journey back to Sofia, the serene countryside transforming into a hazy kaleidoscope of greens and blues as they sped by. The quiet hum of the engine filled the silence, offering a moment of respite from the whirlwind brewing within her.

Kit's thoughts shifted to her upcoming meeting with the accountant in Sofia and what lay ahead in Pristina. Her heart was a mixture of regret and anticipation. The thrill of her encounter with Sergei lingered, but her responsibilities loomed. As the car cruised smoothly along the highway, she decided to enjoy the drive, letting the warm breeze carry her worries away. A new day was on the horizon, full of challenges and revelations, and she felt ready for it.

Chapter Twenty-Two

Sofia, Bulgaria

The sedan's tires murmured against the ancient cobblestones as her driver expertly navigated Sofia. Kit, settled in the backseat, watched the city's façade: pastel neoclassical buildings mingled with sleek contemporary structures, where Sofia's past meshed with its dynamic present. As the car slipped into the hotel driveway, Kit thanked Ivan for his adept driving before stepping out and returning to the hotel.

Kit entered her suite without formalities, the room still echoing her presence from the day before. Most of her luggage were still waiting for her there. She swiftly laid out her ensemble for the afternoon's appointment: a sleek, tailored navy business suit paired with a crisp white blouse. She clasped a gleaming silver necklace around her neck. Leather flats, chic yet practical for Sofia's uneven pathways, completed her outfit.

Standing before the full-length mirror, Kit hoped her reflection embodied the confidence she sought. The navy suit projected authority she was still growing into. Her clear blue eyes aimed for a determined gaze, though a flicker of hopefulness revealed her novice status in international finance and the grey economy's shadowy fringes.

She gave herself an encouraging nod, willing her image to command the serious regard she yearned for. Her leather satchel was packed with a notebook, silver pen, and an eagerness to learn. Gathering her satchel, she left her room and into the elevator. A sigh of anticipation escaped her as the doors closed, poised on the edge of discovery, ready to meet Alexei Georgiev and unravel the mysteries Silver had hinted at.

Kit lingered for a moment in the hotel lobby after calling a taxi through the receptionist, her mind tracing the upcoming meeting's potential paths. When the taxi arrived, she slid into the back seat. The vehicle took her through the city, the historic charm of Sofia's inner city streets giving way to the stark efficiency of its business district. Eventually, it pulled up in front of Georgiev Financial Associates, a block of concrete and glass that spoke of concealed strength.

She handed the fare to the driver, murmured a polite "Thank you," before exiting onto the sidewalk. Shoulders back, suit jacket smoothed down, Kit took a moment to collect herself. Her eyes climbed the facade of the building, taking in the discreet emblems of influence: state-of-the-art security cameras overseeing each passer-by, windows tinted to obscure the workings of the financial powerhouse within, and unmarked black SUVs that lined the curb—a silent confirmation of the importance of those who conducted their business behind those walls.

She made her way to the entrance, a single sheet of frosted glass set in a frame of polished steel. A soft chime sounded as she opened the door, stepping into a world of cool marble, soft lighting, and an atmosphere heavy with hushed importance. Kit took in the polished marbled floors, framed artwork, and the subtle sound of classical music from unseen speakers.

The receptionist, clad in a crisp fitted dress, looked up from her ebony desk and let her gaze linger on Kit's outfit before offering a pleasant smile. Behind her, the credenza had the same glossy finish. The windows on the wall were etched like frosted glass, concealing what was happening inside.

"We've been expecting you, Ms. Chase," she said, her voice carrying the efficiency of an office dealing with fortunes every day. "Follow me, please."

Kit trailed behind the receptionist through several secure doors, each safeguarded by its own unique passcode or key card. The path culminated in a spacious office where minimalist design opening onto an expansive view of Sofia's skyline framed by towering windows. Surveying the room, Kit noted an absence of personal memorabilia or photographs that might offer a glimpse into the life of the occupant—a sign that whoever worked here valued discretion and privacy above all.

And there, behind a sleek mahogany desk, sat Alexei Georgiev. His glacial eyes assessed her sharply, a thin smile playing on his lips. His expensive suit was tailored, the fabric and cut revealing a man who appreciated the finer things. His gaze was calculating, as if he could see the secrets hidden in the shadows. Kit placed him as being around 50 years of age.

"Ms. Chase," he greeted, rising from his chair and extending a hand. "Welcome to Sofia." He spoke in flawless, slightly accented English.

Kit shook his hand, a current of anticipation surging

within her as their eyes locked. This encounter was a mutual assessment, a silent interview where both sought signs of synergy. In the intricate game of international finance, Alexei could be her newest ally.

Alexei gestured for Kit to take a seat at a table within his expansive office. They positioned themselves across from each other, surrounded by a spread of documents that might have been cards dealt in a high-stakes game. Numbers and trends leaped from the print, their full impact shrouded by jargon-laden language.

"I understand you're in search of guidance for your personal financial interests," he began.

Kit nodded, looking at him expectantly to continue.

"Navigating market volatility," Alexei began, flipping through a report with seasoned precision. "Diversification of assets, strategic risk management, and capital preservation—these are the pillars of a robust financial strategy, Ms. Chase."

Kit's smile was polite, serving as a prelude to the true intent of their meeting. "That's accurate, Mr. Georgiev. Your firm's expertise in managing sizeable portfolios is well known, in certain circles. And your work with the Abramov family in Russia has particularly caught my attention. It seems their high regard for your services is well-deserved," she said, allowing her genuine interest to show through the professional veneer. In her mind, she added, Silver's endorsement spoke volumes.

He met her gaze directly, his expression remaining impeccably neutral. There was an astuteness in his eyes, suggesting he had expected this turn in their conversation. Clearly, he was well-versed in navigating these strategic exchanges.

"Ah, the Abramovs," he remarked, a subtle playfulness

touching his tone, though his eyes remained cool and detached. "They are indeed prominent figures within our network. However, as you might appreciate, Ms. Chase, we prize confidentiality in all our client engagements."

"That's reassuring to hear, Mr. Georgiev," Kit replied, her voice steady despite the quickening pulse she felt. "I'm considering a venture and would value your input. The project involves setting up a private entity dedicated to crime prevention—JPI is the working title. It's somewhat unconventional, which means the financial underpinnings need to be just as innovative. I'm seeking guidance on how to finance it discreetly, ensuring my association remains confidential and tax implications are minimized." She paused, watching him carefully for a telltale sign of his thoughts.

The blue depths of Alexei's eyes stayed locked on her, his thoughts impenetrable. He reclined in his seat, fingers steepled together in thought as he pondered her words.

"An intriguing proposition," he said at last, his voice betraying nothing. "Yet, there could be many angles to cover. Financing, execution, legality... every facet demands attention."

His interrogation peeled back the layers of her proposal methodically: funding sources, operational plans, account-ability structures, and control mechanisms. His probing was incisive, targeting the core of her initiative with unerring accuracy. Notably, he steered clear of questioning the origins of her funding. As Kit fielded his thorough queries, it became clear his examination was more than a test of viability—he was assessing the potential risks, benefits, and even her underlying motives. A heavy silence fell over the room, and Kit held his gaze with determination. She was ready for this challenge, resolved to face it head-on.

"I've sensed you may prefer to act without too much delay, which is why I've prepared an initial financial blueprint, taking into account the essentials," he gestured toward a dossier on his desk. "It includes key goals: securing your assets for the long term, implementing strategies to protect your identity and wealth, pinpointing savvy investments to bolster your portfolio, reducing tax exposure, and devising a plan for your legacy."

"You developed all this without my input?" Kit questioned, her surprise evident. *Silver had probably briefed him*, she thought.

"It's based on what we've deduced about your needs. It seemed prudent to discuss it with you in person," he said.

"It looks like you've covered most of the bases," Kit acknowledged, her tone reflecting a grudging respect. "Legacy planning hadn't crossed my mind, I have to admit."

"Forecasting for the future is as crucial as managing the present," he advised. "I've also outlined a tentative strategy for distributing your assets," he added, indicating the charts and graphs stacked in the dossier.

Her eyes quickly perused the list: managing offshore accounts, the mainstay of discreet financial dealings, traditional investments like stocks and bonds, and alternative assets such as real estate and start-up ventures. She paused on a section about art and rare book dealerships, piquing her interest.

"Can I offer you some coffee or tea as you review these?" Alexei suggested, seeing her inunundated by the details.

"Yes, that would be wonderful, thank you," she responded, still lost in thought. "Coffee, black, no sugar."

Alexei moved to his desk and pressed a buzzer. "Do you need a copy of my passport, or other ID?" Kit asked, aware

of the importance of client identification in legal procedures. Yet, she wasn't sure if the same rule applied in the
gray area they were operating in.

"Ms. Abramova has endorsed this securely," he began,
"but we need to take an additional step. If you use our
services, our legal team will review everything. They'll
provide an extra layer of privacy through attorney-client
privilege for all our dealings."

Kit maintained her poker face while internally admiring
the plan. "That's smart," she responded. "Given the private
nature of the operation, protecting our finances and operations is vital." Her legal insight told her this was a clever
tactic for safeguarding privacy and staying within legal
bounds, yet it wasn't foolproof against a criminal investigation, particularly one into money laundering.

Alexei leaned back, his fingertips pressed together,
nodding thoughtfully. "Your project is multifaceted, Ms.
Chase—finances, operations, legalities; all intricate parts to
align."

Kit paused over her coffee, considering the investment
strategies laid out in the portfolio. A diverse mix from hedge
funds to art dealing promised discreet avenues for asset
growth.

"Your assets are impressive," Alexei continued, indicating the document. "Our plan is tailored for confidentiality, strategic objectives, and protecting your mission's
integrity. Here's the financial framework we've devised for
you," he motioned towards the summarized contents of a
detailed folder.

He leaned forward, underscoring the plan's key goals.
"We aim to fortify your wealth, shield your identity, and
maintain a strategic distance from tax scrutiny," Alexei
stated. "Our approach includes establishing a network of

offshore entities and trusts for optimal tax positioning. As an art enthusiast, you'll benefit from the use of freeports, where your valuable pieces can reside tax-free and secure."

Kit spoke with clarity, highlighting a key requirement. "Anonymity is critical," she asserted. "With the level of transparency expected in my role at OIDC, any personal financial moves are potentially open to examination." She leaned in, her intent gaze underscoring the issue's seriousness. "These transactions must be insulated from my career. My reputation and the integrity of my position are at stake; they cannot be compromised."

"Understood," Alexei agreed smoothly. "A structure involving shell entities, private entities, and secure channels will preserve your anonymity. We'll manage your philanthropic funding without attracting any undue attention."

Kit's eyebrow arched in inquiry. "What about Swiss banks?"

Alexei matched her posturing, also leaning in. "Swiss banking is ideal for privacy, given its history and legal framework. Though they adhere to their own standards, they're not under the EU's direct influence, which is beneficial for us. But bank secrecy is just one facet; we must also adapt your portfolio as needed, ensuring compliance with tax laws and supporting your financial progression."

Kit considered this, then asked, "How do I communicate my instructions?"

"We rely on encrypted email and secure telephone lines for most communications," Alexei explained. "For voice, we're starting to use an emerging technology called VoIP— it's secure and runs over the internet."

Kit's brow furrowed at the acronym. "VoIP?"

"Voice over Internet Protocol," he elaborated, seeing her

puzzled look. "It's quite new but promising for safeguarded conversations. Consider it our private channel."

He pushed a heavy-duty cell phone across the table to her. "This phone is configured for secure calls. We'll replace it regularly to ensure security." She glanced at the stack of documents. Carrying them seemed a gamble. Better to review them here, handle what she could face-to-face.

"Essentially, a disposable phone," she remarked, noting its simplicity compared to the multifunctional devices that were becoming more common.

"Please come back in approximately one month," Alexei instructed. "By that time, we'll have the arrangements in place for your final approval, and we can finalize any outstanding details."

Kit broached an essential topic. "What about your fees?"

Alexei detailed their billing approach. "We have a quarterly retainer, which is one percent of the managed funds per year, billed every three months. Additionally, there's an annual management fee of three percent." He assured her, "The returns we anticipate should render these fees a minor detail. We deduct them directly from your assets to maintain discretion in your financial activities."

Standing up, the figures swirled in Kit's mind—a significant sum, indeed. Trust in Alexei's expertise seemed her only viable path. As she rose, a whirlwind of emotions took hold: excitement for the new venture, nerves about the unknown, and the adrenaline of stepping into a covert realm.

Alexei gave her a significant look. "Remember, Ms. Chase, in our line of work, trust is our currency. And discretion is not just a virtue—it's a necessity."

Kit met his gaze firmly, their mutual understanding

unspoken yet solid. "Understood. I appreciate your flexibility in scheduling, Mr. Georgiev. I'm eager to begin this partnership," she said, her voice steady.

After exchanging goodbyes, Kit walked away. The sound of her heels clicking against the marble floor filled the quiet hallway, marking her exit. She could sense Alexei's understanding of the stakes, his grasp on risk, profit, and the game's inherent thrill, lingering in the air as she walked away. As the day faded to dusk, she knew the wheels were already in motion; their covert alliance would be set into motion with a message she would soon receive.

Chapter Twenty-Three

Pristina, Kosovo

Kit stepped off the plane into the brisk Pristina morning. The awakening city stretched its long shadows across the tarmac, a visual echo of the mixed feelings she harbored from her recent dealings in Sofia. The air was crisp, hinting at both the day's potential and the unresolved tension from her financial arrangements with Alexei.

Seeking discretion, Kit chose a nondescript taxi over the official OIDC car service. The city pulsed with the day's early rhythms as she weaved through the streets, consciously avoiding her typical stops and known associates like Owen. She kept her usual phone powered down, intentionally cutting off contact with familiar networks. However, the clandestine phone—a discreet lifeline to Alexei, Sergei, and Silver—lay within arm's reach, a silent guardian of her hidden connections.

By the time Natalia's early arrival from Bucharest brought her to Pristina, Kit was already blending into the city's fabric. As Natalia emerged into the soft light of the morning, her petite frame and the depth of her dark eyes stood out. Her greeting smile was a bright spot in the day, and the colorful scarf in her hair spoke of a vibrant personality beneath her composed exterior.

They regrouped at Kit's car, parked a discreet distance from the airport, to drive into the heart of the city. The Artemis Wellness Centre, adjacent to the verdant city park, promised a peaceful interlude. Natalia entered to discuss the therapist position, while Kit retreated to a nearby café. Here, amid the ambient city sounds, she contemplated Sergei's cryptic summons to Dečani and the strategic intricacies of her next move.

Natalia soon appeared, her interview concluded, a tentative optimism in her step. Kit approached her as they walked to Kit's car. "How did it go? What kind of questions did they ask?" she inquired, her curiosity as much about the interview as about gauging any undercurrents it might reveal.

Natalia flicked a dismissive hand. "The usual drill. They dug into my therapy methods, my PTSD case experience."

Reaching the car, Kit eyed her with interest. "And? Their verdict?"

"I think I nailed it," Natalia responded. "My Jungian approach, the active dreaming—it was right up their alley. I've handled trauma from the battlefield to the boardroom."

Starting the car, Kit gave a wry smile. "Sounds like you caught their attention."

"The dream therapy clinched it," Natalia confirmed, buckling her seatbelt. "I think."

Kit weaved through the traffic, raising an eyebrow. "What about your work with tarot?"

Natalia leaned back. "It came up when we talked about therapeutic imagery. I explained that it's all about unlocking the subconscious."

"Nice," Kit said as they blended into the flow of traffic. "Pristina's no playground, but you're no novice." She shot Natalia a conspiratorial look. "Ready for some covert action? We've got a monastery tour lined up at Visoki Dečani."

Later, in Kit's apartment, the space was filled with the sounds of zippers and the rustle of clothes as they prepared for the trip. Kit leaned in, lowering her voice. "Natalia, I need to tell you something. There's more at stake here than just a monastery visit. Sergei is concerned about Father Peter and something about Rasputin Manuscripts at Visoki Dečani."

Natalia stopped, her hands still, as she processed the information. "Do you think they're in danger?"

Kit folded a sweater, her fingers deft, her mind racing. "If Mal Mala figures out their location, absolutely. He deals in the currency of the illicit, and cultural treasures are his gold. Those manuscripts..." She trailed off, the implications clear—despite the Monastery's fortifications, it had to be vulnerable to determined burglars.

Natalia sealed her bag, her features etched with concern. "Sergei's evasive about those manuscripts, always has been. But bringing them to Kosovo... it's an unexpected move."

Kit's nod was slow, thoughtful. "He speaks of them not as relics, but as conduits—vessels of ancient knowledge and esoteric power. And in the wrong hands..."

A spark of interest lit Natalia's eyes. "This mystery... it

intrigues me. The dreams have been leading somewhere, maybe to answers hidden in these very manuscripts."

"Stay in tune with those visions," Kit advised, her gaze flicking to her watch—keeping an eye on the time. "As soon as we're settled, we join the monastery tour. It's a strategic first step—knowing the terrain, sensing the currents beneath the surface."

Dečani, Kosovo

By mid-afternoon, Kit and Natalia drove up to the Dukagjin Resort in Dečani. Tucked away in a swath of vibrant greenery, the resort hotel offered a serene weekend retreat. The villa was an embodiment of rural elegance, with its rough-hewn stone walls offering a sense of solidity. Inside, extravagance was on display through the expansive windows: floor-to-ceiling glass that framed the lush, emerald landscape outside, inviting the untamed beauty of the wilderness into every room.

"I love it," Natalia declared, her luggage thumping onto the bedroom floor. "I need this break after the gamble I took with the Artemis Centre in Pristina."

"Risks can be rewarding," Kit replied with a wry grin.

Kit and Natalia, having settled briefly in their rooms, made their way to Dečani Monastery. The entrance was secured by EUFOR troops, a clear reminder of the region's tension. They parked near the main buildings, just as a tour bus released a flock of tourists. Without hesitation, the pair slipped into the crowd's wake.

Nestled against a backdrop of cloud-kissed hills, the monastery's whitewashed walls and terracotta roofs shimmered in the amber sunlight. Yet, this beauty was underscored by an unmistakable undercurrent of danger. The monastery's perimeter, marked by a high wall and a reinforced gate, spoke of a need for protection. The incongruity of soldiers stationed by the ticket office, with a German Shepherd dozing at their feet, added to the dissonance.

Once the tourists had advanced, Kit and Natalia approached a robust metal door within the entrance tower. The door, embellished with orthodox crosses and sharp bevels, was clearly intended as a deterrent to invaders. Kit surveyed the surroundings with a critical eye, hunting for vulnerabilities that could be exploited by adversaries like Mal Mala.

Upon entering, a stone church rose majestically, its presence dominating the courtyard, flanked by three-story structures that likely housed the monks. The carefully maintained grounds framed this bastion of spirituality. Its design, featuring narrow windows and minimal doors, betrayed its historical need for defense. Above the entrance, an ornate arch was adorned with a menagerie of stone creatures—centaurs, archers, and birds, with a cunning fox nestled among the intricate etchings, all shielded by a metal overhang.

Kit gestured to Natalia, her eyes on the archivolt's spiral carvings catching the afternoon glow. Memories of her layover in Istanbul flickered in her mind—there, she had scoured the UNESCO cultural heritage site for information on the Visoki Dečani Monastery. The blueprints she had examined online now took on a vivid form before her eyes, lending tangibility to her previous research.

Natalia, equally captivated, whispered, "Incredible," as her notebook appeared in her hands, her pen racing to capture the breathtaking detail.

For the two women, stepping inside to monastery grounds felt like a journey through time. Frescoes and icons, aged yet vibrant, covered the church's interior. An elaborate depiction of the family tree of Serbian Kings linked with the Serbian Orthodox Church wove its roots across the walls.

A black-robed Orthodox priest, his bearded face crinkling into a smile, welcomed them with an overview of the monastery's history. "Visoki Dečani stands as a testament to our faith, built in the mid-14th century and dedicated to the Ascension," he said, his voice softly resonant. "Within these walls are frescoes that chronicle our history and the remains of Saint Stefan of Dečani—his legacy is a beacon of faith through the centuries."

Kit took in the towering marble sculptures and the glint of a gold-clad Bible, while Natalia scribbled notes feverishly. Each piece of history, the priest noted, played a role in the region's past, the monastery itself a repository for artifacts and medieval manuscripts of profound significance.

"The world must recognize this sanctuary's value," he continued, gesturing to the imposing entrance tower. "It has weathered conflicts and grenade blasts, a guardian of heritage and holiness alike. And it's not just the stone and mortar that protect—the devotion and prayers here are as much a shield as these ancient walls."

Kit absorbed the condensed history lesson, the priest's words painting a picture that was both sacred and strategic. She was acutely aware that beneath the surface of his narrative lay currents of potential threat.

The church bore a patina of time; its blackened interior whispered of centuries of prayers by candlelight. Gilded icons cast a luminous glow across the walls, their presence a bridge between a hallowed past and the tangible present. The air was thick with the scent of frankincense, an evocative fragrance that seemed to carry the weight of ancient secrets.

Kit's mind, constantly analyzing, drifted towards the hidden vaults of the monastery. If it were to gain UNESCO World Heritage Site recognition, there would be additional layers of protection guarding its valuable treasures. However, the true value lay in what could be concealed in dark corners—ancient manuscripts and holy relics, each fiercely guarded pieces of history. But the Rasputin Manuscripts were not as easy to find as one might think. Father Peter was a master of puzzles; their hiding place could be as mysterious as their contents.

The sound of silence surrounded them as they walked through the quiet pathways, but a sudden chill ran through Kit's body, breaking her focus. Her instincts warned her of potential dangers, like a whisper on the wind. Despite the tranquil atmosphere of the monastery, there was an underlying unease—a sense of looming threats that couldn't be seen with the naked eye.

The tour group made their way to the monastery's souvenir shop, a small space filled with religious artifacts and handcrafted items. It was meant to be a peaceful break from their sightseeing, but Kit's attention was caught by a stranger in the corner of the shop. He wore a nondescript jacket and a low hat that hid his eyes, and his intense interest in a set of rosary beads gave off an unsettling vibe. Kit couldn't recall seeing him with the other tourists, and she knew he didn't belong there.

At that moment, Kit's trained eyes spotted something metallic hidden under the stranger's jacket—possibly a weapon? Her heart raced, but she kept her composure. She had to protect Natalia and figure out what this stranger wanted. The tour suddenly took on a dangerous tone.

Kit's instincts were on high alert. This man didn't seem like a tourist interested in religious souvenirs; he seemed more like someone surveying the area. If he was working for Mal Mala's crew, it could spell trouble for them. Adrenaline surged through Kit as she leaned closer to Natalia and whispered, "Do you see that man over there? Don't look directly at him, just take a quick glance. Something doesn't feel right about him."

Natalia's eyes widened a fraction before her gaze flickering briefly towards the stranger, "What's our play, Kit?"

"We need to stay alert. Don't let him know we're onto him," Kit instructed. "Start browsing. And keep an eye out for anyone else who looks out of place."

They began to move around the shop, with Natalia drawn to the hand-carved crucifixes as Kit pretending to admire a collection of artisan candles. All the while, their attention was divided between the memorabilia and the man in the corner, tension mounting in the peaceful ambiance. Kit knew she and Natalia needed to stay one step ahead. The tour had taken a sinister turn, and a question mark hung over the safety of the invaluable Rasputin Manuscripts.

As the monastery tour concluded and they made their way back to the villa, a sense of unease wrapped itself around Kit and Natalia, like a chill creeping in at dusk. Their minds were elsewhere, caught up in the day's events —the interred Saint, the mysterious carvings, and the lingering aura of mystery. Despite the rising tension, the monastery's solemnity held a captivating beauty.

Chapter Twenty-Four

Once back in their Dukagjin Resort villa, Kit and Natalia's discussion about the afternoon's exploration of the monastery was disturbed by the discovery of a cryptic note left propped up on the vase of flowers in the middle of the table, where they couldn't miss it. The message was brief but cautious:

"Meeting with Fr. P. arranged for tomorrow. Will collect you outside then at 11PM. Stay alert – S."

Sergei had managed to track them down and enter their private villa to deliver the note. While it might be unsettling for others, Kit found it both thrilling and comforting to know he was close. Sergei had always pushed her boundaries, and this was no different. However, his warning echoed loudly in Kit's mind. The timing of the proposed meeting, so late at night was troubling. Natalia, deep in thought, seemed to be processing the same revelation.

"Isn't that very late for a meeting with Father Peter," Natalia said.

"Talk about cloak and dagger," Kit said, picking up the piece of paper to examine it closely. "If this note was actually written by Sergei. Do you think he has in mind some kind of khash training session where we have to break our limitations, our habitual timetables?"

"We can be sure of that." Natalia's gaze held a flicker of concern. "I suppose we'll find out now soon. But what about the man in the shop? Could he be one of Mala's?"

Kit replayed the scene at the monastery shop in her mind, the man's furtive glances among the curios—a stark deviation from the innocent curiosity of a tourist. "It's possible," she admitted. "We have to keep our eyes open. Mala's influence could reach farther than we thought."

A soft chuckle escaped Natalia's lips, lightening the tone of her voice. "Is Kosovo always this exciting?"

Kit replied with a half-smile. "It's always full of surprises, which is why we need to take advantage of any calm moments we get. Maybe we can use tomorrow morning for a therapy session? It could give us an edge."

Natalia's eyes lit up at the suggestion. "Great idea! And I don't expect any payment; helping others is what I'm passionate about. Your offer to let me stay temporarily is extremely generous. Just give me some space for my tarot readings and we're all set."

"I was actually hoping to learn more about your dream therapy techniques," confessed Kit, rubbing her temples in an attempt to clear her mind. "Lately, everything seems like a jumbled mess and I can't make sense of it."

They both fell into a comfortable silence, each contemplating the delicate balance between remaining professional and forming a personal bond. The looming midnight meeting added an air of mystery to their plans. For Kit, meeting with Sergei again was not the only reason she was excited; she also couldn't wait to unravel the enigmatic ideas of khash philosophy with Father Peter's guidance. This trip was no ordinary visit; it was a careful dance on the verge of danger, with the coveted Rasputin Manuscripts as the prize.

Kit awoke in the morning, feeling refreshed. The alluring scent of freshly brewed coffee, scrambled eggs, and toast wafted through the air. Natalia had turned on the radio, filling the room with soft Kosovo pop music. Kit got out of bed and strolled over to the window, drawing back the blinds to reveal a breath-taking view of the lush green valley. She donned her robe over her pyjamas and slid into a pair of slippers before heading to the kitchen, where Natalia was waiting.

"Good morning," Natalia greeted her. "Are you hungry?"

"Famished," Kit replied. The previous night had consisted of mere snacks and drinks at the hotel bar, hardly a proper meal.

They settled at the table, overlooking the picturesque view. The atmosphere was cozy, with a rustic yet refined style. Kit relished the privacy of being able to talk freely over breakfast without worrying about eavesdroppers.

In the quiet aftermath of the meal, the clink of dishes being set aside filled the space as they prepared to move to the lounge. Kit cradled her coffee, the warmth seeping into her palms, while Natalia retrieved her tarot deck, moving with a practiced and purposeful air. Settling into the embrace of the couch, Kit drew a cushion to her chest. Natalia assumed her position in the commanding, high-backed chair. She lay out a midnight blue silk scarf on the coffee table, a stage for the cards fanned out before them.

"Let's find our theme for today," Natalia instructed, her voice steady. "Draw a card, Kit."

Kit's hand wavered above the arcana before selecting one. The card she revealed portrayed a daunting tower perched on a craggy cliff, being sundered by lightning, with figures plummeting from its heights amidst a chaos of flames.

Kit tensed. "That looks ominous," she murmured uneasily.

Natalia nodded, her eyes fixed on the card. "The Tower —sudden upheaval, a revelation. Does it mirror any turbulence in your life?"

"That tower reminds me of the monastery yesterday. Literally. And yes, my life's been upended recently. My father, long absent, emerged in Bangkok with revelations that have left me reeling. He's got links to Pristina that I didn't know about, and now I'm under security scrutiny because of him—just when I don't need the attention."

Natalia leaned in, her gaze intent. "Such rediscoveries can be shocking just like the lightning bolts in the card. And to be thrust into the limelight of security checks—your privacy could feel invaded, your autonomy questioned."

Kit nodded, her eyes reflecting the turmoil within, the card's imagery a stark representation of her inner storm.

"I'm in a whirlwind of emotions and questions. It's challenging because there are different parts of my life that I'm juggling." Kit shifted uncomfortably. "Can I ask you to keep this confidential. This is a delicate balancing act."

"Of course, whatever we discuss stays between us. I suppose people didn't know what you were doing in Ljubljana, when you were there with us."

Kit shook her head; That was for sure. "I'm torn about the future. New Zealand, Pristina, art sales... it's a mess. And let's not start on relationships," she said, biting her lip.

"Explore your passions, values, desires," Natalia

suggested. "Journaling could help, as could dream analysis. Let's see what your subconscious says."

Kit nodded. "Feels like I'm split into pieces."

Natalia presented a diagram, a circle divided into life's facets, like work, relationships, finances and family. "Rate your satisfaction in each. It's a start."

Kit smiled at the simplicity. "Better than any shrink I've seen."

She glanced at the paper, then at Natalia. "The Tower card from the tarot... it's like it's coming to life."

Natalia's eyes sparkled. "Life can mirror the cards and vice versa. Ready to look deeper?"

Kit inhaled, nerves bubbling. "Let's do it."

She kicked off her slippers and leaned back. A wave of calm hit her. "I think I'll stay like this all day," she joked.

Natalia's laughter was a comfort.

"Relax and take some deep breaths," Natalia said, guiding Kit through breathing exercises. Her voice lowered to a murmur, creating a comforting rhythm. "Picture a place, somewhere that brings you peace. Like a childhood home, a garden, or a sunny beach..."

At the mention of a beach, memories flooded Kit's mind. A pristine lagoon in New Zealand, its silver sands stretching out before her. Lush ferns and a babbling brook nestled in the bush, leading to her private piece of paradise.

Kit sighed, her voice dreamy. "It's like I'm really there."

"That's right," Natalia encouraged her. "Let your worries slip away."

Kit inhaled deeply, a fleeting memory tugging at the corners of her mind. Her time with Sergei in the rose petal room. His smiling face appeared to her, basking in the sunlight of her New Zealand lagoon. She reached for him, but he remained just out of her grasp, bathed in the iridescent glow of the water's reflection.

"He's here," Kit whispered, her eyes still shut tight.

Natalia leaned forward, her interest piqued. "A friend?"

"Yes, a friend," Kit confirmed. "Just standing there, smiling. He's even wearing his speedos." Kit chuckled, breaking the serene atmosphere momentarily.

"Good. Stay with it. Look around, see if there's anyone else." Natalia's voice was a comforting presence, grounding Kit in her vivid imagery.

Turning her imaginary gaze, Kit saw Silver perched on a rock, bikini-clad and carefree. The distinct sound of boots on a gravelly path drew her attention to Owen, appearing from the lush bush in military uniform.

"The whole gang's here," Kit reported, a hint of amusement dancing in her tone. "Owen sticks out though—decked out in army gear and all."

"Who else is there, Kit? Anyone you want to talk to?" Natalia prompted.

Kit's gaze flickered across the imaginary lagoon, settling on the distant figure of her father. "My father Vernon is there, but he's out of reach."

"Understood," Natalia replied. "For now, let's talk with those who are closer. Your father can come later."

In Kit's mind's eye, the hush of the underbrush was suddenly broken by a soft, yet deliberate rustle. In the dimming light of Kit's mindscape, a vixen edged into sight, her coat a blend of reds and golds, interrupted by strokes of midnight black. The fox's eyes, sharp as cut glass, held a reflective quality that seemed to pierce the veil between the natural and the supernatural.

"A fox," Kit breathed out, her amusement tinged with an undercurrent of surprise.

Natalia leaned in, her voice soft. "What's the fox doing?"

"She's... watching," Kit answered, her pulse quickening. She extended a hand, palm down, in a silent overture. With a measured gait that betrayed no fear, the fox approached, a shadow gliding across the forest floor.

The vixen was now close, so close Kit could detect the faintest scent of wild fur, the subtle movement of air as she breathed. "She's right here, beside me," Kit's voice was a whisper, the initial chuckle now extinguished by the moment.

The fox's proximity was electrifying, her gaze fixed on Kit with an intensity that spoke of deeper, unspoken understandings. The air seemed charged around them, the line between Kit's reality and the world within her mind blurred by the animal's almost spectral presence.

In the dreamscape, Kit felt a deep connection to the ancient and powerful spirit of the vixen. More than a figment, the fox was a sentinel, guiding her through the psychological maze she found herself in.

"These figures are projections," Natalia's voice was a grounding force. "They're influenced by your perceptions. Let's see their intentions."

Sergei emanated a magnetic allure. At Kit's inquiry, he offered a cryptic gesture, presenting her with numbers she knew all too well before fading into the mist.

Owen, burdened by his uniform, exhaled a heavy sentiment. "I want your trust, Kit," he said, eyes earnest. "But I feel you're elsewhere." In the warmth of their embrace, his stiff garb transformed into casual beachwear, a softness between them.

"Better," Kit's smile was genuine, even here.

Silver's arrival was heralded by tropical scents. "I'm here to protect you," she whispered.

But the peace was short-lived. The underbrush rustled with a new presence, sinister and menacing. It was Mal Mala, the one whose gang she feared could desecrate the monastery. His intrusion was a blade through the fabric of her sanctuary.

"What do you want?" Kit demanded, her voice steady despite the ice in her veins. This was her imaginary sanctuary. How could Mala intrude?

Mal Mala's sneer was a dark omen. "Step aside or suffer," he growled.

Kit, bolstered by the silent strength of the vixen watching from the shadows, stood her ground. "This is my realm, Mal Mala. I'm the law here, and you're the one trespassing."

His laugh was like a thunderclap, unsettling yet incapable of shaking her resolve. "You think you're safe here?" he taunted, spitting venomously onto the ground. "This is just a preview, Prosecutor. In the real world, you can't hide behind your fox."

As he turned and disappeared down the path, the vixen emerged, her gaze locked on Kit with a fierce protectiveness. The encounter had been a stark warning from the depths of her subconscious.

Kit jolted awake in the Hotel lounge, her breath a frantic rhythm.

"Natalia," she choked out, the echo of Mal Mala's threat still ringing in her ears, "I saw him—Mal Mala. He came for me."

Chapter Twenty-Five

The session with Natalia had left Kit with a lingering shiver, the echo of Mal Mala's threats hanging in the air like a bad omen. Yet, as she and Natalia stepped into the brightness of the day, the sun's rays seemed to wash away the shadows of her mind. They had time, a rare commodity, and Peja's market awaited—a perfect distraction from the darker corners of her thoughts.

The morning sun, now fully risen, bled its warm colors across the hilly horizon. The world outside began to pull Kit back from the brink of her subconscious fears. As they hit the road towards Peja, the hum of the SUV along the rugged route was a comforting counterpoint to the morning's tension. They wove through the lush Kosovo landscapes, with craggy peaks standing sentinel in the distance, as if guarding them from the uncertainties that lay behind.

Peja emerged on the horizon like a scene from a storybook, an old-world gem that promised respite and wonder. Its Ottoman footprints, etched into the architecture, mingled with the vibrant pulse of modern life in a dance of times past and present. Upon entering the town, they were welcomed by the charming clamor of the local bazaar.

The market was a celebration of life and color. Countless stands spilled over with a riot of hues, local fruits and vegetables vying for attention amidst dazzling crafts and fabrics patterned in dizzying designs. The scent of freshly baked bread mingled with the tang of ripe fruits and the bold aroma of strong, steaming coffee. It was a mixture of smells, each thread pulling Kit further from the grimness of her earlier encounter, luring her into the present moment.

Here, amidst the lively banter of vendors and the laughter of children playing between the stalls, Kit found a measure of peace. The weight of her role, the seriousness of her investigations, could be shelved, if only for an afternoon. With each step through the bazaar, the more the market's vivacity infused their spirits, buoying them with an anticipation that was light and hopeful.

The market's vibrancy lingered on their senses as Kit and Natalia wandered through the maze of stalls. Kit's fingers danced over a hand-woven rug, its patterns as intricate as the ones in her mind. Natalia, drawn to the shimmer of local jewelry, admired the delicate filigree, a tangible distraction from the intangible dangers they faced.

They bantered with vendors, while savoring succulent figs and sharp cheeses. Kit allowed the vibrant life of Peja to eclipse the shadow of Mal Mala, her recent vision dissipating like smoke amongst the lively streets. Yet, the reminder of their investigation lingered, a subtle undercurrent beneath the day's pleasant surface.

As the clock hands marched towards lunchtime, they found solace in a quaint taverna. Here, the rich scent of borek and roasted lamb enveloped them, and they indulged in the hearty flavors, letting the local wine carry their conversation on its flowing current.

The return to their hotel was a quiet affair, the day's images still playing behind their eyes. They dined again, more quietly this time, in the hotel restaurant, the echoes of the market's chaos giving way to the evening's calm.

With nightfall came a shift in energy. They prepared for the meeting with Sergei, their movements deliberate, their attire a reflection of the night's seriousness. Kit's black jeans and loose shirt embodied practicality and purpose, while Natalia's black maxi dress and jacket spoke of a stealthy elegance. Together, they wrapped dark scarves around their heads, a nod to decorum and discretion.

They shared a look in the mirror, their eyes reflecting the dual nature of their day—part discovery, part danger. With the night cloaking them, Kit felt the stirrings of adrenaline, the same ancient power that had surged within her during the active imagination session, now ready to be channelled into the night's activities.

Sergei waited below, an enigmatic figure who may hold the key to understanding the turmoil that had been haunting her dreams. Kit and Natalia left the safety of the hotel, fully aware of the stark contrast between the peace of their time there and what awaited them ahead. The descent from their hillside villa was a wordless one, each step bringing them closer to the unknown. The dimly-lit path was lined with rustic lamps, casting long shadows and adding to the clandestine atmosphere of their meeting spot. A sedan sat in the darkness, blending in with Sergei's ghostly figure as he stood beside it. As Kit looked at him, memories of their past encounters flooded her mind, but she pushed them aside for now. The night demanded her full attention.

"That's Sergei. Let's get going," Kit whispered to Natalia, her voice barely audible.

Squeezing into the back seat of the car, they were immediately filled in on the night's plans. Sergei's tone had lost its previous warmth. "We will enter the monastery through an old tunnel that once served as a refuge. It is now our secret passage to Father Peter and the Dečani Monastery."

Kit's whisper was laced with disbelief, "Is this allowed? And what about the guards?"

"The tunnel bypasses all checkpoints. Father Peter has received silent permission from the Abbott to use it and his chapel for our purposes. The soldiers will dismiss any activity they see as part of the monks' nightly rituals," Sergei explained confidently, his words carefully chosen.

Natalia suddenly realized the gravity of their situation. "The Abbott must have great trust in Father Peter."

Sergei nodded in agreement. "Their loyalty to the Russian Orthodox Church compels them to act, even in unconventional ways during these dangerous times."

Kit's curiosity could not be contained. "But why all the secrecy?"

Sergei met her gaze in the rearview mirror, his eyes reflecting a somber certainty. "Tonight, Father Peter will reveal the sacred Rasputin Manuscripts and initiate us into the khash degrees at midnight. We must harness their power when the veil between worlds is thinnest."

A weighty determination settled over Kit. "There's no turning back now. And I wouldn't want to."

"Right," Sergei agreed, his grip on the wheel tightening

as they drove closer to the monastery. Kit took a deep breath, remembering their recent possible proximity with Mala's men at the sacred site. "We might have already crossed paths with them."

Sergei nodded as he turned onto a more secluded path. "We will discuss more later, but this road avoids the main entrance and takes us through the hills to an old hermitage. It's been used as a discreet passage for centuries and will lead us to our target tonight."

The car's headlights cut through the darkness as they followed the secret path known only to a select few. As they approached the monastery, shrouded in mystery and illuminated by moonlight, the air in the car grew heavy with anticipation of crossing paths with both ancient power and present danger.

Sergei expertly maneuvered the black sedan to a stop, its tires crunching gravel under the shadow of ancient stone walls. He turned off the engine, plunging the night into silence save for a few nighttime creatures. The ticking of the engine was the only sound intruding on the peaceful atmosphere.

He glanced at his passengers, darkened silhouettes in the car's interior. With a curt nod, he got out of the vehicle, his worn boots sinking slightly into the damp earth. The entrance to the tunnel was artfully concealed behind a pile of rocks and foliage. Sergei pulled away some of the camouflage before his fingers found the cold, metal handle of a wooden door embedded in the earth. He gave a reassuring nod to the women before pushing it open, revealing the gaping entrance of the hidden tunnel.

A mustiness hung heavily in the air as they stepped inside. Sergei flipped on his flashlight, illuminating the darkness that enveloped them. They moved quickly, the secret door closing with a creak behind them, shutting out any trace of noise.

With every step, the darkness seemed to cling closer, becoming a tangible presence in the small space. Kit's heart raced; the narrow beam from Sergei's flashlight was their only source of light in this suffocating void. Shadows danced along the walls, playing tricks on her mind—rats, spiders—but she pushed through.

Natalia's heavy breathing echoed behind her, the only sound in this eerily silent place. Kit couldn't shake off the feeling of being trapped, with no one else knowing their location or able to help if something went wrong. But she refused to let fear overcome her. Her determination flared and she pressed on, focusing on the light from Sergei's flashlight as their guide through this underground maze.

Sergei suddenly stopped, his voice a hushed whisper, "Stay close. Quiet now. We're almost there."

They nodded in agreement and pressed onward. Eventually, they arrived at a door. Sergei applied pressure to the handle and it groaned under the strain, making its presence known. A refreshing breeze greeted them as they walked through, carrying with it the distinct aroma of aged wine, signaling the end of their secret expedition.

Stepping into the wine cellar, Kit felt her tense shoulders drop a fraction. She exchanged a quick glance with Natalia, whose eyes mirrored the relief in her own. Their hands briefly met in a silent exchange of camaraderie, the reassuring squeeze acknowledging their successful passage through the tunnel.

They moved on quickly, stepping over the creaking floorboards of the wine cellar. The uneven light from

Sergei's torch cast elongated, ghastly shadows of them on the stone walls, adding to the eerie atmosphere.

A wooden staircase led them to another door. Sergei paused at its base, his eyes flicking back towards them once more. With a beckoning gesture, Sergei led them up a rickety wooden staircase. Each step creaked under their weight, echoing in the otherwise silent cellar, as they ascended towards another door, another unknown awaiting them in the heart of the monastery.

Once out of the wine cellar, Sergei led them through a maze of corridors. These were dimly lit, their walls cool and damp to touch, a testament to the monastery's centuries-old existence, although no doubt the buildings had been rebuilt and renovated over the centuries.

The journey through the monastery contrasted with the constriction of the tunnel, swapping the oppressive darkness and rickety wooden supports of the passageway for the serenity of the religious institution. Kit felt her anxiety ease, replaced with a burgeoning curiosity. Father Peter, the enigmatic manuscripts, their very purpose of coming here—everything lay ahead.

As Kit stepped into the secluded chapel, a wave of wonder washed over her. The atmosphere was heavy with the scent of incense and an undeniable sense of the divine permeated every corner. Soft candlelight danced around the room, casting shadows that flickered with each gentle breeze. Father Peter stood alone at the altar, a quiet icon of devotion lost in prayer.

Sergei turned off his flashlight, immersing them in the warm glow of candles. The outside world faded away, leaving only the hushed intimacy of the chapel. Kit's heart raced; in this peaceful sanctuary, she could feel the truth pulsing through her veins, and knew that the danger lurking in the shadows was real.

This small chapel was a treasure trove of faith, far from the grandeur of the monastery. The walls were lined with ancient icons that exuded a stoic beauty. The air was thick with mystical energy, enhanced by the interplay of incense and candlelight against the engulfing darkness beyond. In this ephemeral setting, it almost seemed as though the sacred icons themselves came to life—Saint Michael locked in eternal battle against the dragon, and the compassionate gaze of the Madonna watching over all.

The altar stood proudly, its polished wood gleaming from the countless touches of devotion. Above it, a carved cross darkened by years of oil commanded attention, flanked by gilded icons that caught and cast shards of light around the dimly lit space. An ancient rug, with faded patterns and a history long forgotten, lay at the feet of the figures depicted in the icons. The pews, worn smooth by use, waited patiently for worshippers to occupy their spaces. In this sanctuary, time seemed to slow down and create a bubble where the present could reach out and touch the past.

Father Peter, tall in his austere black cassock, turned to greet them. Without his usual orthodox priest's hat and over-garment, his physical presence felt even more imposing. Kit noticed a brief glimmer of joy in his otherwise stern expression as he stretched out his hand towards Sergei. Sergei respectfully kissed the priest's ring in return, paying homage to his religious authority.

"Welcome to Visoki Dečani Monastery. This chapel is the secret heart in the heart of Kosovo," Father Peter greeted them in a deep and resonant voice. Sergei expressed his gratitude for this exclusive gathering and re-introduced his fellow travelers, Natalia and Caitlin. Natalia nodded in reverence while Kit observed their surroundings intently. Checking her watch, she noted that it was almost midnight. *Just a few minutes left*, she thought to herself.

"You must be wondering why I have called you here at this late hour," Father Peter began, his smile cryptic. "Midnight, when our world is closest to the unseen realm. In these times of great internal and external threats, we must abandon secrecy and embrace openness. Tonight, I present to you a portion of the Rasputin Manuscripts, with the hope of guiding you on a spiritual journey towards unlocking your divine potential."

Sergei nodded respectfully, his demeanor more serious than Kit had ever seen. The air filled with anticipation as they all turned to face an oblong table made of dark wood against the right wall. A lamp cast light onto the ancient folio that rested atop it—finally, the Rasputin Manuscripts! They were a compilation of various documents carefully preserved and curated by Rasputin's followers, later discovered by one of his sons. The pages contained mysterious symbols, images, and texts that seemed to hold profound spiritual meaning, some appearing to have been added over time.

Kit's heart raced as they followed the priest towards the table. This was the moment they had all been waiting for, the pivotal point of their mission. Her excitement was almost palpable. Father Peter's deep voice resonated throughout the room, filling Kit's mind with every word.

"Khash philosophy is like a masterful chess player navigating through life's maze," he declared. "Until now, you have been mere pawns, novice khashes barely grasping the bigger picture. But tonight, you stand on the brink of transformation—from apprentices to adepts. The game intensifies, and we must quicken your induction. Time is not a luxury we can afford. Beyond adeptness lies the domain of masters, the Svetoch—the Illuminated ones. Sergei is on his way to achieving this zenith, but tonight he too will face the crucible of Adept initiation. The teachings of khash are not just stories; they hold keys to unlocking profound energy, finding balance within the psyche, and elevating consciousness towards spiritual evolution. It is a journey to the immortal essence of one's soul. Remember, this path is treacherous and requires patience not only as a virtue but as a necessity."

Father Peter's his silhouette was stark against the flickering candles as, with great care, he unfurled ancient parchment scrolls, laying them out on the table in a cryptic pattern that hid its secrets within overlapping edges.

"Select a page, guided by your intuition. The one that resonates with you the most," he instructed them. Kit and Natalia exchanged a knowing glance, recognizing the similarity to their recent tarot card selection.

"Proceed in the order of your acquaintance with the khash philosophy. Sergei, you first. Select a page and pass it to me without glimpsing its face," Father Peter instructed. Sergei reverently moved forward, hesitated briefly before selecting a page, then handed it over to the priest.

Natalia went next, and then it was Kit's turn. As she stepped towards the table, a wave of dizziness washed over her, the dancing light from the lamp giving her a surreal feeling. She took a moment to collect herself before adopting the same strategy as in a tarot reading, letting her hand float above the table until it gravitated towards a particular parchment. The rough texture of the paper brought back memories of her days at the British Library, carefully handling valuable manuscripts while wearing protective white gloves.

Guiding them back to the pews, Father Peter invited them to sit, placing their chosen parchment next to each. "I will pray and anoint you. At my command, you are to reveal the face of your page. I will provide brief interpretations for each symbol, following which you should internalize the symbol and meditate upon it," he explained. "Each of us is connected to a unique khash power, one that aligns with our individual paths and our deepest selves."

The chapel air vibrated with Father Peter's sacred chants, a resonant backdrop to the ritual unfolding at a breakneck pace. Kit's skin tingled as the priest's thumb, slick with fragrant oil, traced a symbol on her forehead in a swift, purposeful motion.

He began by addressing Sergei in Russian, effortlessly switching to English so that everyone could understand. He showed them a symbol, the Eye of Tomorrow, which glowed with a brilliant blue light and had countless paths stemming from its center. "Sergei, your special ability is foresight," he announced confidently. Sergei's attention was locked onto the symbol, his eyes filled with a longing desire to unravel its mysteries.

Natalia received her symbol next, the Tree of Dreams, a page depicting a network of silver branches and roots reflecting her inner world. "This will enhance your connection to the subconscious, Natalia. It will enable you to navigate the secrets of the dream world with ease," Father Peter said in a solemn voice. She was visibly moved, her face a canvas of awe. Tears glistened in her eyes as she took the page, grateful for this gift that would deepen her connection to herself.

At last, Father Peter's gaze connected with Kit's, and he

turned the parchment around to display a striking image of a russet red fox leaping through moonlit skies. "This is the Tracer Fox, Caitlin," he declared, pressing the image into her hands. "It represents strategy." The symbol seemed to radiate energy that sparked something within Kit, igniting a newfound sense of determination and quick thinking.

Each symbol held a deeper meaning, unlocking hidden powers and revealing the vast potential within the soul. The fox's eyes, shining in the dark silhouette, etched themselves into Kit's mind—a silent promise of the strategic mastery she was about to acquire.

Kit's grasp tightened on the aged parchment, its ink whispering tales of ancient wisdom. Its worn edges spoke of countless seekers who had sought its guidance throughout history. The Tracer Fox leapt off the page, a symbol of the cunning and insight needed to navigate their game of shadows. This was not just an artifact; it was a map to true mastery.

The symbol sparked a rush of vivid memories. She recalled her daring escape from the fugitive Raco through the Sharri mountains, with a wild fox as her companion when she needed help. Another memory flickered—a shadowy fox leading her through winding alleys, away from danger once again. And in a moment of refuge, Anubis, the jackal god, stood guard against her pursuers in a museum. Even during her active imagination session with Natalia, the fox remained a constant presence in the shadows.

Kit's connection to the fox was primal—calling forth her innate skills for strategy and survival. With Sergei and Natalia both absorbed by their own symbols, a silent bond formed between them on this shared journey. As they sat under Father Peter's watchful gaze, they were no longer mere players—they had become architects of their own destiny.

The stillness of their meditation was shattered, disrupted by a sudden chill that filled the previously calm atmosphere. An ominous feeling seeped into the chapel, causing the newly initiated adepts to raise their heads. In hushed whispers, they acknowledged a shared dread, "They're here."

Chapter Twenty-Six

Muffled voices and a sudden thud against the door made Kit jolt with fright. Father Peter, acting swiftly, gathered the scattered manuscript pages, slid them into a portfolio, and securely tucked it away in a box folder with a sturdy handle. The three initiates stood, their reverie shattered. Kit's eyes swept across the room, hunting for another exit. But, as she feared, the private chapel had only one way in and out.

Sergei muttered a curse under his breath, his voice barely audible. It was an unexpected profanity in the previously solemn atmosphere.

The door to the private chapel flew open, exposing Mal Mala and his crew—a band of thieves, well-versed in their trade. Clad in black attire with faces camouflaged by dark paint, they appeared as ghosts against the monastery's stone walls. Kit's heart raced as she caught a glimpse of the intruders. She had seen Mala at the casino before, but he looked completely different now. His sleek suit was replaced by tactical gear, every inch serving a purpose in the art of stealthy movement. His hair, once perfectly styled, now blended into the darkness that clung to his skin. The intense look in his eyes betrayed his intent to rob the Church of its wealth.

The brief moment of silence was shattered by Father Peter as he confronted the unwelcome visitors. He moved with a quiet grace, his tall figure casting an almost supernatural shadow across the cold stone floor. His robe flowed behind him like the wings of an avenging angel as he stood before the trespassers.

"Desecrating this holy place is a sin you will pay a price for," he declared, his voice rumbled as if with a seismic force.

Kit's attention flicked to Sergei, his hand subtly betraying the shape of a concealed pistol. But Father Peter's keen eyes missed nothing and made an imperceptible gesture that stopped Sergei from drawing his weapon.

Mala sensed the tension in the room and changed his tactics. "There's nothing for us here," he spoke smoothly, taking a step backwards. With a wave of his hand, he directed one of his henchmen towards the main church and the others to search for the treasury. His mind was already planning their escape route. "Meet at the rally point immediately," he whispered to his gang as he backed out of the room.

Kit's mind raced as she realized the threat to the monastery's treasures. "We can't just stand by," she urged, her voice filled with determination despite the overwhelming odds. The intruders were not only experienced in street battles, but they also seemed well-prepared, possibly having studied the monastery's layout beforehand.

"Perhaps the military can help," Natalya ventured,

although the thought of being arrested themselves was a concern.

Sergei's grip on his pistol tightened. "I say we confront them directly."

A rapid exchange of strategies ensued, prompted by the urgency of their predicament. They concurred: Natalia would trigger the alarm, sending reverberations throughout the sacred walls, while Sergei, pistol ready, would hurry to the fortified tower, the sanctuary of the most revered relics. Father Peter would initially join Natalia, then bolster Sergei's defense at the tower. They would reconvene at the tunnel's entrance, posthaste, after the alarm's echo.

Yet, this left the main church vulnerable. "I'll secure the church," Kit announced with resolve.

"No, it's too perilous alone. Stay with Father Peter and Natalia. Besides, we cannot afford a confrontation with EUFOR," Sergei objected.

But Kit had made up her mind. "I have the element of surprise—and the Tracer Fox," she said, invoking the symbol of her newly honed strategic cunning. Her tone left no room for argument, her intent as clear as the conviction in her eyes. The others, recognizing her mind was made up, nodded reluctantly, understanding that her move was a calculated one, and there was no time to argue.

As Father Peter deftly concealed the box file containing the manuscripts behind a hidden panel in the chapel, they ventured out. Kit slipped into a shadowed nave, her figure merging with the darkness. A wave of adrenalin washed through her, spiking her senses. Her online research on the Monastery's layout was about to pay off. Coupled with their earlier orientation visit, she felt secure enough to navigate the unfamiliar corridors.

As the group moved ahead, Kit deliberately branched off into a side corridor. Sergei's well-meaning vigilance often bordered on suffocating, yet by now, he should have recognized a fundamental truth about her: Kit was a lone wolf at heart.

Misleading silence filled the monastery courtyard, in contrast to the drama unfolding inside. Kit surveyed the church, its silhouette loomed against the night sky. A faint glimmer of light inside betrayed the possible presence of thieves. She needed to delay the looting until Natalia's alarm could summon the guards. Adjusting her black head-scarf and securing her satchel, she moved swiftly toward the side entrance. The door opened with a soft creak, an indica-tion of her presence she couldn't avoid. Kit slipped through the gap into the church's stillness.

The interior was awash with a subtle glow. Kit advanced, the soles of her shoes silent against the cold stone. Rounding a corner, she spotted a figure. Mal Mala hunched over a table, his torchlight illuminating the valuable artifacts before him. "Game's up," she declared, her voice steady. "The guards are on their way."

He turned slowly, his confidence undiminished by the prospect of capture. "I don't know what you think you're doing here," Mala said, a calm hunter facing down his prey. "I suggest you leave while you still can."

"I have unfinished business," Kit replied, her tone even but her mind racing. Her recent initiation into the Tracer Fox teachings echoed within her, bolstering her resolve.

Mala simply shrugged and turned back to his looting. Kit took a steadying breath and approached the sarcophagus at the main altar. Her hand trembled as she reached out to steady herself on the sarcophagus that housed the saint's mortal remains. As her fingertips made contact with the surface, without forethought, she closed her eyes, her lips moving in silent prayer for help and guidance. She didn't know if it was her nerves or the power of the initiation a short time ago, but a warmth began to spread from her fingertips up her arm. It seeped into her, making her feel more confident, more connected with her instincts. She withdrew her hand, her gaze sweeping over the room.

Kit's mind raced, the teachings of the Tracer Fox whirling through her thoughts. *Observation. Intuition. Strategy.* Her heart pounded in sync with these echoed words, her eyes keenly assessing Mala, seeking a weakness to exploit. He seemed absorbed in the precious artifacts he greedily collected, paying little attention to her scrutiny.

Her Tracer Fox skills rippled to life, reminding her of the art of concealment and misdirection. The church's play of shadows and secretive nooks became her allies in evasion and distraction. She swallowed hard, feeling a knot of apprehension twist in her stomach. Fear was a luxury she couldn't afford now.

Opening her eyes, she assessed Mala, noting his focus on the artifacts, his back to her. Emboldened, she stepped forward. "Mala, you're out of your depth. We know who you are; we're always a step ahead." Her words, though sharp with confidence, belied the fear within.

At her challenge, Mala straightened, annoyance flashing in his eyes. "Who the hell are you?" he snarled.

Her distraction had worked. She retreated, her fingers finding the switch to the night lights and plunging the room into darkness. Now only the moon's glow and Mala's disorienting torchlight remained. She heard him curse, perceived the confusion in his movements.

Using her heightened senses, she navigated the darkness, her Tracer Fox training at the forefront. She closed in on Mala. As she neared him, she tripped him deftly, her hand darting out to snatch the artifact-stuffed bag from his grip.

Mala fell with a surprised grunt, momentarily dazed. Kit pivoted, her heart hammering against her ribs as she sprinted toward the church entrance, the stolen bag clutched tight. Her plan had worked—for now. All she needed was to stay ahead until help arrived.

The alarm bell rang out suddenly, its haunting echo reverberating through the monastery, throwing Mala's crew into further confusion. The lights from the soldiers' stations flashed on, as did strong, overhead spotlights. A siren split the night. She had to get out now or risk arrest herself.

Kit bolted to the private chapel where the group had met earlier, her breaths shallow as she slid the bag of rescued artifacts into the secret cavity behind the panel—a hiding place she'd seen Father Peter use for the Rasputin Manuscripts. Her gaze lingered on the hefty manuscript box, its fastenings inviting. The allure of the forbidden pages pulsed through her, a siren song tempting her to lift just one folio. Her fingers edged closer, her intent murky even to herself, when the door's hinges creaked.

She whipped around, her face a mask of innocence as Sergei and Natalia entered.

"We need to move," Sergei urged, a hint of urgency in his voice. "The guards are on their way. What are you doing down there?"

She gestured towards the bag. "Hiding these artifacts I managed to grab from Mala. They'll be safe here with the manuscripts," she explained, hoping her voice sounded steadier than she felt.

"Smart," he acknowledged, stepping beside her to shove the bag deeper into the alcove. As they sealed the panel,

Kit's shoulders dropped, the weight of her unacted desires lifting invisibly. The manuscripts were out of sight, out of reach, and the temptation dissolved into the cool air of the chapel. "Father Peter is still out there with the other monks, but the EUFOR guards have been alerted. We need to get out of here."

As they regrouped, Kit felt an inexplicable warmth coursing through her body. She smiled, realizing that she's unwittingly touched the Saint's remains and somehow managed to outwit Mala. She silently thanked the Saint, feeling in her heart that a miracle has just happened.

Once safely out through the tunnel, they reach the waiting vehicle without further incident. Kit allowed herself to take a deep breath and relax slightly. Natalia was still wound up tightly.

"Are you okay?" she asked Natalia, who nodded, her arms still nervously wrapped around herself, but otherwise unharmed. Kit turned forward. "Sergei, what's the deal with this 'Tracer Fox' title?"

Sergei navigated the car with a careful focus, his words measured. "Kit, a Tracer Fox is the khash epitome of stealth and insight. It's a recognition of a skillset that borders on the preternatural—anticipating moves, remaining unseen. You'll be able to 'foresee' possible scenarios and predict patterns and reactions, almost like having a sixth sense."

"I'm not sure I can live up to that," Kit admitted.

"Patience," he counseled, his tone a blend of command and comfort. "Your abilities will emerge. Trust in that."

Shadows moved over them, cast by the branches under the weak streetlights. The car pulled up to the hotel. It was now well past midnight. Sergei cut the engine and switched off the head lights. The conversation was now shrouded in the hush of the car's interior.

Natalia broke her silence, "And what about my symbol, the Tree of Dreams?"

"It's a key to unlocking the subconscious, akin to your dream therapy. We traverse its branches in our minds, interpreting symbols that guide us in the conscious world. The roots connect us to the subconscious and the ground of being," Sergei answered after considering for a moment.

They had escaped the monastery by the skin of their teeth, slipping like shadows through a network of tunnels, unnoticed, moving with a speed born of adrenaline. Now, parked under the anonymity of night, their conversation seemed like from another lifetime.

"Now, here's what's unique. A trained khash operative can intentionally navigate the Tree of Dreams, not just interpret it. This can enhance their intuition, foresight, even their reaction times. It's a potent tool if harnessed correctly, but it requires deep understanding, patience, and lots of practice."

After Sergei concluded, Natalia's voice held a soft wonder, "I love that. It's as if our chosen symbols connect us on a deeper level."

Kit nodded, her mind weaving through the night's revelations. She glanced at Sergei, the dim light casting shadows across his contemplative face. "And your symbol? What was it, again?"

Sergei paused, a deliberate hush in the cramped space of the car. When he spoke, the words "The Eye of Tomorrow" sounded like it was filled with hidden depths.

"The gift of foresight?" Natalia whispered. The car's interior felt suddenly more intimate. A shiver of intrigue danced up Kit's spine—a cocktail of trepidation and thrill.

In the quiet, Natalia's fingers moved as if to trace the edge of her own Tarot deck, the gesture betraying a flicker of envy as if she was thinking about her own Tarot predictions. Her gaze lingered on Sergei with an intensity that was hard to read, the interplay of dim light and emotion painting a complex portrait of her thoughts.

"You don't need it, dear. You've already got that gift," Kit said, lightly touching Natalia's arm in reassurance, before turning back to them both. "After we split up back there, I faced off with Mal Mala. Got back the artifacts. And there was this moment with Saint Stefan's sarcophagus…" she trailed off.

Sergei's breath hitched. "Saint Stefan? His touch is said to work miracles."

"I didn't believe until…" Kit hesitated. "I asked for help, any help. And it came. I suddenly felt I could out manoeuvre Mala, and I did."

"That need might have been the key," Natalia said.

Kit's confession slipped out, "I almost looked at the other Rasputin manuscript pages."

"But you resisted." Sergei's eyes met hers in the rearview mirror.

"Your arrival stopped me. I'm not sure what I was going to do. Mal Mala's probably arrested by now, but what happens next? What if they tell EUFOR we were there…"

Headlights pierced the dark as a car approached in the distance. Sergei's voice was urgent. "Time to go. Lay low at the villa and let this storm pass. We were lucky tonight."

Kit's fingers tightened on his arm. "Tonight was unforgettable, thanks."

"And Father Peter…?" Natalia queried.

"We'll see him soon enough. He'll be okay. Now, go," Sergei said with urgency, bringing their discussion to a close.

As they parted, the remnants of the night's ordeals—the

chase, the ancient relics, the brush with the sacred—intertwined in a thick silence. Each moment, a thread woven into their shared experience, lingered in the air, an unforgettable pattern of memory and mystery that clung to them as they moved away.

Chapter Twenty-Seven

Pristina, Kosovo

Kit and Natalia, having narrowly escaped their adversaries at the monastery, spent a night in restless silence within the sanctuary of their hotel rooms. By morning, they checked out, their demeanors betraying none of the previous night's chaos. The return to Pristina was marked by calm, the unsettling events with Mal Mala's gang and EUFOR receding with each passing kilometer.

Days later, Kit was on the road again, making her way towards Adriatiku, a restaurant located on the peaceful shores of Batlava Lake. Taking the scenic route out of Pristina, Kit arrived at the restaurant early, the off-the-beaten-path journey allowing her a respite from her responsibilities. She appreciated the serene drive, her thoughts clearing as the cityscape gave way to natural vistas.

She had chosen the location both for its authentic cuisine and its reputation for discretion. Here, she would meet Matt. Faced with allegations after a mission gone awry, his career hung in the balance, but Kit had a strategy to vindicate him.

As she parked her car near the lake, Kit braced herself for the pivotal conversation ahead. The stakes were high, not just for Matt but for their covert team. Batlava Lake, a remnant of Communist-era infrastructure now a scenic retreat, seemed the ideal backdrop for such a decisive meeting.

Approaching the jetty, Kit noticed Matt seated alone, a solitary figure against the placid backdrop of the lake. With the lunchtime crowd sparse, the scene was set for their discussion—a moment that could shape their next move and the future of her covert operations.

Approaching Matt, Kit greeted him, "Hey Matt, what's up?"

The signs of distress were visible on his face. His healing bruises and the discoloration around his left eye painted a picture of his recent ordeal from the cave explosion. His usually neatly combed grey hair was unkempt, and his weight loss was noticeable. Despite this, he smiled when he saw her.

"Hey, Kit. Not much. How about you?"

"Not bad," she replied, "You know—fighting crime—battling the bureaucracy... How's Sylvie? When's the baby due?" Spotting the waiter lingering at the far end of the jetty, close to the kitchen, Matt signaled him over.

"In a couple of months," he replied. "She's flying back to the UK for the birth to be close to her parents for support."

"Considering the circumstances, you could take the chance to go back with her," Kit suggested, scanning the menu. After a moment of discussing their choices, Matt relayed their order to the waiter—soup for Kit and a pizza for himself.

"Yeah, that's one way to look at it. I guess you've heard that I'm temporarily out of work," he said. "Of course, the police force back home will take me in."

"Of course," she said. "But it's a pity to see you leave under these circumstances. Do you have any updates on the investigation into the cave incident?"

"These things can take a while. They've interviewed me a couple of times. I've been put on administrative leave with pay, as you probably know."

Kit nodded, sipping her water and waiting for him to continue.

"They're interviewing everyone, even reaching out to Scotland Yard!"

"Why would they do that?" Kit asked. "They weren't at the scene."

"They're trying to ascertain the standard procedure in such instances."

"But you went by the book, right?"

"I think so. But it was far from a conventional situation."

"You couldn't have known there was someone nearby with a detonator."

"We're meant to secure a perimeter before advancing."

"The perimeter was secure, but the suspect showed up later. I saw it myself," Kit added.

"They'll probably interview you in the next few days. They've assembled an investigative team, which includes personnel from other missions and the headquarters."

"I'm sure they will, since I'm an eyewitness. They've taken the case off me because I'll have to testify in court. But I'd much rather be prosecuting than giving testimony."

"Damned politics!" Matt said, finishing his beer and signaling to the waiter for another. "My conviction rate is better than anyone else's. This whole situation is just wrong. No one could've foreseen that explosion in the cave. With terrorists and organized crime involved, it could happen at anytime."

Kit recollected times when Matt had supported her and Eva. He was an exceptional team leader. His current predicament seemed tremendously unjust.

"I think I'll join you for a drink," she announced. "A glass of house white?"

Matt nodded, placing the order. They both admired the serene blue lake and the lush green forest beyond for a few silent moments.

"What kind of options are you considering?"

"I could rejoin the force in the UK, obviously. But I still feel I have more to contribute here in Europe, particularly Kosovo. Plus, I prefer to have choices than be railroaded out."

"Ever thought about consulting work?"

His green eyes, troubled and on the verge of tearing up, shot her a sharp look. "What sort of consulting work are you suggesting?"

"You know, like security consulting, policy advice..."

"I did consider it, but the market is fiercely competitive. You have to hustle for assignments constantly."

"Consider this," she said, carefully. "We're aware that Kosovo isn't a sovereign state but an internationally administered territory. Maybe there's a chance to strike a deal to work with the ministry or even EUFOR, when the situation demands."

"But how would they foot the bill?" he retorted. "Kosovo already maintains a police force, and a EUFOR law enforcement team exists. How could a third-party even find room to operate?"

Kit looked down, then out over the undulating surface

of the lake. "In the US, governments are increasingly employing private security firms for their services. It's not exclusive to the US, either."

"Hmm," Matt said thoughtfully. "That's a valid point—it could be feasible for us to outsource services to the relevant authorities—or rather, have them outsource to us."

"Exactly," Kit agreed.

"But how could they manage the expenses?" Matt pressed. "Seems like a Hail Mary to me."

"A contact of mine mentioned that there might be a foundation willing to shoulder much of the costs. The contracting party, say the Kosovo Government, could then compensate with a much reduced or even symbolic amount. It might be under the table for a while." She found herself nervously fidgeting with her mobile phone, eventually placing it on the table as their orders arrived. Lunch was welcome distraction from trying to figure out whether Matt was buying into her narrative. A risk in dealing with investigators and lawyers, be they police or legal analysts, was their knack for spotting inconsistencies or loopholes. But Matt didn't look dubious. He stretched out his legs with a relaxed chuckle.

"Under the radar—that's our style, isn't it?"

"Exactly," Kit replied with a chuckle. "This looks delightful," she commented, dipping her spoon into the creamy broccoli soup. He nodded to the waiter who set down his pizza and salad.

"If your contact can materialize something by the month's end, I'd consider it. Otherwise, I'll be heading back to the UK, taking a breather before rejoining the force there."

Kit flashed a smile. "Excellent," she said. "I'll relay the message." She glanced up at Matt from beneath her lashes, trying to gauge his reaction. He was thoroughly enjoying his pizza. He seemed to accept her story. Or could it be that he saw through her, suspecting her involvement to be deeper than merely through a 'contact?' Surely, he should want more specifics, a name at the very least. Or perhaps he would bide his time, waiting to see what she could deliver.

"I have something else to discuss with you," she said tentatively.

He glanced up at her as he chewed on his pizza, washing it down with a swig of beer. "Hmm?" he mumbled between mouthfuls.

She drew a deep breath, gathering her thoughts. "I'm not sure if I've shared much about my family situation back home in New Zealand."

"You mentioned your mother and boyfriend back home, not much else," he said.

"My parents divorced when I was young. My father left New Zealand to work as a security consultant in Australia. We lost touch—until quite recently. He reached out to my mum in Auckland, saying he wanted to reconnect with me. After two decades of radio silence, it was jarring. But I thought, why not? His absence had left a gaping void in my early life, and I wanted to see how things had worked out for him."

She now had Matt's full attention. "What made him reach out after so long?"

"I did reconnect with him, briefly," she said, withholding the part of the story about their rendezvous in Thailand. "He expressed a desire to rekindle our father-daughter relationship. However, there were two interesting complications. One, the Australian Secret Service intends to run a thorough security check on him for his work, and they're interested in his family members. Secondly, there's an extradition request to Australia from Kosovo for a Serb accused of war crimes, for which he's the case manager."

Matt's interest in his meal dwindled. She could practically see his investigator's mind whirring, assessing all possible implications of the information she'd just imparted.

"What's your father's name?" Matt inquired.

"Vernon Chase."

"And his current whereabouts? Occupation?"

"I believe Melbourne. He still works in security, now as a consultant."

"That would a first, extradition to Kosovo from Australia. Who's the accused?"

"Petr Simić. He led a Serbian military battalion charged with war crimes in northern Kosovo. He went to Australia some time ago."

"So, your team in Eva's office are extraditing him?"

"No, all this was news to us. He said the plan is to establish a war crimes tribunal in Pristina. While the idea has been suggested previously, we were oblivious to any tangible plans. He said the Kosovo authorities are pushing to get things rolling, at least for initial suspect interrogations."

"So, Australia is planning to send Simić to Pristina, where he will be interviewed and detained awaiting trial. Is that right?"

"Seems to be. I'm a little skeptical about my father's sudden interest in me. I suspect it could be to do with this case, or perhaps he wants to prevent any unexpected backlash against it."

"You suspect he's worried that it might tarnish his reputation if his estranged daughter opposes the extradition trial, given your influential position with the chief prosecutor's office."

"Something like that. Honestly, I'm not sure what to believe."

"And how was it when you met?"

"He does look like he could be my father, as far as I can remember him from all those years ago. He's got the same complexion as mine. He did suggest a paternity test, if I wanted."

"That might not be a bad idea—you're dealing with a near stranger."

"Yeah, maybe. But to answer your question, our interaction was, under the circumstances, okay as far as it went. It's not easy, you know, after so long. He's a stranger and I still resent how he abandoned me and my mother."

"These things can happen," Matt mused, lost in thought for a while. "Are you seeking my view on this?"

"I'd value your insights, Matt. You have a keen eye for character assessment. I think we both can agree that the sudden appearance of my father raises questions. If it's not too much to ask, I was wondering if you could use your Scotland Yard contacts for some discreet inquiries? I'd be really grateful."

"Consider it done," he assured, already composing a message on his mobile. "I'll contact a friend over there."

"I can't thank you enough, Matt. I'm also uncertain about when he's arriving with Simić. Just consider it a heads-up. They'll probably keep it low-profile, I guess."

"Possibly," he agreed. "But keeping things under wraps in Pristina is like trying to hold water in a sieve. It's only a matter of time before the news leaks."

After their coffee, Matt paid the bill. As they prepared to leave, Kit casually suggested Matt should start considering priorities for a contract justice task force, in the event they could pull it off. She recalled Dua's comments about the dogfighting rings and the plight of restaurant bears. Focusing on environmental and animal protection could be a promising start.

"I'll give it thought, Kit. You know, I rather like the idea."

They exchanged a handshake, and she embraced him briefly. A wave of optimism washed over her as she approached her car. They truly did live in interesting times.

Kit sat at her cluttered desk, the glow of computer screens casting a pale light on her face. Her fingers flew over the keyboard as she communicated with Sergei, Alexei, and Silver in hushed tones through encrypted messaging apps. Disposable phones and secure technology were their only means of communication, a necessity to protect their plans from prying eyes.

Natalia had become a constant companion in Kit's apartment, her belongings slowly transferring from Romania to Kosovo. She respected Kit's need for privacy and kept her distance, offering only a nod of understanding as she entered the room where Kit was clearly preoccupied.

Under the guidance of Silver, Kit began to consider liquidating her assets. Sergei, utilizing his knowledge from his dealings in Chechnya, suggested creating a trust based in Fiji—a remote location that would attract less attention. Meanwhile, Silver's plan involved establishing a shell company in North Macedonia, where the difficult-to-access Cyrillic records would deter any potential investigations by English-speaking regulators. Their methods were pushing the boundaries of legality, but their determination for justice remained unyielding. If Kit's superiors in Berlin or New York discovered her tactics, there would be serious consequences. However, Kit was resolute in her pursuit of justice.

Eva stood out with her badge as Chief Prosecutor, starkly contrasting Kit's covert maneuvers. Facing a crucial decision, Kit had to either resign or cleverly conceal her wealth—especially with Australian officials closely examining her father's security status. A brief chat with Alexei set their plans into motion. Each option—Fiji or Skopje—held its own risks and rewards. A text from Sergei appeared on her screen, giving his support: *Clearing the chessboard, Kit. Creating your reality. I'm proud of you.* The warmth of his words was a rare comfort. *Thanks. Without you, none of this would be possible,* she replied.

Let's see where this leads, he typed back.

Matt's lack of suspicion was a small mercy. Eva, however, was another game. *Fooling Eva... that's a tougher play,* Kit confided.

It's in your hands. You know the board best, Sergei replied.

Various explanations for her sudden wealth raced through her mind. A lottery win, perhaps? Or an inheritance from a distant relative? Sergei seemed to favor the latter option.

"The EUFOR's financial struggles could make your 'inheritance' a welcome solution. It could even serve as a test run for larger plans," he said.

Alexei, always cautious about surveillance, had become somewhat of a ghost in their network. But their upcoming meeting promised to solidify their plans. Kit hesitated before typing. *I've messaged Alexei and suggested Fiji or Skopje as potential bases,* she eventually wrote, her thumb hovering over the 'send' button before finally committing.

As she let out a sigh and bit her lip nervously, as she

typed another thought, *Sergei, when will we see each other again?* The words on the screen made her feel vulnerable. *Dečani was amazing, but we never got the chance to talk.* She hit send before any more doubts could take hold. His reply came quickly. *I've got some trips coming up. Let's aim for Bulgaria or Slovenia. We'll find time.*

Kit nodded, her professional roles vying for attention in her packed schedule. *I'll make it work,* she typed back.

Then, Sergei's next message veered into unexpected territory. *Have you ever tried phone sex?* His bold question caused a tremor of shock to pass through her.

The cursor blinked mockingly as she struggled to process his words.

It's about staying connected... across the distance, he clarified after a pause that stretched too long.

Kit's reply was hesitant, a stark contrast to her usual assertiveness. *I've never... it's not something I've done.*

I want to see you, he wrote, the subtext as palpable as if he had whispered it in her ear.

A visceral reaction uncoiled within her, a warm wave that Sergei had always managed to stir, regardless of the miles between them. Her reverie was shattered by the shrill ring of her other phone, the one reserved for the mundane realities of life. Coffee splashed over her hand as she startled, cursing softly.

"It's Owen," she recognized the tone instantly. *Sergei, I have to go. We'll talk later.*

Kit remained still, the sound of the ringing phone a stark reminder of the duality of her life. Owen represented a stability, but Sergei... he ignited something else, something just as real and terrifying in its intensity.

The phone fell quiet, surrendering to voicemail. She couldn't face Owen now, not after the door Sergei had opened. It left her questioning her desires and the secrets that weighed on her conscience.

With a deep breath, she decided against returning Owen's call. Instead, she texted Natalie who was out with her new co-workers. *Do you think we could fit in another therapy session soon?* Sorting through the tangled threads of her life had become urgent—a puzzle she could no longer delay piecing together.

Chapter Twenty-Eight

L ocated on the outskirts of Pristina, the unremarkable gas station existed in a jurisdictional limbo, straddling both the fringes of the city and the administrative checkpoint leading to Belgrade. This was the perfect spot for Driton Kupi to meet with his associates, away from the prying eyes of law enforcement and the watchful gaze of Pristina's underworld.

Parking his VW Golf strategically, he selected a spot with outdoor seating that gave him an unobstructed view of the café entrance. With a brief nod, he signaled for a waiter and ordered an espresso with a single shot, along with an ashtray. As he sipped on his bitter coffee and smoked a cigarette, the scents mingled together, creating a familiar aroma.

Before long, a car pulled up and Fatmir and Andrea arrived, Driton's trusted lieutenants. They exchanged quick handshakes and pats on the back before joining Driton in a corner booth. In this dimly lit space, they were almost invisible to anyone passing by. After exchanging pleasantries, Driton quickly brought up the explosive incident at the caves that had resulted in the deaths of several law enforcement officers. "Why was Briz even at the caves when the police arrived?" he asked.

Andrea's concern was evident as he leaned in closer. "Someone on the inside tipped him off—my cousin's brother-in-law works in the military police office and keeps us informed on the quiet."

"And you made a decision without involving me?" Driton's eyes narrowed suspiciously.

Andrea stubbed out his cigarette in the ashtray and shifted uncomfortably. "Boss, you said phones were compromised. Briz was only supposed to observe. But he... he took it too far with the explosion."

Driton blew out a plume of smoke, his gaze unflinching. "From now on, we'll discuss everything here. This is our conference room," he motioned to the dingy surroundings. "We blend in with our surroundings here."

"Understood, boss." Andrea nodded while Fatmir played with a box of matches, his silence weighing heavily in the room.

"And did the blast erase all traces of our involvement?" Driton leaned back, already strategizing.

Andrea nodded. "Everything incriminating went up with it."

Fatmir spoke up, his voice low. "There's chatter at the precinct. Searches, suspicions. But no solid trail leads back to us. They've got nothing."

In the dim light, Driton's determined gaze pierced through the haze of smoke and uncertainty. In this in-between space, they were safe—at least for now.

"Make sure our contact in the military police keeps a close watch on the evidence logs. If there's any suspicious activity or mention of our case, we need to know immediately," Driton said in a low voice.

Fatmir, who had been quiet until now, leaned in closer and spoke in a hushed tone. "And if something does come up?"

Driton quickly surveyed their surroundings, checking for potential eavesdroppers. "Let's just say, a sudden fire in the evidence room wouldn't be unheard of," he hinted, leaving the rest unsaid.

Understanding passed between Andrea and Fatmir with slow, deliberate nods. "Fatmir, I need you to gather information on the EUFOR evidence room—security protocols, guard rotations, layout of the building. Is it possible to start an 'accidental' fire?" Driton asked.

"On it, boss," Fatmir responded confidently.

Driton continued, "Check for any off-site backups. And scrutinize the main building's condition. Old wiring could be our friend."

"Some evidence might be off-premises, in a storage unit on the military base," Andrea said.

"Then that's part of your recon. Understand? We need all traces gone," Driton emphasized. "It's better to eradicate the evidence than face these charges in court."

The men fell into a comfortable silence, taking drags of their cigarettes and sipping on coffee while checking their smartphones. Driton sent loving messages to Lira, then confirmed his plans for the upcoming weekend with another woman: his fiancée.

Returning to the main issue, he stated, "Remember to stick to the alibis for the time of the café and cave incidents. Were there any witnesses who saw Briz at the cave?"

Andrea shifted uncomfortably. "One of the prosecutors —she saw him."

"The Italian?" Driton's tone was sharp.

"No, the one with red hair," corrected Andrea.

Driton's hand tightened around his extinguished cigarette. "Her sighting connects us to the explosion. Were there casualties among the officers?" A solemn nod from Fatmir confirmed it, and a heavy silence descended upon them.

"We need information on her," Driton finally broke the silence. "Who is she?""Caitlin Chase, from down-under somewhere. Not long in Pristina but already on high-profile cases. She's involved with a Brit from the military police," Andrea reported.

Driton's mind raced, calculating the new risk. The redhead could unravel everything they'd built. She would have to be watched closely.

"We need to manage this," Driton mused, lighting another cigarette. "Surveil her for a few days. We might be able to execute a drive-by or get rid of her some other way. Let's neutralize the threat and pin it on Mal Mala."

"I'll handle it," Andrea volunteered,

Driton nodded in acknowledgment, understanding Andrea's eagerness to redeem his previous lapse in judgement—the missteps that led to the latest explosion and the consequential police fatalities that plunged them into a deeper quagmire.

"And what are Briz and Milon up to?" Driton inquired about the two absent team members. The others informed him that Milon was currently out of town visiting relatives, while Briz was laying low in the aftermath of the recent bombing incident.

"In that case, Andrea, take Briz along when you shadow the redhead," Driton said, his voice firm. "Together, I expect you to figure out a foolproof plan to clear her from our trail."

Andrea nodded, absorbing the information before posing his own question. "What's the latest on Mala?"

"He got the message loud and clear from the café bombing," Driton said with a sardonic smirk. "He'll be keeping his head down for a while. Besides, I've heard through the grapevine that the fool landed himself in cuffs trying to knock off the Dečani Monastery treasury over the weekend. The sheer stupidity!" His laughter punctuated the quiet. "That place is as well guarded as Fort Knox."

A flicker of concern crossed Andrea's face as he leaned forward slightly. "Boss, you're aware Mala ordered a hit on you, aren't you?" he probed cautiously. "Do you think he's called it off now?"

"I believe he now realizes that any further attempts on my life will result in dire consequences for him," Driton stated, his tone filled with grim determination. "In the meantime, our priority is to keep out of prison. And of course, keep our women satisfied."

His final remark drew laughter from the men. "And ensure that our women keep us satisfied in return." Fatmir chuckled. With that, they stubbed out their cigarettes, emptied their coffee cups, and headed towards their respective vehicles. As the dusk deepened, it cloaked their movements, rendering their departure from the roadside café practically invisible to all but the most observant onlookers.

Chapter Twenty-Nine

K it carefully put each piece of her outfit together, fully aware of the significance of her meeting with Visar Dreshaj. As both the Minister of Energy and Deputy Minister of Justice, he held immense importance for her goal of establishing a private law enforcement unit. Plus, she intended to gather information about the upcoming war crimes tribunal in Pristina.

Combining approachability and sophistication was her aim, as she swapped out her jeans for black trousers with a subtle red pinstripe—a nod to her iconic red heels. A sleek black camisole and a stylish leather jacket kept her warm against the evening chill, while a bold red handbag and lipstick added a pop of color to her ensemble.

Her choice of jewelry radiated an air of refinement; a white sapphire pendant and diamond stud earrings highlighted her professional demeanor and unwavering determination. Visar had chosen the All Gem Hotel as their designated meeting place. It was a luxurious establishment, rumored to be funded by foreign investors. Kit's involvement in a complex money laundering scandal had made her aware of the intricate financial ties between Austrian capital and Pristina's most prestigious hotel.

Her host had arranged for a driver to pick her up from her apartment, sparing her from navigating the city's uneven streets in heels or finding a taxi. Driving herself would have been too conspicuous and could have revealed her destination at the All Gem Hotel. The ride was brief, and upon arriving, Kit noticed the driver's familiarity with the hotel staff through their silent acknowledgments. He led her past the opulent lobby and crowded terrace to a secluded dining area where a table had been set up for their private meeting.

Visar was already at the designated meeting spot, absorbed in a phone conversation. His relaxed manner and charming personality hid his complicated past, involving both military and academic experiences. Despite their previous tense interaction at the casino, Kit felt confident about the evening ahead—as long as history didn't repeat itself.

Upon Kit's arrival, Visar ended his phone call and put out his cigarette. He stood up to greet her with a hug and kiss on each cheek before pulling out her chair. He then signaled to his driver who moved away but remained close enough to keep an eye on them. Knowing from past experience, Kit guessed there were likely additional security personnel nearby.

"Kit, my dear, you look stunning tonight," he complimented her smoothly with a smile.

A knowing smile played on her lips—she was adept at this dance of charm and strategy, ready to engage. However, she knew that tonight's success would require more than just allure. Before entering the meeting, she silenced her phone to avoid any interruptions from Owen or Sergei. She refused to let their calls or texts break the carefully culti-vated ambiance she aimed for. Despite any concerns, she maintained a radiant smile as she confidently met Visar's gaze.

"Thank you for making time in your busy schedule to meet with me," Kit said, extending her hand towards Visar who delicately took it. He gently pressed his lips to her wrist, subtly inhaling the scent from her pulse point. Kit couldn't help but notice the European flair in his manner, perhaps influenced by his Albanian roots.

As they settled into their seats, Visar wasted no time in ordering a pair of aperitifs, setting the tone for the extrava-gant evening ahead.

"I hope you've come hungry," he said with a smile, hinting at the indulgences to come. "I have prepared a special selection—oysters, champagne, and more to satisfy your appetite."

Kit's eyebrow raised in surprise. "Oysters, in landlocked Kosovo?"

"Yes," Visar confirmed. "With the right connections, one can enjoy these delicacies even here. They were flown in fresh from Tirana."

"Perfect," Kit replied, her voice smooth, tinged with appreciation. "I had a long day at work and no the chance for dinner."

Visar's face lit up. "Then you'll love the menu I've prepared for us. We'll start with the delicious bruschetta, followed by fresh oysters, and then your choice of herb-crusted lamb or grilled sea bass for the main course. And for dessert, we have chocolate mousse and strawberries." His description hinted at a well-thought-out meal, balancing both light and indulgent flavors.

"Visar, you're really treating me tonight. What brought this on?"

"We've been friends for a while now, Kit. I think we understand each other well and enjoy each other's company. I wanted to show my appreciation for our friendship and thought a special dinner would be fitting," Visar explained, his gaze softening.

Kit couldn't help but feel a flutter in her stomach at his words—an unexpected yet pleasant sensation.

"That's true," she responded. "I hope you won't this this is an overstep of our friendship, but there is something I wanted to discuss."

"Ah yes?" He arched an eyebrow at her. As per their unspoken agreement, they had steered clear of the usual pleasantries concerning family or spouses. Kit was aware that he was married, but his wife largely confined herself to her domestic life, seemingly indifferent to her husband's affairs outside the home.

"A friend of mine from New Zealand had this idea. She has connections with a charitable trust that focuses on improving legal systems in regions recovering from, or preparing for, conflict." Kit stopped speaking momentarily, observing Visar's facial expression before continuing. "Her suggestion was to bring in security experts as consultants in Pristina, and they would receive a modest fee to help cover their costs. She wanted to know if the government would be interested in such a partnership." Her proposal lingered in the air, a bold yet carefully planned proposition, waiting for his reaction.

He leaned back in his chair, observing her closely. "Security consultants? What exactly does that involve? We already have EUFOR and the prosecutor's office, as well as our local law enforcement."

"Well, there have been discussions about budget cuts for EUFOR, which raises concerns about future international support," she explained. "I thought that Kosovo could benefit from having its own informal, adaptable, yet efficient law enforcement capability."

"I've heard of similar initiatives in this region before. Does it involve any of your colleagues?"

She couldn't help but smile slightly. "It might..."

"And this friend of yours, where is she getting their funding from?"

She took a sip of her aperitif, feeling its warmth spread through her body and help her relax. "She didn't specify the source of the funds. This person has recently come into money and, I believe, prefers discretion," she explained.

"The funds aren't from Kosovo, I trust?" he probed.

"No, the benefactor mentioned a Central European connection," she assured him, just as a bountiful platter of oysters and hors d'oeuvres arrived at their table. The sight triggered an unanticipated hunger within Kit.

"I'd entertain the proposal if it were presented in a confidential document. It's something I could discuss with the Minister of Justice and the Prime Minister," he suggested, seemingly lost in thought. "An auxiliary enforcement capability could prove handy, considering the unpredictable nature of internal affairs. The recent bombing case accentuates that point. Rumors of a rogue police unit being involved are circulating, but proving such theories is a tall order."

"Indeed," she concurred, letting an oyster slide down her throat, chased by a sip of champagne. It didn't match New Zealand's Bluff oysters, but it was satisfying nonetheless.

"Undoubtedly, this initiative would necessitate us

working together more closely than we currently do. That means I'd need to coordinate closely with your friend, too," he stated, knowingly.

He was astute enough to realize that her 'friend' was a cover, and Kit was the real mastermind. Yet, he indulged her, providing both of them a face-saving out should the plan not materialize.

"Such coordination was on my mind," she responded, lightly dabbing at her lips, mindful of her lipstick.

"And could you shed light on your friend's motivation to invest in Kosovo?"

"I believe our benefactor sees potential in Kosovo and thinks extra support for the government could prove beneficial. The decision to cut EUFOR funding seems premature, considering the ongoing institution-building process."

"And the chain of command—would it link back to, say, British military intelligence?"

"No, the concept revolves around an independent task force," she clarified, stopping short of suggesting accountability to Visar—she couldn't promise that.

"So, essentially, mercenaries?"

"I'm not fond of the term 'mercenaries.' I envision a team underpinned by a respect for the rule of law and a commitment to community service."

"The concept has potential," Visar mused. "A pilot project might be prudent, to observe how things unfold. If word got out, we could face criticism. You know how the public clings to the familiar old guard."

"But you are old guard," Kit countered playfully. "So, we're safe there."

"Would you classify me as old." He laughed.

"I didn't imply age. I meant that you're a trusted figure within the leadership," she clarified.

Visar smiled warmly at her. "We could continue our conversation with greater privacy upstairs, considering its sensitive nature."

Her silence was her response. He had pre-emptively reserved a room—probably adjacent to his security detail.

"You're always one step ahead, aren't you?" she said, returning his smile. As they both got up, Visar signaled to his driver, indicating the side elevator. The driver promptly motioned to a security agent seated nearby

She took a deep breath. She was doing this for the cause, she told herself. But at the same time, she was excited at the prospect of a more intimate evening with Visar, after all these months. Would this mean? She'd have to confront any fallout later. *It's now or never*, she thought.

The flow of events that seemed to inexorably move her and Visar forward towards an intimate encounter was broken by a voice that Kit recognized all too well.

"Caitlin Chase, what are you doing?" It was Owen, bearing down on them in his army fatigues, face flushed red, hands balled into fists at his side. Kit turned to face him, speechless for a moment.

"Owen, what are you doing here?" Kit said at last, looking around behind him to see who was watching this confrontation.

"I asked first, what are you doing?" Owen demanded, inching menacingly closer.

"Owen, this is not your problem," she snapped, raising her voice. Despite the mens' comparable heights, Owen had the more muscular build. She couldn't quite tell who would come out victorious in a physical altercation—Visar's elegant appearance concealed his battle hardened experience. She observed as Visar's security team quickly closed in on them. The driver jumped out of his seat in a rush to join the tightening circle of protection around Visar.

Kit found herself rooted in place. Composure was critical in this instant. This confrontation could jeopardize her entire plan for Justice Pursuit International. The room had fallen eerily quiet except for their drama, the onlookers' eyes widened with curiosity and concern. Any intervention on her part could exacerbate the situation, adding fuel to Owen's rage and drawing more unwanted attention. On the other hand, her departure could distract Owen from the confrontation that loomed.

"Apologies, Visar. I must leave now. I appreciate the dinner, but duty calls. We will touch base on the matter we discussed," Kit announced, quickly extracting herself from the escalating tension. She turned and walked out of the room with deliberate dignity, looking neither to the right nor to the left. The driver kept pace with her as she exited the hotel, leaving behind a bewildering scene.

Back in her apartment, Kit sought refuge beneath the comforter draped over the couch. The echo of her encounter with Owen and Visar Dreshaj at the All Gem Hotel lingered. Her ploy had worked; Owen had tailed her to the hotel driveway but no further. More importantly, she clung to the hope that her maneuver hadn't sabotaged her plans for JPI, despite the possibility that the incident might push Visar Dreshaj to keep his distance.

She freed her hair from its band, shaking it loose. Fingers kneading her scalp, she willed the burgeoning headache to recede from her temples. Amidst the throbbing, her phone chimed—a message from Silver asking about her meeting with Visar Dreshaj. Silver was privy to her scheme of enlisting Visar for the covert task force, financed by her swelling fortune. Hesitant, her fingers paused above the phone's keyboard. After a brief contemplation, she chose transparency over sentiment.

The meeting went as planned, more or less, until Owen showed up and I had to cut things short. Visar is considering the proposal. Updates to follow. Sending the message, she let out a sigh, momentarily shedding the complexities of her personal entanglements to concentrate on the mission ahead.

Kit pulled herself off the comfortable couch and walked over to her desk. Her mind was consumed with thoughts of the task force and Visar Dreshaj, as well as her situation with Owen. Despite the uncertainty of their future, she valued his perspective and didn't want their bond to weaken too much. Determined to focus on the task at hand, she pushed away her pounding headache and swirling thoughts about Owen. She had a goal to achieve: making the task force a reality. She knew that she was on the brink of something important and nothing – not even her own confusion about her personal life—would hold her back. She turned to her laptop, ready to work through the night. The future may be uncertain, but Kit was certain of one thing: she would shape it in her own way.

Her laptop displayed a half-finished proposal for the JPI task force. Kit had devoted herself to the concept, imagining a group of skilled and ethical individuals working beyond the usual boundaries of law enforcement to forge a new chapter of justice. Her financial enterprise was her lever for transformation, to carve out possibilities free from the limitations and prejudices of existing systems. Yet, she was aware of the hurdles ahead. The possibility that her vision might be met with skepticism or opposition loomed large.

. . .

By the following morning, the storm seemed to have passed. Kit slipped into her professional outfit, a sleek ensemble of black slacks and matching jacket, the crisp linen of a white shirt contrasting against them. Her choice of black loafers completed the look, but it was her red patent leather bag and matching Hermes scarf that injected a fierce pop of color. She misted herself with an elegant, understated perfume. In this outfit, she felt every inch the formidable lawyer.

Yet, as she made her way to work, an unsettling quiet loomed. Owen and Visar remained silent, not a word since their confrontation the night before. An ordinary observer might have seen this as a return to peace, but Kit knew better. The tempest hadn't passed; it was merely gathering strength. She couldn't escape the feeling that the consequences of their altercation were far from over. Still, Owen's actions were his own, and she refused to accept blame for his lack of control. For all he knew, she and Visar were just sharing an innocent business drink—a common occurrence in their world. The fact that they had intended to take things further that night was neither here nor there, she reasoned.

Once at work, she sought solace in routine, burying herself in the teetering piles of files and unending flow of emails. She had to prepare a monthly brief for the regional and global OIDC headquarters in Berlin and New York on the main legal, as well as a status update on all the pending prosecutions. The familiar rhythm of her responsibilities brought a welcome distraction. But then, there was a snag. Owen's involvement in some of her cases now presented an obstacle. She had not foreseen how a personal disagreement could encroach on her professional terrain.

Kit pondered the possibility that Zena, perhaps taking quiet satisfaction in Kit's clash with Owen, might become a crucial intermediary in Matt's office should Owen persist in his silence. The idea of Zena delighting in the changing dynamics, however, unsettled her. As these thoughts swirled in her head, she hoisted a bulky legal file in one hand, the other cradling her morning coffee, preparing herself for whatever the day would bring.

But the comfort of routine, and the peace it offered, was short-lived. The jarring ring of her phone punctured her bubble of normalcy. It was Angel from the front office.

"Good morning, my dear," Angel said.

"Hey Angel," Kit responded. "What's going on?"

"Eva would like a word. Can you pass by her office?"

"Sure," Kit agreed, her attention already drifting back to her tasks. She nudged the file to one side, her grip on the coffee tightening.

Eva was engrossed in the morning newspaper when Kit found her, mission reports stacked to one side. Bambino, her canine companion, lay calmly in one corner, a bowl of water and chew toy nearby.

Eva glanced up, greeting Kit with a simple "*Bon giorno. Good morning.*" Without waiting for a response, she started right in, "Have you seen the news today?"

Kit shook her head. "I haven't had a chance to review the media briefings yet."

"You, Owen, and the Minister for Energy have all been mentioned in relation to an incident at the All Gem hotel last night." Eva peered at Kit over the rim of her chic black reading glasses.

Kit faltered, "They... they are?"

"The head and deputy head of mission want a briefing ASAP. Once one news outlet has it, the rest will follow suit."

"Shit," Kit muttered under her breath.

"So, what happened?" Eva asked.

Kit swallowed hard, grappling with the sudden, stark realization of her situation. "Well, I was just having a meeting with Visar. We occasionally meet for a drink to coordinate, as you know. But then Owen barged in, flying off the handle. I made a quick exit."

Eva cut her off, "It's all on camera. Someone from the hotel leaked it, and now it's circulating online. *Madre Mia!*"

"Th-there's not much to see," Kit stammered, scrambling to form a coherent response.

Eva gestured towards her computer, its screen displaying a snapshot of the events. Kit's eyes widened at the sight of her and Visar heading towards the VIP elevator, his hand on her lower back, and Owen storming towards them, fists clenched in visible fury. The urgency of Visar's security detail rushing to intervene filled in the untold part of the story.

"But there is something to see, especially concerning Owen," Eva observed dryly.

"I'm not sure what more I can add," Kit responded, feeling cornered.

"Right now, it's about damage control. Incidents like this can tarnish our reputation. Surely, you could've chosen a more discreet location for your rendezvous with Mr. Dreshaj?" Eva suggested, her tone coolly reproachful.

"I'll remember that—if there's a next time," Kit retorted, her voice tight. "He suggested it," she added.

"And, you should have informed me about the incident immediately. Damage control is crucial in these situations. I could have briefed the mission leadership and avoided them being blindsided by these media reports."

"You're right, Eva. I apologize. The entire episode just left me... rattled. I suppose I was hoping it would simply blow over," Kit admitted.

Eva's immaculately manicured nails drummed a steady rhythm on the table. "Now, this episode has sparked widespread speculation about your relationship with a government minister, and why Owen behaved the way he did."

"Storm in a teacup," Kit said dismissively.

"Pristina thrives on storms in teacups," Eva retorted. "But that's not the only news. Here's the second piece. I'm unsure which one will rattle you more: your father arrives today, and he's bringing the extradited Mr. Simić with him."

Kit's eyes widened in shock. "What!? How is that possible so soon?"

"Well, you did warn me about your father. Apparently, they're intending to conduct preliminary interviews. In the weeks to come, they're pushing to enact legislation that will establish a special war crimes chamber in the Pristina court. It seems Mr. Simić is set to be the first defendant."

"I didn't know he'd be here so fast!" Kit exclaimed. "Vernon made it sound like it could be weeks or even months in the future."

"No, Simić is arriving today, escorted by your father," Eva confirmed.

"What time?"

"I believe early afternoon. You might want to be at the airport to welcome them. There could be complications with border control, and it's better to be proactive."

Kit was torn between shock and relief. Shocked at her father's unexpected arrival, yet relieved that she wasn't facing immediate suspension or investigation following last night's fiasco at the hotel. Despite the history she shared with Visar, who had confidentially supported their work in the past, her task force plans required careful re-evaluation. Would Visar still be a willing player? Should she include Eva in the operation?

As Eva began to speak again, Kit focused back in. "You're currently held in high regard by mission leadership, thanks to your successful handling of events at the cave explosion. Otherwise, I shudder to think of the outcome. Owen is now on administrative leave, pending an investigation into his conduct. The video footage of him threatening the Minister of Energy could lead the police to press charges for disorderly threatening behavior."

"Oh no!" Kit gasped.

Eva nodded. "This situation shows the complications of mixing business and pleasure. It becomes less acceptable when it nearly results in an assault on a minister."

"I was only maintaining contact with Visar because of his contributions to our work," Kit said defensively.

"I understand," Eva replied. "We need to find the best way to present this to the mission leadership. They detest scandals involving OIDC staff. Security footage can be manipulated, of course, but the presence of numerous witnesses complicates matters. You did the right thing by leaving when you did."

"Testifying in either case isn't something I look forward to," Kit admitted, adding, "Thanks for understanding."

"One more thing," Eva said. "How did Owen find you and Visar at the hotel? Did you inform him?"

"In retrospect, I should have told him, but I didn't," Kit admitted. "Either he stumbled upon us by chance, which seems unlikely given our discreet location, or he was tailing me."

"Or someone at the hotel tipped him off," Eva suggested.

Kit was mulling over these possibilities when an uproar of ringing phones and approaching sirens shattered the quiet. Even Eva's dog perked up, sensing the commotion.

"Angel, check what's going on?" Eva called out to her assistant. "Contact the intelligence unit."

After a few tense minutes, Angel returned. "Two fires have been reported—one at the EUFOR military police headquarters in the top floor evidence lock-up. The other's at the off-site evidence storage area at Camp Sunrise."

Kit and Eva shared a look of shock. "Seems like Owen's outburst can wait," Eva said, her tone dry. "There's a real emergency to handle. Our bombing case evidence is at those sites."

"This could be a bold move to destroy evidence," Kit observed.

"And dangerous," Eva echoed.

"I need to see what's happening," Kit said, rising.

"Perhaps you'd better keep a low profile after last night's fiasco," Eva suggested.

"You're probably right," Kit said. "But I'm going anyway."

"The rebel we know and love," Eva said. "Just try calling Matt's office first, see who's going there."

"With neither Matt nor Owen around, I guess I'll try Zena," Kit agreed. Eva was already treating Bambino to some treats, indicating their conversation was over.

Chapter Thirty

With a sigh of relief for the temporary escape from a confrontation with senior management about last night's debacle, Kit weaved through the parking lot, sidestepping oil-slicked puddles that reflected the weak spring sunshine. The brisk wind that tugged playfully at her hair served as a brisk reminder of the turmoil in her thoughts, just as chaotic and untamed.

Why, during her moments of guided visualization with Natalia, had Owen appeared, seeking more commitment? His accusations about her secretive activities the previous night were accurate, yet she dreaded the thought of losing him. Owen was her stability, her constant, whereas Sergei was like a storm, captivating yet dangerous with his unpredictable moves. Silver was a constant enigma, unchanging. And Visar—she had nearly lost herself with him, or was it he who was nearly ensnared by her?

Her hand rummaged through her bag, eventually clasping the cold metal of her car keys. With a swift pull, she pulled open the door and sank into the driver's seat, her bag thumping onto the passenger seat. Kit took several steadying breaths, her forehead resting against the steering wheel's cool leather. The rhythm of her heartbeat slowed, revealing an unsettling clarity—she harbored love for each of them, but each stirred a different part of her soul. Was she a mosaic of affections, each shard able to love autonomously? Or had her past left her too fragmented to offer her whole heart to anyone?

Her hand found its way to her phone as she sat in the stillness of the parking lot. Regret welled up inside her as she remembered the tumultuous events of the previous night. Owen's instincts had been right, she had been on the precipice of cheating on him with Visar, all in the name of launching the new task force.

Her phone screen illuminated with a string of unread messages from Owen. She drew a deep breath, her fingers hesitating above the screen before she finally began to type a response. *Sorry about the misunderstanding last night. Please forgive me. Are you okay?* She hit send, a knot in her stomach. The idea that Owen's career could be in jeopardy because of their personal drama filled her with guilt.

Eva's words echoed in her mind and she considered reaching out to Matt's office for information. She quickly dismissed the thought; she couldn't stomach the idea of asking Zena for anything right now. Maybe one of her own coworkers would be there, like Axel, but she would rather face the scene of the fire alone than risk running into him. She made up her mind; she would go to the fire and see for herself what was going on.

A soft tap on the window pulled her from her thoughts. Dua was peering in, a question in her eyes. Kit rolled down the window.

"Eva said that you're going to the fire," Dua said, her

voice filled with a mixture of concern and excitement. "Can I come?"

"Sure, why not," Kit replied. Dua's energy and helpful nature was a welcome distraction. As if on cue, her phone chimed with a new message from Owen. *Sorry I acted like an idiot last nite. Let's talk.*

A wave of relief washed over Kit. The lines of communication with Owen were still working. Despite her dangerous dance with Visar, she didn't want it to ruin what she had with Owen.

Sure thing hon, she texted back. As she looked up, she saw Dua observing her, an eyebrow arching quizzically.

"It's just Owen," she explained.

"You guys are still talking?" Dua inquired.

Kit sighed. "Has the news reached everyone?"

"More or less," Dua grinned cheekily. "You know what they say—all publicity is good publicity."

"I'm not so sure about that," Kit replied, her lips curving into a smile despite herself.

"Come on, it's kind of romantic having two men fight over you. Maybe Owen will challenge Minister Dreshaj to a duel."

"Don't even think it! If that idea gains traction, he might just try." Kit chuckled. With her spirits slightly lifted, she fired up the engine, maneuvering the vehicle past the security guards, and into the traffic. The traffic was unusually dense, and an ambulance wailed past them, forcing its way into the crowded lanes. The majority of the vehicles were older, showing signs of wear, though interspersed were newer cars, likely driven by visiting diaspora members. Expertly navigating the potholes, Kit drove towards the city center. Ahead, a plume of greasy grey smoke billowed above the cityscape.

"What do you think happened to start the fires?" Dua asked.

"I'm not sure, but it's suspicious that two evidence lock-up areas caught fire at the same time."

"Do you think the same gang responsible for the bombing is trying to eliminate evidence?"

"It seems likely," Kit replied. "They've already set off an explosion in the café and at the cave site. Their best option now is to eliminate any evidence linking them to these crimes."

Dua glanced at the horizon to their left. There, in the distance, lay the military camp perched on a rise overlooking the city. A column of smoke was also visible there.

"So, what's our plan?" Dua asked.

"We'll conduct a preliminary inspection," Kit said nonchalantly. "I want to view the scene first hand. You should try to discretely take some pictures of the area and the crowd."

"I'll use my phone," Dua agreed, retrieving it from her bag.

Traffic had come to a crawl. The main road was blocked, and police were redirecting traffic into side streets. Kit slowed the vehicle, presenting their ID cards at the police checkpoint.

"Good morning, Officer," she greeted, "We're from the chief prosecutor's office, here on official duty." The young Kosovar police officer studied their IDs before nodding them through the barrier. Kit found a parking spot about half a block away from the site of the fire.

The moment Kit switched off the engine, a hushed silence enveloped them, momentarily masking the distant crackle of encroaching flames. As she reached for the door handle, Dua's hand on her arm stalled her—a silent warning that she chose to ignore. Kit's attention was momentarily caught by a white van, oddly out of place and angled strangely amidst the chaos, an anomaly that lingered at the edge of her consciousness.

With Dua's grip still lingering, they edged through the crowd that had congregated to watch the fire's spectacle. Fire engines barricaded the front of the threatened building, firefighters in a controlled rush to deploy their hoses towards the waiting hydrants.

The crowd was held back by a line of police, their presence a barrier against the tide of onlookers. Dua's touch again, less a warning now and more a clandestine communication, drew Kit's eyes to the phone in her hand. With a subtle nod, Kit gave the go-ahead. Dua slipped away, her movements casual as she pretended to take a call, all the while her phone's camera discreetly capturing the pandemonium and the vulnerable faces descending the building's shaking emergency ladder.

The air was pierced by sirens, as police units and ambulances stood ready for action. A woman, battling the effects of the smoke, leaned on a firefighter for support down the fire escape. Others, enshrouded in protective blankets, bore looks of dismay. Billows of smoke persisted in their surge from the upper windows, menacing the antenna array crowning the five-story edifice.

Kit's attention drifted to the periphery of the onlookers where she noticed two men standing apart, their gazes unsettlingly intent upon her. The first, with a neat military buzz cut, had a look of stern focus accentuated by the shadow of stubble on his jaw. His eyes, unwavering, seemed to carry the weight of a silent resolve. Beside him, a younger man possessed a sharp alertness in his dark eyes. His hair, a modern contrast of length and shave, added an air of calculated style to his appearance. Kit felt the weight of his interest like a tangible force, his gaze dissecting her movements with an almost clinical curiosity.

Britz's inquiry sliced through the ambient noise around them. "Do you think we should we tell Driton that the fire was set as planned?"

"Not yet," Andrea replied, his eyes still focused on Kit. "Our calls might be monitored. He'll see it in the news."

Britz nodded, his expression a mix of satisfaction and anticipation. "Our man inside did great work. Given the building's aged wiring, he found it simple to rig an ignition —just a little tampering, and the place was ready to light up. His compensation will certainly match the risk."

Andrea grunted agreement. "Seems like the second team was equally successful at the military camp." The ominous plume of smoke spreading from the hill behind the city center was evidence enough.

"See that redhead over there. That's the one on Driton's blacklist. The Albanian woman she was with earlier seems to have disappeared," the younger man pointed out.

Peering intently, Andrea commented, "Let's focus on the redhead." He gestured subtly towards a white Combi van, its rear windows obscured with paint. "She's getting close to our van."

"Are we thinking the same thing?" Britz inquired, a hint of anticipation in his voice.

Andrea's gaze met his sharply. "We take her now? The fires could provide us with the perfect smokescreen."

"Exactly, but shouldn't we get Driton's approval?"

"Again, the communication issue. If we move fast and cover her face, she won't see us. Driton appreciates initiative."

"We'd better get moving then. Soon she'll be past the van."

The biting wind had intensified, aiding the spread of the flames and carrying the acrid smoke through the air.

Kit walked towards the edge of the carpark area, trying to get a view of the side of the burning building. Perhaps the suspects were there to observe their handiwork, and Dua could get a photo of them. A nondescript white van was parked at an erratic angle. There was an alley way on the other wide that might allow a better view of the side of the building. She passed beside the van and was about to step up on the crumbling pavement from the road, when strong hands grabbed her around the waist and lifted her off the ground from behind.

Kit's Krav Marga training kicked in, and she instinctively went limp and heavy, dropping towards the ground, then kicked out hard behind her. She heard a crunch as her heel connected with her assailant's knee. He cursed and lurched back, and she prepared to run. But she was caught again from the side, her arms pinned close to her body and dragged towards the white van. She couldn't see who her assailants were. Kit struggled hard using legs, elbows, and fists. One man shouted to the other in Albanian, and she felt someone grab one of her legs. She was forced into the back of the van and pinned down by a hard knee to the small of her back. He quickly twisted masking tape around her wrists and then ankles. It was a difficult task, since she was flailing and screaming hard. He pushed her face hard down onto the base of the back of the van. He shouted more instructions in Albanian, and she felt her head pulled back by the hair, and a tape roughly placed across her mouth.

Someone wrenched her handbag out of her grip and tossed it onto the ground outside. The doors slammed shut and in a few moments the van lurched forward, roughly bumping over the pavement and then back onto the road.

"Damn, you hurt my knee," said the man roughly in accented English.

She tried to scream, and kicked back hard with both legs, but didn't connect with anything. She hated being separated from her handbag and in particular, her mobile phones. No one would know where she was, although Dua would start looking for her pretty soon. She heard one man speaking to the other and then someone put a sack over her head so she couldn't see anything more. She tried to make a sound, but her voice was muffled by the tape and the sack over her head, as well as the noisy engine. However, she could hear that voices were raised at the front of the van and the two men seem to be having an exchange of views.

They travelled for some 10 to 15 minutes. With lack of suspension in the van, the potholed roads and the smell of petrol fumes, Kit started to feel nauseous. A horrifying real-ization hit her: if she were to vomit now with her mouth sealed, she could choke on her own bile. Sweat trickled down her forehead. She pressed it against the coarse sack in an attempt to wipe it off and tried to take calming breaths.

However, it was not long before the van stopped. The men continued to argue in curt Albanian. She heard the door open, and she was roughly pulled out of the back of the van. They hustled her into a building. By the sound of the echo suggesting an open space, she guessed it might be a warehouse. Trying to calculate possible location based on the length of the trip she guessed that she might be some-where on the outskirts of Pristina, perhaps even towards the airport, where she knew there were several warehouses used by importers and exporters.

Chapter Thirty-One

Dua meandered among the spectators gathered to observe the firefighters, making a show of texting and speaking on her mobile while discreetly capturing photos of the crowd and the firefighting efforts. The acrid tang of smoke still lingered in her nostrils despite the fire now seemingly under control. The EUFOR military police had arrived, but it was odd to find Matt and Owen absent. Both men were currently on suspension, yet the military police operated as usual.

After about thirty minutes, Dua started looking for Kit, expecting to spot her nearby. Yet, there was no trace of her. Dua shot her a message, but it went unanswered.

With concern growing, Dua stepped away from the crowd to phone. The call rang, unanswered. But from a distance, she heard the familiar ringtone. Perplexed, she redialled, following the sound around the corner. There, near a car park, lay Kit's designer bag with the ringing phone inside. Rushing over, she retrieved the bag, her heart sinking like a stone as she pulled out the still ringing phone. There was no sign of Kit.

With a heartbeat hammering in her ears, Dua called Eva, her words spilling out as soon as the call connected. She explained how she and Kit had split up to canvas the area more effectively and her subsequent discovery of Kit's deserted bag.

Eva was silence for a moment, heavy with implication. "She might have been taken," she said at last. "Given the bombing case suspects and Kit witnessing their actions at the cave, they're the likely culprits."

Panic edged Dua's question, "What should I do?" as her breath caught in her throat.

"Find a café, somewhere public. I'm calling Matt. His badge may be on the shelf today, but his expertise isn't," Eva said. "Keep Kit's bag with you—Don might need it for Max to try to find a scent, even though their trail likely went cold with a vehicle getaway."

Dua acknowledged, her gaze darting through the deserted streets, the need to leave the vulnerable area pressing upon her. "There was a white van here before parked at an odd angle. It's gone now."

"That could be the one. I don't suppose you got the plate number."

Dua thought for a moment. "No, sorry. It might even have been missing plates."

"Once you're safe, send me the location," Eva continued, clearly making an effort to keep her voice level.

Dua's thoughts drifted to the chaos she had photographed at the Police HQ, the flames still gnawing at the structures, with EUFOR and emergency services swarming around the scene. "The assignment Kit gave me, the crowd photos—it all seems so trivial now. We should have stayed together," she murmured, her voice trailing.

"We'll find her. Driton Kupi must be the key," Eva said.

"But we need to move quickly. Matt will work with Owen and Don. We'll loop in the Kosovo Police as needed. Can you alert Axel and the others, then wait at the café?"

"Heading to the Black-and-White café, now," Dua said, already walking. "I'll wait there until I hear from you or someone from the team comes to get me. Do you think Kit will be okay?" Dua's voice hitched.

"I certainly hope so," Eva said before disconnecting.

As Dua continued on her way, she scanned her surroundings, but there was nothing suspicious. A few passers-by were headed towards the fire, drawn by the spectacle. Clasping Kit's handbag tightly under her arm, she made her way to the Black-and-White Café. Outdoor tables were already set out to welcome the warmer spring weather, but Dua opted for a seat inside, close to the window, wanting to avoid attention.

Once settled, she ordered a macchiato coffee and messaged Eva that she had arrived safely, before scrolling through her phone. There were several unread messages from Besim, but she couldn't bring herself to respond yet. Her thoughts whirled in a continuous loop, but she felt like she was treading water. Sitting idle while waiting for someone from the team was a struggle. Her hands, restless, fidgeted with her coffee cup, turning it aimlessly. If only the coffee grounds at the bottom could reveal Kit's whereabouts, but she had no talent for such divination methods.

To pass the time before her coworkers arrived, Dua distractedly rifled through Kit's handbag in the unlikely event that there was something that might offer clues about her location. As her hand brushed against Kit's phone, the idea occurred to her that it might hold some information about her friend's predicament. Part of her felt uncomfortable about intruding on Kit's privacy, but urgency won over. After booting up the device, Dua was met with the anticipated lock screen. She sighed heavily and spent a moment trying to open the phone, without success.

As she was about to return it, she noticed another object wedged at the bottom of the bag, concealed in a crumpled paper bag. She carefully extracted it, revealing a cheap disposable phone, the kind one could buy off the streets of Pristina or Tirana for a few euros, no registration required. This phone was unlocked, perhaps due to the impact damage it had sustained or just its throw away system hadn't merited a lock. Its systems were basic, but effective enough, offering less security compared to modern smartphones. The number was unfamiliar to Dua, certainly not one she knew Kit used. Opening one of the messaging apps, she found a thread of texts with individuals named 'Silver', 'Sergei' and 'Alexei.'

Her hand shaking, Dua threaded her way through Kit's private texts. The messages with Silver revolved around investments, massive amounts of money traversing the lesser-known corners of the internet, and casual remarks about bypassing anti-money laundering measures. As the chilling understanding settled in, Dua whispered, "Oh, my God." Could it be possible that Kit was entangled in illicit transactions? Cryptic discussions with someone named Alexei alluded to shell corporations and freeports in seemingly improbable locations. Fiji, where was that exactly? Dua pondered.

Turning her attention to the messages exchanged with Sergei, Dua was reminded of a suspect by the same name who had slipped through their grasp in a past investigation. He was the one that evaded an Interpol arrest warrant.

With a sinking feeling, Dua tried to reconcile this information suggesting a close association the mentor she thought she knew. Recollections of Kit's frequent out-of-town trips and Owen's recent jealous outburst surfaced, forming a disturbing pattern. She tried not to jump to conclusions. Surely there had to be a more reasonable explanation.

She was left wondering how far Kit's secret life extended. Was she leading a double, or even triple life? The extensive investments were a stark contrast to her modest prosecutor's salary. And her involvement with Sergei, a potential criminal, raised a slew of uncomfortable questions.

Scrolling through other messages, Dua discovered references to therapy sessions. Considering the magnitude of her secret activities, that Kit needed professional psychological support seemed plausible.

Dua realized that the phone itself was unlikely to reveal Kit's current whereabouts, which was the most pressing concern. She would need to address these revelations later. She was torn about whether to confront Kit about the second phone or to simply dispose of it, pretending ignorance of its existence. The latter option would undoubtedly simplify matters, avoiding office disputes and potential damage to her career.

Lost in her thoughts, Dua glanced up to see Owen and Zena striding toward her, evidently alerted by Eva to her location. Owen looked perturbed, and Zena was struggling to keep up with his pace. A surge of anxiety washed over Dua. She swiftly turned off the phone and slipped it into own her bag just as the pair reached the table, putting off a firm decision about what she had discovered until later.

Dua rapidly recounted to Owen and Zena what had happened. Owen, his eyes taut with concern, grasped Kit's bag and began an impromptu investigation.

"Where's her phone?" he said as he rummaged with increasing frustration through the bag's contents.

Dua averted her gaze and shrugged. "Isn't it in there?"

Zena commandeered the bag and upended its contents onto the table. Spilled out before them was an array of items that painted a portrait of Kit: her wallet housing cards, her keys, a tube of lipstick, a black legal notebook, her OIDC ID, and an elegant pen.

Zena's fingers closed around Kit's smartphone. "Got it," she said. She attempted to unlock the device, but the security code thwarted her efforts as it had Dua's. "Nothing we can use right now. What did she say during your last conversation?" Zena asked Dua.

"She just asked me to scan the crowd that had gathered to watch the fire. Said we'd reconvene in a bit."

"So, she never said where she was going?"

"No," Dua confirmed, her eyes scanning the passers-by outside, as if expecting Kit to appear at any moment.

Zena pressed on. "How did you find her bag?"

"I began searching for Kit when I hadn't heard from her and followed the path back to where I'd last seen her. I'd dialed her number and heard the ringtone. In the car park, I found her bag on the ground. I contacted Eva, and... you know the rest."

Owen yanked out his own mobile phone and dialed Kit's number. As the call echoed through the phone lying before them on the table, it went unanswered, eventually leading to voicemail.

Dua shifted uncomfortably as she questioned whether her decision to hide the second phone was wise. It could hold clues that might help track Kit. On the other hand, she was pretty confident that Kit wouldn't appreciate her private exchanges regarding financial dealings with Silver or the heated messages with Sergei being made public. Dua had acted on instinct and she desperately hoped her gut feeling had steered her right.

She promised herself that she would scrutinize all the messages later for any potential leads. For the moment, however, it seemed more plausible that their suspects had abducted Kit, especially considering she could positively identify at least one of them from the cave bombing, and her disappearance had nothing to do with the contents of the burner phone.

Meanwhile, Owen dialed Matt who informed him that they had successfully located Driton Kupi. Evidently, Kupi had bolted from his apartment and was now navigating the city streets at an alarming speed, with Don in hot pursuit.

"Let's hold on for a few minutes," Owen suggested, "We'll get an update on Kupi's movements. He might lead us to Kit."

Within the hour, Dua was hunkered down in the back of a Jeep, the hum of Owen's steady driving the only sound. Matt rode shotgun, while Zena, her blonde hair falling over her face, sat beside Dua, the tension palpable as they pulled up outside the nondescript building in Pristina's industrial outskirts. They were a mismatched convoy of Kosovo police, EUFOR officers, and undercover diplomatic cars, all unnoticed by the news crews for now. Smoke from distant fires smeared the sky, a perfect cover.

"Major Hackman and Owen aren't exactly on active duty," Zena remarked, her voice low and conversational. "Yet here they are." She shot a glance under her blonde fringe at Owen in the driver's seat. Zena's whisper barely cut through the cabin's hum.

Before Dua could respond, Owen cast a look over his shoulder, his voice a gruff growl, "Damn straight." Matt only responded with a noncommittal grunt, his attention seemingly absorbed by the barely discernible figures he could make out through his military-grade binoculars inside the warehouse.

Don approached their vehicle with an update. "Kupi's in there with at least two others. We still aren't sure where Kit is," he said, indicating the warehouse.

"Do you think she's in there?" Owen said sharply.

Matt kept his eye on his scope. "That's where the trail leads."

Dua spoke, her tone low and urgent. "Kit's the main witness in the cave bombing—she saw the bomber with the detonator."

"She should've been under protection," Owen said. "We knew the risks to her."

"I did my best. She turned it down," Matt said. "We can't force her."

Dua's gaze snapped to a white van parked nearby, a chill running down her spine. "That van... I remember it from the lot where Kit disappeared."

A beat of silence, then the realization settled like a storm cloud.

"They could have snatched her in that," Matt said. "I'll call Kupi and see what he says. Sargent?" he queried looking towards Owen.

Owen retrieved Kupi's phone number from his notebook, entered it into his phone, and then passed it to Matt.

Zena lent forward between the two men. "Are you planning to call him?" she asked. At Matt's affirmative nod, she continued, "I've trained in hostage negotiation. Let me handle it."

"And what would you say to him?" Matt asked.

"I'll figure it out once I connect with him," she said.

After a beat, Matt handed her the phone. "Alright then, go ahead."

Zena, phone in hand, flashed them a cheeky grin. "Wonder if I should use my midnight DJ voice?"

Owen eyed her skeptically, "Your what?"

She just waved him off, still smiling. "Never mind. It's an FBI negotiating technique—to sound chill and get the target to relax."

"What kind of nonsense are they teaching at these courses?" Owen grumbled under his breath.

But Zena, her hand resting lightly on Owen's shoulder in a calming gesture, had already initiated the call. She hit the call button.

Several rings later, a gruff voice broke through the silence in Albanian. "What do you want?"

"Hello, this is Zena Letalova. I'm a liaison officer with EUFOR. How are you today?" She maintained a relaxed and friendly tone that surprised Dua.

The voice on the other end of the phone grunted. "I've had better days," he said, switching to English. "Why are you calling?"

"Has he looked out of the window recently?" Owen muttered. Lena signalled him to keep quiet.

"I was wondering if we could help each other," Zena said. She was looking intently at the warehouse window ahead of them, the smoke-filled breeze blowing strands of blonde hair across her eyes and mouth.

"How's that?" Kupi said.

"Well," she said slowly, almost lazily. "It looks like maybe you have something we want, and perhaps we can do something for you."

"What are you thinking of?"

"You said you were not having a great day. Perhaps I can help with that."

"Officer Letalova—is it? You've got my number, so I suppose you know I'm a senior detective with the Kosovo police. I am interviewing a confidential informant here. I don't need interruptions, I need a little space."

"You need a little space." Zena repeated after him.

"That's right. I see you've got this place almost surrounded—you can send the vehicles back to base. I've got everything under control."

"How could I do that?"

"Just tell them the situation's under control. That Driton Kupi's got things under control."

"Maybe we could do that," Zena said. She mouthed to Matt, "Get them to pull back a bit. A few vehicles could wait around the corner out of sight."

Matt looked at her in a way that expressed some doubt, but he nodded to Owen to go and see what he could do. Dua beckoned him to come close to her as he exited the vehicle. "Hostage negotiations 101—establish a rapport with the kidnapper."

"What do you mean?" he asked with some irritation.

"That's what Zena's doing. Trying to develop some kind of understanding with Kupi."

Owen shrugged, but his whole body was tight. "Hostage negotiations 101—get proof of life."

There was a stifled cry coming from the room, audible over the phone, a woman's voice, starting to call for help and then silent again. Owen started to come back towards the vehicle, his voice raised.

"That's Kit!" he said.

Zena waved him away and pointed to the vehicles he was supposed to get moved further back.

"Actually," Zena responded, her tone hinting at a light-hearted curiosity. "We're looking for our legal officer, Caitlin Chase. Haven't seen her around, have you?"

"What makes you think so?" came Driton's guarded response.

"We have reason to believe someone in that building could help us locate her. Perhaps." Zena let the statement hang in the tense silence. The stillness was finally broken by the noise of a few vehicles retreating.

"Give me a moment, I need to consult with my people. Can you wait? I'll call you back," Kupi suggested.

"Absolutely," Zena assured him, allowing a hint of warmth seeping into her tone. "I can do that."

As the call ended, Zena put down the phone and locked eyes with Matt. "Not entirely bad," she assessed. "He seems open to a dialogue."

Matt, however, seemed less than convinced. "Sure, but we heard what sounded like Kit screaming. He didn't even confirm she's in there."

In that moment, Owen returned to the vehicle, his resolve evident. "I'm going in. I have to get her out."

"Hold on," Zena interjected. "He's engaging with us— let's see what he offers."

Matt turned to Owen, holding a hand up to halt his movement. "Sargent, we're all worried about Kit. But right now, we need to wait for the next move. Storming in might provoke a reaction we can't control. Ms. Letalova, what's your plan now?"

"We wait for his call," Zena stated calmly. "This might take a while. Those who aren't needed here should head back to headquarters. I'm sure there's work piling up."

Dua was quick to object. "No way, I'm staying."

Zena shrugged.

"The press might show up any moment. I could, you know, liaise," Dua offered.

Chapter Thirty-Two

Hauled out of the white van, Kit had kicked and thrashed as two men carried her inside the warehouse. They deposited her in a warehouse corner, leaving her bound and gagged. Time dragged on as they discussed in Albanian, with only the discomfort of a bright spotlight for company, its glare making her eyes sting and clouding her ability to think.

Under that harsh light, sweat pooled at the small of her back and trickled down her forehead. Around her, the sounds of agitation were unmistakable: chairs scraping against concrete, the restless movements of her captors. A sharp cocktail of oil, paint, adhesives, and building materials assailed her senses, punctuated by the distinctive odor of cigarettes as the men lit up. Invisible from her position, their presence was betrayed by the striking of matches and the smell of smoke, which seemed to lend a measure of calm to the tense atmosphere.

The dull, cold light of spring penetrated the grime on the windowpanes, hiding the world outside. Her hands, strained against their bonds, twisted in vain, only tightening the tape's cruel grip on her flesh. The bonds around her ankles were just as unyielding. Connecting the dots now seemed straightforward; these men were likely accomplices in the bombing case. She recalled being spotted at the cave right before the suspect triggered the explosion. It was only logical they would target her, despite her persistent dismissal of cautious advice, opting to decline special protection. Thoughts raced through her mind—could anyone possibly discover her location?

The older captor's abrupt action broke her focus as he ripped the tape from her mouth to speak.

"What's your name?" he demanded.

The question seemed like a trap to her. Revealing her true identity could seal her fate more certainly than if she feigned being the wrong captive.

"Caitlin," she replied eventually, calculating that they must already know who she was.

Meanwhile, Kupi was on the phone, conversing in English with a woman. The distant hum of vehicle engines filtered in, kindling a faint hope of rescue. Yet, it was possible her presence remained undetected. Overcome by a sudden urge, Kit screamed for help, her voice soaring, her body straining against the restraints. But as Andrea leaned over her, he absorbed the full force of her cry. His response was swift; his hand, now a tight fist, struck Kit's chin. Her head snapped back, colliding with the concrete. The blow didn't bring pain, just a severe jolt, a scatter of stars behind her eyelids, and then a descent into darkness.

She found herself thrust into the lush forest clearing she had conjured during her therapy session with Natalia. A sudden sensation of falling swept over her, plunging her backwards into a lagoon. The imposing trees and lush ferns of the native New Zealand bush swirled around her, the spiraling tableau pressing down as she broke the water's surface and began to submerge. Her eyes opened to shafts of sunlight piercing the blue-green water, transforming into ethereal beams beneath the lagoon's surface.

Struggling for breath, she fought against the oppressive water, but her limbs refused to respond. The suffocating sensation of drowning began to overwhelm her, and her hair, freed from its confines, billowed around her face. Disorientation seized her, nausea curled in her stomach, and the world above her blurred through the algae-tinted water.

The silhouette of a figure cut across the sun, pulling her further into the shadowy depths. As a second wave of nausea roiled through her, her wavering consciousness threatened to slip away completely. A voice, muffled and distorted by the water, murmured nearby. The figure dove, hands slicing through the water and reaching for her. The light splintered into a kaleidoscope of shards, piercing her eyes and head with their brilliance.

Suddenly, she was yanked upwards, back towards the surface, breaking through into the realm of breath and life. She gasped, coughing, a violent expulsion of the bile still lodged in her throat.

A man's voice echoed in her ears, soothing and familiar, yet elusive. "Kitten, come back, I've got you."

"Kitten?" Struggling against the blinding light, Kit narrowed her eyes, willing them to open. In a heartbeat, she was catapulted into the sunlit memories of her childhood, chasing her sister within the rainbow mist of a lawn sprinkler. Their laughter, pure and unrestrained, wove through the air, mingling with the steady hum of their father attending to the smoky grill. His voice, warm and inviting, called them to join the feast, the tantalizing scent of barbecued chicken and sausages intermingling with the crisp aroma of garden-fresh salads prepared by their mother.

"Kitten, come here, it's time to eat," he beckoned, his voice a lifeline in the haze of her mind.

She reached for her sister, their hands clasped in shared merriment as they shuffled toward the picnic table, their giggles competing with the promise of the meal ahead. Abruptly, the scene morphed, and she was engulfed in water, yet not alone. A sleek, vivid presence cut through her peripheral vision—the Tracer Fox, her power animal, its fiery coat a stark contrast against the aquatic blues and greens. With grace and intent, it weaved through the water, leading her upwards, toward the shimmering surface.

As if in echo, her father was there once again, his face etched with effort as he pulled her from the watery depths. She surfaced, gasping, a sharp pain stabbing through her temples. With the fox as her beacon, she was ushered back to the threshold of consciousness, back to the reality of the battle that awaited her.

Outside, Zena was back on the phone with Kupi.

"Hi Driton, if I can call you that," she said. She gulped slightly and cleared her throat. It was difficult to keep the relaxed, even tone of voice that they taught in the FBI training, the midnight radio DJ. After hearing Kit scream, she wondered what was going on. They had yet to provide proof of life, or really offer anything of significance.

"What is it?" he replied gruffly over the phone.

"We moved the vehicles back, like you asked. I know you've got everything under control and there—but I'm just wondering, could you just let us know whether Caitlin Chase is in there with you?"

Before anything else could be said, Matt grabbed the phone from Zena. "Hello, Detective Kupi," Matt said. "It's Major Hackman here, from the EUFOR police. We've been looking for Caitlin. I just received word that her father has arrived in Pristina. It's been a long time since Mr. Chase saw his daughter, and it's really important..."

At first Zena was surprised when Matt took the phone off her, but when she heard his play, she gave him the thumbs up and shrugged.

"Major," Kupi said. "I think we met a few months ago. So, her father is here, you say?"

"Yes, he just arrived from Australia. Actually, he's bringing a Serbian war criminal—accused war criminal, I should say, being extradited to Kosovo."

"Ah, yes, I think I heard something about that," Kupi said. Now it was like they were two colleagues chatting over the phone. "That was a great job bringing that Serbian back here. Simić, I think his name was, wasn't it?"

Dua heard a vehicle arrive and turned around to see who it was. An armored OIDC vehicle pulled up behind them. Eva got out, dressed in her lawyer's black suit, followed by Christina and a redheaded, middle-aged man that Dua doesn't recognize. He had a well lived in, weather-beaten freckled face that had been burned too often in the sun. Dua slipped out on the Jeep and went to meet them.

"*Ciao*, Dua," Eva said. "What's going on?"

Dua quickly bought Eva up to speed.

"So, do we know that Kit is in there?" Eva asked.

"We're not sure, but we think so," Dua said. "Zena and Major Hackman have been trying to talk to Driton Kupi inside, trying to establish a rapport, I think. We heard a woman scream." Dua looked away, biting her lower lip.

"Right," Eva said. She glanced at the man beside her.

"This is Caitlin's father, Vernon Chase. He's in town on other business."

"The extradition case," Dua said.

Vernon looked surprised.

"Everyone knows everything here," Eva quickly explained before guiding him towards Matt and Owen.

Not everything, Dua thought, remembering Kit's phone in her bag with its clandestine messages.

Owen got out of the Jeep and further briefed Eva and Vernon about what had been happening. Christina went to talk to Dua, who was hovering behind Eva and Vernon, trying to hear what was being said. Vernon asked Owen if they had schematics of the warehouse.

"I'll try to get them," Owen said. He called a number on his radio telephone and requested headquarters to send a map of the area, and, if possible, plans of the building at their GPS coordinates as soon as possible. Like many streets in Pristina, it did not have a formal address. "They should be able to do it in a few minutes, I hope," Owen said.

"What are you thinking?" Eva asked Vernon.

"Well, I was wondering if there was a back entrance, or even access through windows that might not be visible to the kidnappers immediately."

"In case we have to breach," Owen said. Vernon nodded but said nothing as he squinted intently towards the building.

Matt was still talking in circles with Kupi, who continued to be evasive. Kupi had requested transport away from the current location to take his suspect back to his Police station for interrogation. Owen checked his phone and opened the attachments to the message. There was a diagram of the area and plans for the warehouse.

"Good old former Yugoslavia," Owen muttered. With

its bureaucracy still intact, there had been more regulations before the break-up of the former Yugoslav Republic into its composite territories and republics.

"Can I see, mate?" Vernon asked his broad Australian accent.

Owen handed him the phone, with the open schematics. "I might just take a copy, if you don't mind, so I can take better look."

"Go ahead," Owen said, and Vernon keyed in his own phone number, forwarding the message.

Matt clicked off the call and sat for a moment and passively gazing towards the battered exterior of the building.

"How's it going?" Zena asked.

"I thought we were getting somewhere, but Kupi just rung off on some pretext or another." Matt said. "I'd really like to get this done before nightfall."

Eva introduced Vernon to Matt, and the two men shook hands.

"He's accompanying Simić, who is being extradited from Australia for trial in Pristina on war crimes," Eva said. "But now we have a more pressing problem. We think they've got Kit inside. These are our prime suspects for two fatal bombings and she's a key witness."

Vernon was studying the plans of the building on his phone.

"aYour negotiations have stalled, is that right?" Eva asked.

"It seems so," Matt said. "I'd really prefer that we do something before nightfall. As far as we know, they've got no food or water in there. Tempers can fray. It's possible that Kit is injured."

Vernon looked up with concern written over his face. "What makes you think that Kit might be injured?"

"We heard a woman scream, that was cut off and nothing since," Owen said.

"And we weren't able to speak to her," Zena said. No proof of life. "He did more or less admit that they have her in there. Kupi was asking for transport, but then he broke off."

"Nothing for it, but to start again, I suppose," Vernon said. "It seems like things might take a bit longer. If you don't mind, I might give the office back in Canberra a call. Let them know that I arrived in Pristina, and Simić is okay, at least. I delivered him into custody before I came here."

Matt nodded. "We'll try calling Kupi again. Zena can try those FBI negotiation tactics again."

Vernon nodded. "I'll be back in a few," he said quietly to Eva and stepped back away from the vehicle. After a few moments, Dua announced that she needed to stretch her legs. She walked back across the parking lot, in the same direction that Vernon had taken.

From a measured distance, Dua shadowed Vernon, curiosity fuelling her pursuit. Their companions were engrossed in their fraught telephone negotiations with Driton Kupi, the front warehouse occupied their focus. No one seemed to pay much attention to her departure.

Vernon stopped in front of a building to the right of the parking lot. He pulled out his phone, checked some messages and then dialed a number. He made a few short comments, perhaps just leaving a message and then rang off. Dua positioned herself behind a nearby car, and waited there, occupying herself with her own mobile phone messages, glancing up occasionally out of the corner of her eye towards Vernon.

He checked around quickly, before ducking down an alley way close to him.

Rapidly pocketing her phone, Dua pursued Vernon with brisk, quiet steps. By the time she peeked around the alley's edge, he was already vanishing around the far corner.

Dua's heart raced she realized that Vernon was attempting a stealthy entrance into the back of the building where Kit was imprisoned. A moment of hesitation gripped her—the option to call for backup beckoned, but she dismissed it almost immediately. Involving the others could spell disaster, compromising Vernon's covert approach or, even worse, escalating the situation. The waning daylight underscored the urgency; with each passing moment, Kit's peril grew.

Kit had not only introduced Dua the intricacies of international law, but also modeled to her a strong sense of independence and determination. Now, it was Dua's turn to step out into uncharted territory. She trailed behind Vernon with a renewed sense of purpose, knowing that if his lead turned out to be a dead end, she could always regroup with the others. But if it led to Kit, this could be Dua's chance to repay her mentor by diving headfirst into danger.

Sure enough Vernon looped around the warehouse. He had obtained the building's blueprints from Owen, and Dua surmised he had pinpointed an alternate entrance to the warehouse. Late afternoon shadows were stretching longer with the encroaching dusk. A biting chill, accentuated by the acrid scent of smoke from nearby fires, pierced the air. Bracing against the cold, Dua pulled her denim jacket's collar closer to her neck, her hands seeking warmth in her pockets as she quickened her pace after Vernon.

She came across a metal grey door that had been left slightly ajar. There was no sign of Vernon further up the alleyway. The door seemed to mirror its counterpart on the opposite side of the warehouse, the one leading to the parking lot where the team was waiting and negotiating with Kupi. She looked around her for a last time, then slipped inside, leaving the door as she had found it.

It was even darker inside, as scant light was getting in through the grimy windows. Several doors led off a corridor, and through one of them, she could hear voices. Unlike many of the other OIDC staffers, she could understand Albanian. Slowly, placing one foot carefully in front of the other, Dua crept quietly closer to the open door. Across the other side of the hallway, she could see a number of boxes, stacked and scattered, partly blocking the hallway. As she got closer, a shadow detached itself from among the boxes and blocked her path. A jolt of adrenaline stuck in her throat, and she froze on the spot, her body telling her to prepare to flee. As the figure, a man in a jacket, became clearer, she recognized him. He angled his face slightly towards the light, and she could see that it was Vernon. Surprised that he realized she had been following him, her throat relaxed and she drew shaking breath.

He pressed a finger to his lips, signalling for silence. She nodded, and quietly stepped closer to the wall, following his lead she melted into the shadow. The moments dragged on into minutes, and they listened and strained to see what was happening inside the large room. There were three men, one on the telephone, while the other two stood or paced impatiently.

Dua could just make out the crumpled figure of Kit slumped in the corner of the room. She was wearing a blindfold, her hands and ankles bound with masking tape, but apparently was not conscious. Her head lolled to the side, partly supported by the wall. She could see a trickle of blood pooling where Kit slouched. Dua remembered that in many ways, Kit was a master of subterfuge. It was possible that she was fully conscious but trying not to attract the attention of the kidnappers. Still, she couldn't fake the blood. She really was injured.

Kupi was speaking English over the phone, Dua assumed to Matt or Zena. He was trying to arrange for transport and continued to be evasive about Kit's presence or otherwise in the room.

Dua looked at Vernon questioningly. They had to do something, but she wasn't sure what.

In the echoing silence, he raised a hand, motioning for a halt. A silent command to wait. Dua watched as his gaze swept over the room, mapping the locations of entrance and exit points. His scrutiny extended to the men present, their stances, the weapons they bore. Like many Kosovars, they wielded guns with a familiarity that came from the necessity of living on the edge. Their status as police officers, albeit rogue, provided them an entitlement to firearms.

Vernon's assured demeanor told of the operations he'd tackled as a seasoned field operative. Yet, for Dua, a multitude of questions loomed unanswered. She watched him, her nerves humming with anticipation, her mind racing with uncertainties. This was a game of high stakes, and the odds were far from promising.

Kit emitted a soft groan, her body stirring. She was tucked near the door where Dua and Vernon were concealed, her form partially hidden from the room's occupants. Dua found herself indifferent to the fates of the men. Seeing Kit, bound and gagged, sent a wave of nausea sweeping through her.

She allowed her mind to wander to a better future—coffee meetups in the office cafeteria or the Black-and-

White Café, with Kit and a fully recovered Besim. Maybe one day, Kit would take Dua into her confidence and share the secrets of her clandestine life. However, Vernon's actions derailed her train of thought, demanding immediate attention.

Vernon pulled out his phone, quickly silencing it to prevent any accidental sounds that might expose their presence. His fingers moved swiftly across the screen, dispatching a message—Dua prayed he was asking for backup. He then dialed a number and slipped the still-connected phone into his breast pocket, leaving the line open. He gestured toward the men before directing her attention to Kit.

To ensure she understood, Dua mimicked his actions, pointing first at herself and then at Kit. Vernon responded with a slicing gesture. Grasping his intent, she retrieved a small folding knife from her handbag, a versatile tool for fruit, letters, or as it turned out, potential rescue missions. She brandished the knife towards Kit, repeating the cutting motion. Vernon gave a confirming nod.

Vernon's phone hummed silently against his chest, signaling an incoming message. Pulling out the device, he quickly scanned the contents. His eyebrows lifted in a silent affirmation and he turned to Dua, nodding. The next move was about to commence. Vernon's predatory features broke into a grin, laughter lines appearing around his eyes. Dua watched as he seemed to relish in the looming danger, almost as if this was a performance he'd been rehearsing. Slowly, exuding an undeniable presence, he rose to his full height and stepped into the space where Driton Kupi and his associates waited.

"Gentlemen, Vernon's the name," he announced, his hands elevated, palms forward, to display their weapon-free status. The three men swiveled abruptly. Kupi's phone clattered onto the table from the surprise, his hand immediately drawn to his holstered pistol.

"No need for concern," Vernon said smoothly, navigating further into the room, distancing himself from the door he had come through and drawing attention away from Dua and Kit. "I'm fresh off the plane from Australia. Word on the street is that you fellas are top-tier police."

While Vernon became the center of the men's attention, Dua took her opportunity. Stealthily, she slid into the room, inching closer to Kit, the compact pocketknife ready in her hand. Shielded by the wall, she was largely hidden from the men's sight. She murmured a silent prayer, beginning the careful task of slicing through the tape binding Kit's ankles. She yearned to reassure Kit, but the silence was essential. Despite the blindfold, Kit emanated a quiet alertness. Dua suspected that Kit must recognize her father's voice, even after their prolonged separation.

As the bindings loosened, Kit carefully flexed her legs. Meanwhile, Vernon continued his performance, weaving words of friendship between Australia and Kosovo.

"And why are you here?" Kupi demanded, his voice slicing through Vernon's jovial chatter.

"I'm hunting for intel," Vernon began, his broad grin and open posture continuing to disarm the men, even as his words spun a web of vague explanations. "You see, I recently extradited a Serbian war criminal back to Kosovo for trial. And I had a hunch that you guys might hold a key or two to the crimes he committed."

While Vernon engaged the men, Dua quietly continued her mission, her blade sliding through the remaining duct tape binding Kit like butter. Once she reached Kit's head, she dared to whisper, "It's me, Dua."

Her voice barely rose above a breath, a secret exchange masked by Vernon's boisterous diversion. The men remained oblivious.

Gently, Dua removed the blindfold. A gasp caught in her throat as Kit's condition was revealed. One eye was an alarming shade of red, likely from a burst blood vessel caused by a fall or a hit. A menacing bruise was emerging on her temple, a hint of the treatment she had endured.

"Are you alright?" Dua breathed, a mere whisper of sound in the dimly lit room.

A weak nod was Kit's only reply, but it was enough. Her body shifted, limbering up, testing the limits of her newfound freedom. There had been no time for an elaborate plan. Dua knew that surprise was their best shot at escaping unscathed.

"We need to run for it," Dua murmured, "Can you stand?" She was aware that their cover was tenuous at best. Any curious glance from the men would expose them. However, as Kit locked eyes with her father, Dua saw a flicker of determination ignite within her. The fog of trauma was lifting.

"Yeah, I think so," Kit replied, her voice barely audible. "I might have a concussion."

Dua nodded, extending her arm to Kit. "Hold onto me," she said. With Dua's help, Kit got up unsteadily, her determination outweighing her physical state.

"Can you kill the overhead light?" Kit requested, wincing at the harsh illumination. "It's blinding. I need to alert the Tracer Fox."

Dua didn't grasp Kit's cryptic comment, but the request about the light was clear. Flicking off the nearby switch, she plunged the room into a softer glow. When she turned back to Kit, her companion looked decidedly more composed, her gaze darting around the room, assessing the situation with newfound clarity.

"I'm ready," Kit confirmed, her voice steadying. Without a moment's hesitation, she maneuvered towards the exit, her intuition guiding her along the path Dua had taken earlier.

Their progress was interrupted by a gruff shout from across the room. "What's going on here?"

"Hey, over this way!" Vernon shouted to distract the men. He sprang towards the opposite end of the room, away from Kit and Dua, pulling an object from his pocket and tossing it several meters behind him. It was a military-grade flashbang, smuggled in without their knowledge.

"Take the shot," Vernon commanded into his phone. The statement must have been clear, for moments later, the shattering sound of gunfire echoed through the room as bullets tore through the windows. Vernon dropped to the floor as the room erupted into chaos. One of the men fell, struck by a bullet. Driton, swearing violently, moved to the window, returning fire with his police-issued firearm.

In the tumult of shattering glass, Dua and Kit made their escape, slipping out of the room before anyone could register their departure. Casting a final glance behind her, Dua saw Vernon rise again, low to the ground, running towards the exit. He, too, was armed, ready to fight his way out if needed. Dua gulped. All that mattered now was to get Kit out of the building. They were going as quickly as they could down the hallway, when Owen burst through the entrance through which they had originally entered.

"Is she okay?" Owen asked.

"Yes, I think so," Dua said. "She might have concussion though. Vernon—he's still in there."

"Matt was following him over the phone, once we realized where he'd gone. Let's get Kit out first," Owen said. "They're going to breach the front entrance."

Dua's relief surged as they emerged from the building, the open sky above them offering a breath of freedom. Yet, the threat of unseen bullets from behind loomed. The clamor of a door being battered down and the shattering of glass peppered with shouts reached her ears. The likelihood of pursuit seemed to dwindle with each passing second.

As they approached the exit back to the parking lot, chaos greeted them. Police vehicles had formed a barricade in a tight semicircle, sealing off the entrance. Signs of the raid were clear: doors forced open, windows shattered. The sporadic echo of gunshots underscored the tension inside. An ambulance stood poised, its medical team on edge. Dua, with Owen's help, steered Kit towards the promise of aid. Eva and Zena quickly followed.

"How is she?" Eva asked with concern.

"Seen better days, I'm afraid," Owen confessed. The medical crew had helped Kit into a wheelchair and had hoisted her into the ambulance. Despite her insistence that she was fine, her protests fell on deaf ears. A noticeable change came over Owen, his previously taut shoulders slowly relaxing as the medical crew set to work, checking Kit's vitals and examining her head wounds.

"She probably has concussion," the lead medic said. "We need to get her to a hospital immediately for a scan. There's a risk of subdural haemorrhage. Even in the best case, she'll need to be monitored for a day or two."

"We won't hold you back then," Eva said, stepping aside. Turning to Dua, she added, "Could you find out which hospital they're taking Kit to? We'll want to follow up on her progress later."

"Sure," Dua said, rummaging in her bag for a notebook and pen.

"Well done," Eva said to Dua with approval. "I appreciate this kind of initiative in my officers."

"Officers? But I'm just an intern," Dua protested, taken aback by the compliment.

"We've got a new position opening up soon—you could be high on the list of candidates. I'm sure Kit would back that," Eva said. "Don't make a habit of rushing off by yourself into danger, though." Turning her gaze around the scene, she wondered aloud, "Where's Kit's father?" It wasn't long before she spotted Vernon observing from a distance.

She signalled him to join them. "What happened in there?" Eva asked Vernon, her tone shifting from relieved to stern.

"I simply kept them occupied while our young hero here managed to free Kit. Your team was then able to apprehend them," Vernon explained with a shrug.

"I want a full debrief later—I need to know exactly what happened," Eva said.

Chapter Thirty-Three

Kit sat up in her hospital bed, cradling a plastic cup of cool water, when Dua breezed in with a burst of color—flowers in one hand, chocolates in the other. Tucked into one of Pristina's best hospitals, Kit reaped the benefits of comprehensive scans and constant monitoring. Her private room had a window framing a park.

Kit's eyes sparkled at the sight of Dua's gifts. "Thank you so much," she murmured, despite the IV-line snaking into her vein and the monitor beeping its steady rhythm beside her. A deep bruise marred her left eye

"They're a little cheer from everyone," Dua explained, setting the gifts down. "Thought the chocolates might lift your spirits."

Kit chuckled, a wistful glance at her abdomen. "I'll indulge—once I'm free from this IV."

With a sympathetic nod, Dua placed the chocolates on a nearby bench, proceeding to find a spacious vase in the cupboard. After filling it with water, she arranged the bouquet.

"How're you holding up?" Dua asked.

Kit rewarded her with a small smile. "I've been better, but they're treating me well here. They predict I should be back on my feet within the next few days."

"Did they confirm concussion?"

"Yes. Concussion and a small fracture."

The two women chatted, and Dua updated her on what was happening in the office.

"Did your father come in to see you yet?" Dua asked.

"Actually, you're the first," Kit said. "I expect he will sooner or later—I am very grateful to both of you. If you hadn't come in when you did, I don't know what would have happened."

Dua reached out and touched her hand, squeezing it warmly. "You're welcome—" Dua paused and looked out the window briefly. "You know, I think maybe I should model myself on you."

Kit laughed. "I don't know if that's such a good idea. Ask my former fiancé about my track record with relationships. What happened to those guys that kidnapped me, the Kupi gang?"

"There were three of them. One was shot and is recovering in hospital."

"Not this hospital, I hope"

Dua laughed. "No, he's in a military hospital at one of the camps, under guard. The other one was arrested and is being interviewed. But Kupi himself got away."

"Any idea where he went?"

"No, he seems to have disappeared for now. Who knows, he might end up reporting back to the police station. He kept up with the pretence that he was investigating a case." Dua paused, and looked like she was struggling to find the right words. "You know, there's something else I wanted to talk you about," Dua said and paused again.

"What's that?"

Dua reached into her handbag and pulled out Kit's second phone. She placed it on the bed beside Kit. "I was looking for clues where you might be and I found this in your bag." Dua said.

Kit gasped and grabbed the phone. "Thank goodness, I thought I'd lost it!"

"Of course there was your other mobile phone. But it was locked. That was how I discovered you'd been taken. I called and I heard the phone ringing, it had fallen out of your bag. But this other one was tucked right in the bottom."

"And..." Kit looked at Dua piercingly.

"That's what I wanted to tell you." She looked sheepish. "That phone was not locked—I was able to read the messages." She went on quickly gabbling a little. "I was looking for information about where you might be."

Kit took a deep breath, and slowly exhaled. Finally, she asked, "Did you show this to anyone else?" But she thought that she would have certainly heard something had Dua shared the information on the phone to Eva, Matt or Owen. She hoped she hadn't mentioned anything to her friends.

"No, I didn't tell anyone," Dua said. "I was looking at it when Owen and Zena arrived, looking for you. They wanted to see everything in your bag. I slipped your burner phone into my bag and I didn't say anything about it to them. I don't know why—I just felt it was the right thing to do. But, I wasn't able to find anything on it that would help us locate you. And after having read what was there, I thought you'd want that information kept private. They took your other phone, though."

"You got that right. So, what did you read?"

"I read your messages with a guy called Sergei and someone called Silver, and one or two others."

"And, what did you think?" Kit crossed her arms across her chest. Suddenly her injuries receded in importance compared to someone having cracked open her private life.

"Well, I didn't know what to think, at first." She laughed nervously. "I wondered if Sergei could be that Russian officer that was posted here in Pristina and that we had a red notice out for him—about those killings. But then I thought, it couldn't be. And then with Silver talking about millions...."

At that moment a nurse came in, pushing a trolley with medications, and holding a clipboard. Her glossy dark hair was tidily pushed back, and she moved with practiced efficiency. Kit made a nervous motion with her hand, telling Dua to stop talking.

"Ms. Chase, how are you feeling today?" asked the nurse. She checked Kit's head under the dressing and took her temperature and pulse.

"Feeling better, thanks nurse," Kit replied.

"I'll make a note of that and let the doctor know," she said, making a note on the clipboard. "We'll be bringing your afternoon snack soon. I'll just leave your afternoon medication here for doctor who will be doing his rounds in about half an hour. He'll check everything and give you your anticoagulant and antibiotics shot." She laid the hypodermic syringe and two vials on the bedside table in a small stainless-steel pan.

"You treat me like a princess here," Kit smiled.

"We do our best," the nurse said and continued on her rounds.

The two women sat in silence for some moments.

"I think everyone is entitled to their privacy," Kit said, finally.

"Absolutely, I agree," Dua said. "I admit that I was

upset about Sergei at first—you know we Albanians are not the greatest fans of Russians. But I'm guessing there's probably good reasons for what you've done—whatever it is you have done."

"I thought there was," Kit said. "But you know, I'm thinking of leaving the organization."

"To spend the millions you were discussing with Silver?"

"Well, I was thinking of setting up a task force. A criminal justice—rule of law kind of thing. We could work for the Kosovo government, as well as for OIDC. Or any other body that we thought was worthwhile."

"I'd like to be part of that," Dua said. "I'd like to be like you, Kit." She paused. "Maybe not with the Russian, but knowing what I want out of life and going after it."

"Robin to my Batman kind of thing." Kit laughed.

Dua laughed too. "Maybe, yes! What about some animal protection projects?"

"Absolutely," Kit said. "What do you have in mind?"

"You know that Besim and his friends—they're working in their spare time for an animal protection NGO. And we're all very worried about the conditions of bears being kept in restaurants and on public display. We've been talking to an organization outside of Kosovo, who might be able to help with some funding."

"I'm sure there's something we can do to help," Kit said. "Are you thinking about some kind of wildlife refuge, perhaps?"

"Exactly," Dua said. "But first we have to rescue the bears, and then have somewhere to keep them."

"I've got a friend in government, who might be willing to help."

"Yes, we can't really do anything without the authorities at least being willing to turn a blind eye."

"I think that is a great idea. You have to promise me one thing though" she said.

"Yes?"

"Keep what you saw on that phone to yourself." Kit paused and took a breath. "It's very important to me, to keep that side of my life private. And, as I mentioned, I probably I won't be with the organisation for that much longer anyway.

"Don't leave!" Dua exclaimed. "I won't tell anyone, I promise. Take your time to make your plans. Just let me be part of them. I don't want to end up working for Axel or Christina—they're nice, but... I don't feel that they're thinking along the same lines as us. Plus, Eva said she's like to keep me on the team with a better contract."

Kit pondered for a moment, weighing the pros and cons. It would be comforting to have someone by her side who truly understood what she was going through. However, it could also spell disaster if Dua turned out to be untrustworthy. Kit's entire career could be destroyed in an instant.

"I need you to understand how crucial this is, Dua. If anyone finds out, we will both be in serious trouble. But if you agree to keep quiet, I'll make sure you get the next open position in our office."

Dua's head nodded slowly as she processed the weight of Kit's words. "You have my word," she said.

"Then maybe I can bring you onto our covert task force. A few of us have been working off the record for some time now—although they aren't fully aware of my situation.""Who are the others in the group?"

"Me, Owen, Matt, Eva, Angel, Don."

"Not Zena?"

"No," Kit replied, letting the word hang in the air. She didn't feel like delving into the tension between her and Zena that revolved around Owen. It was clear that even Zena had been fighting to keep Kit safe from Kupi's gang. Maybe it was time for Kit to loosen up a bit and let things go. But not now.

"And what about you and Owen?"

"You know what," Kit said, "The worst thing about this place is that they don't serve alcohol with meals. A stiff drink would be much appreciated right now."

"I completely understand—I'll try to bring you a small flask of spirits next time I visit."

"Great idea. I know I won't regret making you part of the team, Dua." They both laughed.

"I think Owen and I will be okay—we've been through some rough patches, like any relationship." Kit said.

Dua nodded. "Does he know about Sergei?" Dua asked, looking down and then up again. She was too curious to let it rest.

Kit was silent for a moment. She remembered the time that she had met with Sergei at the castle overlooking Ljubljana. He and Owen had only just missed each other by a few minutes. Finally, she said "No—not yet. I might tell him about Sergei, in time. Although, it might do more harm than good. You heard what he was like when I had a drink with that local politician."

Dua smiled. "Yes, I heard about that. He was very jealous, apparently. It earned him a suspension."

"That was an overreaction on his part. You can probably imagine how he would react if he found out about Sergei. But I'll tell him when the time is right. Hopefully, he'll get back to work soon."

"It's nobody else's business—I apologize for prying.

Both Matt and Owen were there for you when it mattered most, putting themselves on the line. I hope they're both back at work soon," Dua said with a sympathetic smile. "And your father... I only met him briefly, but I really like him, Kit. I hope you two can have a better relationship in the future."

Kit nodded. But she knew for a fact that serious questions would be asked at the highest levels if it came out about her secret relationships with Sergei and Silver. No, it was too risky. It was becoming clearer and clearer that Kit would have to resign sooner rather than later. And what's more, she didn't know how Sergei and Silver would react if they knew that Dua was aware of their role in her life. That could be dangerous—primarily for Dua, if they decided that she was a threat to their operations. Silver had been quick to draw a knife on her former psychotherapist Maria Montenegro when she had threatened their operation, and Kit had had to talk her down from using it. The best protection might be to draw Dua in much more closely—but that would make her complicit in what could technically be described as money laundering. Natalia's role in the situation also needed to be considered and their relationship with Father Peter and Sergei's Khash group.

"Well, let's both think about the situation. For now, I trust you to not mention, or even hint about any of this to anyone."

Dua nodded. "I understand," she said.

"I'm really pleased that you're on board with all this, Dua. We can work much more closely together in the future. I'll suggest to Matt and Eva that you come to our next task force meeting. And about my father—that was a bolt from the blue. I never thought I would see him again, but here he is. And the way that you and he came to my rescue—I'm so grateful." Kit smiled and looked up at Dua. "I really do owe you, both of you. I know Matt and Owen—and Zena, for that matter, had the best of intentions, but they didn't seem to be getting anywhere negotiating with Kupi and his gang."

"You're welcome," Dua said. "Don't worry, your secrets are safe with me. I really hope I can get on this task force, and we can work together on animal protection projects—that would be so cool."

Kit released a deep sigh of relief as Dua left, sinking into the hospital bed. She needed to reconsider her plans, and perhaps Dua could be of use. After all, Kit did owe her and Vernon. What were the chances of him showing up just when she needed him? It was almost too perfect, like her vision from the beachside lagoon had come true. Maybe she could introduce Dua to Natalia and bridge the gap between her dual lives.

As Kit drifted off into her thoughts, an orderly entered the room, dressed in scrubs and a surgical mask. He locked the door from the inside and pulled the curtains closed behind him. Kit's heart jolted as saw Driton Kupi. She recognized him instantly but decided to stall, buying time to come up with a plan.

"Excuse me, doctor," she said, trying to keep her voice steady. "Have we met before?"

Driton's expression softened slightly as he removed his mask. "My apologies for the deception," he said regretfully. "I'm not actually with the hospital. I'm Detective Kupi from the police department."

Kit's voice trembled slightly as she reached for her phone, hidden on the other side of her hospital bed. "A detective," she said, trying to maintain a calm demeanor.

"I got the call yesterday, when you were... taken," he

admitted, his face betraying his unease as he nervously clenched and unclenched his fists. He glanced out the window, anxiety written all over his features.

"I appreciate your involvement," Kit replied, flipping on her phone and frantically typing a message to Owen. "Unfortunately, I didn't see much—they blindfolded me most of the time, until I collapsed. I woke up here with hazy memories."

"Ms. Chase, I find your story difficult to believe. I must insist that you come with me to the station."

"My doctors haven't cleared me yet. They diagnosed me with a severe concussion."

He responded curtly, "I insist."

Kit hit send on her message to Owen: *Help*.

"But why do we have to go to the police station?" Kit asked, stalling as she inched her hand towards the assistance bell by her bedside.

"I'm afraid I can't allow that," he interrupted, standing in front of her and casting a dark shadow over her. Kit felt trapped and vulnerable, lying in bed with an IV tugging at her arm. She quickly considered the distance to the door, wondering if she could escape by ripping out the IV, jumping out of bed, and reaching the door before he stopped her.

"Why not?" she asked.

"It's better if we're not disturbed," he replied, his face now hidden in darkness as his broad shoulders blocked the light from the window. As he leaned closer, Kit caught a whiff of his overpowering cologne mixed with a hint of body odor. He seemed agitated.

"In fact, maybe we should just end this now," he said as he reached for the pillow on the nearby chair. In just a couple of steps, he would be right on top of her.

She went to untuck the bed to extract herself from that terrible looming shadow. But he caught her and started to push the pillow down on her head, covering her nose and mouth. The deceptively soft pillow weighed heavier and heavier on her mouth and nose, cutting off her breath. Malevolent red and sickly yellow stars flashed against the dark screen behind her eyes, and her concussed skull shot her head with pain as he pressed against the fractures. Her hand grasped on either side, stretching frantically with failing strength to find something to defined herself with.

Her fingers found the cold, sterile touch of the hypodermic syringe beside the bed. With her waning strength, she maneuvered it upwards and plunged it into Kupi's chest. His hands, pressing down on her, had left his ribcage open to her assault, and the needle slid in effortlessly. As the pressure eased, Kit drew a shallow breath, then shoved the needle in deeper, puncturing his left lung. A grunt escaped him.

The reaction was immediate; he recoiled, struggling for breath. Taking advantage of his shock, Kit shoved him hard. He stumbled backward, desperately clawing at the needle now embedded in his chest. His breaths came in ragged gasps, each one sounding more strained than the last.

He gasped, staggering back in shock. She took advantage of his momentary weakness to break free from the sheets that were restraining her and take a deep breath. The sensation was glorious after being confined for so long. With a wince of pain, she yanked the IV drip out of her arm, barely feeling it amidst the rush of adrenaline. Grabbing her phone, she bolted towards the door. It was locked, but she quickly flipped the latch open.

But Kupi was not giving up yet. He threw away the bloody syringe and lunged at her as she opened the door, pushing it shut again with all her might. A sharp pain shot through her head, threatening to blur her vision, but she fought back tears and mustered all her strength fueled by adrenaline. She delivered a swift blow to his windpipe, followed by a knee to his groin and a forceful push on his chest, sending him tumbling onto a medical cart.She wrenched the door open and fled in her nightgown out into the hallway.

"Help!" Kit screamed at the top of her voice. Two police officers, who were supposed to have been watching the room but instead were down the hallway at the coffee machine, saw her and sprinted towards her.

"Arrest him! He tried to kill me," she exclaimed, pointing at Kupi as he made a run for it down the hallway. The officers wasted no time in chasing after him. Owen appeared from the elevator with a look of shock and concern on his face. Kit pointed in the direction where Kupi had fled, her words coming out in a rush, "Kupi was here! He tried to kill me!" Owen must have arrived quickly, meaning he was probably waiting outside the hospital.

"Where did he go?" Owen asked, his body tense with adrenaline.

"That way!" Kit's voice echoed through the corridor, her finger indicating the direction for Owen to go. Without hesitation, Owen sprinted off in pursuit. It wasn't until this moment that Kit took in her surroundings: cold linoleum beneath her bare feet, a flimsy hospital gown doing little to protect her from the chill.

She reached up to touch her head wound and saw that her hand came back covered in blood. A dull ache began pulsing through her head, gradually intensifying into sharp jolts of pain that seemed to radiate throughout her skull. Nausea churned in her stomach, threatening to overwhelm her, as her vision blurred and she wavered on the brink of passing out.

In an instant, the nurse was by her side, wrapping an arm around Kit's waist to support her and keep her from falling over. With a quick signal, she called for an orderly who helped them make their way back to Kit's room. The nurse acted as both guide and support system as they walked slowly down the hallway.

Kit was gently lowered onto the hospital bed, her arm reconnected to the IV drip. As her consciousness faded and the world around her became hazy, she knew she was slipping into unconsciousness. The beeping of the heart monitor was the last thing she registered before everything went black.

Chapter Thirty-Four

After being discharged from the hospital and returning home, Kit lay in bed next to Owen. She reached over and felt his warm body, breathing deeply as he slept facing away from her. She cuddled up to him and whispered, "I owe you one," then planted a gentle kiss on his shoulder. She wrapped her arm around his waist and added, "I'll explain everything soon, I promise." She nuzzled against his skin.

"Is that so?" Owen replied with a gravelly voice, still half asleep. "When exactly do you plan on doing that?"

Kit propped herself up on her elbow and playfully swatted his arm. "You were supposed to be sleeping."

"Didn't you know? The Welsh always sleep with one eye open."

Kit let out a soft giggle. "I've never heard that before."

"It's an old shepherd's tale," Owen explained.

"I think you just made that up," Kit countered with a smile.

"Maybe you need to teach me a lesson, then," he said, and pulled her on top of him. The warm, sleepy weight of their limbs tangled together, and Kit found herself lost in Owen's deepening kiss. *Surely nothing could ever feel as good at this*, she thought. The mood was interrupted by the persistent ring of her phone.

"Let it ring," murmured Owen, his voice thick.

Kit sighed heavily. "I wish I could ignore it..." With reluctance, she peeled away from his warm embrace and reached for the phone that was abandoned on the nightstand. It was Eva's name that flashed on the screen.

Kit's eyes darted to the clock, and her heart sank. "Oh no, look!" she blurted, springing from the bed with a newfound urgency. She jabbed a finger towards the glaring green digits of the alarm clock. It read 10:05. "We were supposed to be at a meeting at ten!"

"A meeting? With who?" Owen's voice was now tinged with concern.

"Eva," Kit said, now fully aware of their lateness.

"On Saturday?" Owen asked, sitting up and rubbing his eyes.

"Criminals don't take weekends off," Kit replied with a mix of humor and stress as she quickly grabbed her jeans, T-shirt, and jacket from the dresser and threw them on. As she dressed, she couldn't help but notice the tender red mark on her arm—a reminder of where she had been hooked up to an IV not too long ago.

"*Bongiorno*, Kit," Eva's voice greeted her with a teasing lilt. "Was that Owen I heard in the background?"

Kit's voice was muffled as she pulled a T-shirt over her head. "Yeah, it was him. We both just woke up, overslept actually."

Eva chuckled on the other end of the line. "Well, you missed the start of the meeting, but we're all here waiting. Dua is here too; I invited her to join our task force after you vouched for her. We're just enjoying coffee and croissants. Get here when you can," she said before ending the call.

Owen was already on his feet, shaking off the sleepiness quickly. "We'd better hurry," he said, a smile spreading across his face despite the urgency. "Oversleeping won't stop us from fighting crime."

Kit mirrored Owen's smile, feeling the rush of adrenaline coursing through her body. Their partnership was complex, filled with both unspoken secrets and a deep level of trust. But moments like this reminded them both of their shared determination, overshadowing any tensions. Oversleeping was a small setback in their larger commitment to their cause and each other.

Glancing at Owen, still entangled in the sheets and only partially dressed, she urged him to get up. "Come on, we need to move. There's a task force meeting waiting for us—complete with breakfast."

Owen responded with a mischievous smirk as he swung his legs out of bed.

"I'd better put on my big boy pants," he joked, their playful banter undiminished by the morning's chaos.

The aroma of warm coffee and freshly baked pastries wrapped around Kit as she stepped into Matt's urban apartment, where comfort and professionalism coexisted. Owen, a silent pillar of support, shadowed her closely.

"Apologies for the delay, everyone. Concussion side effects," Kit quipped, an attempt to lighten the undercurrent of tension.

Dua, bright-eyed and eager, handed Kit a steaming cup. "Welcome, Kit," she beamed.

"Morning, Kit, Owen," Matt's greeting cut through the casual scene, his uniform absent today. Don, relaxed as ever, acknowledged them with a stroke to Max's head and a casual "Hey," briefly distracted by the simple pleasure of pastries.

Owen, stirring a freshly brewed coffee leaned against the counter, his smile easy but his eyes sharp. "Are we here for more than coffee and croissants? Not that I'm complaining."

Matt's serious tone grabbed their attention once again. "I have some news," he announced, with a determined look on his face. "I'm in the clear. The investigation into the cave bombing is complete, and I've been cleared of any wrongdoing."

A relieved whistle from Don echoed through the group. "That's great news!"

"Congratulations!" exclaimed Kit, raising a fist in the air.

Matt nodded at Eva and gave her credit for helping him with his case. "Eva's review of my brief made all the difference."

"It was just a matter of following standard operating procedures," Eva shrugged off any praise.

"It also helps that we've got both the Kupi and Mala gangs in custody, and water-tight cases against them. The two guys in Kupi's gang who took Kit hostage are cooperating in return for a reduced sentence. But Mala had a weird story about events at Dečani monastery before his arrest for burglary," Owen said.

Kit held her breath. Her role in the Dečani monastery incident was something she hoped would never see the light of day.

"What was that?" Angel asked, curious.

"He had some story about a woman in a black head scarf who stole his bag in the church," Owen said.

"Were all of the artifacts retrieved?" She hoped her question would shift the focus away from the mysterious woman that had just been mentioned.

Angel chimed in, "That's a relief. Maybe the guy Mala was just out of his mind. Trying to steal from Dečani Monastery? That's ridiculous with all the security protecting it."

"According to the other gang members," Owen added with a furrowed brow, "there was some sort of fight with a tall priest and a novice at the Tower."

Eva made no comment but kept reading through the notes on her legal pad. Kit often had the impression that Eva suspected more than she let on.

"But let's get back to the main point," Matt interrupted. "The time off work gave me a chance to reflect. I realized that my priorities were all wrong, so I made the decision to retire early."

"No way," Owen protested. "You're too young for that."

"Well, according to the UK police pension scheme, I'm old enough to receive a decent, albeit partial, pension. And spend more time with my family."

"This doesn't make sense," Owen argued. "You're one of the best operational leaders I've ever worked with."

"But," Matt said slowly and deliberately. "It also opens up other possibilities for me."

"Such as?" Owen inquired.

"Maybe Kit can explain it better…" Matt trailed off.

All eyes turned to Kit. *It's show time*, she thought and took a deep breath.

"I recently reconnected with an old friend of mine in Australia," she began, trying her best to maintain a neutral tone. "She mentioned a foundation that funds international rule of law projects. I believe our task force could qualify for independent funding through this organization." She felt a flush rising on her cheeks, since she knew the funding was coming from Silver's shrewd manipulation of the interest from their anti-money laundering operation.

"Who is this friend?" Eva inquired.

"She wishes to remain anonymous. But rest assured, everything is completely legitimate. She may have access to funding from a deceased relative's estate," Kit explained.

"Interesting," Eva noted, jotting down some key points in her trusty legal pad. "I would like to see more details on this potential funding. How much money are we talking about?"

Kit shrugged, "It's hard to say for certain, but potentially around $300,000 to start with. Of course, it would depend on each individual project and its needs."

"Does she—or you, have any projects lined up?" There was something about Eva's manner that made Kit feel she suspected that the story might not be completely true.

"We've been throwing around a few ideas," Kit began, her words falling flat even in her own ears. "Dua mentioned something before, but we haven't had a chance to discuss it yet. I know it might seem like I'm just rambling, but hear me out. There have been discussions about organized crime and their involvement in animal mistreatment—bears being kept in cages, dogs being abused. No one has really prioritized it because there are more pressing issues, but my friend suggested this could be a good starting point. And it would also help address the problem of organized crime."

"That would be amazing, Kit," Dua said eagerly. "Besim and I have been working with an animal protection NGO to rescue the caged bears in Kosovo. We could definitely use help getting them out of captivity and into a safe sanctuary."

"It would be hard to do anything like this without support from the government. Although I think I know someone who might be able to help with that." Kit couldn't help but glance over at Owen, curious to see his reaction. She was referring to Visar Dreshaj, and Owen's frown confirmed her suspicions. Memories of their confrontation in front of Visar resurfaced, but luckily the media coverage had died down amidst other breaking news. The senior management had decided to give Owen a warning note in his personnel file, but no further action was being taken against him.

"Before we move on to that, there's one more thing," Matt interjected. "We have a special guest joining us today. I figured you wouldn't mind, Kit, since he helped us out of a sticky situation." He checked his watch as the elevator doors opened. "Right on time," Matt noted with satisfaction.Kit scanned the faces around the table but they all seemed as surprised as she was. It was a today was full of unexpected twists.

Vernon Chase emerged from the elevator, sporting a wide grin as he looked at the group. "You have quite the setup here, Matt." He was still dressed in his travel attire and carried a backpack on his shoulder.

"Welcome, Vernon," Matt replied, rising from his seat to greet him. "Have a seat and I'll get you some coffee. How do you take it?"

"Black with one sugar," Vernon answered, settling into a chair at the table. "Hey there kiddo," he greeted Kit. "You look much better than when I saw you last."

"Dad, you could have given me a heads up that you were coming today," Kit scolded.

"Well, at least you called me Dad. That's progress," Vernon joked as he accepted the coffee from Matt. Kit couldn't help but notice that this might be the first time she had seen Matt make coffee for someone else. Was he already transitioning out of his military leadership role or was he just trying to make Vernon feel welcome?

"I thought Vernon could update us on the work of the new war crimes tribunal in Pristina since he brought their first defendant here," Matt explained.

"My pleasure," Vernon replied, clearing his throat. "The tribunal is an important step towards accountability, and both the local and international communities will be closely monitoring its progress. With Simić's extradition, it's imperative that we avoid mistakes. The defendant has been under strict supervision at a secure facility since arriving, and we've collaborated with multiple agencies to ensure the integrity of the proceedings."

"I'm still upset that our office wasn't notified," Eva interjected.

"No offense intended," Vernon assured her. "The operation's security was top priority, and we couldn't risk any information leaks. After the fire at the Police evidence storage, communication had to be cut off until Simić was safely transferred."

"Yeah, because whoever set that fire probably had inside information," Owen added skeptically.

"My primary concern now is security for the upcoming hearings," Vernon continued. "We're briefing witnesses and taking precautions to ensure their safety. We're also carefully reviewing courtroom security protocols due to the high-profile nature of the case. Experts from the International Criminal Court are advising us, and we're implementing their recommendations on site."

Eva's lips tightened, a visible sign of her irritation at this overstep. "I want the names of these so-called experts later," she said, her voice steady but cool—a clear indication she was not one to be side-lined, especially in matters of her own jurisdiction.

"Vernon also said he could be interested in some contract work on the side," Matt added, looking at Vernon. "Maybe with this task force we were talking about. Justice Pursuit International. It has a ring about it."

"Indeed," Vernon agreed with a nod. "My experience with the tribunal could provide valuable insights for your task force, especially when dealing with transnational justice issues."

"Does this mean we can start planning for the restaurant bears rescue?" Dua asked, her voice hopeful.

"Yes, I think so," Matt confirmed. "And with Vernon's expertise, we could extend our reach beyond local cases. The task force could use his knowledge to help with international liaisons and perhaps provide judicial assistance in similar cases elsewhere."

As Vernon detailed the logistics of managing such a high-stakes operation, the room listened with attention.

This morning, Kit had been close to handing in her resignation. However, with all the unexpected turns that have occurred, things were getting more intriguing. She might stay a little longer to see how things played out with her father present. It was important for her to make sure everything was set financially with Alexei. And she also wanted to give herself time to see where things went with Owen. The room was filled with excitement over new opportunities and satisfaction over closed cases. But as the task force began to feel a sense of completion, an underlying dissonance crept in—a jarring note that only Kit seemed to notice.

"Looks like Australia is moving on Pristina in force," Kit said with a wry twist of her lips. "Molly at the Australian consulate in Skopje has been pushing for mutually beneficial briefings, whatever that entails."

Eva, always strategic in her thinking, leaned back in her chair and began to contemplate the potential outcomes. "We'll have to figure out how to make the most of this," she pondered. "A bit of diplomacy could prove useful, as long as it remains within the public eye."

Kit agreed with a nod, but her thoughts were elsewhere. Molly, an associate at the Australian consulate in Skopje, possessed knowledge that could jeopardize Kit's carefully planned maneuvers. The thought of Molly being more knowledgeable about the shifting tides than Kit herself was unsettling.

As the group began to disperse, each to their new roles and continued missions, Vernon raised his hand, signaling he had one last thing to share. "Hold up, before you all scatter, there's one more piece of the puzzle I need to place on the table."

The team halted, their interest piqued as they turned to Vernon. "I've been approached by a US Army liaison. They're orchestrating what I'll term a 'special access program' here in Kosovo."

Kit's eyebrow quirked, sensing the deliberate ambiguity in Vernon's words. "What sort of special access program?"

With a careful sweep of the room, Vernon considered the weight of his revelation. "They're pioneering a remote viewing program—highly classified, experimental stuff. They're looking to recruit individuals with certain... talents, for intelligence purposes."

Skepticism mingled with curiosity rippled through the room. Remote viewing, the purported ability to see distant or unseen targets, straddled the line between speculative fiction and fringe science.

Eva recovered her poise swiftly. "You're suggesting that the US Army is launching a psychic spy operation right here, in Kosovo? How are we implicated in this?"

Vernon nodded. "They suspect that some of the pending war crimes tribunal cases might intersect with sensitive intel, accessible only via these... unorthodox strategies. They want to know if we've come across any individuals who might possess such abilities."

Kit quickly processed the information. "I'm not sure about all this psychic stuff, but if it can help us find our suspects, it could be extremely useful."

Owen interjected, "Like uncovering the mastermind behind the Black Sun syndicate."

Kit nodded in agreement, a possible plan forming in their mind. "My friend Natalia has an incredible sixth sense. She may be drawn to this kind of thing. Though, working with the military is not typically her style. But if there's a new game being played, we can't just sit back and watch."

Vernon fixed his gaze on Kit and spoke with a cryptic smile, "I had hoped for your open-mindedness. Welcome to the brink of discovery, where intelligence tactics are reimagined. Let's see what comes of this new intel frontier."

As the group disbanded, Kit couldn't shake the feeling that they were entering unknown territory. This revelation wasn't just a plot twist in their ongoing mission—it marked the beginning of an entirely new battlefield.

-THE END-

More books by Tasmin Turner

The Crime Scene Kosovo series continues with *In Plain View*.

In the next book in this series, Kit Chase faces her most intriguing case yet, delving into the world of organized crime. Her professional life is a labyrinth of moving parts and secrets. But her personal life is equally intricate. With a boyfriend and an old flame still in the picture, Kit must navigate the turbulent waters of love while upholding justice. The stakes get even higher when her long-lost father reappears, bringing with him a whole new set of challenges.

In Plain View is a captivating legal thriller that will keep you on the edge of your seat. Don't miss out on this must-read book! Coming soon in ebook and print formats.

The Crime Scene Kosovo Series

Thanks for joining Kit in this adventure. If you enjoyed the book, please rate and review it on your favorite platform! It's always much appreciated.

The Crime Scene Kosovo books will includes the following:
The Missing Diary #1
The Price of Justice #2
Explosive Reprisals #3
In Plain View #4
Join my newsletter to be notified of new releases, give-aways, and pre-release specials at
www.wish-books.com or email joann@dreamlifenz.com

About Tasmin Turner

Tasmin Turner is the author of the Crime Scene Kosovo Series, which is based in the early 2000s in post-conflict Balkans. Tasmin lives in the heartland of New Zealand, after two decades living in Europe and the US. She's passionate about writing and enjoys frequenting cafés.

Author's Note : Information about Kosovo

The Crime Scene Kosovo series is set in a fictional post-conflict Kosovo, with fictitious characters, organizations, and events. The information below is a brief account of Kosovo's real historical background.

Kosovo is a self-declared independent country in Europe's Balkan region. Although many nations—including the United States and several members of the European Union—acknowledge its 2008 declaration of freedom from Serbia, Russia and some other countries, including some EU states, do not recognize Kosovo's independence. Most inhabitants are Albanian, and the minority are Serbs, together with other ethnic minority groups. The official languages are Albanian and Serbian.

The name Kosovo is derived from a Serbian term meaning "field of blackbirds." After serving as the heart of a medieval kingdom of Serbia, Kosovo was governed by the Ottoman Empire from the mid-fifteenth century to the early twentieth century. This was an era when Islam grew in importance and the number of Albanian speakers in the region grew. Then in the early twentieth century, Kosovo was incorporated into Serbia (later part of Yugoslavia). By the second half of that century, Muslims of Albanian origin outnumbered Eastern Orthodox Serbs in Kosovo, leading to frequent interethnic tensions in the province.

In 1998, an ethnic, Albanian-led secessionist rebellion escalated into a global crisis, resulting in NATO's 1999 air bombardment of Yugoslavia, which at that time was a remnant state comprised of Serbia and Montenegro. Peace was restored afterwards, and Kosovo was administered by the United Nations and supported by several other international and regional organizations during post-conflict times.

A landlocked country, Kosovo is flanked by Serbia to the north and east, North Macedonia to the south, Albania to the west, and Montenegro to the northwest. About the same geographic size as Jamaica or Lebanon, it is one of the smallest countries in the Balkans, with a population of less than two million people in 2021, predominantly of Albanian descent. The capital, Pristina, is also the largest urban area. Albanian and Serbian are spoken languages, with most Kosovars adhering to Sunni Islam.

The information in this description is drawn from the following source: Allcock, John B. , Young, Antonia and Lampe, John R.. "Kosovo". Encyclopedia Britannica, 8 Nov. 2022. https://www.britannica.com/place/Kosovo. Accessed 16 January 2023.

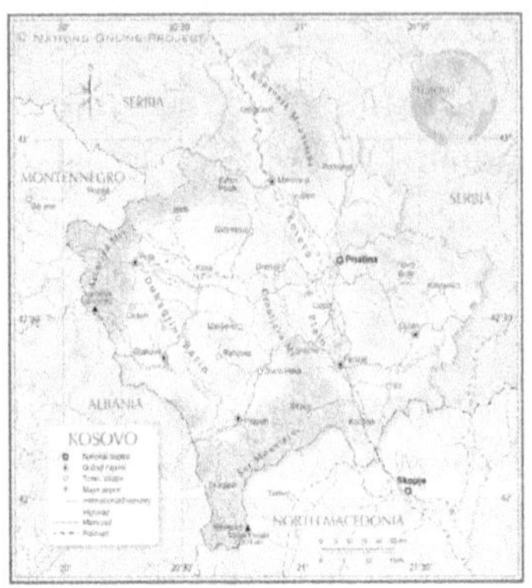

Map of Kosovo

The source of the map is Nations Online Project accessed 10 January 2023 https://www.nationsonline.org/oneworld/map/Kosovo-map.htm